EMMA WHITEHALL is a introvert from the North East of England.

Her work has been published in anthologies and magazines in the UK, USA, Ireland, and Mexico, and she has performed her stories in various pubs, cafes, radio channels and heritage centres in the North East. A former Waterstones bookseller turned indie bookshop champion, Emma writes fun, emotion driven fantasy, with characters that you'll want to take for a coffee. Or wrap in a blanket. Or both. Emma lives in Tyne & Wear with her cat and an ever-growing to read pile.

You can find Emma at emmawhitehallwrites.squarespace.com, or on Instagram and Twitter at @pensandpizza.

HERETICAL

EMMA WHITEHALL

NORTHODOX PRESS

Northodox Press Ltd
Maiden Greve, Malton,
North Yorkshire, YO17 7BE

This edition 2024

1
First published in Great Britain by
Northodox Press Ltd 2024

ISBN: 9781915179777

This book is set in Caslon Pro Std

For all the Generals, Pisces Risings, and Lily Volts.

You won't hold us back.

'Don't come crying

I am nobody's moral centre...'

– Dream Girl Evil, Florence and the Machine

Chapter One

Some students in Ignatia Heretical's classes were wide awake at six, ready for a Green Goddess smoothie and a workout before the sun had even risen. Starting the day the way young Heroes should. Not Ig. She rolled out of bed quarter of an hour before she needed to, stuffed a protein bar in her bag and bolted to class like the devil was after her.

That was how she ended up sweating through her uniform before Flyer Class had even started. She scrambled around in her holdall, looking for the can of deodorant she thought she'd stuffed in the bottom of her bag that morning. She could've sworn she remembered doing it – but she'd been in such a rush…

'Alright, girls,' called Coach Cloudspear, 'I want you out here and ready to fly in three minutes. Not four, not three and a half. Three. Got it?'

'Yes, Coach,' replied the eleven other girls in the changing room; all Heroes in training like Ig, all shivering in the cool air of the changing room as they bundled their holdalls into lockers and wriggled into identical gold-and-white shorts and t-shirts. But even though they were all Academy students, Ig often wondered if the others were even the same species as her. Ig's hair was scruffy and short, her clothes were always too tight or ballooning off her, and she had a phobia of eye contact that had crossed over from *'shy'* to *'are you actually able to look at anything but the floor'* a loooong time ago. These girls were glossy and confident, their laughter flowing as they joked and gossiped and made friends as easily as breathing–

'God, Heretical's out of breath before she even gets her Power

Lender on!' laughed Petra Pribhakr, tossing her long black braid over one shoulder. 'Sunita, make sure you're on my team so I don't have to work with her today.'

There weren't many classes she was particularly enjoying right now. But Ig hated Flyer class most of all.

'Did you leave your deodorant in the dorm again?'

Ig looked up, straight into the sea-blue eyes of Pisces Rising; her dorm-mate and literally the most perfect girl in existence. No, literally. She was perfect. She was everything a student at the Lunalist Academy For The Gifted and Talented – the best school for Heroes in the country – should be. From the second Ig had arrived at Lunalist, she'd known that Pisces was absolutely flawless. Even her imperfections were perfect – she had a freckle under one eye that was shaped like a fish. If Ig had a pound for every time, she'd imagined pressing a kiss right there, just above her cheekbone, well… she'd be stupidly rich.

A lot of Lunalist students had the potential for a Power running through their veins because one or both of their parents were Heroes. It was a genetic trait that unlocked Power Lenders and finally blossomed into a singular ability when you turned sixteen. Pisces' parents, however, were a cleaner and a nurse; she'd been discovered by Lunalist when she fell from a climbing frame in first school and bounced – all Heroes (and Villains, unfortunately) were a little harder to kill than civilians. She was a real Cinderella story; plucked from obscurity, destined for greatness. Who wouldn't fall in love with her?

'Here,' Pisces said, flicking her wavy red hair out of her eyes and handing Ig a white spray can. In Ig's mind, rose petals fell around her pretty, slim shoulders and violins started to play in the background. 'Take some of mine.'

'Um,' Ig said, pathetically. *Stop blushing*, she thought. *It's deodorant. You're going to stop blushing… now. Now. Right now. Now. Dammit.*

Pisces didn't get up at six for her workout. No; she left

their shared dorm at five, so she could squeeze in a round of meditation. She was intelligent, athletic, and utterly devoted to becoming her best self. A self she could be proud of, no matter what her Power was revealed to be. And you know what the worst part of it all was? Pisces was nice. Ever since they started rooming together in their first year, Pisces was the only student who seemed to tolerate Ig. Most of the time. Which, of course, had led to Ig spending more than one sleepless night imagining herself saving Pisces from a burning building, or from drowning in shark-infested waters, a gentle embrace and a breathy *'you saved my life,'* as her only reward…

More stupid, useless daydreams.

'You're welcome, Iggie,' Pisces sang as Ig sprayed herself liberally – even though Ig hadn't in fact got around to saying thank you yet. 'That's what roomies are for, yeah?'

'I, um, suppose so,' Ig said. 'Hey, so are you looking forward to–'

'Pisces!' squealed another girl, crashing into their shared space. 'Oh my god, girl, are you ready to Tear. It. Up on the relay tracks today?'

Lily Volt; she of the perfect skin, rounded cheeks and vibes as warm and comforting as a glacier. Rumours were already bouncing around school that Lily was being courted by some expensive makeup company to be the face of their dewy-finish foundation line once she graduated, no matter what her Power turned out to be.

'You bet I am,' Pisces said with a smile, detangling herself from Lily's clutches.

'You're gonna be on my team, right?'

'Oh, if you think you can keep up!'

'Ugh,' Lily scoffed. 'So rude. Like, wow.'

Ig didn't know why Lily talked like that. With that cheerleader-ish, 'oh-my-gaaahhhd' American accent. Lily Volt was from *Middlesbrough*. But the popular kids – and some of the teachers – ate it up. Like she was already a celebrity or something. And

Pisces didn't seem to mind it, either; she was already being drawn into Lily Volt's little crowd, laughing about how easy today's race would be. If you needed someone fast and graceful, Pisces was the girl for you. Climbing, flying, jumping – you name it, she was born to do it.

'Oh,' Lily said, her gaze flicking to Ig, 'and you're here. You're gonna remember not to cheat, right?'

Ig felt herself bristle. 'What does that–'

'I mean you might forget,' Lily simpered, running a hand through her long, blonde hair. 'You know. It's second nature for someone like you.'

'Come on, Lily…' Pisces murmured.

'Girls!' yelled Coach Cloudspear. 'Time's up. Get into two teams of six. Line up on the turf, prepare your Power Lenders and make sure you have your bands on, ladies; I will not wait for anyone who needs to go back and get it.'

That was one time, Ig thought bitterly.

Lunalist Academy For The Gifted and Talented sat along the River Tyne; a glittering, shining example of excellence, of discipline and studiousness and order, complete with state-of-the-art classrooms, a gigantic pool and a sprawling, astroturfed field where physical lessons – like Flyer Class – took place. Ig's mam said the school looked like a giant disco ball. But it was the best Hero school in the country; and besides, Ig's dad had gone there. It had been a no-brainer for Ig when it came time to pick out her future; her dad had been showing her photos and telling her stories of Lunalist since she was five. It was just a shame that he wasn't here to take her classes for her. Ig's dad was constantly sunny, confident and had an amazing ability – as well as being the fastest man in the North – to befriend anyone within a six-foot radius. All qualities Ig was sorely lacking. Not like she'd tell her dad that. She was going to make this place work for her if it killed her.

Ig trailed behind Pisces as she squealed and hugged a cluster of the other athletic girls as if she hadn't seen them for weeks. Ig swallowed.

She wasn't jealous. Envy wasn't a very Hero-like emotion.

Once they were lined up, Coach Cloudspear walked down their row and slotted an eggshell-blue disc the size of a thumbnail into the white silicone band around their wrists. Each Power Lender chirped out a pretty, beeping tone as he did, making it sound like the class were surrounded by robotic birds.

'Power Lender Activated.'

'Power Lender Activated.'

'Power Lender—'

'Power—'

'Power—'

'Power Lender Activated.'

As Coach Cloudspear clicked the disc into place on Ig's band – giving her a stern look she couldn't quite read as he did – she smiled at the familiar, funny feeling of suddenly being assigned a real, honest-to-god Power; a cool, pricking tingle, like having a mint in her mouth but *everywhere*, that ran up and down her arms and up her spine. Then, the feeling of weightlessness that came with flight washed over her limbs. Of course, she didn't get wings. They were a status symbol more than anything; flight was a very marketable power. But she could levitate, and push herself through the sky – well enough, at least, for a forty-five minute lesson. In other classes, she might have the energy of fire rush through her veins, or a tiny tornado forming in her palms. It was the only way kids like her, whose potential was still malleable and unrealised, could try out Powers before their own was revealed to them at sixteen. It was also Ig's favourite thing about school; the feeling, for a second or two at a time, that she was powerful, and purposeful and knew what was expected of her.

'Thank you, sir,' Lily Volt simpered as she floated an inch off the ground, and Coach Cloudspear chuckled as if she'd said something funny.

It was a good day to fly; the air crisp and cool and still. There were markers placed along the pitch; like giant white basketball hoops, sticking straight up. The game was to fly up and out to each marker as quickly as you could, fly back, and hand the baton you were carrying to the next member of your team, Easy enough, right?

'I want a good, clean race, alright ladies?' Coach Cloudspear said, raising an eyebrow in Ig's direction. Ig blinked hard, trying not to let the embarrassment show on her face. For months now, she felt like she was constantly being told off for something she hadn't even done – and, even worse, no-one would tell her what she was accused of; instead giving her vague hints and *'you know what you did'* vibes, and getting annoyed when she didn't fall to her knees and beg to be expelled. She was on trial for the crime of being Ig Heretical, seven days a week.

Ig slotted herself in second to last – with Pisces bringing up the rear, her breath terrifyingly close to the back of Ig's neck – and cast her eyes down the line of girls that made up their opposing team. Okay; they had Sunita Clarkson. She was speedy, but she wasn't very tight on her turns. Petra Pribhakr was definitely going to get a Flying Power when it came to her Power Revelation Ceremony, so she was a one to watch out for…

'Iggie… Ig…'

But then they had Melanie Marks, who was much more suited to something like Animal Communications than physical classes like this one…

'Iggie! Go!'

Ig blinked. Pisces was ushering her forward like an unruly sheep, while the girl who had just flown for their team – a lean, dark-haired girl called Jessie Jameson – was tapping her foot and raising an irritated eyebrow. 'For god's sake,' she muttered under her breath. 'Coach, this isn't fair…'

Oh, crap. She'd missed her turn to fly. With a shout of frustration, Ig lurched herself upwards, scrambling through the sky, the markers seeming a million miles away…

Suddenly, a redheaded streak whooshed past her, making Ig

pull up mid-air to avoid a collision.

'Come back!' Jessie Jameson screamed at Ig. 'Come back!'

As she floundered her way back to the starting line, Ig watched as Pisces zoomed through the markers, straight as an arrow, speeding back towards the ground – before twisting her body like a swimmer and launching back into the sky for a second lap, soundly beating both Ig's opponent and her own by a mile.

Oh, Ig thought. *Well, that's… that's good. We won.* The sound of her team erupting into whoops and cheers as Pisces carried them to victory hurt her ears and her heart. Pisces did a pretty loop-de-loop in the air before barrelling straight into her teammates for an emotional hug. 'We did it, guys!' she laughed. 'Look at us! Beth, you were amazing! So were you, Jess – your turns are getting so much better, oh my god.'

'Oh my gahd, Iggie,' Lily Volt simpered, as she passed Ig on the way back to the changing rooms. 'I'm so glad you were on our team. You were suuuuper helpful.' She gave Ig's shoulder a shove that was a little too hard to be friendly.

'Uh-huh,' muttered Ig, dabbing the sweat from her face with the bottom of her T-shirt. Coach Cloudspear always said ignoring bullies would make them stop once they got bored. Lily Volt, Ig had discovered, very rarely got bored with anything.

'Yeah,' Lily said, trying to hold in a snigger. 'It makes us look so much better to Coach Cloudspear when we win with someone like you on the team. You're, like, a handicap, y'know? Like in golf.' She banged her elbow into Ig's side, hard. 'Aren't you glad you had Pisces to babysit you out there today?'

'Oh *stop,* Lily,' giggled Jessie, 'don't be so mean.' She pouted in Ig's face, her voice all sugary-sweet and fake. 'Don't you know she fancies Pisces? That's why she's always tagging along after her. Isn't that right, Iggie?'

Ig bolted for the safety of the showers.

Chapter Two

'You're not angry, are you, Iggie?' Pisces said quietly, as they got changed back into their white-and-gold uniforms after a brisk shower. 'It's just, you know, every second counts, right? And Beth and Jessie and the girls have been working so hard to improve.' Pisces' face went soft, her eyes wide and coercive. 'They really deserved the win, and...'

Ig pulled her shirt back over her head and shrugged at the same time, her whole body wriggling about like a worm on a hook. 'It's fine, Pisces. Really.'

Pisces smiled, relieved, and wrapped one long arm around Ig's shoulders. 'I knew you'd get it.' She leaned in close, and Ig felt like a million bolts of static were coursing through her veins. 'And Lily's just looking for attention, you know that. Talk to Coach if she's bothering you.'

'Yeah, that always works so well,' Ig said sarcastically, shoving her shorts back into her holdall. A month ago, one of the girls in her class had told the tutors Ig was copying her homework – which was a lie, and Ig had told the tutor as much. The other girl had cried, and Ig was sent out. In the corridor, where everyone could see her, Mr. Sunspot had given Ig a lengthy lecture about how Beth Carmine was a very promising young Hero in training, and if Ig felt the need to accuse her of cheating, then perhaps she should assess where those feelings of inadequacy and anger were coming from. Nothing changed, and Ig didn't bother going to the teachers anymore.

'That's my Iggie,' Pisces chirped brightly, turning away to wave at Jessie and Beth and – *ugh* – Lily Volt. 'I'm coming, hold on...'

The room was suddenly alive with static as the speaker in the corner of the room blared into life. *Ignatia Heretical: The General wishes to speak with you. Ignatia Heretical, to the War Room immediately.'*

Ig started at the sound of her own name being squawked over the tannoys. Everyone in the changing room turned to look at her, as if expecting a reason why her name was suddenly interrupting their social time with Pisces. As if Ig herself had any idea.

'Um,' she said. 'That's me. I guess I should… um, let me just grab my bag…'

The straps had fallen between the slats of the bench it was resting on. Of course. That gave her an extra twenty seconds of everyone in the room staring at her.

'What do you think she's done?' she heard someone whisper.

'Who knows?' another voice hissed back, as if she wasn't even in the room anymore. 'Could be anything, knowing *her.*'

'You know who her mum is, right?'

Ig flinched.

'I bet it's nothing,' Pisces whispered, as Ig finally yanked the strap free and slung her holdall over her shoulder. 'You'll be fine.'

Ig managed to give her friend a nod, mouth set in a tight line. Sometimes she hated Pisces for being so bloody nice. But that was what they were all here for, right? To learn to be good?

'Ignatia Heretical–'

'Alright, alright,' Ig cringed, grabbing her bag and wrenching open the door. 'I'm coming, I'm coming, no need to shout.'

They always used her full name. Like anyone else here was called *'Ignatia'*, for God's sake. Her mam thought it was a pretty name. Ig wasn't sure she agreed.

It wasn't until she was out the room and on her way that she realised her holdall wasn't closed properly. The zip caught sometimes; Ig made a mental note to fix it in the lift up to the War Room.

Lunalist's corridors were well-lit, with shining tiled floors and murals of famous Heroes from history painted on the walls by local artists. One of them was of Ig's dad. Luca Peterson; The Streak. Based on a photo that was clearly taken before he became a dad, The Streak wore the same bright, beaming smile in two dimensions as he did in three. Ig passed it on the way to the lift and felt a little sick. Guilt, she supposed.

'Miss Heretical?'

Ahead of her, walking the opposite way, was Ig's Agility & Ability tutor, Miss Pineda. 'Miss Heretical, come here, please.' Ig did as she was told. 'Are you on your way to the War Room? They've been calling for you.'

Where else would I be going? Ig thought. But, instead of saying that out loud and getting in trouble for 'insubordination' – again – she nodded.

'How are you finding your homework this week?'

'I… er… ugh.' Ig took a deep breath and fixed what she hoped was a Pisces-worthy smile to her face. 'It's coming along, Miss.'

Miss Pineda clicked her tongue in a way that Ig assumed was meant to be sympathetic but came across as pitying. 'You know, if you're having trouble, The Base is always open.'

The Base was the after-school-hours club for students struggling with their homework. Attendance was marked on your report for the end of the year. Ig would rather sit on a porcupine.

'I'm okay, Miss. Promise.'

Miss Pineda cocked her head to the side, bird-like. 'If you're sure?' she said, her tone sing-song-y and patronising. Ig felt a tic of irritation spark up in her jaw but covered it up with her sunniest smile and said nothing.

'You know, I understand how hard this must be for you,' Miss Pineda continued. 'Being the first person in your family to study as a Hero, after all.'

What? 'But I'm *not* the–' Ig began, before Miss Pineda interrupted her, waving her off irritably.

'I mean the first *girl.* I know your dad.'

Of course you do, Ig thought, that tic in her jaw worsening.

'I want you to know that all the tutors are here for you, especially if you're struggling–'

'It's fine! Positive, Miss!' Ig chirped Miss Pineda scowled, clearly annoyed at her speech being cut off. But Ig really, really didn't have time for the sympathy parade. 'I'll have my homework ready for next lesson. After I've been to the War Room.'

'Is your holdall broken?' Miss Pineda took a step towards Ig, reaching out to take her bag from her hands. 'Do you need me to close it for you?'

Ignatia Heretical–

'I have to go, Miss. See you later!'

Off Ig went; skidding around a corner, narrowly avoiding bashing her hip on the wall. She wasn't late; not yet. She could still make good time up to the War Room if the lift was waiting for her.

And, of course, the stupid thing was cruising back down from the top floor at a snail's pace. Perfect. She could fiddle with her bag now, while she waited; but knowing her luck, the lift would come as soon as she tried. Better to wait.

Imagine Miss Pineda asking where she was going. As if she didn't even recognise her own name. And like she couldn't even zip up her own holdall right – as if everyone hadn't had their stupid bag break at least once–

'…worry about that girl, you know.'

Ig's ears pricked up. She glanced behind her; Miss Pineda was leaning against the door of a classroom, talking to another teacher. Talking to another teacher about her.

'…shuffle her back down to Basic last week, did you hear?'

'Ugh, that must have been such a nightmare for you.'

Classes at Lunalist were divided into three; Basic, Intermediate, and Advanced, depending on the student's abilities and potential for that specific class to be a staple of their eventual Power. Was Ig a mystical fighter, or a healer, or a shapeshifter? Was she going to save the world with her speed, or her wits, or her charms? She didn't know – and her teachers shuffled her from Basic Classes into Intermediate and back again as a result. Once, a really hopeful teacher placed her in Advanced Strategics, only for her to go totally off-piste at her first assessment and start talking about how she'd thrown away the map she'd been given and started again, because she'd noticed a flaw in the Villain's lair she had been assigned. It wasn't designed to be breached by a flying Hero, like she'd been told – it was a water-based lair! There must have been a mistake. So, she'd drawn up a new version of the lair, but set it amongst the clouds, so her fictional Hero had a better chance of success. She was kicked back to Intermediate before the class had finished.

Ig turned back towards the lift doors; face bright red, pretending she couldn't hear. Why was this lift so bloody slow?!

'Her dad's been called up so many times to talk to The General about her, I don't know how he copes.'

'Isn't the mother in the picture?'

'Oh yes. But you know who she is, don't you? The Witch Queen?'

'I mean; it's obvious with that hair, once you know.'

Ig pulled on the ends of the fluffy, black bob curling around her ears. Everyone said stuff like that, and she didn't know what they were talking about. Her mam's hair was beautiful.

The lift opened behind her with a soft woosh.

'*Ignatia Heretical–*'

Ig leapt inside and slammed the Close Door button before the hot tears of shame could begin to fall. She crammed all her files and notebooks a little further down into her holdall, fumbling with the clasp before throwing it on the floor in frustration, letting the papers and pens and Flyer Class kit scatter across the floor. Then she picked them up, guiltily. It wasn't the bag's fault, after all.

Everyone knew who Ig's mam was. The beautiful and terrible Witch Queen, with her murder of crows and her wicked smile, causing chaos throughout the early 2000s all over the United Kingdom until, suddenly, she settled down with a Hero and had a baby with him; finger painting and changing nappies instead of manipulating the entire world to her whim. She was the great love and the worst embarrassment of Ig's life.

Safely inside the lift, Ig tried her best to breathe. Anger and shame swirled in her stomach, bouncing off each other and mingling in her gut. Being here was all she'd ever wanted. And it was going so badly. She was The Streak's daughter – she should be following in his footsteps! And he'd told her so much about his time here; all the fun he'd had, all the friendships he'd made, all the hilarious scrapes he'd got himself into and out of again with a roguish grin and a wink. He'd been so excited for her to come here, and whenever she called home and he asked her how things were going, she'd say they were fine and hope he couldn't tell she was lying. Because most people here took one look at Ig – with her pathetic attempts to fit in and her awkward, pained smile – and decided she must be The Witch Queen come again, not The Streak's daughter. And when she wasn't terrifying and gorgeous and lethal like her mam, they discarded her and labelled her a failure.

He must be so disappointed. No matter how well he hid it from her.

As the lift silently whooshed her up to the War Room, Ig noticed a hot, tingling feeling in her palms. She forced herself to open her eyes; her hands, braced against the lift's console, were blotched with dark purple spots, collecting across her knuckles like bruises. It happened when she got stressed, or annoyed, sometimes; Mam said it wasn't anything to worry about. 'Just bad circulation, love,' she'd said once, after Ig had come to her crying because the pads of skin under her fingernails had turned black. 'Your grandad was always the same. Try and shake it out. Your hands won't fall off, I promise.'

So that was what Ig did. Shook out her hands one by one, counting to eight under her breath as she did. The bruising had faded a bit by the time the lift pinged open; the doors sliding away to reveal a huge, well-lit room, filled with desks and computers and people bustling about in *important* looking uniforms and staring intently at important looking screens. But Ig shoved her hands into the pockets of her uniform all the same. Just in case. She didn't need to show herself up. Not today, of all days. Because, in the middle of the room, a woman with iron-dark hair and an iron-cold expression was staring her down.

'Ignatia Heretical,' The General said. 'You're late.'

Chapter Three

In the eyes of the world, The General *was* the Academy. Attending her Power Revelation Ceremony at the tender age of fourteen – two years before most students were even considering being ready for such an honour – she'd used her amazing, once-in-a-lifetime strength to help her teacher Apex defeat the Midnight Movement – the most famous collective of Villains in the United Kingdom. She was a legend in the making… and, after graduating, she gave it all up to come back to the Academy and pass on her drive, her passion and her integrity to the next generation by working her way up from teaching assistant to become the school's most famous headteacher.

Ig's mother hated her.

The General was constantly being featured in glossy magazines, in interviews and on posters advertising the school – her muscles still rippling under the material of her suit, her grey hair cut neat and short – and every student got a letter from her personal desk when they were accepted into Lunalist. Ig had framed hers. The General organised the lesson plans, kept tabs on every student and, most importantly of all, she was there when you had your Power revealed to you. Every student, in the moment their life changed forever – like so many before them – had The General at their side, guiding them forward.

When Ig had first arrived at the Academy – hair neat, uniform ironed to within an inch of its life, her father at her side laughing with the tutors about the old days – The General had passed them by and looked down at her with an appreciative nod of the head.

'Miss Heretical,' she'd said. 'I attended this school with your father. He's a good man. You'll make us proud, just like he did.'

The next time The General saw her, Ig was face down in the mud after attempting a jump in Agility & Ability that was far too high for her. Ig had never forgotten the expression on her headteacher's face. The disappointment. The regret. The distaste. Now, every time Ig flubbed a test, or her marks weren't quite high enough, or people like Lily Volt looked down their snooty, pretty noses at her, she imagined that expression and let herself feel the pain that it brought. *One day*, she would think, *I'll earn back my potential. I'll change how The General looks at me.* And now, she was here, in the War Room – right at the very apex of the Academy's curving roof, where students were usually forbidden to go. What did that mean?

Ig crossed the room, legs heavy and awkwardly stiff underneath her. People passed by her; clutching tablets, jabbing at the screens and talking to each other in fast-paced, technical jargon. Over in a corner, a girl – a new graduate who was picked up for the War Room team because of her hacking skills – prodded her co-worker in the shoulder, and the pair watched as Ig climbed the two steps onto the main raised podium, head held high. She wouldn't show fear. She was brave. She was a Hero! But then The General cast a look her way, eyebrow raised, and Ig felt embarrassment heat up in her stomach again. 'Sorry,' she began, hands twisting over one another nervously. 'The lift took ages to arrive, General, and – well, I was in my Flyers kit when you called for me, and I had to get changed, so...'

'A poor management of your time does not excuse lateness, Miss Heretical.'

'I... sorry, General.'

'Quite alright. Every failure has the chance to be a learning experience, hm?' The General held out a hand, and someone slotted a tablet into it. 'Now, we have a lot to discuss.' The General strode off, leaving Ig to trot behind her to keep up. Around them, the glass walls of Lunalist were painted eggshell blue by a sunny, springtime sky, filled with fluffy white clouds.

'I'm sure,' began The General, 'that you are aware, Miss Heretical, how important this school is. The Academy houses the best of the best. Under this school's guidance, students like yourself grow into caretakers for the entire planet.' She cast a meaningful look down and to the side, directly at Ig – but exactly what that meaning was, Ig wasn't sure. 'This school prizes strength, discipline, and ability. I'm sure you know that, Miss Heretical. Take your hands out of your pockets, please.'

Ig tucked her hands behind her back, making sure not to glance at her fingers and give the game away. The tingling had stopped, so hopefully the bruising had too.

She was definitely here to be reprimanded for something. Something big. Had she forgotten some homework? That used to happen all the time, until she got a planner. But the problem with the planner was you needed to remember to fill it in. Ig had been so sure she'd been doing better recently, but obviously she was wrong, clearly she'd messed up again and she was about to be expelled–

'Have you ever heard, Miss Heretical,' The General asked, turning finally to face Ig, 'of the Shackleton School for Villains?'

Ig only knew what everyone knew. Tucked away in some half-forgotten part of Northumberland, Shackleton was the Academy's darker half. A place where students went in, and Villains came out. A very, very bad place.

The General leaned down into Ig's personal space. 'Do you know anything about their methods? Who teaches there, any of their alumni?' Ig shook her head. 'Interesting,' The General sniffed. 'I assumed, with your background, that you would know of it.'

Ig winced. Of course The General knew that The Witch Queen had gone to school there; she was The General, after all. But apart from a few old photos, her mam really hadn't shared much of her Shackleton days with Ig. To be fair, Ig had never asked.

The General shuddered; a barely-there shake of the shoulders, as if repressing the memory of something disgusting. 'Shackleton Academy is a place, Miss Heretical, where children are groomed to become the next arbiters of chaos and disaster by the very people who have tormented graduates of Lunalist for years. Decades, even.'

The General paused, turning, feet together, to stare out of the window at the river and the sky surrounding them. Ig took the opportunity to take in her headteacher while she was distracted; tall, with broad shoulders and an imposing jawline, her clasped hands resting on the small of her back. Not a stray thread, not a loose hair out of place – apart from the broad spiderweb of scarring across her right wrist. A trophy from her days as the country's youngest working Hero; every year group had a new theory about what they thought had happened. The latest one she'd heard from the first years was that The General had had her entire hand cut off in a fight with Laseria, and doctors at the RVI in town had sewed it back on. Which was silly. The RVI didn't deal with reattachment surgery. Pisces' dad worked there; Ig had heard him talking about work during their once-a-week, hour-long phone call. Ig was much more partial to the theory that The General's scar was a burn; potentially from the famous incident at the Tyneside Cinema when The Roxy suite caught fire during a showing of The Shape of Water – ironically – and The General had saved five old ladies who went on the record as saying they weren't really enjoying the film, anyway.

'For most of our history, Lunalist and Shackleton had, shall we say, an almost-friendly rivalry,' The General said after a long while. 'After all, you are children, and we tutors are working in a professional capacity. Then,' she strode away, her face an ivory mask, 'there was the Incident in '92.'

'The Incident?' Ig jogged a step or two to keep up. The staff around them gaped at her as if she'd asked for clarification on the moon landing – clearly giving away that they were listening in. *Sneaks.*

'On the first day of Autumn Term, 1992,' The General filled in; still not looking in Ig's direction, 'a Shackleton student attacked Lunalist. They disapproved of our methods; jealous of our results, the calibre of Hero we were putting out into the world, the way we constantly knocked back their schemes once they graduated into the real world. And so they invaded, hoping to sabotage us. They actually got into the dorms. Where we *sleep*.' She peered at Ig, who shrank back. 'You really didn't know about that, Miss Heretical?'

Ig didn't dare move, for fear that the wrong sort of blink could be interpreted as her having travelled back in time and committed the crime herself.

'Fascinating. They were apprehended quickly, but one student was seriously injured in the resulting conflict.' The General's jaw set. 'Life-changing injuries, the poor girl never recovered. But all the same, they were driven back. Since then, there has always been a monitoring between the two schools – and of course, there is a sense of competitiveness once our alumni make their way into the world. Boasting about a graduate's skills, lamenting their defeats. But nothing beyond that.' The General cleared her throat. 'However, one of our reconnaissance teams have reason to believe that Shackleton is planning something. Another assault against Lunalist.'

'Planning something?'

'Yes. Shackleton–'

'Like what?'

The General slowly – terrifyingly slowly – turned to face her. 'Miss Heretical. You know better than to interrupt.'

'Sorry, General.' She did know better. Normally. But something important was happening, and she still had no idea why she was here! She needed answers! Patience, Ig had learned while studying at Lunalist, was not one of her strong suits. She folded her hands behind her back and looked out of the window. 'Please continue. I won't speak again. Until you want me to, that is.'

'Very well. Shackleton sits outside a very small rural community in Northumberland called Rossborough; the villagers let the students run feral with no accountability or monitoring; provided their actions stay firmly on school property. Because of that, our reconnaissance teams couldn't glean any extra information about the school from the locals. I was not willing to risk the safety of our students, so I made the decision to call off the mission and report back so we can regroup. Talia?'

A beautiful girl with short-cropped hair stepped up from basically nowhere to stand beside The General. She was one of the older students who was giving their gifts and their expertise back to the school that had raised them; she'd probably be a teacher someday, like The General. Folded neatly against her back were a set of huge, feathered wings. 'Hey, kiddo,' Talia said, reaching out to ruffle Ig's hair.

'Um,' Ig replied, eyes downcast and bashful. She'd never wash her head again. Pisces was the main object of her affections, but anytime Ig was in the vicinity of a pretty girl who was even remotely nice to her, she was useless.

'Talia here,' The General was saying, placing an affectionate hand on the older girl's shoulders, 'is the leader of our main reconnaissance team. She can tell you everything you need to know.'

Everything *Ig* needed to know?

'So,' Talia said, leading Ig over to a huge holographic projection in the centre of the War Room, 'This is what we know about the layout of Shackleton. One building, four storeys tall; but we do wonder if there's an elaborate basement system.' She tapped the screen, and four extra levels blipped into existence below the foundations. 'No way students and faculty are all sleeping and studying in that small space. Perhaps the students are housed above ground, and the, er, *lessons* are done down below. That's part of what we need to find out. The basement theory also means we have little to no idea what they're teaching their students.' Talia reached back and touched one of her wings. 'That, and the thorns.'

'Talia and her team can't get too close to the grounds themselves,'

The General explained. 'Part of the school's fortification is a wall of briars and bramble thickets around the perimeter.'

'Like in Sleeping Beauty?' Ig added – more so it sounded like she was listening than anything else. She was listening! She just needed to *show* that she was listening, which was a whole different skill. After a long pause, The General nodded.

'I suppose so.' The General flicked her hand at the hologram screen, and it changed to a line-up of faces; people with masks and sneers, wild smiles and deadly serious glares. 'The faculty. Not too much intel to gain about them; they're all established Villains, we know who they are and how they operate. But the students?' The General narrowed her eyes. 'Wild cards, all of them.'

'Wild cards?'

'They're unknowns to us. Unpredictable, in the most literal sense of the word. They could be planning anything. That is our main goal. Learn more about the students.' The General flicked the screen back to the layout and looked at the foundations of Shackleton long and hard, before turning briskly on her heel and walking away. 'Dana!'

The hacker girl slid over to Ig, still in her chair, and pressed a silver, compact mirror-shaped device into her hand. 'A communication device,' Dana explained briskly. 'You can call the War Room directly on it. It also has a dictaphone app, for note-taking and reconnaissance.'

'Um… okay?' Ig turned the device this way and that in her hands. 'Cool,' she offered. Dana curled her lip.

'Your uniform will be provided for you by the faculty,' The General continued, 'however, anything else you wish to take with you – clothes, books – must be packed away and sent down to the office before tomorrow evening. One term; you can arrange contact with the device Dana gave you once a month – three times in total – to give you ample time to gather intelligence. We'll assess then, to see if we need you in place for a longer period.'

There were two rooms off to one side of the War Room; both

with simple, frosted-glass panelled doors. The General opened
the door on the right. 'Now; step into my personal office and
we'll iron out the details.'

Wait. *What*?!

'General,' Ig stammered, 'I… I'm a bit confused. What… who
is… am I…'

The General, Dana and Talia gave Ig a look. A strange mix of
pity, frustration and confusion that Ig had known for most of
her life. 'You're going to Shackleton,' Talia said, talking ever so
slightly slower than she had before. 'Undercover.'

…*Oh*.

Chapter Four

'Awww,' Pisces cooed, throwing her arm around Ig's shoulder, 'but what am I going to do without my favourite roomie?'

'Ahaha,' Ig said – not laughed; she *said it*, like an idiot – 'I'm sure you'll be fine without me.'

'Nooo, I'll miss you!' Pisces rested her cheek on the top of Ig's head, and suddenly the hallway seemed to have all its oxygen removed in one fell swoop. 'You'll have to make a recording of your snoring, I don't know if I can sleep without it.'

'…wh-what?'

Pisces had been briefed on where Ig was going, but no-one else at school knew; Top Secret, according to The General. In The General's office, Ig had been told to act normally for her last full school day at Lunalist. Then, she'd be whisked away before morning lessons started. Great. If only Ig knew how to act normal. Especially when she was around Pisces.

'Okay, ladies and gents,' their teacher, Mrs. Owlish said, interrupting Ig's thoughts about Pisces and beds, 'take your seats, we have a lot to go over today.'

Ig found her usual seat in her Press Conference and Promotional Material class and tucked her holdall under her chair. This was a more standard classroom experience at Lunalist than Flyer Class; a neat, orderly room with a state-of-the-art touchscreen whiteboard at the front and a fussy, bespectacled teacher trying to wrangle the attention of twenty or so teenage Heroes in the making. Ig's seat was right by the window, so she got a perfect view of the world outside the Academy; the silver, curving Millenium Bridge just outside the school's perimeter, the kittiwakes wheeling through the air, the busy people bustling to and fro – all safe in the knowledge that there would always be new Heroes to protect them.

This would probably be the last time Ig saw this view for a while. Ig rested her head on her chin and thought back over everything The General had said to her. All the information she'd been given about her new…mission? Did this count as a mission? Yeah; it did. Of course it did. *Take that, Lily Volt; I have my first mission already. Have fun in Flyer Class without me.*

'Iggie… Ig…'

She needed to pack. She'd have to remember her toothbrush – who knows if Villains even cleaned their teeth regularly enough to supply her with a new one if she forgot? And she'd have to pack her pyjamas, and her shampoo, and…

'Iggie!'

In the same instant that Pisces tugged on the sleeve of her uniform, her pretty brow creased with concern, Ig's attention snapped back into the classroom with a crash of panic. Every single person in the classroom was staring at her – including their teacher, tapping her foot rapidly against the tiles in irritation.

'Miss Heretical,' Mrs. Owlish sniped, peering over the top of her wire-rimmed glasses at Ig. 'You've finally blessed us with your attention.'

A giggle rippled around the room, and Ig felt her face grow hot. She swore that Mrs. Owlish didn't even *need* glasses; she just wore them so she could make patronising faces at people. 'Sorry, Miss,' she murmured under her breath. 'Got lots on my mind.'

'Hm. I'm sure you do.' Another classroom-wide giggle; louder this time. Mrs. Owlish's foot tapped all the harder on the tile. 'I was asking if you were ready?'

Ready for what? Ig thought. *To go? Am I going now? No; I thought The General said I had 'til tomorrow morning…* When she paused; tongue pressed against her teeth, mind raking through possibilities for what she might possibly have missed,

Pisces leaned over and whispered in her ear.

'Your project.'

Oh. That was right. Today was PCaPM assessment day. Yay.

'How,' Mrs. Owlish said, turning back to address the entire class; eager to turn Ig into a learnable experience, as if this weren't embarrassing enough already, 'can you – any of you! – expect to become the best Heroes you can be – to serve the citizens of this world properly! – if you can't listen to instructions? It isn't hard, children; there's always a right way to do these things.'

And *that* was exactly why this was Ig's least favourite lesson. No matter what she wrote down, she always seemed to do it the *wrong* way. Press Conferences were always about six times longer than they needed to be – either the mission went well, or it didn't, right? Why did that need to take up so much time that could be spent actually fixing the problem?! Ig didn't understand, and no-one seemed to be able to give her an answer; they just glared at her and moved on with the lesson. To make matters worse; for this assessment she'd had to write three – *three*! – different press releases for three outcomes of the same mission! One for a failure, one for a success, and one unforeseen circumstance. It had been like pulling teeth. But she needed this Assessment to go well, or she'd be shunted back down to the Basic Class when she came back from Shackleton. Another reshuffle of her schedule, another letter home, and one less class with Pisces? No thanks.

Also, 'children'?! Ig was *fifteen*. She wasn't a baby anymore.

'Miss Heretical? Are you ready to show us your–'

Oh, crap. Ig hadn't moved. 'Um,' she sputtered, bursting into life and rifling around in her holdall, 'hang on, just a second. It's in here, I didn't… get it out of my–'

The communication device The General had given her fell out of its pocket with a clatter. Ig picked it up and inspected it; she couldn't break the bloody thing before she'd even left the school grounds – and forgot all about what she was looking for

for ten precious seconds.

'Oh, right – sorry, Miss, I'll be just a–'

'Alright, that's enough,' Mrs. Owlish interrupted with a roll of her eyes. 'Miss Rising, why don't you give us your presentation first? While Miss Heretical… composes herself.' The tutor shot Ig one last withering look over her glasses. 'I know cunning and manipulation runs in your family, Miss Heretical, but if you are stalling for time over an incomplete assessment, you'll be in detention for a week.'

Ig abandoned her bag; sinking slowly into her seat, embarrassed. She wasn't stalling for time – she just hadn't been prepared to go next. Times like these, Ig wished with all her heart they made Power Lenders for Acting Like A Competent Human Being.

'Miss Rising? Are you ready to present?'

'Yes, Mrs. Owlish.' Pisces stood up, flicking her auburn hair over one shoulder as she did. Someone at the back of the class wolf-whistled – before getting smacked by his friend – while someone else called out *we love you Pisces!*'

It was true. Everyone did love Pisces. Including Ig. She was… she was just so *impressive*, wasn't she? Pisces shot Ig a sympathetic look before striding to the front of the classroom, million-watt smile in place.

'Okay. Now, Miss Rising,' their teacher said, visibly relaxing now that she could focus on a *real* student, 'what was your project? Remind the class.'

Pisces tucked a lock of hair behind her ear, rolling her eyes in an '*oh, little old me?*' sort of way that made Ig want to punch a pillow. 'A Power Revelation speech.'

A chorus of 'oooh's – as if Power Revelation speeches weren't the same every single year. Ig had been watching them on TV since she was little, she could practically recite them. Mrs. Owlish gestured for her to begin, sitting at her desk with a big, wide smile that made something inside of Ig twist painfully.

'*Welcome, students,*' Pisces began, after clearing her throat, '*To your*

Power Revelation ceremony. You attended the Lunalist Academy For the Gifted and Talented to discover your strengths – and hone your talents – in the most prestigious school on the planet. But from this moment on, you are no longer students. You are Heroes. Last night, each of you attended a special ceremony with your tutors – and The General, of course.' (another hushed "oooh". Of course Pisces namedropped The General to get the crowd on side.) *'In that hallowed space, your chosen Power was revealed to you.'* Pisces clasped her hands earnestly at her chest. *'You are all shining examples of what Lunalist students can be, and should all be very, very proud. When your name is called, you will join me up here, on this stage…'* Ig swore her eyes were shining with emotional tears, *'and show the world what you have achieved. Ladies and gentlemen; may I present, for the very first time, your new Heroes!'*

The entire class applauded, and that was the moment Ig knew she was done for. Her assessment project, sitting crumpled at the bottom of her satchel, was full of points and counter points, facts and information about the fictional mission she'd been given. She'd even made the sentences short and snappy, to ensure she kept everyone's attention. But she couldn't smile and cry and *connect* on command, the way that Pisces did. Goodbye, Intermediate PCaPM. Any dreams she had of showing up Lily Volt went up in smoke before her eyes. She'd really have to impress them on this mission to claw her way back to respectfulness, wouldn't she?

'Don't worry about your grades, Iggie,' Pisces said to her, as they made their way to their next class. 'When you've absolutely smashed your first mission, no-one's going to care about some stupid PCaPM assessment.'

'You think so?' Ig said. Pisces looped one long arm around her shoulder.

'I know so. Forget all about it,' Pisces said breezily, 'and think about what movie we should watch tonight. You need a leaving party, after all – I'll grab us some popcorn from the mess hall after school finishes for the day, and we can watch whatever you like! How's that sound?'

'Thanks. Yeah, it sounds good. Um, Pisces,' Ig said, stumbling over her words as her gaze plummeted to the floor. 'Before I go to Sh – um, before I leave, I wanted to say, well, I'm really going to miss–'

'Pisces!' Coach Cloudspear called from halfway down the hall, 'you remembered about Swimming Club tonight?'

Pisces winced; her arm still draped over Ig's shoulder. 'Bloody Swimming Club,' she muttered. But as Coach Cloudspear wandered over to them, her arm slipped away. She straightened her back, and Ig felt a chill run up her back as Pisces' smile turned bright and cheerful, her voice jumping up an octave when she said 'Hi Coach! Were you talking to me?'

'I was.' Coach Cloudspear said, folding his arms. 'You've remembered it's your first session at Swimming Club tonight, yeah? I really think it'd be good for you. Plus, I know the girls are heading into town to go for iced coffee first?' He winked, and Ig wanted to vomit. 'Special perks, we call it 'team building' so I can get you out of lessons to go have some fun. It'll be good for you to, uh,' Coach shot a look in Ig's direction, 'mix with some other girls.'

Off to one side, a group of girls – all Swimming Club girls, Ig supposed – saw who Coach Cloudspear was talking to and began to wave manically and squeal meaninglessly in their direction. Among them was Lily Volt, who raised her hand to her lips and blew Pisces a sickeningly sweet kiss. Pisces flicked her fingers in a greeting, and her lips twitched into a shy smile.

Pisces didn't like swimming. She hated getting her hair wet. Ig had known that for years. But all the same, she watched her friend turn to Coach Cloudspear, grin with all her teeth and say that '*yeah, of course she remembered! She couldn't wait!*'

The amazing thing to Ig was that she really sounded like she meant it. Pisces was a marvel, in more ways than one.

Coach Cloudspear's smile was big, genuine and relieved. 'Good. Good! The girls are all heading up to Planet Mocha soon; the one at Monument? You should be able to catch them.' He cast a look over Ig, and the smile faded. 'Work on your take-off for next lesson,' he said curtly. 'Please.'

As their teacher turned and walked away, Ig leaned into Pisces and whispered; 'Iced coffee? Swimming Club? But what about movie night tonight? I leave in the morning, Pisces…' Pisces' face fell. 'Oh. Oh, Iggie, I forgot. I forgot all about Swimming Club, I am so, so sorry–'

'No, it's okay.' Ig swallowed her disappointment – and, as much as she hated to admit it, her frustration. She'd be spending her last night at Lunalist for a whole term all alone? *Really*?! 'We'll celebrate the night I get back. Like a welcome home party.'

'Okay.' Pisces said, relieved. 'It's a promise, okay?' She leaned in and gave Ig a big hug. 'I'm really going to miss you!' For one fleeting second, Ig allowed herself to close her eyes and dream. Maybe when she returned – or after their Power Revelation, when she was a real Hero – she could finally confess to Pisces how she felt. And, once she'd proven herself, she could be the type of girl that Pisces would like back. Maybe, after they left Lunalist, they could go on adventures together; even save the world together. The great, infamous Hero team of Ig and Pisces, wondrous and powerful saviours who kissed each other mid-air and The General would officiate their wedding and Lily Volt would be so jealous she'd spontaneously combust and… 'Bye, Iggie. See you when you get back! Enjoy your film!' And Pisces was off, running on her long, colt-like limbs towards the other group of girls. She disappeared into the crowd, rounding the corner and vanishing from sight.

Chapter Five

'*Iced Coffee.*' '*Swimming Club.*' Bah.

Ig couldn't even remember the last time she went across the river into the city centre. Oh, wait; it was when she went to see Phantom at the Theatre Royal with her mam. But that didn't count, right? Going into town with your parents was different from going for '*iced coffee with the Swimming Club girls.*'

About twenty minutes' walk from the school was the centre of Newcastle, where generations of teenage Heroes had loitered aimlessly during their free periods, basking in everything their city had to offer. Discounts on clothes and makeup in the shopping centre, free drinks on their birthday at Planet Mocha, tourists eager to take their picture so they could say that they met a Hero before they made it big – all revolving around the gigantic stone monument to Earl Grey like it was the spoke of a wheel. Pisces loved going into town, she went every chance she got. It was so different from the quiet, orderly halls of Lunalist – full of life and noise. And Ig was stuck in her bedroom, trying to work out how many socks she needed to pack.

That night, instead of watching the film she'd planned to share with Pisces, Ig had called home; curled up under her weighted blanket, her beloved, battered shark plushie held tight in her arms, her phone propped up on the pillow.
'Hey, sweetheart!'

'Hi, Dad!'

Luca Peterson looked like a surfer from a film set in the Nineties; broad and smiley, always cracking jokes in his thick American accent and making strangers into friends. Ig remembered begging her parents to let her bleach her hair, so she'd look more like him. She and her dad had got as far as the tub – a towel wrapped around her shoulders, Dad examining the instructions on the back of the box – before her mam had come home and gone ballistic. Now, Ig was sort of glad they'd never gone through with it. She could cut her hair, so it didn't look like her mam's infamous, waist-length locks. But try as she might, she couldn't fake her dad's sun-kissed, California gold.

The Streak charmed people. The Witch Queen terrified people into loving her – or, with Ig and her father, loved them so intensely that they simply couldn't resist her. Ig seemed to just make people vaguely confused.

'How's my girl doing?' Luca Peterson held his tablet at what his daughter called 'The Old People Angle', all nose and chin. 'Oof; I see Finnie. That bad, huh?'

'Just… a lot going on. Is Mam about?'

'I think she's doing her yoga in the living room. But I can get her? Baby! Ig's on the phone–'

'No! No, Dad,' Ig protested, waving her hands in front of the screen. 'I have something to tell you, but Mam can't know.' The General had made her promise. For security reasons.

'Oh… sure. Sure. What's up?'

Over the next ten minutes, Ig told her father about her first ever assignment – 'It's a reconnaissance mission,' she'd said, with a frisson of pride, 'they want me to, ah, infiltrate this Villain, um, compound. And see what they're planning.'

'Oh, for real?! Honey,' her dad cried, snatching up the tablet and spinning it around so Ig felt like she was flying, 'that's amazing!'

Her dad's favourite word; *amazing*. Everything was *amazing*, from news reports of the latest Hero to save the world to her mam's pasta bake. Mam said it was because he was American; Ig thought it was because he himself was amazing. He was the best dad in the world.

'My little girl, on her first ever mission!' Ig's dad flopped back into his seat. 'Oh, I can't wait to tell the guys – oh, hold on. I can't, can I? Darn. And you're sure your mom can't know? It's 'coz she's a Villain, right? You know she wouldn't ever rat on you, Ig, she wants what's best for – oh. It's Shackleton, isn't it?' He winced. 'You're going to Shackleton. They think your mom would have, whaddaya call it, hometown loyalty.'

'Yep. But it's a secret, Dad. Please?' Ig should have known she couldn't keep a secret from her dad for long. Luca Peterson was super speedy – in every way. He could run, swim and talk ten times faster than any other human on the planet when he wanted to, and his brain worked in a similar way; leaping from thought to thought like a spider monkey. Ig felt a little of that same pull in her brain, from time to time – it was part of why her grades fluctuated so much. It had basically been a given that Ig would have a Power, some day; something like ninety-five percent of kids born to a person with a Power had one of their own, and Ig had two supernaturally talented parents for the price of one. But, even so, Ig didn't fit. She was awkward, and the teachers didn't know what to make of her. This mission would change that, though. She'd make sure of it.

'Well,' her dad said after a long moment, 'as long as you're safe, I'll keep my lips zipped. It's school business, after all, right? Your mom did promise to steer clear.'

'Right.'

'So why'd they choose you, honey? Your grades finally starting to stabilise? I knew they would, I was telling Grant and John on the driving range just yesterday that–'

'Um. It's something like that.' Ig said, hugging Finnie a little closer.

'We've informed Shackleton that you're transferring,' The General had said in her office, 'because Lunalist wasn't the right fit for you. You needed an education that was more your...' The General's gaze flicked over Ig, 'more your tempo.'

Ig felt stupid for wincing at those words, forcing her shoulders to relax as The General continued talking. Because they weren't true, right? They were a cover story for her real mission. An act. A way for her to be of use to her school.

'And with your last name, and your resemblance to your mother,' – Ig's hand went to her hair, but she bit her tongue – 'this operation should go off without a hitch. If there's one thing I know about the faculty at Shackleton, it's that they lunge at every chance they get for a new recruit.'

There was more. As The General filled out the forms, citing the reasons for Ig's supposed transfer out of Lunalist, Ig had read – upside down – that there was a blank space for any 'Reasons Not Pertaining to Academia' for her departure. 'Put in there,' Ig had said to The General, snatching up a pen out of her tutor's pot to gesture with, 'that I got bullied. Here. Um, please.'

The General had looked up from her paperwork with a slow blink. 'Miss Heretical,' she said, 'we have a zero-tolerance policy on bullying at Lunalist.'

'Right, yes, I know,' Ig had said, furiously clicking the pen as she thought. 'And I'm not! Being bullied, I mean.' *I mean, she thought, Lily Volt is a massive pain in my backside every single day, and she did try and get one of her little boyfriends from the year above to pretend he fancied me. At least that one backfired when they found out I like girls. And people still say I'm a cheat who copies homework. But that's not bullying. They never hit me, or anything.* 'But if they think I have been – bullied, I mean – then they won't assume that I, you know, like anyone at the Academy. Why would I be communicating with anyone from a place where I got, you know, my head stuffed down a toilet or something every day? Plus, it'll help with that, um, tempo thing you mentioned.'

The General had sat in silence for a long moment. Then, she'd nodded, and written something down in the box. 'Very good, Miss Heretical,' she'd said softly, and Ig's heart leapt into her chest with pride. 'You could have potential here at Lunalist yet.'

A knock at her father's bedroom door. 'Is that my daughter I hear?' called a woman's voice.

'We're just talking school stuff, baby,' her dad called over his shoulder. 'Be out in a minute.'

'Well, wrap it up. I want to talk to – ugh, Luca! Do you really have to dump all these receipts on the coffee table? Coffee, petrol, coffee again *in the same day…*'

'I gotta have my frappe!' her dad said with a laugh. 'Ig, listen to this; I went to Planet Mocha for a frappe; they tried to give me it on the house again, can y'believe that?!'

Ig could believe it.

'Said it was an honour to have The Streak as a regular. *Sooo* embarrassing – I'm your regular Average Joe, these days.'

The door behind him opened. 'Yes, dear,' Ig's mam said, rolling her eyes into the camera as she flicked her fingers in greeting at her daughter. 'So very average.'

'I told the girl behind the counter, I said—'

'*You guys are the real Heroes,*' Ig's mother chimed in, waggling her head in a perfect imitation of her husband when he thought he was being funny. 'Hello, poppet.'

Ig laughed, covering her mouth to muffle the giggles. 'Hi, Mam.'

Only The Witch Queen could make yoga pants seem intimidating. Her long, dark hair was piled up on top of her head, tied with a green ribbon. Her eyebrows were dark and arched, her eyes naturally a piercing emerald shade. Ig's were more like the colour of old moss. In her hand was a mug shaped like a black cat – filled with what Ig knew was herbal tea – which she drank from like a haughty queen sipping on a cup of wine as she decided which her subjects could live another day. 'So,' Viola Heretical said, 'what is it I can't know about my own daughter?'

Ig groaned internally. When she'd started *applying* for schools, her mam had dropped some subtle hints about wanting her to go to Shackleton – in the form of pamphlets about the school being 'coincidentally' left at the dinner table, in the car, and even in the shower for Ig to peruse. When Ig had picked Lunalist regardless, she'd pouted for a week – calling every raven in the county to their doorstep to rustle their feathers menacingly and poop on her dad's car – but eventually, she had accepted it. Begrudgingly. She'd even promised Lunalist in writing that she'd never set foot on the school grounds; meaning Dad had to drop everything whenever there was a Parent's Evening or a 'little chat' about Ig's grades. He'd left so many missions, missed out on so many opportunities, so he could sit in a chair that was too small for him and listen to Ig's teachers say she still wasn't applying herself. When she did! She really did, all the time; she just couldn't make it work.

'Ig,' her dad said, beaming, 'has an assignment. It's all very hush-hush, but it's gonna lead to big things!' He looked over his shoulder. 'We're so pleased for you,' he said, making eye contact with The Witch Queen. 'Aren't we, baby?'

In the background, Ig watched her mother steel herself with a deep intake of breath. 'That's right, darling,' she said, smiling into the camera. 'We're really proud of you.' She smiled, thin as wire.

'Good!' beamed Ig's dad. 'Good. Everyone's happy.'

'Um. There's one last thing,' Ig said, bracing herself. 'So I can't use my phone, because it could get tracked. I've got a new thing to use -' she waved the communication device Dana had given her in front of the camera – 'but, um…'

'Your mother's knowledge of our mission,' The General had said, 'should be limited. She was a Shackleton student, after all. Some of the 'teachers' there were employed as far back as 1990; I would hate for her to use her connections to sabotage the flow of information.'

'Mam can't…um, talk to me. At all. All term.' Ig cringed. 'Sorry, Mam.'

'What?' Ig's mother thundered, outraged, as Ig clutched Finnie tightly to her chest, tears of guilt and embarrassment pooling in the corner of her eyes. 'A whole term? This is absolutely ridiculous – no, Luca, it is, don't 'c'mon, baby' me.'

Darkness began to gather around her, and her hair began to vibrate with energy.

'Mam…'

'You're only fifteen, Ig; that's no age to be totally on your own, somewhere I can't find you.' Oh, god. Was she levitating? She was levitating. She really was mad. 'I don't know who that General thinks she is; interfering in my family life, making plans with my daughter without informing us. We're still her parents, Luca–'

'Mam!' Ig held her hands up to the camera lens – going for calm and placating, but coming across as pleading. 'Please. It's just for a little bit. I promise. Please. It's important, Mam. For me.'

Ig watched her mother pause, and exhale; weighing up her options. 'Fine,' she said, eventually. 'Because I love you, I won't get angry. But I'm not happy about this, Ig. At all. Your dad will be bringing it up at the next Parent's Evening, on my behalf. Perhaps he'll even be withdrawing his annual donation that we can't really afford to give anyway, *Luca*.' She glared, and Ig's dad winced.

'Anyway, honey,' he said; 'we better go. Your Auntie Memoria is coming over tonight, and I promised her I'd make my famous hummus. And you know that woman never forgets…'

As Ig sent her best to her godmother, ended the call and turned over in her bed, Finnie the shark cuddled up under her chin – she'd have to remember to put him in her bag for tomorrow; she couldn't leave him behind for a whole term. She knew she was doing the right thing. Her mam would understand, eventually. She closed her eyes and tried to focus on her breathing, but she couldn't sleep; she was thinking about her future; a world where no-one would have anything to laugh about. Where the name Ignatia Heretical wouldn't be followed with 'the Villain's daughter' anymore. No, she'd be Ignatia Heretical; Hero. A world where she would never, ever feel like she wasn't good enough again. It was all just a term away.

Chapter Six

'Miss,' said the chauffeur, 'please stop. The noise is distracting me from the roads.'

'Oh.' Ig forced her hands to stop fiddling with the clasp on her new bag – an old-fashioned leather satchel in deep, woodsy green. 'Sorry.' She pushed the bag onto the floor of the car and gazed out the window at the thick, dark woods flashing past her. Rain lashed against the windows, leaving fat droplets to race along the glass. The car had been waiting for her at Rossborough Station; her last contact with anything to do with the Academy for three whole months. It already felt as if Ig was in another country, not just a different part of the North East; she'd audibly gasped as they passed through farmland and she saw cows for the first time in years, grazing underneath a rolling grey sky. It felt like she'd been taken into a fairy tale. But not a cute, glittery one from the films, with talking animals and songs. More like the weird, scary ones that her mam told her at bedtime when she was small, with fateful bargains and unhappy endings.

The car drove up a long, winding road – more like a paved lane, really, with tight turns and stomach-lurching bumps. A rabbit dashed in front of the car, and the driver had to slam on the brakes, cursing.

'Did we hit it?' Ig asked, concerned. She unrolled her window just in time to see a white tail flash as the rabbit ran into the hedgerows.

'What do you care?' the driver grumbled, as Ig sat back in her seat. 'You're a Villain now, aren't you? I bet you'll be experimenting on cute little bunnies like that before breakfast.'

'Oh. Right.'

The sky was beginning to grow dark as the car finally crunched over the gravel road that led up to Shackleton School for Villains. Ig turned to look out the back window of the car – as if someone from Lunalist was going to run up behind them, yelling that this was all a big mistake, that Ig was going to prove herself in a much less risky way. Something like swimming the entire length of the Tyne, or telling Lily Volt she had a spot on the end of her nose. But, of course, no-one was there.

Ig was on her own.

Shackleton was all wrought iron and dark brick; with spires reaching up into the sky like stalagmites, sharp and dangerous-looking. The windows were all huge and ornate and, as the headlights of the car swept over them, Ig swore she caught forty or fifty sets of eyes staring down at her. Then she blinked, and the faces pressed against the glass vanished. The car came to a stop, and Ig took a deep breath, checked her bag one last time, and stepped out of the car.

Someone was standing under the huge, carved arch that made up the entrance of the school, waiting to meet her. An adult – a little younger than Ig's mam, if she had to guess – with a neat, dark pinstripe suit on and the most perfectly sharp eyeliner Ig had ever seen. 'Ignatia Heretical?' they asked, taking a step forward as Ig unloaded her suitcase from the car boot, dashing around the side of the car and under the porch roof to try and stay out of the rain. 'I'm The Nyx, your new headteacher.'

'Hi,' Ig said, a little out of breath and very conscious that the small amount of mascara she put on that morning in her dorm (oh, she missed her dorm already) was probably streaking down her cheeks.

'I'm glad you made it in one piece,' said The Nyx. 'Those roads are treacherous. Did you come through the village or over the hills?'

'Um. Hills. I think. I didn't see a village.'

'You couldn't miss it.' Their voice was low and musical; it sounded like they were holding in a laugh the entire time they spoke. But not in a mean, Lily Volt sort of way; more like they were sharing a private joke. 'It's probably best if you came the hills way; nice and inconspicuous, we don't need anyone knowing about your arrival that doesn't need to, yes? Alright, Mr. Lunalist Driver; we'll take it from here.' They raised a perfectly manicured hand in a wave, and the car pulled away without a backward glance. Ig's stomach fluttered with nerves. The Nyx placed a hand on Ig's back, and guided her into the school. The doors swung shut behind her, and Ig felt as if she'd been swallowed by some gigantic beast.

'Now,' The Nyx was saying, 'since you're fifteen, you will have access to the village unsupervised, though I think for your first time you should be accompanied by one of your peers. Shackleton students have, ah, a reputation in Rossborough.' The Nyx gave Ig a sly look. 'Mayhem is looked down upon, but mischief is welcomed. Do you understand my meaning?'

Ig didn't have a clue. But she nodded anyway.

The main hall of Shackleton School for Villains was grand, dark and sweeping. On either side of Ig were ornate oil paintings of past Villains, vases filled with blueish, thorny plants and a gigantic staircase – complete with shining wooden bannisters, a well-worn green-and-black carpet running up the centre, and two actual suits of armour standing guard at the bottom – that split in two on the first floor and curved dramatically into separate hallways. And lining each hallway – whispering and hissing amongst themselves as they stared down at Ig – were the faces she'd seen at the window, smiling down at her with all the glee of a shark noticing a new fish in its tank. Ig was definitely not at Lunalist anymore.

'Students,' The Nyx said, softly but firmly, 'line up.' The giggling and whispering stopped, replaced by the sounds of shuffling feet scuffing against the hardwood floors and down the stairs. The students arranged themselves into a line, stretching from one side of the room to the other. Nearest to Ig and The Nyx were the younger kids – about twelve years old, standing straight and tall, desperate for approval and vibrating with unspent energy. At the other end of the line were the older students, about Ig's age; still standing tall, but with the easy confidence of students that had done this a million times. 'Why don't you join your peers at the end?' The Nyx asked Ig. Blankly, Ig nodded, walking down the long line and feeling every set of eyes watch her pass. Sizing her up. Even in her new uniform – a dark purple blazer with green accents and a matching skirt – Ig felt almost naked. A boy with curly hair and a sharp smile winked at her, which made her double her pace for a multitude of reasons, though for the most part she was met with looks of curiosity and scepticism. If only they knew why she was really here. Finally, she found the end of the line; next to a girl with bright green hair and a dusting of freckles across her nose.

'Hi,' the girl said, smiling with too many teeth. Ig straightened her back and started forward, saying nothing. The girl shrugged and turned to look down the row at the boy who'd winked at her. 'Students,' The Nyx was saying, walking up and down the row of children, 'even when we have a new arrival to our school, we must be professional. Even our best and brightest, Miss Section.' The girl with the green hair snapped back to attention; though Ig noticed her hands were twitching. 'And part of that professionalism is the recitation of our school motto. Students?'

'*Semper Scelestus*,' said the students as one; all staring forward, their voices clear and crisp as a knife in the gut. *Always wicked*. Ig swallowed hard. The brainwashing on display was disgusting her, and she'd been here five minutes.

'*Good*. Now, let's give our new classmate a chance to breathe, please. Back to your studies – or your dorms, if you are on free period. Please.'

'Yes, Professor Nyx.' One by one, every student disappeared, vanishing somewhere in the many halls and rooms surrounding the staircase. 'Forgive them, Miss Heretical,' The Nyx said, turning to face Ig once more. 'We don't often get new arrivals in the middle of a school year; usually our First Years arrive all together at the end of the summer. Now, we have some things to address, before you become adjusted. Please,' they said, gesturing with a long, slender arm to a large wooden door off to the side of the stairs, 'can you step into my office for a moment?'

Ig stiffened. Was this it? Was Ig found out before she'd even unpacked? It did sound like something that could only happen to her. The Nyx ushered her into a small room tucked under the stairwell that smelled of incense. It was filled with globes, papers, and high bookshelves stuffed with old leather bound photo albums. 'All my old students,' The Nyx said, waving a hand at the nearest shelf when they caught Ig staring. 'I like to keep the yearbooks. It's quite nice to look back and see who I've taught – once they're out causing havoc in the real world.' They took a seat behind a huge, dark oak desk. 'Your mother is in there somewhere; though of course I didn't teach her. I was a little younger than her, but she really took me under her wing – so to speak. She was like my big sister, back in those days.' Their smile became wicked; conspiratorial, eyes flicking up to the albums again. 'Let me know if you ever want to see The Witch Queen when she still had braces and pigtails.'

The thought of her mother as an awkward teenager made something in Ig's brain short circuit, so she shook her head. But The Nyx had already moved on, shuffling papers around on their desk. 'I wanted to tell you privately, Miss Heretical, that your peers don't know exactly which school you transferred from. Let them assume it was a civilian one for now, for your comfort as much as theirs. Though with the family resemblance and your unique last name, they may work out that you're a legacy pupil soon enough.' Ig tugged shyly on her hair as The Nyx continued, oblivious. 'Let me see; your timetable is right here. And this is your lesson planner; you'll be expected to show you have it at the beginning of every school day, or you spend your breaks and free time in solitary confinement. True chaos can only come from a base of organisation, otherwise it's just messiness.'

That… was… surprisingly good advice.

'Here are your notebooks, you can pick up more when you need them from the little shop in the dungeon, and–' they produced a familiar, slim silicone band from a drawer, 'of course, you'll need this. For a little while, at least. Already registered to your Student ID, ready to use.'

They reached across the table and placed a Power Lender in Ig's outstretched hands. Ig gawped at it. It looked exactly the same as her old one at Lunalist, apart from…

'It's black,' Ig said, thumb running over the tiny, plastic buckle. She'd only ever known Power Lenders to be white – though the colour change did make sense, she supposed.

'I know; how dull. But they are customisable, once you reach a certain grade,' The Nyx said, misreading Ig's expression. 'Decals, stickers and such – there was a trend last year for doodling on them in gel pen, but that seems to have died off. Once you discover your Power, they become nothing more than nice keepsakes, so each one being a little different makes sense at that point.'

Ig looked up from her fidgeting. '*Discover*?' Did you say, 'discover' my Power?'

But The Nyx ignored her; steepling their fingers and staring right at Ig. 'Now, Miss Heretical; it says in your transfer paperwork that you were bullied at Lunalist. Is that correct?'

Oh, crap. Was this a test? Were they trying to catch Ig out, see what she could remember from her own paperwork? If Ig was now technically a Shackleton student, would The Nyx take an accusation of bullying against her as an affront to the school? Would they ask her for names? What was The Nyx's power, anyway? What if they could explode someone like Lily Volt from a county and a half away?

Actually, that didn't sound too bad.

'Miss Heretical?'

'Mm-hm!' Ig said, her mouth a tight smile, bobbing her head up and down instead of speaking. The Nyx's gaze softened, and they nodded.

'Well, I want you to know, if anything like that happens here–'

Here we go. 'I want you to know if anything like that happens here, those students would actually never do something so awful, so maybe you should think about your own behaviour because remember, Miss Heretical, we have a zero-tolerance stance on bullying.'

'Make sure you hit them twice as fast and three times as hard, okay? And when they come to apologise, shake their hand – but never forget. *Semper Scelestus.*'

What. The. Hell?

'Good lass,' The Nyx said, clapping their hands together and rising from their chair. 'Right then! I suppose it's time for you to see your dorm, yes?'

Chapter Seven

Ig followed The Nyx out the office and up the winding staircase.

'I'm afraid your dorm is on the third floor,' they said, as Ig huffed and puffed behind them, lugging her suitcase behind her.

'It's okay!' Ig chirped, sounding false even to her own ears. 'Lots of… lots of exercise. Hooray.'

A few younger students were still hanging around – consulting their planners in loud, staged voices and darting looks Ig's way. The Nyx raised one eyebrow in their direction as they reached the top of the staircase, and the students scuttled off with a muttered apology. *They don't know you're a Hero*, Ig reassured herself, as one girl nearly fell down the stairs because she was craning her neck so hard to look backwards at her. *Stay calm*.

'They're just curious,' The Nyx said, the students whispered and glanced back at her. 'We don't encourage celebrity here – not until you've done something worth the infamy.' They gave Ig a wry smile, and she blushed. 'The student you'll be rooming with,' The Nyx said, changing the subject as they straightened a portrait of a smouldering woman with diamond-shaped pupils and an alligator draped over her shoulders, 'is in most of your classes. I thought it would be helpful for you if you had a buddy, at least for your first few weeks, so you can acclimatise to how we do things at Shackleton.'

'Okay. That's… okay. So,' Ig said, in between deep, burning lungfuls of air, 'you said the third floor, right?'

'I did.'

'Are all the students up there?'

'No.'

'Oh.' Ig leaned against the banister as casually as she could while a group of girls her own age passed by, chatting and giggling. 'I mean,' she said trying not to stare as one girl peeked through her curtain of long black hair and glanced back at her, 'I supposed that, you know, there would be a floor for students, and somewhere for the teachers to sleep, and then that just left, like, a floor and a half at most for classrooms.' The Nyx stared, one immaculate eyebrow raised, so Ig continued, rapidly losing steam as she did. 'And well, um, that's not a lot of room, is it? For all the different classes. That you do. Here. And I was wondering, um, if that was right?'

After a moment, The Nyx stooped down to Ig's level, looking right into her eyes. Ig flinched, suddenly very focused on the green-and-black patterned carpet under her feet. 'You,' The Nyx said, 'are a very smart young lady, Ignatia Heretical.' And with that, they plucked Ig's timetable from her grip, folded it into quarters, and closed their hands around it. Pale blue light began to seep out from between their fingers and, as Ig watched, The Nyx slowly unfolded their hands to reveal a tiny, paper version of Shackleton Academy resting on their palms.

'There are certain criteria to being headteacher of Shackleton,' they said, their voice low and musical. 'And that is this; you must be a master manipulator.' As they spoke, they opened their palms further, fingers fanning out from each other. 'Of space, I mean.' And the tiny Academy began to stretch. Outwards and up, somehow growing taller and longer without seeming to take up any more space. Inside the tiny windows, Ig could see rooms spiralling out from one another like delicate, miniscule fans. She gasped, lowering herself into a squat so she could take a better look.

'Wow. How do you do that?'

'It's my Power, Miss Heretical.' The Nyx smiled, sphinx-like. 'It means we here at Shackleton have unlimited possibilities for learning. A student arrives without warning? There is a bed waiting for them, somewhere. When my students wish to learn something new, there will be a classroom available for them – though I still need to hire staff. I can't create them, obviously.'

They gave Ig one last glance, then clapped their hands together again. Ig jumped as the tiny Shackleton collapsed back into a flat sheet of paper. 'It also means the layout is unable to be mapped by anyone but me. Helpful, no?'

Ig flushed red and agreed. The Nyx straightened, brushing their hands down their expensive, pressed trouser legs. 'I'm glad you're so interested already though, Miss Heretical. Curiosity is a valuable trait, here.'

I bet it is, thought Ig.

The Nyx cocked their head, listening. As Ig strained her ears, she could hear the distant throb and whine of electric guitars off in the distance. The Nyx smiled. 'Come along, Miss Heretical; your dorm-mate is waiting for us.'

The entire room was filled with plants. Huge, leafy fronds spilling out from earthenware pots; squat succulents in soup tins and vines creeping up the supports of the bunk beds that, Ig noticed, looked a lot shabbier than the ones at Lunalist. Ig could even see something green sitting in the sink of the tiny en-suite bathroom off to her right, the tap dripping steadily into the soil. And every single leaf in the room shook with heavy, slamming drums and the screech of electric guitars.

'Vivian,' The Nyx called. 'Vivian, I'm here with your new dorm-mate.'

Nothing. A singer with a voice like barbed wire sang about digging through the ditches and burning through the witches. The Nyx tapped their expensive-looking nails against the door frame.

'Vivian. Vivian. *Miss Section!*'

'Coming!' Off to one side, near the back of the room, some plants shook a little harder than the rest. 'I'm coming, I'm just a bit stuck. I'm–'

A girl fell out of the plants. The girl from downstairs, with the green hair and the toothy smile. She was short – at least a head shorter than Ig was – with a waterfall of bright green hair that went down to her waist, naturally golden skin and freckles that were half-hidden by a bright pink blush daubed on her cheeks and nose. Ig's mam had read her a book when she was little about pixies. She'd told her about how they were beautiful, but treacherous and cunning. Ig decided immediately that her new roommate was *definitely* a pixie.

'Ugh, hang on – this hair, I should've put it up.' The girl rolled up through her spine and flicked her hair backwards from her face. 'Pffffbt. That's better. Hi! I'm Vivi.' She beamed at Ig, who took a step backwards. 'Nice to meet you properly!'

'Uh. Hi.'

'Miss Section is in most of your classes, Ignatia,' The Nyx was saying, as Ig tentatively pushed a gigantic watering can aside to place her suitcase down. 'Apart from Poisonology and Ms. Schwab's classes – though she's more than welcome to join you in Advanced Monologue if she stops talking to her plants long enough to learn her lines.' They smiled teasingly at the girl, who pushed her hair out of her eyes, blowing a self-conscious raspberry.

'Professor Nyyyyyx, don't embarrass me in front of – oh, sorry, what do you like to be called? And was it Miss? She/her pronouns? I want to get it right.' The new girl – Vivian – got right up in Ig's face, their noses almost touching. As if she could sniff out Ig's gender.

'Um. Miss. She. And it's Ig, not Ignatia. Please.' Not even her mam called her Ignatia, unless she was in trouble.

Vivian grinned, snapping her fingers happily. 'I can remember that. Ig. Like Ignorant. Or Ig-sinificant! Ha, I guess that one doesn't work. And I go by Vivi, not Vivian.'

Ig narrowed her eyes. 'So Vivi… Section. Like… like what they do to animals.'

'Yep!'

Okay. Ig could definitely remember *that* name. She would bet any money this was the bunny-torturer the driver was on about in the car.

'Vivian can show you around Shackleton,' The Nyx was saying, 'and help you find your classrooms. My hope is that the two of you will become–'

'Woah, woah, woah, hold on!' Vivi said, shooing Ig away from a wicker basket full of pretty yellow flowers. 'No touching the Widowsworts. Suuuuper poisonous, kill you dead in six minutes. I'm should have put them in their press to dry out overnight, but um,' she shrugged, 'I didn't. I forgot. I'll move them before tonight, I promise.' She smiled guiltily. 'No such thing as a bad first impression, right?'

This girl is going to kill me, Ig thought.

Chapter Eight

Not long after that, The Nyx made their departure. 'Miss Section will take care of you from here,' they'd said, and Ig was sure they were suppressing a tiny smirk as they left. Possibly because Ig had already nearly been poisoned, bitten, stung and swiped by every plant in the room. The door closed behind them, and Ig was left alone with this…this botanical psychopath she had to bunk with for the next term. Her dorm back at Lunalist looked positively spotless compared to this, even with all of Ig's protein bar wrappers on the floor. But the mission needed her to suck it up and get on with it.

Currently, Vivi was repotting a succulent. In her school clothes. Ig had made sure her blazer made it to the school perfectly pressed, not a thread out of place. Vivi's, by comparison, had a smudge of pollen on the lapel, a button missing, and a badge shaped like a cactus that read 'Free Hugs!' on the breast pocket.

Ig would not be following that badge's instructions.

'The Nyx brought you here during my free period,' Vivi said, packing in the soil around the plant with her fingertips. 'So, we've got all the same lessons for the rest of the week. I'll show you how to work out where your classes are, how the corridors work and stuff – it's pretty easy – but then on Monday first thing I've got Poisonology, so you'll probably have to find your way to your Monologue class on your own, okay? But you'll be fine. What do you think?'

She whirled and practically shoved the plant pot in Ig's face. It had a skull and crossbones painted on it. Badly. Ig smiled as warmly and naturally as someone passing a kidney stone.

'It's… great.'

'I'd usually pick up a cute pot in the village, but this little guy needed replanting ASAP.' Vivi flicked one of the succulent's spiky leaves and giggled affectionately. 'He's one of my own creations. Part Agave, part Crassula Ovata – soon I'll be able to harvest the syrup and use it in – oh, I dunno – in cocktails, on cupcakes, as a dressing on salads… all sorts of things!'

'Oh,' Ig said, relieved. 'That actually sounds quite interesting.'

'It is!' Vivi smiled at her sweetly, as if Ig had made her day. 'And the symptoms will be even *more* interesting!'

'…symptoms?'

'Oh yes.' Vivi bounced up and down in place; the safety pins down the right side of her skirt jingling merrily. 'Vomiting, diarrhoea, depressive episodes, sleeplessness – and because of the sweet, syrup-y consistency, it should be virtually undetectable!' She rubbed her hands together fiendishly. 'No-one will ever suspect the cupcakes. *Mwahaha.*'

'Oh,' Ig said weakly. She patted her hip, finding solace in the communication device she'd tucked away in her skirt pocket. The first chance she got, she'd make a note about poisoned confectionery coming out of Shackleton.

Vivi placed the pot on their huge, wooden double-desk with a loving pat. 'My ticket to top marks on my test next month. Come on,' she chirped, plucking a red flower from a nearby plant and slotting it behind her ear; 'we'll have a nice slow walk along the corridors and get you to our next class with time to spare.'

As they walked down the corridor out of the dorms – back towards the staircase – Ig couldn't shake the feeling she was being watched. It wasn't exactly a new feeling – the usual whispers that had always followed her were still there, along with the wide-eyed gawping. But that didn't make it any less uncomfortable.

'So there's the breakfast nooks,' Vivi was saying counting off rooms on her fingertips, 'the classrooms, obviously, the gardens, the assembly hall – oh, and that's Solitary Confinement.'

She pointed to a dark iron door that seemed to be embedded deep into the wall. Ig could have sworn she heard screaming from behind it. *I never thought I'd miss The Base,* she thought with a shudder.

'So,' she offered, desperate to change the subject, 'how do we get to, um,' she glanced at her timetable at her first lesson of the day, 'Torture Management?'

Oh my god.

'Well, the trick is,' Vivi was saying, arms swinging by her sides, 'to know where you're going.'

Wasn't that the trick to getting everywhere? Ig thought.

'Stride with purpose!' Vivi stuck out her legs like she was marching, the flower in her hair bouncing. 'If you know you need to be at the first floor for Poisonology, and your feet are telling you that you need to go right this time and not left – no matter how many times you've gone left before – you'll find it every time! But if you doubt yourself, you'll end up in some dumb staircase to nowhere for half an hour. Speaking from experience. Show the school no fear, and you'll be fine.'

'That's easy for you to say,' muttered Ig. To her, all the corridors – with their patterned carpets and endlessly repeating wallpaper – looked exactly the same. She couldn't even use the portraits lining the walls as markers; how many glowering, arrogant faces glaring down their noses at the viewer did one school need?!

'Hey, Ig?' Vivi turned and took Ig by the shoulders, staring earnestly into her face. 'You're gonna be alright here, okay? It must be hard, coming to a school with totally new values and classes and stuff. I'll teach you everything you need to know.'

Injured pride and embarrassment sparked in Ig's chest. Who was this girl – this Villain! – to think she knew Ig within half an hour of meeting her?! *And was she wearing purple mascara? Madness. Utter madness.* 'I don't need a babysitter,' she said.

Vivi shrugged. 'Okay, okay. But since we're going to the same classroom right now, why don't we walk together?'

Ig shrugged right back. 'Fine.'

'Fine!' Vivi parroted, sticking out her tongue. 'I bet you'll be roaming these corridors with the pros before the end of the day, won't you? Because you're so clever.'

'That's right,' sniffed Ig. 'I will.'

'You'll be finding whole new classrooms before the week's out!' Vivi made a picture frame with her forefingers and thumbs. '"The Ignatia Heretical Hallways", they'll call them. I can see it now. Only accessible if you have never asked for help in your entire life. Otherwise, you're locked out and shamed in the cold.'

Ig disliked how... friendly this girl was. Making jokes and chatting before they'd had the chance to work out where they stood with one another. It was a trick, she knew that. Trying to catch her off guard. Well, Ignatia Heretical wouldn't be caught so easily.

'Come on, then,' Vivi was saying as they walked. 'Tell me; what would your classrooms be for? On The Ignatia Heretical Hallways.'

'For?' Ig asked. 'Well, um, I don't know. What, um, sort of things do you, er, learn here?'

Smooth. But instead of giving an answer that Ig could subtly repeat into her dictaphone when they got to class, Vivi just tilted her head. 'Did your mam never talk to you about this place? When you were going to the normal school, I mean.'

Ig jolted in surprise. 'How do you know about my mam?' She resisted the urge to blurt out an entirely fictional backstory about how she used to go to a civilian school – where was a civilian school near home?! Gosforth Academy, that would do – and how she suddenly decided to follow in the family footsteps and... and...

Don't say anything, said an unexpected voice inside her head. *Let her tell you what she knows, then act.*

Vivi raised an eyebrow. 'How many Hereticals do you think there are, Ig? Everyone knows about her.' Was she blushing? This was getting weird. 'I used to have such a crush on The Witch Queen. Those pictures from when she took over

Newcastle and turned it into a crystal city in 2009? Swoon!'

'Did you just say 'swoon' out loud?' Ig asked. But Vivi didn't seem to hear her; spinning in a tight circle, books clutched to her chest. 'Also, you know… that's my mam.'

'Oh; right, right.' Vivi stopped spinning and collected herself. 'No, I get it; it's probably weird to have a thing for your friend's mam, isn't it?'

'Probably. Plus, you don't know her like I know her. She's properly cringey in real life.' Ig started counting on her fingers; a vicious, gleeful little feeling sparking up in her chest. This random, green-haired girl thought she knew everything. 'She leaves her coffee cup on the counter instead of putting it in the dishwasher, she sings along to old 90's music in the shower, she clips her toenails on the sofa while we watch TV…'

'Noooo, stoop!' Vivi cried, clapping her hands to her ears. 'I get it, I'm officially uncrushed.'

Ig grinned. 'Ha; told you.' Then the smile vanished from her face, any good feeling she had suddenly swamped by shame. That wasn't a nice thing to do. Or even a mature thing. She should know better. Her gaze wandered back over to Vivi. Between the hair, and the unkempt blazer, and the safety pins down her skirt, she couldn't look any more different from what Ig was used to. The students here really were wild cards. Not like her; she was a pillar of order and discipline. She was a Lunalist student, no matter what blazer she was wearing. The pair walked in silence for a while, before Ig cleared her throat.

'Also, we're not friends,' she said, attempting to make her voice firm and reasonable. Better to let this girl down easy now, rather than further along the line once she was giving information to The General. To her surprise, Vivi laughed.

'So, I have this issue with knowing when people like me. Like, when does Someone You Know become a Friend? And is that the same as a *Best* Friend? What if you just talk to them in one class, is that still a friend? It was always a problem when I was little, so my mams said I should start off calling everyone my friend, and then, when I know them a little better, I can change them to Best Friend, or Schoolfriend, or They're Ok, I Suppose.' Vivi shot Ig a sly, sideways look. 'Or My Enemy.'

Hm. Ig had never considered doing things like that before. It sounded… tidier. But also incredibly naïve. 'Are there many people in the Enemy camp?' she asked. Vivi scowled.

'Well, there was this goose back on my mams' homestead. He thought I was after his eggs, so he'd chase me all the time. And I'm like, 'I don't want your babies, Kevin! I'm only six, I'm not ready to be a mother.' She shrugged, blinking at Ig with her big, guileless blue eyes. 'Apart from that, no-one yet.'

Despite herself, Ig sputtered out a tiny laugh. This girl was so, so strange.

Chapter Nine

To Ig's surprise, the Torture Management classroom was pretty normal-looking, if a bit old-fashioned. Twenty individual desks – huge wooden ones with a pencil holder built in and a lid that slammed shut in a satisfying way – with a large chalkboard and a bigger desk for the teacher at the front. A teacher who hadn't arrived yet, so Ig and Vivi entered a classroom full of chattering students; all leaning across desks, flying paper planes and loudly insisting that if Mr. Throttler doesn't get here in ten minutes, we're legally allowed to go back to our dorms. Ig's mam had taken her to a historical site when she was little, where people lived out being from the Victorian era. The actors playing the teachers would shout at you and teach you times tables, but you got to keep your easel and chalk as a souvenir. It reminded her of that.

Vivi took Ig's hand and pulled her towards a pair of desks by the window. 'First class!' she beamed. 'Your Villain career starts right here! Isn't it exciting?'

Ig kicked her satchel under the table and knotted her hands together awkwardly. She'd never been in a classroom without a teacher before. Was talking like this bad? Would she get in trouble on her first day? A student near the front of the class – a broad, wolfish-looking boy with the beginnings of a beard (and fangs) – realised who Vivi was talking to, and nudged the girl on the other side of him. Who nudged the person on the other side of her. Slowly, silence fell across the classroom, as each head turned in Ig's direction.

Perfect. Just how I wanted this to go.

Then, someone stood up and pointed. 'You're The Witch Queen's daughter–!'

The door banged open, and the most terrifying man Ig had ever seen stepped in. He was gigantic – at least seven feet tall – wearing a dark tunic and a cowl. Where his face should have been, there was a leather mask with a cruel, hooked beak and two glowing copper eyes. Slowly – painfully slowly – he turned his head and regarded the entire class; impassive, cold and unyielding.

Forget Vivi, Ig thought to herself. *This guy's the one who'll kill me.*

'Good morning, Mr. Throttler,' chimed the class, now sitting nicely in their seats. Mr. Throttler nodded once, then stepped up to the chalk board. Then, his head jerked up, like he was sniffing something on the wind. He turned towards Ig, who shrunk down in her seat.

'Haha,' she laughed awkwardly. 'Hello, Sir. I'm the… the new student.'

Mr. Throttler regarded her in silence. Ig had never felt quite so exposed in all her life. Then, he took up a piece of chalk, wrote 'Mr. Throttler; Torture Management' in ragged text on the board, and held out one gigantic hand towards Ig.

'He wants you to tell him your name,' Vivi said out the corner of her mouth.

'Oh. Oh, r-right.' Ig stood up *(why did she stand up?!)* and cleared her throat. 'Ignatia Heretical,' she said, with a hand on her heart. 'I just started here, and… I…' Mr. Throttler shook his head slowly, and a chill went down Ig's spine. 'I'm sorry,' she squeaked.

'The board!' Vivi hissed. 'Go write it on the board.' Ig did as she was told; scooting up to the board with that awkward, terrified smile still in place, writing her name in tiny, shaky script under the teacher's. She looked over her shoulder at Vivi, who gave her a beaming thumbs up. Her hands were shaking; the chalk squeaked on the 't' in 'Heretical' and Ig winced in pain. The sound went right through her. She turned and looked up at Mr. Throttler. He nodded, and ushered her back to her desk.

'It's easier for him to remember things if they're written down,' Vivi whispered, as Ig took her seat again.

'Right,' Ig said, as Mr. Throttler started to write '*Match the Torture Method to The Hero – One Point for Each Correct Answer*' underneath both their names. 'That's really, um, reassuring to know, Vivi.'

The next five minutes consisted of watching in silence as Mr. Throttler wrote the names of torture devices on one side of the board and different descriptions of Heroes on the other. Then, from watching what Vivi started to write in her notebook, Ig deduced that she was meant to write down which Hero would succumb best to which device. You know; a normal, wholesome school activity.

'Okay,' she breathed, taking up her pencil. 'First act as an undercover Villain. Easy! Here we go.'

Waterboarding was first up. That probably wouldn't work best on an aquatic-Powered Hero. So it wasn't that option. But there was a fire-throwing Hero on this list. Ig supposed they wouldn't be able to use their Power to get away, so she scribbled her answer… and then took a second to absorb the fact that she was plotting the demise of her own side and jotting it down. For *points*.

It's all for the mission. Just keep thinking about the mission. About your Power Revelation ceremony. How proud Dad's going to be. What The General will think of you. Seeing Pisces again. It'll all be worth a little bit of discomfort now. Okay; a Hero with super strength. What would work best on them..?

Before Ig realised it, half an hour had gone past. It was actually quite enjoyable – in a sick and twisted sort of way – to get so lost in a task. To pretend she was someone else for a while – someone evil, cold-blooded and calculating, not the awkward mess of a girl she really was. Although about halfway through, she had glanced at Vivi's page, saw that she'd connected each Hero to their impending doom with swirling lines drawn in brightly coloured pen and, in a panic, borrowed a purple fine liner to draw some skulls and crossbones around her work, to give them a little evil flair. But apart from that, it had been a pretty uneventful first lesson! One last Hero to match up and–

There were no torture methods left to use. Just one word, floating aimlessly in the middle of the page.

'Stalwart.' That wasn't even a type of Power! It was an adjective. They might as well have written 'has long hair.' Ig stared at the word for a while – narrowing her eyes to see if that helped at all. It didn't. She looked back up at the board, in case she'd missed something – and immediately caught Mr. Throttler's eye. He tilted his head at her, regarding her with his cold, metallic eyes, and Ig winced, looking back at her paper with a squeak. She'd missed something. There was a piece of the puzzle she was missing. Was she meant to pick one of the answers to use twice? This happened all the time at Lunalist, but she hadn't expected to mess up in the first lesson-!

There had to be something she was missing. Some piece of the puzzle. Ig looked around at the classroom walls, wondering if there was a clue somewhere. There wasn't; just posters of guillotines with phrases like 'keep your head in your studies!' She looked at Vivi, who was happily still connecting her answers. She hadn't done anything with 'stalwart' yet.

Besides, Ignatia, said a miasma of teachers' voices inside Ig's head; *cheating is bad. Eyes on your own page.*

'Stalwart.' What did the word mean? Well, it meant loyal, brave and true. Someone committed to their Heroic cause. Someone like that wouldn't be easy to break. You couldn't really force information out of someone like that with brute force; you'd turn them into a martyr. You'd have to use something sneakier, more devious…

Something inside her brain went 'click.' Ig blinked. It was awful. It was heartless. It was definitely the right answer. She paused, putting the tip of the pen to her lips – making a face when the metal at the end of it scraped against her teeth. She thought one more time about what she wanted to write, letting it roll around in her brain in case she was wrong – but, in her heart of hearts, she knew she had it. Sick with guilt and hating every word she wrote, Ig answered the question.

'A Stalwart Hero won't be broken with any of the methods listed here. Find out what – or who – they are loyal to, and use that to your advantage – maybe a Psychic Villain could help here?'

Wow, that was clunky. But it got her point across.

A shadow fell across her paper. Ig started with a yelp, shoulder crashing against Vivi as she looked up into the emotionless, copper eyes of Mr. Throttler. Paralysed with nerves, Ig watched in horror as he took her paper in one huge, gloved hand, and brought it close to his face. Reading her answers.

This was it. Something in what she'd written would give her away. Ig was sure of it. She was too soft, too kind, too Heroic for a class like this – she didn't belong here, she needed to get back to Lunalist before this guy popped her head off her shoulders –

Mr. Throttler took a pen from his pocket and wrote something across the top of her page. Then, from the same pocket, he attached some sort of marker and, after pressing it into the top corner of the page…walked away without looking back, letting the paper flutter back down into Ig's lap. Hands shaking, Ig picked it up and smoothed it back out across her desk, trying to breathe normally in case her teacher could sense her fear.

Scrawled across the top of the page, in that now-familiar ragged script, was a message.

'Clever choice with the Psychic Villain. Sorry for giving you a tricky one on your very first day. Looking forward to having you in the class!'

Underneath that was a sticker. A smiling, cartoony shooting star, the words *'well done!'* written across its tail in glitter.

'Wow!' Vivi hissed in Ig's ear. 'You got a sticker? On your first day? Lucky!'

Ig let the paper drop onto the desk and stared into space for the rest of the lesson, listening to her heartbeat slamming against her ribs – feeling for all the world as if she'd been approaching the gallows before being suddenly swept away for chocolate ice cream instead.

Working out this place was going to be tougher than she thought.

Chapter Ten

'Look at you go!' Vivi crowed, skipping ahead of Ig on their way to the next lesson. 'Getting on Mr. Throttler's good side already! How does it feel?'

Awful, Ig wanted to say. *Like a betrayal. Like I don't even know who I am anymore. Like the person I always thought I would be is sitting on my shoulder right now, wailing in disappointment as I blunder headlong into getting a Torture expert's approval and, and… and on the other shoulder is someone new. Someone who feels sort of good about it.* Ig had never, ever got a sticker back at Lunalist. She didn't even know if stickers were a *thing*. How would she know? Maybe Pisces had a whole binder full of brightly coloured tokens of approval from all her tutors.

Ig's heart twisted a little at the thought of Pisces. Was she missing her right now? Ig wasn't sure what would be better; if Pisces was crying into her pillow every night thinking about how she missed her chance to confess her undying love to Ig… or if she was totally fine without her.

Suddenly, all the lights in the corridor went out with a click and a hum of electricity – followed immediately by a crack of blinding, blue-white light that shot out from under a closed classroom door.

'Did lightning just strike inside that classroom?' Ig asked.

'Oop,' Vivi said, snapping her fingers in Ig's face. 'That reminds me of someone else you need to meet.'

'Someone else?'

'Well. *Someones*.'

Vivi took off at a jog towards the end of the hall – to a

classroom where smoke had begun drifting out from under the door in thick, dark plumes. Ig followed, the Rescue and Escape Protocol Lunalist had drilled into her sounding in her head. It occurred to her with a shock of panic that she hadn't seen a fire extinguisher the entire time she'd been here.

'Right,' she stammered, 'but you didn't answer my question. Was that lightning? Inside? In a school?'

'Oh!' Vivi said, her eyes lighting up with understanding. 'Yeah! But don't worry; that's just–'

'At last!' a voice cackled from the offending classroom, 'my magnum opus is complete! Now the world will forever tremble at the name of *Mercutio von Ryan!*'

'Ah…yeah,' Vivi said, with an affectionate eyeroll. 'That's the classroom where Mercutio usually hangs out. Along with–'

'Pietro! Are you documenting this?'

A non-committal mumble could be heard under the rumble of thunder.

'Pietro–!'

'I'm on it, I'm on it. God. Gotta put my book down and everything. Where's my bookmark gone? You seen it?'

'You're in the presence of greatness and you're more concerned with losing your place?!'

'It's the best part, Merc! Desdemona is about to confess her undying love to Lord Kristan! It's been four books in the making! Do you know how long it took me to read four books?'

'You're here to help me, Pietro! What sort of inept, off-brand assistant are you?'

'*One who wants to read his book, Merc!*'

Ig turned to Vivi. 'Do I really want to know?'

'Yes!' Vivi cried, dragging Ig towards the danger by the wrist. 'How else will you learn if science is your calling?'

'Vivi…Vivi stop…Vivi–!'

As Vivi and Ig wrenched open the door, a carpet of thick, vaguely purple smoke billowed out around their shins. Ig stepped into the doorway to see a tall, brown-haired boy – eyes eclipsed by a pair of lab goggles – towering over a squat, square cage, sitting on a long wooden bench; one of five that ran from one end of the classroom to the other. The cage was connected by a pair of jump cables to a gigantic mess of sparking wires and tubes shifting suspiciously green liquid back and forth.

'You better start paying attention, Pietro,' the goggle-wearing boy was saying – more to the air than to the other student, who was flicking through a well-worn paperback with his feet up on the teacher's desk. 'Because this – this very moment! – is about to go down in Shackleton Academy history!' He raised his hands above his head, chin tipped towards the ceiling. 'For I, Mercutio von Ryan, have wrung life from that which was dead, and bent the consciousness of the creature to my will!' With a flourish, he opened the cage door. 'Behold, assistant; the first of my new army of loyal super soldiers. Be free, my undead minion!'

Out of the cage hopped a rabbit. A fluffy, lop-eared bunny rabbit, the only blemish in its snow-white fur being a long, angry-looking scar that ran down one side of its face.

'Awwwwww!' The other boy – Pietro, Ig assumed – put down his book and crept over to the rabbit. Once they were standing side by side, Ig realised that the two boys were virtually identical; apart from the fact one was dressed like something from a low-budget Frankenstein remake. 'Hi, little fella.'

'She's a girl, Pietro.'

'Oh. Sorry. Hang on; where did you get a rabbit from? Especially a slightly dead but very cute *pet* rabbit?'

Mercutio shrugged languidly. 'Accidents happen all the time. Some people aren't prepared to be pet owners. Don't worry about it.'

Ig thought back to the rabbit that was nearly flattened by the car that brought her here and winced. So the driver had been right, all along. They were experimenting on innocent little creatures.

'I always worry, Merc. That's my job.' Pietro tapped the rabbit on the nose. 'Boop.'

The rabbit sniffed Pietro's finger and turned away dismissively. 'See?' Mercutio said smugly, folding his arms as she hopped towards him with her fluffy tail twitching. 'Loyal.'

'Doesn't look particularly evil, though,' Pietro muttered, prodding the bunny between the ears. Mercutio paused for a moment, looking down at the rabbit as if he'd seen it for the first time.

'I mean... I only had certain options for... the... she was the only rabbit that was fresh enough to... the next one'll be bigger,' he finished, wilting slightly under the other boy's smirk.

'Ooooh, maybe a Pomeranian or something! Vicious.'

'Shut up, Pietro.' Mercutio fished around in his lab coat pockets and produced a tiny eyepatch. 'There,' he said, affixing it to the scarred side of the rabbit's face. The tips of the angry, puckered red skin still poked out from either side of the patch. 'Evil. I shall call her Onslaught.'

The other boy, growing bored, realised they had company. In one swift movement, he was bounding towards the door.

'Viv!' he cried, wrapping Vivi up in a hug, lifting her a few inches off the ground. 'Oooooh,' he growled into her hair, swinging her back and forth. 'I missed you; I missed you so much.'

'Pietro!' Vivi giggled, 'I saw you in assembly this morning!'

'Yeah! And that was hours ago! How's your new assignment coming? Operation Befriend The... ah.' Pietro stepped back from Vivi, finally catching sight of Ig as she lingered in the doorway. 'Here she is now, I suppose.'

Even though he was technically identical to the boy staring at an undead rabbit, frantically making notes and chewing vigorously on the end of his pencil, Ig noticed that Pietro carried himself totally differently; his limbs were more fluid and his stance less rigid. Mercutio had, frankly, gorgeous hair; softly curling around his temples, conditioned within an inch of its life . His brother's hair was wild; sticking up from his forehead like he'd shoved his fingers through it instead of brushing it. Pietro's smile was wide and easy and, from the way he was looking Ig up and down, he was a total and utter flirt.

'Cute,' he said. 'I'm Pietro von Ryan. The one with the rabbit eating his hair is my brother.'

'I am not *your brother*,' drawled the other boy, having clambered up into the table with the rabbit in his arms. 'You are *my clone*.'

Pietro flapped one hand in a '*blah blah blah*' gesture, rolling his eyes at the girls. 'Then why am I so much more handsome than you, Merc?'

'I – wha – you are not more handsome than... we have identical DNA, Pietro!' Mercutio juggled the rabbit into the crook of one arm and pushed the goggles up onto the top of his head indignantly. 'There is objectively no way one of us is more handsome than...Vivi,' he trailed off, finally acknowledging that the two girls in the doorway existed.

'Hi, Merc!' Vivi chirped, waving so hard that she lost her balance and bumped into Ig.

Whatever was powering the bluster and manic energy coming from Mercutio von Ryan was suddenly gone – as if a switch had been flipped. His eyes were wide and slightly vacant, and a flush of red had begun creeping its way up his neck. Slowly, as if his arms were heavier than he expected them to be, he lowered the rabbit down and in towards his chest; unaware as it happily snuggled against his collarbone.

'Hi. Um... hi.'

'Isn't Viv looking nice today, Merc?' Pietro said, widening his eyes meaningfully at his brother. 'She's done something new with her hair, hasn't she?'

'Um,' Mercutio reiterated. Vivi patted the flower in her hair bashfully.

'Maybe it would be nice to, you know,' Pietro inched closer to his brother, grabbing him by the lapels and jerking him down to eye level, 'say something about it. *Like a person would*.'

'It's... a... oh!' Mercutio brightened, snapping a finger in Vivi's direction. '*Lycoris radiata*. Red Spider Lily, yes?'

'That's right!' Vivi squeaked, clearly thrilled. The flush on Mercutio's neck grew darker.

'Well,' Pietro grumbled, tipping his head towards Ig in a conspiratorial way, 'I meant he should say that it was pretty or something. But whatever, it worked.'

'I had to put my best foot forward, didn't I?' Vivi reached out and grabbed Ig in a tight side-hug. 'First impressions are important after all!'

'Von Ryan,' said a voice behind Ig; a teacher she hadn't seen before was leaning into the classroom, peering through spectacles with lenses as thick as a glass bottle. 'You need to be clearing out of her here in five, remember? I need the room.'

Mercutio straightened. 'Yes, Miss Genetica.'

The teacher looked over at Onslaught, who was nudging Mercutio's hand in pursuit of scritches. 'Is that your latest project?'

Mercutio nodded.

'Any rigor mortis this time?'

'No, Miss Genetica.'

'Impressive. Did you enhance her biological advantages, or did you graft on new ones to her genetic material?'

'She's got an eyepatch,' Pietro offered cheerily. Miss Genetica looked him up and down.

'Shouldn't you be clearing up?' she asked witheringly.

Pietro sighed. 'Yes, Miss.'

'Well, it was nice to meet you, Merc,' Ig said, finally shrugging off Vivi's embrace and striding forward, hand outstretched. The General always said a Hero had to be charismatic and forthcoming in meeting people; especially those who seemed a little awkward. 'I'm Ig Heretical.'

Merc looked at her hand like it was a dead bug. 'It's Mercutio,' he deadpanned, raising one perfectly sculpted eyebrow. 'Or, preferably, von Ryan. I don't know you. Come, Onslaught.'

Ig's face fell. Mercutio hopped down from the table and, with a swish of his lab coat, left the room; bunny still in hand. Pietro watched him go, then turned to the girls and shrugged.

'He's a sweetheart, deep down.'

'Pietro!'

'Coming, boss. I'm coming.' Pietro clicked his tongue and pointed double finger-guns at Vivi. 'See you at lunch, babe. Bring the new girl.'

'See you then!'

Pietro blew air kisses all the way down the corridor; walking backwards until he disappeared out of sight around a corner. 'So,' Ig said, nudging her classmate as they turned and walked the other way, 'Pietro seems…nice.'

'He is!' Vivi beamed.

They had to be dating. They had to be. People weren't just… like that with each other.

'So, you two are… close, yeah?'

'I've known him since we were five. My mam knows their uncle. He's their guardian. So, I maybe thought I could show you where Monologue Class is, for Monday–'

'Yeah, but is Pietro your…' Ig flailed her hands awkwardly for a moment, searching for a way to talk around what she wanted to ask. At Lunalist, you couldn't shut the other girls up when talking about their crushes. Now, faced with starting the conversation herself, she didn't know where to begin. In the end, she decided to awkwardly bump her hands together in a heart shape. 'You know.'

Vivi kept walking for a disconcertingly long amount of time before realising what Ig was getting at. 'Oh! Oh, no no no; Pietro doesn't go out with anyone,' she said, tucking her hair behind one ear. 'He says he's never wanted to. He can't ever see himself, you know, being someone's boyfriend or whatever.'

'But he's s–'

'Flirty?'

'Loud.'

'He's just like that. He'll be blowing you kisses by the end of the day, too.' Vivi looked down at the ground, bashful. 'It's actually Mercutio that… that–'

'Needs to warm up to me? Can't see that happening anytime soon,' Ig interrupted, laughing loudly at the mental image of the scientist blowing her deadly serious kisses. 'Or, you know, ever.' Somehow, even though both boys were identical, it was impossible to imagine Mercutio behaving anything like his brother. Clone. Whatever. It was like layering ice over a warm fire; simply impossible. Vivi looked at her for a second, then laughed – a little too loudly.

'Yeah! Yeah, that's what I was going to say. What a…what a meanie. Come on, we're going to be late.'

Chapter Eleven

The rest of the day passed in a haze. Ig felt like her head was filled with cotton wool; stuffed full of information until nothing else could fit. She trailed around after Vivi from class to class, taking nothing in – and hating herself for it. Was this going to be how it was, here? One terrifying lesson, a brief meeting with a mad scientist and his assistant and she was rendered useless?

Maybe she wasn't right for this job after all. Maybe she should tell The General she picked the wrong student for this mission. Maybe–

'Ig? What do you think?' Ig snapped out of her daydream to find herself walking out the main doors of Shackleton with Vivi at her side. Where were they going? Was Vivi escorting her out personally? 'Um,' she replied. Vivi laughed and knocked her knuckles against her own head.

'You've got a lot going on up there, haven't you?'

'…have I?' Ig said weakly.

'All day you've been on edge,' Vivi replied, shouldering her backpack a little more. 'Are you feeling overwhelmed?'

Like I'd tell you, Ig thought. Why did she care so much, anyway? It made Ig suspicious.

'Don't worry. There's plenty of time to take these things in. What I was saying,' Vivi continued, 'was should we have our break in the courtyard? It's pretty, and there's a nice fountain we could sit under.'

A nice fountain? On the drive up here, Ig had been imagining what the place she'd call home for the next term or two would look like. 'Nice' didn't exactly factor into it. But hey – it would be an excuse to see more of the grounds. So she nodded.

It was a fairly pleasant day; the sun shining through the clouds and turning everything around them, including Vivi's hair, a vibrant shade of green. 'Are you allowed to have your hair that colour?' Ig asked, as Vivi produced a scrunchie from her pocket and tied her hair back in a ponytail. She shrugged, and Ig felt silly for asking.

'I did it before I got here,' she said, twirling the ends around her fingertip. 'When I get home, my mams have a new box of dye sitting on the side of the bath, waiting for me. It makes me a little less sad about leaving here, you know?'

'You get *sad* when you leave here?'

Vivi shrugged again. 'You didn't get sad when you leave your old school for the summer?'

Ig said nothing. Usually, her dad picked her up. They sang along to the radio all the way home, then walked through the door to their house in Gosforth to a plate of what they called 'Mam's Welcome Home Pancakes' – Ig's mam always felt left out when she couldn't come along on the drive home, so she made Ig's favourite breakfast when they got back. She didn't think of school a lot while she was at home. Apart from when she missed Pisces.

Pisces. What was she doing, without Ig there? Did she have a new dorm-mate already? Was it lonely, without her there? How was she going to sleep tonight, without the sound of Ig gently snoring in the bunk below hers?

'Hm, I suppose not,' Vivi said; filling in the gaps in the conversation herself. 'Not if you're getting bullied.'

Ig flinched. 'Who said I was getting bullied?'

'Whoah! Defensive,' Vivi said, making sure the red flower in her hair was still in place with the flat of her hand. 'The Nyx told me.'

Oh. Right. Ig's plan to make her transfer to Shackleton seem more natural. 'What else did they tell you?'

Vivi twisted her mouth. 'Not much.'

The landscape of the gardens around Shackleton was wild – but, as it seemed to Ig, strategically so. The grounds were made up of corridors of tall, thick briars, as well as all sort of plants and flowers and trees that Ig didn't know how to name; not exactly a maze, especially not after the school's actual hallways, but high and thick enough that you could wander around and no-one would know where you were. Ig made a mental note, wishing she'd brought her communication device. She hadn't realised until after Vivi had shunted her out the dorm that she could have turned it onto dictaphone mode in her pocket and recorded entire lessons without even trying.

The thorny corridor they were walking down opened up into a paved courtyard; dark, thick slabs of concrete, with an ornate fountain of a dragon in the centre of it. The beast was rearing up on its hind legs, wings stretched out…but instead of breathing fire, this dragon spat an arch of shimmering water into the air, which tinkled back down to the pool the sculpture was sitting on. Vivi sat on the lip of the fountain, and Ig followed her lead.

'Sorry,' Vivi said, pulling one leg into her lap and playing with the ends of her shoelaces. 'That was a bit blunt, wasn't it? Just now, I mean. I get like that, sometimes. Overly familiar, is what my Mami calls it. I have a Mam and a Mami,' she explained. 'I have two mams–'

'I remembered,' Ig said.

'And calling them both Mam would be confusing. And Mami is from Colombia originally, so…what was I talking about?'

'Being overly familiar,' Ig said, pressing her lips together so she didn't smile.

'Right.' Vivi smiled back shyly. 'Sorry I blurted out about you being bullied. The Nyx told me because they thought I could look after you better if I knew. I quite like looking after people. I haven't told Pietro or Merc. Need to know basis only, I promise!'

'I don't need to be looked after,' Ig said, her pride prickling. 'I'm not a baby.'

'I didn't mean it like that!' Vivi cried, holding up her hands like she thought Ig was going to hit her. 'I just meant… that… oh, crap. I'm not making a very good first impression.'

She looked so sad that Ig had to laugh. 'You're fine,' she said, surprising herself when she realised she meant it. 'I'm not the best at the first impression stuff, either.'

'Really? 'Coz I think Mr. Throttler was ready to adopt you by the end of that lesson.'

'He's so scary!' Ig said. 'I've never had a teacher like that before.'

Vivi made a show of looking around her for witnesses. 'Did you know he breeds kittens as a side hustle?' she stage-whispered.

'No!'

'Ragdolls. Big fluffy stupid things. My Mam says I can have one if I graduate with good marks…'

As the two were talking, another group of students rounded the corner into the courtyard. Ig supposed, if guys were her thing, the boy leading the charge would have been handsome. In a snooty, well-groomed sort of way; eyes shining, dark skin, hair perfectly oiled and combed. 'Vivian Section,' he called, striding towards the fountain, 'I challenge you to a Villain War!'

'Ugh,' Vivi groaned, rolling her eyes at the boy. 'Falcon, I've told you. Villain Wars aren't a thing–'

The boy – Falcon? – jutted his chin out towards one of his followers. They stiffened, eyes widening and turning vague. 'You know the stinging nettle vines in the Poisonology classroom?' he said mildly.

'Yes, Falcon,' the other student replied in a daze.

'Go salt the earth it grows in.'

'Yes, Falcon.'

'Falcon, come on!' Vivi screeched, leaping to her feet. 'That's my Hybridisation assignment! It took me months to get it to grow! You wouldn't dare!'

'Try me,' smirked Falcon. Ig did not like this boy one bit.

'Fine,' Vivi growled, eyes narrowed. 'Call your crony off and I'll–'

Falcon raised one slender hand and clicked his fingers together. Instantly, Vivi stood up on the lip of the fountain and, eyes glassy, made a farting noise with her hand and her lips. Then, she gracefully turned on her heel, bent over, and smacked her bum three times in succession. The crowd around the newcomer laughed, delighted, and Ig scrambled back in terror; taking care not to tumble straight into the water. This was it. The students were showing their true colours. They were attacking – they were attacking each other! – and Vivi was under their command. This boy clearly had some sort of mind control Power. Ig was caught behind enemy lines, alone. What was she going to do?! She had to do something! She had to–

'Very funny, Falcon,' said Vivi, shaking her head as if to wriggle out of the trance she'd been put in. 'Fart humour – and you're what? Sixteen?' Falcon turned to his crowd, who were still hyping him up, and bowed. 'Well,' Vivi said darkly, pulling the red flower from her hair, 'if you're so into toilet humour, get a load of this.'

Ig watched, frozen, as Vivi closed her eyes, tightened her grip on the flower, and blew. A cloud of reddish spores drifted away from the flower, crossing the courtyard and hitting Falcon – and only Falcon – right in the face. He tensed, eyes narrowing slightly as the pollen went up his nose. 'Ugh,' he said, shuddering. 'That smells disgusting. Are you making aromatherapy warfare now, Vivi–'

Falcon's entire body went rigid. His hand flew to his mouth. He gagged. Then he ran to the fountain, leaned over the side, and vomited straight into the water. 'Ewwww!' cried the collective of Villains behind him. Ig managed to leap out of the way before getting splashed, retching herself as she did. Vivi, now miles away from the site of her attack, crowed with laughter.

'What do you think, Falcon? Warlike enough for you?'

'Very… *bleurgh*… impressive.'

'So I get your dessert for a week at lunch, like usual? I think they're making sticky toffee pudding this week; with big fat dates and loads of sauce…'

'*Oh don't mention food…*'

Vivi leaned towards Falcon's back. 'I can't hear you,' she trilled in a sing-song voice, patting him on the shoulder.

'*Fine okay you can have my stupid desse – bleeeurgh!*'

'Yes! Another round goes to Vivi Section!' Vivi spun in a circle, arms outstretched with a beaming smile. A smile that fell away as soon as she saw Ig's face.

'Y-you,' Ig began, before swallowing hard and catching her breath. 'You're the same age as me…you're not meant to have a Power yet, I-I don't understand…'

Only special cases had their Power revealed early. The very best, the brightest, the ones who needed to get out into the world and start helping people. They certainly didn't just…stay at school! This awful school was letting Villains run around with Powers, unsupervised? Why hadn't The Nyx told her that her new dorm-mate was a biological weapon waiting to go off?

'Hey – woah, hang on, deep breaths.' Vivi approached her, hands splayed out like she was calming a skittish animal. 'You're right, I've got my Power, but it's fine. I… look, let's get away from all this puke-smell, and we'll talk. Okay?'

Ig paused. 'You're not going to make me throw up?'

'I won't make you throw up. Promise.'

A promise from a Villain was worthless. Ig knew that. But what were her options? To go it alone? To ingratiate herself with Falcon-the-puppet-master and his band of howler monkeys? Or stick with the girl that, at the very least, she had the best chance of getting a handle on? So she allowed herself to be led away, into the maze of thorns.

'Okay,' Vivi said, when they found a decent bench to sit on. 'Soooo, yeah. I have a Power – have had a Power, I mean. Since I was thirteen.'

THIRTEEN?!

Vivi drummed on her legs shyly while Ig stared at her, open-mouthed. 'I know! I know. I'm a prodigy, The Nyx says so all the time.'

'A prodigy?!' Ig squeaked. 'A prodigy – you're an, an outlier! You and that boy back there, Kestrel or whatever he's called, you're both… deranged!'

A flicker of hurt crossed Vivi's face, and Ig instantly regretted her choice of words. 'Sorry,' she said before she could take another breath. 'What I mean is… my dad says no-one gets their Power early. You get told what it is when you turn sixteen, at your Revelation Ceremony.'

'Really?' Vivi tucked her legs up under each other. 'That must be really hard on the people who know when they're younger, like me.'

'But you don't know!' Ig protested. 'That's the point!'

Vivi laughed. 'It seemed like I knew how to make Falcon Reeve splatter his breakfast all over that poor fountain, didn't it?'

She had Ig there. 'How did you do it?' she asked, curiosity getting the better of her. The Red Spider Lily was still in Vivi's hand; slightly crumpled, but still pretty. 'Was it the plant? Did you control it?'

'Not 'control', not really.' Vivi uncurled her fingers and let the flower rest in her palm. 'It's like – okay, how do I explain – I can manipulate the plant. Not into becoming something else, and I can't shoot vines from my hands or anything weird like that. It's more like I can ask it to be the worst version of itself. Spider Lilies can cause vomiting if you eat them, and so I suggested to this one – with my mind, not out loud – that having spores that did the same thing but way, way worse would be a really, really good idea…so it did it for me.' Vivi looked down at the flower. 'It's like they love me so much they'll do what I tell them to.'

'Have you had a mission yet?'

Vivi laughed. 'Oh, no. I'm not ready for my debut.'

'Debut?'

'Oh, you know.' Vivi fluttered her hands around her head theatrically. 'When you burst onto the world's stage in all your terrible glory. Merc's been preparing for his since he was seven. But I'm really not there, yet; it needs to be special, right?'

'Oh.' Ig didn't know what else to say, so she didn't say anything. At Lunalist, you were given your Power at your Revelation Ceremony, and that was that; you were a Hero, report for duty. Maybe not the same day or anything, but soon after. That was what the Power was for, wasn't it?

The two sat there in a silence that turned from awkward to comfortable over the next five minutes, as the birds chirped overhead and a sweet, clean scent filled the air. Ig breathed it in deeply, feeling her lips relax into a smile.

'What's that smell?' Ig asked Vivi.

'There's a mint plant under the briars over there. I asked it to smell a little stronger for us.' She gave Ig a strange, sideways look. 'I'm a Villain, Ig. That doesn't mean I'm out to get you.'

'I know,' Ig said, not knowing anything. The silence turned awkward again. Then, she nudged Vivi in the shoulder. 'That Mercutio guy, though–'

'Oh, Merc would definitely kill you,' Vivi laughed. 'I say that with love; he's just not good with new people. Oh, okay, listen to this; so he has his Power, but Pietro doesn't – isn't that strange? Even though they're the same, they're so different.'

'I suppose so; so what's Mercutio's Power?'

'It's not so much a Power as a calling; Merc is really good at making things. Living things. Like that bunny – I really need to ask him where he found a pet rabbit that was, um, not quite alive anymore. I hope he hasn't been raiding the village pet cemetery again!'

'Oh! Okay… wait, did you say 'again'?'

As Vivi talked, Ig wished again that she'd had the presence of mind to bring her dictaphone. All this stuff would be very useful to The General.

Chapter Twelve

Ig had planned to use her bedroom as a base for communicating with The General. But after two days, Vivi was yet to leave her sight, even at the weekend when her chaperone duties were null and void; a constant, yammering thorn in Ig's side. Plus, after learning what her dorm-mate's Power was, Ig wouldn't put it past Vivi to have a whole spy ring of Venus Flytraps working overtime in their dorm.

'Your first solo lesson is on Monday,' Vivi chattered, while Ig checked out the (lacking) privacy standards in the bathroom. 'So you've got the entire weekend after today to prep – you'll be fine, though. And we'll catch up later, and you can tell me all about it. Monologue isn't my thing – it's actually my only Basic level class. I overact, you know?'

'Mm-hm,' Ig said, knocking on the cubicle walls and listening, dismayed, to the echo carrying across the room.

'I'm sure you'll crush it, though. You're picking things up so fast! You would have never thought you were a normie a week ago. Guess it really wasn't right for you!'

Ig swallowed her first instinct to be offended. She was getting annoyed with all of Vivi's relentless, tactless support. Being complimented by Vivi felt like having a brick covered in glitter thrown directly at your face. Unwanted, garish, and painful.

There was simply nowhere she could contact home safely. Every classroom was full of students on their free periods, working on some lethal-looking project or another. The halls were always crowded, and the bathrooms were… well, a zoo. At least she'd managed to record a few lessons to report back to The General about – until Vivi wanted to use Ig's 'hand mirror' to check her makeup, and she had had to hide it in her satchel again. The communications device was the last thing she wanted Vivi to see – she'd probably feed it to one of her insane carnivorous plants. As the weekend approached, Ig found herself becoming increasingly annoyed, until Vivi finally suggested she 'go explore' by herself, after Ig had groaned and huffed and stomped so hard a few leaves had fallen off her stupid Widowswort plant. Ig took the hint, and the opportunity, gladly.

As soon as she left the dorm, she took a wrong turn and promptly lost her temper. Ig was sure she was heading towards the main staircase, and had walked into a supply cupboard instead; colliding with a broom and sending it clattering to the floor. With a growl, she picked it up and shoved it back into the cupboard – dislodging a still-damp mop as she did, the pail falling over and slopping mucky water onto her shoes. Ig yowled in anger, stamping her feet and causing one of the younger students to stick their head out the room.

'You okay out here?'

'I'm fine!' Ig snapped, piling the mess back into place and shutting the door on it before she could cause any more damage. The student disappeared back into their room.

How was she going to feed back what she'd learned if she didn't have any privacy? Ig whirled, trying to get her bearings. She needed air; she needed space to think. How was she going to get out? Spinning in a circle, she spied, at the far end of the corridor, a tiny shaft of light, shining onto the carpet.

The window wasn't the biggest Ig had ever known, and she probably wasn't the smallest person to ever try and use it as an escape hatch. But still, it ended up working. After a lot of undignified wriggling and some very coarse language. She landed with a crunch on the gravel that surrounded the building, and set off towards the thickets of briars and hedges.

It was late afternoon; the sun was beginning to set, setting the sky alight with fiery oranges and deep pinks. Once she was safely in the gardens, Ig took a moment to pause and enjoy the view. They didn't have sunsets like this one at Lunalist. In the city centre, the sky was usually grey, or dirty pale blue. Ig wondered what the sunset was like, high above the North Sea tonight. Eventually, she found herself back at the fountain – which was much cleaner and nicer-smelling than it had been when she and Vivi had been here last. Ig felt sorry for whichever cleaner had stumbled across the aftermath of Falcon and Vivi's 'war'. Did this school have cleaners? It must, surely; even the relatively small amount of students here made a lot of mess. Especially with those experiments they did in their free time – as well as witnessing Mercutio von Ryan's rabbit-based necromancy, Ig had already seen a classroom fill up with some sort of green foam, and heard a horrific shriek coming from another. She hadn't had the courage to investigate.

This place was a nightmare.

Ig sat on the lip of the fountain and collected her thoughts. The sound of the gently rushing water behind her soothed her frazzled nerves. Drawing her knees up to her chest, she chewed on her lip as she took in her surroundings. The quiet felt like a cooling balm on her brain; she could finally think clearly, see clearly, notice things she hadn't seen the last time she was here – like the chip right at the tip of the dragon's muzzle, like someone had put their weight on it and the stone hadn't held. Or like the fact she could see sparrows darting in and out of the hedgerows like tiny, dun-coloured shadows, or that there was the outline of a door etched into the red brick of the school wall off to the right of her…

Hold on. There was a door?

Chapter Thirteen

It was almost impossible to see; the brickwork around it matched up perfectly, and there was no doorknob, no windows. But the door was there, if you knew where you were looking. Ig hopped down from the fountain and walked towards it, pressing the flat of her palm against the brick. After a good, hard shove, the door creaked open; slowly and painfully, like it hadn't been opened in years. Ig squeezed through the gap she made for herself, and the door closed behind her with a muffled thump. Ahead of her, barely visible in the dark, was a set of gently curving stairs, heading up and to the right towards… what?

Curiosity got the better of her. This felt like a secret; like something no-one else she'd encountered at Shackleton knew about. Vivi certainly hadn't included it in her grand tour of the grounds. *'Here's the place where I inflict chemical warfare on my enemies, my favourite patch of dandelions and, oh yes, the secret door.'* And if there was nothing at the top of those stairs, Ig could call The General in the dark with her back to the door, listening for eavesdroppers. The steps beneath her feet were made of stone, and there was a carved handrail that was covered in dust that caked Ig's hands. As she climbed, she realised that the room ahead was actually growing lighter, relatively speaking: the sun was almost set. But she could see the last of the light creeping through cracks in a slanted trap door – like a sunroof, but made of wood – above her head. The only piece of furniture on the tiny landing at the top of the stairs was an old, battered, three-legged stool that Ig used as a stepping-stone to push her way out of the trap door and up into the wide, open Northumberland sky. She gasped as she realised that she'd made it all the way onto the roof – the trap door opened up onto shingles and old bird's nests and, below her feet as she settled herself into a sitting position, an old gutter that was in dire need of cleaning. But beyond that was the entire world.

She could see over the stretch of fields and woodland she'd been driven through on her way here from the train station, and beyond that was the village of Rossborough, nestled against the shining Coquet river. If she tilted her head back, even a little, all she could see was sky. It was perfect. Ig slung her backpack off her shoulders and fished out her communication device; sitting snugly in the bottom of her bag, under a pile of granola bar wrappers. One thing she did enjoy about Shackleton was the unlimited supply of healthy-ish snacks – even if they were dished out from a hatch in the floor that led to a dark, dripping dungeon, staffed only by a staff member with a motherly expression and an impressive, bat-like wingspan. She'd smiled toothily as she'd given Ig her granola bars, then plucked a beetle from the walls and stuffed it into a glass jar labelled 'sweets'. Ig had beaten a hasty retreat after that.

She pressed the Call button, then keyed in the access code she'd been told to memorise. After a second or two of the gold-and-white Calling screen playing its connecting tune at her, a face flashed up onto the screen. Not The General, but a girl Ig recognised from her briefing; the hacker, Dana. 'War Room,' she said, her voice clipped and professional.

'Um,' Ig replied. 'Um, it's, ah, Ignatia Heretical. Reporting in. For The General?'

Dana blinked, then tapped on her screen, squinting at whatever she'd brought up. 'We weren't expecting a report.'

Ig flushed. 'Oh. W-were you not?'

'No. Not yet.' The hacker looked into the lens, face carefully blank. Ig felt like she was being absorbed into the shingles below her.

'I, er, I have to check in once a month. I'm the student on the…' she cleared her throat. 'The reconnaissance mission?'

'I know who you are.' The sudden feeling of being perceived, and found lacking, made Ig's stomach contract. 'She's in a meeting, but I can – oh, no, here she comes, actually. General–!'

'Is that Miss Heretical?' said a voice off in the distance. Ig's breath left her lungs in a long, relieved woosh. The General. She'd be glad to hear from her. It felt good to be back in touch with someone reliable again, after the week she'd had. Sure enough, The General's strong, reliable, serious face came into view; the hacker girl backing away so they could speak, thank goodness. 'Miss Heretical?' The General asked again. 'You have something to report?' Ig nodded. 'But it's been less than a week.'

Ig opened her mouth, and then closed it again. 'Were you… were you not expecting me to update you when I'd safely established my cover? I thought, um…' *I thought you might be worried about me. I thought Pisces might be worried about me.* 'I thought you would want to know what I've learned so far.'

'Of course,' The General said, after a beat of silence. 'Of course I do.' She settled into a tall, white leather desk chair. Ig heard a subtle click as she placed her tablet into a stand. 'Ready to receive information, Miss Heretical.'

'Okay,' said Ig, digging in her bag for her notes. 'So, you were right; the school is packed with wildcards. They're all so weird here, General – there's this one boy bringing things back from the dead! Oh, yes, that's right,' she continued, as if The General had doubted her, 'the students here come into their Powers just… whenever! There's no structure, General, it's anarchy. And this boy, *Mercutio*, he's apparently really good with, um, with dead things. He revived this rabbit – she was dead, like dead-dead, and he brought her back to life under his control! Isn't that insane? And he's got this *clone* – this whole other boy who runs around after him and makes weird little comments like–'

'The von Ryan twins.' The General nodded. 'Rayner von Ryan's adopted charges. We're aware of them.'

'…oh.'

'Rayner von Ryan has been under Hero surveillance since he

was seventeen. It's good to know they are still contained within the school,' The General conceded, 'but we have extensive records dating back to the original boy being put under von Ryan's care, and then again when the supplemental boy was created. Have they achieved anything else?' Ig could have sworn The General wrinkled her nose. 'Besides the, er, rabbit.'

Truth be told, Ig hadn't seen either of the von Ryans since that incident in the classroom. 'No.'

The General folded her hands on her lap. 'Let's move on,' she said, her voice brokering no argument.

Embarrassed, Ig tapped at the screen of her communication device. 'I - I recorded some of my lessons…'

'Wait, Miss Heretical, if you come out of the communications app – listen to me – *Miss Heretical*!'

Ig froze, finger poised over the screen. 'If you come out of the communications app,' The General said, her tone suddenly tense with frayed patience, 'you'll end the call. The dictaphone is for note-taking. Can you remember any of your findings?'

'Um… no. But I have my, er, timetable, here…' Ig produced her crumpled, battered planner. 'Torture Management, Minion Husbandry, Vivi goes to something called Poisonology…'

'Are you learning about how they plan to attack the academy?'

'…no.'

'Let's move on, then.'

This was not going as Ig had planned it. 'Um, er…oh! Okay. So there are secret passageways! I found one just now,' she scooted in a circle to show The General that she was on the roof. 'It led me up to this rooftop, it's really isolated, perfect for contacting you and home… well, my dad.'

'Hm. Well, I'd suggest,' The General said, 'that you don't contact your father until you have a little more to tell him about your mission. It would make sense, wouldn't it Miss Heretical?'

Ig had been planning to call home straight after she'd talked to The General. She thought her dad would be excited to hear from her. But The General was right. Of course, she was. It was too soon. She could see that now. 'Yes, General.'

'Continue. Please.'

Ig turned the camera around so she was showing The General the grounds. 'So, from here you can see that the thorns make up a mazeway. If I can map the entire thing, then maybe I could send it to you, and the flyers or someone could use it to get in?'

There was a silence, and Ig contemplated throwing herself off the roof to end her suffering. Maybe she'd land in the fountain and drown.

'Interesting,' said The General. Ig brightened. *Interesting?* She could work with interesting!

'I haven't been everywhere, yet! But there are markers, definite landmarks that could be used to co-ordinate meeting points, plans of access to the school, flanking groups that could hide out while–'

'A very good place to start.' The General nodded. 'Yes, that could be useful information to have.'

She'd clawed it back. Ig couldn't believe it. It had been worth getting in touch so soon! She'd given The General information she thought was useful! Emboldened, she ploughed on ahead with thoughts she'd only just started working on – about how the school itself operated under The Nyx's spell. 'The school building is a bit more complicated. The Nyx – the headteacher? – uses some sort of Power to, um, compress the school? But they also draw it out, and they put rooms in…the, the corridors have more rooms than they…usually do.'

'The corridors have more rooms than they usually do.' Great stuff, Heretical.

The General raised one eyebrow. 'It sounds like you have the beginning of a hypothesis, there. But it needs work.' Ig shoved her notes back into her bag and nodded, eyes stinging. 'Well,' The General said, as gently as a parent talking to a toddler, 'why don't you make that your priority, to work out exactly how The Nyx manipulates the space of the school.'

Ig nodded again, shame rolling round in her stomach like a stone. 'Is that all?'

Ig nodded for a third time. 'Well,' she said haltingly, 'I was wondering, um… if Miss Rising had left a message for me? Or inquired if you'd heard from me, or..?'

Please, Pisces. Please, ask how I am.

'Miss Rising is very busy with her studies,' The General said. 'She joined the Swimming Club after you left us, and that takes up a lot of her time, as you can imagine.'

'Yeah,' Ig said sadly. Of course she was busy. Pisces was going to be something amazing, one day. How selfish of Ig, to demand Pisces make time to miss her.

'On the subject of studies,' The General said casually, 'how are you finding yours, Miss Heretical?'

A chill ran down Ig's spine. She couldn't exactly say *'oh, brilliantly, General! I got a sparkly sticker in Torture Management!'*, could she? But she couldn't lie, either. Lying to The General was like lying to the Queen, or to God. So she settled simply for nodding tightly and making a bright, cheery 'Mm-hmm!' noise in her throat. Her dad had this cartoony bobblehead of himself in the study that wobbled about if you flicked it, and Ig knew exactly how it felt right now.

'Ah, well,' The General said, as something over her shoulder distracted her. 'Don't get disheartened. You can't expect their horrendous practices to come naturally.'

Had Ig given the impression she was doing badly? She'd been going for a happy medium. Maybe she'd made the wrong head movements or something; non-verbal communication was never her strongest suit. Did she look stressed? Maybe she looked stressed. 'I–'

'Remember you only need to achieve enough to keep your cover. We don't expect much more. I must go, Miss Heretical – next month; those schematics of the maze and school, yes?'

'…yes, General.'

The screen went blank.

Chapter Fourteen

Trying to sleep in Vivi's room (which was Ig's room too, she realised as she looked up at the leafy fronds stretching over the window, backlit by the full moon rising over the Shackleton grounds) was like trying to sleep in a rainforest. Something was always rustling – had Vivi actually confirmed that there weren't creatures living in here with them? – or the gentle tinkle of a watering fountain made Ig desperate for a pee every half an hour. And that was to say nothing of the smells. Oh, they weren't bad smells – lots of pretty flowers and clean, soft earth – but there was so *much* of it. Ig tossed and turned, tried hugging Finnie tight and throwing off all her sheets. Nothing helped.

And it totally wasn't because she had other things on her mind. Sickly, guilty, shameful things.

Her meeting with The General had not gone the way Ig had planned it. She'd been too eager to report back, and either bombarded The General with information she already knew or threw out interesting tidbits without any sort of context. The look on The General's face as she brushed off Mercutio's experiments with the rabbit would haunt Ig's dreams, if she could ever get to sleep. She'd never been so embarrassed.

She needed to focus. She needed to collect real data, use her dictaphone app properly, draw out her schematics of the school and stop cosying up to other students and performing so bloody well at these… these unhinged training sessions. They weren't what she was here for. It wasn't what was expected of her. Of course it wasn't.

'Ig?' came a soft call from above her head. 'Ig, are you awake?'

'No,' Ig grumbled.

'I can hear you breathing. It's definitely not sleepy breathing.'

'I'm fine.' Ig threw herself over onto her side and pulled Finnie in close to her chest, closing her eyes so tightly it hurt. She was calm. She was asleep. She was dreaming.

Pisces hadn't even asked how she was.

With a frustrated growl, Ig flung herself onto her other side and gripped her cuddly shark so hard she thought her fingers would go right through his fabric fin. She wanted her dad. She wanted to call him and have him make her laugh and bolster her mood and tell her that everything was gonna work out... but she should wait. Until she actually had something to tell him about. And anyway, she wasn't really sure that it would help her feel better. If she kept sending The General dud intel, she might get pulled back to Lunalist in shame. Then she'd never get a Power. Then Pisces would never want to talk to her again. Then she would have to leave and go live with her parents again and they'd be so disappointed in her and Mam would get to gloat about how she always knew Lunalist was a bad idea and–

'Okay. You're totally not asleep.' The rungs of the ladder up to Vivi's bed squeaked. 'I'm coming down.'

'Vivi, please don't.'

'Too late.' A pair of tiger-print socked feet hit the floor. 'I'm going to make us some tea.'

'You really don't have to do that.'

'I can't sleep either. I've got some lavender I've been cross-pollinating with honeysuckle for flavour; it makes a really good sleepytime tea.'

Indignation rankled in Ig's head. 'I don't need a sleepytime tea, I'm not ninety.'

'...now, I think I plugged the kettle in behind the monstera, let me just...' Ig winced as pots were shoved aside and piles of books clattered to the floor. 'Oops.'

'You're noisy,' Ig snapped, pressing Finnie over her ears, 'you know that?'

'Yep!' came the chipper reply. 'My Mami's always telling me I'm like a pet elephant.'

Ig huffed under her breath, annoyed that her attempt to hurt Vivi's feelings had been thwarted. Not very Heroic of her, she supposed; but then, people apparently weren't expecting much from her right now. Vivi re-emerged a moment or two later, with two steaming mugs of tea. 'I gave you the Mothman mug,' she said, handing Ig a black mug with red eyes painted on the front and wings for handles. 'It's the cutest one. I suppose I'll settle for a normal, boring cuppa.'

Ig curled her fingers around her mug; noticing, as she did, that her knuckles were starting to bruise. That stupid stress reaction from her grandpa's side of the family. She hated it. It made her hands look ugly; like some dead thing. Vivi probably had some cure for that, too – made from nettles and suffering or something. 'I didn't want tea.'

'It's fine. You need to rest properly, since you've got your first solo class tomorrow.'

Ig was getting angry now. 'Vivi–'

'I promise, it won't make you throw up – I only do things like that to idiots like Falcon. Until we graduate, that is! You won't spew up all over Miss Schwab, don't worry.'

'Vivi, stop it–'

'Not that you'll do badly tomorrow, anyway. You've done so well so far, it's like you're a natural Villain–'

'For god's sake, Vivi!' Ig snapped, slamming her mug down on her knee. 'Stop being so bloody *nice* to me!' Vivi reared back in shock, but Ig barely noticed; she was blind to everything, but how terrible she felt, how guilty and angry Vivi's kindness made her feel. 'Stop being so nice to me,' she said again, enjoying how good it felt to be so awful to someone as sickeningly upbeat – so unrelentingly positive and chatty and *vapid* as this green-haired weirdo in front of her. 'I don't want to be your friend, okay, so just stop – just stop being so nice, I don't want it.

Okay? What kind of useless Villain are you anyway, being so—'

The mug cracked under her grip. Ig looked down as hot, sweet-smelling tea leaked onto her purpling palms, the crack splitting right between the Mothman's beady red eyes. The world suddenly rushed back in. She looked up at Vivi, who was still staring at her, open-mouthed; tears forming in her eyes. Ig stood up and blundered to their tiny en-suite bathroom, dumping the mug and the remains of its contents into the sink.

'Vivi,' she gasped, watching the purple bruising spread along her fingers, 'Vivi, I'm sorry—'

'Is this about your mission?'

Ig's head snapped up. She looked back to where Vivi had climbed onto her bed, hugging her own mug tightly; as if she were scared Ig would destroy it, too. 'What did you say?' Ig asked.

'Your mission,' Vivi said again, looking down into her tea. 'To get information back to the Hero school? Is it not going well?' She shrugged, a high-pitched noise a little like laughter escaping through her nose. 'I mean, I should be glad. But I could have told you that and saved you all the bother.'

'How,' Ig stammered. 'Wh… but… I…'

'Me and the boys worked it out,' Vivi said, not looking away from her tea. 'Like, obviously you didn't go to a normal school. With your parents? Something had to be up. That's why I volunteered to be your dorm-mate. I mean; why else would one of you come here if it wasn't to spy on us awful Villains?'

Ig hovered in the bathroom, tea drying sticky on her hands. 'So why haven't you told anyone you know? The Nyx, or one of the teachers?'

'Because,' Vivi said, taking a long sip of her tea, 'there's nothing for you to find. Shackleton is a place for us to train, Ig. The teachers have always seen it that way. When we get out there—' she gestured towards the window with an arm, 'it's us against the world. I mean, a few of us form societies, groups like The Midnight Movement and stuff, but there's no real chance for us to learn anything at all once we leave here. No one to teach us. So, for us, all that good and evil rivalry crap waits until we graduate.' She looked up through her hair at Ig. 'I don't exactly think it's the same where you come from.' Something like embarrassment flared in Ig's stomach; but with none of the angry fire of before. Now, she just felt shame. Because she knew that part was true. 'So I sort of hoped that you'd get bored and go home if I showed you how the school operated. Tell your boss or whatever that there's nothing going on, and that there are better ways to spend all that grant money you get from the government. But then we became friends – or I thought we became friends.' Vivi angrily swiped a tear from her cheek. 'I thought you might just give up on your own.' Those two words – '*I thought*' – cut through Ig with a sharpness she wasn't expecting.

'Isn't that a bit naïve?' she asked. 'Hoping that the power of friendship will mean that I give up on my mission?'

Vivi looked up at her through the curtain of her hair. 'About as naïve as assuming that everyone is super-duper jealous of you and wants to destroy you because you've got a nice pool and a God Complex.'

Ig opened her mouth, then closed it again. Vivi sighed, and Ig watched the ripples on the top of her tea dancing. 'Ig…you aren't going to find anything. I promise.'

Ig didn't believe her for a second. But that didn't mean that her heart didn't twist at the sincerity in Vivi's eyes.

'But I know you aren't going to give up. So, I want us to be friends,' Vivi said. 'Do you think maybe, while you're here, we can be friends?'

Ig swallowed hard. She looked back at Vivi's cutest mug, broken in the sink, sadly leaking sleepytime tea. Then, almost against her will, she nodded. 'When we graduate,' she said, trying to lift her voice into something light and airy, 'and we're real Heroes and Villains, maybe we can be arch-nemeses or something. Wouldn't that make a great backstory?'

Vivi coughed up a laugh and spread out her arms as if she were putting up a gigantic movie poster. 'Former friends, torn apart by circumstance. Forced to battle to the death–'

'The death?!'

'Or, you know. Maybe until one of us draws blood. And then you can apologise to me for being such a massive idiot and thinking everything's always about your stupid fancy Hero school.' Vivi clambered to her feet and stuck out her hand. 'Shake on it. Peace for now, at least.'

An order, not a request. Ig had a sudden vision from her days spent watching old American films with her dad, and spat on her palm and pressed it against Vivi's; delighted at the scandalised squeals it elicited from her dorm-mate.

'Ignatia Heretical, you are disgusting!'

Ig smiled a wobbly smile. 'I know. But that was my first ever deal, so I wanted to make it count.'

'Can I go back to bed, now? Or are there any more confessions we need to make?' Vivi flattened her face into a mask of seriousness. 'One time, I helped an old lady cross the road. It was the most Heroic thing I've ever done. It haunts me to this day.'

'No, I'm done. Thanks, Vivi.' Ig wasn't entirely sure why, but her chest felt a lot lighter, even though this thing with her and Vivi could only last so long. 'Night.'

'Night, Ig.' Vivi began to climb back up into her bunk, then paused, swinging by one arm off the wooden rungs of the steps. 'Oh, and Ig?'

'Hm?'

The sunny expression vanished from Vivi's face. 'If anything happens to my friends because of you, I'll hunt you down myself. I'm not joking about that. 'kay?' After a long moment (and some mutually uncomfortable eye contact), Ig nodded.

Vivi disappeared into her bunk and was snoring within seconds. Ig climbed back into bed; clutching her sheets, staring up at the patterns the leaves left across the dorm room ceiling, not exactly sure how she felt.

Chapter Fifteen

Monologue Class was her first class without Vivi.

She had walked her there, of course – Ig had protested, hoping to use the time alone to snoop a little around the hallways. But Vivi had insisted, taking her right to the door of Ms. Schwab's Mologuing class. Ig felt like she was being distracted; like a toddler being led away from the toy aisle. The tension from lingered in the air in their dorm room, despite their handshake and promises of peace. Oh, Vivi had smiled and said good morning, just like usual – but then her gaze had snagged on the broken remnants of her mug in the sink, and that smile had faltered. Ig had attempted to apologise again, but Vivi had said it was fine; turning up her music and singing along as she lined her eyes with what looked like purple crayon. It was hard to talk over an entire arena in Brazil howling along with a guitar riff from the eighties.

Arguments like last night always unsettled Ig; she was never sure how to get back to normal. And what was normal, anyway, with a girl you'd known for less than a week? Whatever it was, Ig was astonished to find that she wanted it back.

'You'll be fine,' Vivi said, mistaking Ig's silence for nerves. 'And oh! I forgot to tell you! You'll have some friends!'

'Friends?' Ig asked, looking around. Already waiting outside the classroom were the von Ryans. Pietro had his nose in a book; novel splayed open over his long palm, with his and Mercutio's bags slung over one shoulder while Mercutio brooded moodily in the doorway; fingers drumming against one hip, a single dark curl falling into his eyes. Ig had to admit, the boy would look good in front of a camera someday. Probably after being arrested for burning down an orphanage.

When he saw the girls, Pietro burst into a wide, sunny grin. 'Amigos! You been moved up to Advanced, Viv?'

'Nah,' Vivi said, punching Ig affectionately in the shoulder. 'Just dropping off the newbie!'

Ig nursed her shoulder with a nervous laugh. Another mark against Vivi being okay with her, which stung as much as the punch. She bruised easily. 'That's right. Hiii, haha.'

'You?' asked Mercutio, looking down his perfectly straight nose at Ig. '*You're* in the Advanced Monologue Class?'

Ig was as confused as Mercutio was. After all, it wasn't exactly like she had a track record for excellent public speaking. Maybe it was all part of The General's plan? So she could spy on the best and brightest? Ig was sure it would all be clearer to her if she was smarter. Mercutio snorted and looked away, clearly done with the conversation after a single sentence. 'Be nice, Merc,' Vivi said, bumping him affectionately with a hip. 'She's new.'

Mercutio jolted like he'd been electrocuted, then covered it up with a toss of his dark-chocolate curls and a dismissive huff. 'I shan't make any promises, Vivi.'

'Hello, my darlings!' trilled a sweet, musical voice from down the corridor. A wispy, willowy woman in a tie-dye, floor-length skirt and more than an acceptable amount of bangles floated down the hallway towards them. The only thing that made her look like a Villain was the rattlesnake tail trailing along the floor behind her. 'Are we ready to create together today?'

'Yes, Ms. Schwab,' the class intoned dutifully – even Mercutio. Ms. Schwab nodded, hands clasped in front of her lips, before turning to Ig and Vivi. 'Oh my goodness! So you must be the infamous Ignatia Heretical.'

'Hi,' Ig cringed. She was infamous?

'I cannot wait,' Ms. Schwab said, leaning right down into Ig's space, 'to learn how you think, Ignatia.'

Ig balked, but Ms. Schwab had her hands in a vice-like grip. As she smiled, Ig noticed her delicate, pearly-white fangs. 'Let's go in and get warmed up.'

Vivi gave all three of them a hug before she went, which made Ig feel like a five-year-old being dropped off for her first day at school. Then, she was gone, and Ig was alone. She was glad to be rid of Vivi. She missed her already.

Ms. Schwab's classroom was devoid of desks, chairs or blackboards. It was basically an empty wooden square, with glossy varnished floors and, strangely, a ceiling-to-floor mirror on one wall. 'Okay, darlings!' the teacher said, clapping her hands. 'Put your bags down by the wall, shoes off, and let's get warmed up.'

'*Getting warmed up*', apparently, meant breathing deeply and humming through your nose – while Ms. Schwab insisted that you '*imagine your voice moving in a straight line*', whatever that meant – before doing endless full-body rolls and balancing on one leg while twirling the other one out in front of you. Ig felt ridiculous. And off-balance; she fell more than once. Her only consolation was that, across the circle from her, Mercutio seemed to be having even less fun than she was. While his twin threw himself happily into every single exercise, Mercutio von Ryan set his jaw and stared into the middle distance, suffering his torture nobly. Maybe they did actually have something in common.

'Very, very good work,' Ms. Schwab said, finally relenting and letting the class sit on the floor together in front of the mirror. 'Now, we're going to be working on our improvisation skills today–'

The entire class groaned, and Ms. Schwab's tail twitched in admonishment. 'Now now, darlings; there won't always be time to work on what you want to say. You must be equally menacing when a Hero suddenly infiltrates your lair, as you will be when a long-plotted scheme comes to fruition.' She rose to her feet, the tiny bells at the bottom of her skirt glinting in the sun. 'Miss Kanaan, why don't you start us off? Let me think of a scenario for you…'

An impossibly gorgeous girl named Katalina with the longest

legs Ig had ever seen plonked a chair down in front of the class and purred and growled her way through a *'you don't really want to turn me in, do you?'* sort of speech, where she made some very valid, succinct points – or so Ig had thought, anyway. Once she'd remembered how to breathe. No matter where she went, she was apparently always weak for a pretty, talented girl.

'Excellent work!' Ms. Schwab said, applauding wildly as Katalina dipped into a shy curtsy and scurried back to her friends. 'You've clearly been working on your projection. Well done. Okay, let's see… Mr. von Ryan?'

Pietro pulled a water bottle out of his bag and handed it to his brother. 'Lubricate first, Merc.'

Mercutio grinned down at his brother and took a swallow of water. Something in his body language had changed; he seemed more confident than he had during warm-ups. Ig's hopes of bonding over their shared hatred of speaking aloud vanished.

Ms. Schwab gave Mercutio the prompt of *'you've taken over the airwaves and are issuing an ultimatum to the Hero'* and, to Ig's disgust, Mercutio was brilliant. He mocked, he pontificated, he stalked around the space making puns and grand allusions to his own greatness…before letting it all drop away in an icy, deadpan stare to the 'camera' as he made his demands of the imaginary Hero. Ig suddenly could see him – years from now – making those threats to someone like her (or like Pisces), and her blood ran a little colder. She glanced around the room; everyone else was spellbound, or furiously taking notes. Ig attempted to catch Pietro's eye, but he was focused on his brother – chin resting on one knuckle, smile shifting from proud to something smaller, more wistful.

But, to her surprise, Ms. Schwab seemed unimpressed as Mercutio turned to her for feedback. 'Mr. von Ryan, darling,' she sighed, over the top of the applause that rippled through the audience, 'it's very *good*. It's always very good. But it's always very *classic*. You're settling into a very classic Villain archetype – and I get it, it fits you,' she said, holding up a hand as Mercutio went to interrupt her, 'but I really wish I got to see you experiment a little more in these classes, you know.'

'Yeah, Merc,' heckled Pietro. 'Next time, you've got to be all sexy like Kat!' He made a pouty face, and earned a smack from Katalina, who was sitting to the side of him. She glanced over her shoulder, and Ig found herself mouthing *you were great* and giving a thumbs up, before immediately regretting every life decision that led to that moment as Katalina gave her a tiny smirk and looked away.

'For that remark, Pietro,' Ms. Schwab said sternly, 'I'm putting you in charge of making sure he really does develop. Run some warmups with him, make sure he's working on finding some new inspirations before next week. Okay? Okay. Go sit down, darling.'

Mercutio nodded stiffly, and returned to his seat, scowling. Pietro clapped him on the back and offered him more water, which he declined. Ig suppressed the urge to roll her eyes. He was never happy with anything, was he?

'Alright, alright, settle down,' Ms. Schwab said, fluttering her hands over the class. 'I think it's time to see what the newest member of our cast can do.'

What?

'Miss Heretical, would you like to have a try?'

What.

'Come come, come come,' Ms. Schwab cooed, beckoning Ig up towards the mirror. 'No need to be shy, this is a safe space.'

Funny. Because it felt like being thrown to the wolves.

'Let's see,' Ms. Schwab said, looking Ig up and down. 'What role should you play... how about... oh! How about this; it's the end of your battle with the Hero, and you've won. All hope is lost. This is your big moment; your nemesis is beaten and broken in front of you, and you're delivering the final blow – with your words. Nice and easy, nice and fun.'

Easy? Fun?!

'Whenever you're ready.'

Oh. My. God. Everyone was looking at her. Pietro was beaming in a way that Ig assumed he thought was encouraging, but actually just looked manic. His brother, however, simply narrowed his eyes, jutting out his jaw in a gesture that clearly screamed '*go on; impress me.*' But Ig had never impressed anyone in her life! What was she even going to *say?*

'*You only need to achieve enough to keep your cover,*' echoed The General's voice. '*We don't expect much more.*'

'Okay. Okay, um… I'm, uh, I'm starting now.' Ig cleared her throat, and imagined her opponent standing behind the rest of the class. She couldn't actually look anyone in the eye – that was madness. At least a fictional person couldn't judge her too harshly.

'Right. So, um. It's, uh… over. You've lost. Everything you've worked for has been for nothing.' No-one stopped her, or laughed, so she kept going – her eyes fixed on the invisible person at the back of the room. Maybe they were beaten up a little – a broken nose, the blood dripping steadily onto the ground. Maybe they were shaking a little with the effort of standing. Maybe they couldn't look her in the eye as she spoke to them, humiliated and broken after thinking they were so high and mighty. Maybe it was Mercutio. Stupid, smug Mercutio, who thought he was so smart and made her feel so inadequate for literally no reason..!

'Look around you. You can see that there's nothing left. No-one's going to come and save you, or make it better. There's no way to come back from this and win. So, um, I hope you feel really stupid. For going up against me.' After a moment, when no more words came, she turned to Ms. Schwab. 'That's it.'

To Ig's utter shock, Ms. Schwab actually shivered. 'Oooooh, Miss Heretical – that was downright creepy!'

Creepy?!

'What do we think, class? Wasn't that creepy? The way Miss Heretical used her body language, her tone – so bleak, so hopeless, am I right?' The class murmured sentiments like '*yeah*' and '*I've got goosebumps*' and '*she didn't blink, like, at all.*'

Ig gawked at them, stunned. 'I mean,' Ms. Schwab was saying, shaking her gently by the shoulders, 'there's definitely room for improvement, mostly in trying not to stammer or pause as much, but that comes with confidence. A very strong start! You did so much with very, very little. I hope you're pleased with it.'

Ig wasn't sure; and when she said that aloud, the whole class laughed, which didn't help. She retreated to the back of huddle of students, keeping her head down. There was a smattering of applause, and Pietro let out a single whoop as she passed him, but the real validation – the one that caught her a little off guard – was the look Mercutio von Ryan shot her as she crossed her legs and listened to the next student perform. A raised eyebrow, a cutting glance out the corner of one dark eye – an expression filled with intrigue, envy, surprise and, Ig noticed, a begrudging sort of respect.

It's not very Heroic, Ig thought, as Katalina giggled to her friend and shot Ig an appreciative look, *but I could get used to this.* 'Hiii, von Ryan,' she mouthed, waggling her fingers in a wave. Mercutio looked away. Ig sat a little taller and allowed herself a smile.

Chapter Sixteen

After class, Ig hung about awkwardly; fussing with her shoelaces, her backpack, checking her hair in the mirror. Her bob was starting to turn fluffy, which was the first sign it was growing out. She'd have to get it cut before she went back to Lunalist.

Thinking about the school made her wince. She didn't like remembering her painful conversation with The General, how inadequate she'd felt climbing back down those secret, winding steps – and, of course, the fight with Vivi. Poor Vivi. In the cold light of day, Ig looked back on how she'd behaved and shuddered. She'd lashed out – embarrassed at how eager she'd been for recognition, for comfort, for support – and it had hurt the feelings of the one person who had shown her any real kindness in this place. Not very Heroic at all. The thought of Vivi not speaking to her again, besides from awkwardly ferrying her to and from lessons, filled her with a dread she found hard to describe. She had to make it right. But how? Ig couldn't remember the last time she'd raised her voice to someone else; did you walk up and apologise outright? Did you pretend it never happened? What was the right course of action, here?

'What is our next lesson, Pietro?'

Ig's ears pricked up at the sound of the von Ryan twins walking past her.

'Let's see… oh, it's the second Monday of the month. So, Villain Accounting.'

'Oh, huzzah. Maths.'

'Gotta be done, brother. Not everything is unnatural experiments and showing off.'

'Well, it should be.'

Of course! They were Vivi's friends, weren't they? They'd know how to smooth over this whole messy situation. She hauled her backpack over her shoulders and jogged to catch up with the pair. 'Um, hey. Hey! Pietro?'

Mercutio turned to glare at her. 'Oh, look,' he said dryly, 'it's the ingenue.'

Pietro, however, was already bounding towards her, his mouth quirking into a smile. 'And the Oscar goes to… Ignatia Heretical!' He handed her the water bottle he was carrying like it was an award. 'Speech, speech!'

'Um. Actually,' Ig said, gently pushing the bottle aside, 'I wanted to ask for your help.'

Pietro pretended to pout. 'But I wanted a speech.'

'Well, um, okay…'

'We don't have time,' Mercutio interrupted, leaning into the conversation and snatching back the water bottle, 'to help you with… whatever it is you need help with. Go to The Nyx with your problems, that's what they're there for.' He flicked his gaze disapprovingly over Ig's face and then spun on his heel, clearly expecting Pietro to follow. His brother smiled at Ig, shrugging.

'He's the boss, I'm afraid. Ciao!' He turned away to catch up with Mercutio, and Ig felt her chances of having anything but an awkward, lonely few months at Shackleton slipping through her fingers like sand.

She didn't want to be lonely again. At least, not for a little while.

'It's about Vivi!' she shouted.

Mercutio paused. 'What,' he said darkly, turning back to face her, 'have you done to Vivi?'

Knew it, Ig thought, allowing herself to be smug for half a heartbeat. Mercutio von Ryan might be as pleasant and approachable as a wall of ice, but even she could tell he had a soft spot for her dorm-mate. 'Nothing,' she said. 'I mean, I had an, um, accident. And I broke something of hers. A mug.'

Pietro slapped his hand to his heart. 'Not the Mothman mug, surely?' Ig nodded grimly. 'Oh, Merc – you know how much she loved that mug!' The corner of Mercutio's left eye twitched, and Ig sent Pietro a silent prayer of thanks. He already felt like a co-conspirator, even though he had no real reason to be on her side. 'Oh, she'll be so *sad*, isn't that right, Ig?'

'Th-that's right,' Ig said, picking up on Pietro's cues. 'She's really upset about it, and I want to make it up to her. So I was wondering if you knew what I could do so that she isn't, well, sad anymore, or upset with me, or...'

Ig trailed off as Mercutio strode towards her, towering over her and folding his arms as if passing judgment. Ig willed herself not to step back. 'What time is your free period?' he asked, without blinking.

'Um.' Ig scrabbled to grab her planner out her satchel. 'One 'til two.'

'Ours too. Meet us at the main entrance.' Mercutio spun away again, lab coat tails flowing behind him. 'We're going into town.'

And that was how Ig ended up walking along a winding, paved road – more of a glorified path, really – down a steep hill into the Rossborough. It was a sunny day, and the thick foliage on either side of the path was lush and green, flecked with bluebells and dandelions and wild rhubarb. Beyond the path, fluffy white sheep grazed lazily in their fields while their tiny lambs frolicked and played at their sides, hemmed in by deep irrigation ditches and thorny blackberry hedges. Ig felt like she'd stepped out of a horror novel into a picture book. *Vivi must love it here,* Ig thought, and a pang of remorse resounded in her chest.

'You ever been to Rossborough before?' Pietro asked, swinging his arms casually at his sides. Ig shook her head. She'd barely been out of Newcastle; she'd grown up a twenty-minute Metro ride from the city centre, and then Lunalist was right on the mouth of the Tyne. All she knew was the hustle and bustle of the city; she was still unused to all this quiet and greenery. 'It's cute,' Pietro continued. 'Little shops, a bakery that does the best pull-apart cheesy bread you've ever tasted, and a village full of people who are too scared of us to be a bother.' He reached down, without breaking his stride, and picked up a fallen pinecone from the side of the road. 'So,' he said, tossing it from hand to hand, 'what were you arguing about?'

'What?' Ig started. 'We weren't arguing. I, um, dropped her mug on the floor. By accident.'

Pietro tilted his head at her; his hair falling into his eyes. 'Ig,' he said. 'Vivi already told me you'd had an argument. She just didn't say what it was about.'

'Oh,' Ig replied.

'I'm just looking out for my friend,' Pietro continued. 'And, against my better judgment, I don't like seeing you sad, either. You have a kicked-puppy thing going on, it's rather bothersome. No wonder Vivi decided you were her latest pet project.'

'I…' Ig watched a grey squirrel dash out in front of them, run down the path a little way, and then vanish into the greenery. She didn't want to tell Pietro everything. But she did want his advice. 'I might have told her to stop being so nice to me.'

'Ah. That'll do it,' Pietro said. 'Vivi… Vivi can't help being who she is. None of us can, in the end.' He tipped his head back and looked at the sky. 'I bet her showing you affection makes you uncomfortable. You think it makes her weak. Or maybe you think it makes you weak. But either way, it doesn't. When she needs to be, she's lethal. She can make a nerve-damaging spore from a daisy and a dream, after all.'

Ig nodded to herself, chewing anxiously on the inside of her lip. She really had underestimated Vivi. She'd seen what Vivi could do firsthand – and had still thought of her as a useless Villain, when she was clearly much more capable than Ig herself.

'And people like us – Villains, I mean – don't have a lot of friends, out there in the world.' Pietro waved his arm towards Rossborough. 'So when we find them, we hold onto them tightly.' Pietro rolled the pinecone around in his palm. 'You might even grow to like being friends with a Villain, if you gave it a chance, you know. Before you go running back to that eyesore on the Tyne and forget all about us.'

'So why haven't you turned me in?' Ig asked. 'Vivi said you and her worked out who I really–'

'Because Vivi asked me not to, and I've been friends with Vivi since I was create – since I was five,' Pietro said. 'She seems to think you're going to get bored once you find out we're too busy with our homework to think about what you do up at your fancy school.' He cast her another look; eyebrow raised. 'Plus, if you get too uppity, she'll paralyse you for the rest of term and we can chuck you in a broom cupboard and forget about you.'

'Oh. Okay.' The pair walked together for a long time, saying nothing. Off in the distance, ducks quacked on the river. 'You're pretty smart, aren't you?' Ig said at last. Pietro shrugged.

'People always seem so surprised when they work that out.' As if snapping out of a dream, he looked around, spinning in a tight circle on the road. 'Hang on; we're missing one. Merc?'

They'd left Mercutio behind by accident; he was a few feet back, stooped over and staring into a bush. Pietro lobbed his pinecone at his head. It bounced off his goggles. 'Hey! Science boy! Come on. We only have one free period.' Merc wafted a hand in his direction, clearly distracted. As Pietro and Ig approached, she saw what he was looking at; a crop of lavender, alive with hard-working bumblebees.

'So,' Pietro said, shifting his weight onto one hip and crossing his arms, 'whatcha working on?'

'A theory for how to turn bees in to a swarm of deadly assassins,' Mercutio said nonchalantly, not taking his eyes from the insects in front of him. 'For Minion Husbandry.'

'Oh, of course. How silly of me not to realise.'

Mercutio looked at the bees as they stumbled from flower to flower, glowering as if they were a particularly tricky puzzle to be cracked. 'If I can make the larvae imprint upon a robotic Queen, they'd follow her into battle and protect her. My only stumbling block so far–'

'Won't the bees die after they sting someone?' Ig asked. 'Their stingers break off after they use them, and it kills the bee. Right?'

Mercutio raked his hands through his hair with a groan. 'That's exactly it!' he cried, clearly too distracted by his problem to remember to be awful to her. 'Exactly right, Heretical.'

Pietro nudged Ig in the side, waggling his eyebrows. '*Exactly right, Heretical,*' he whispered with a grin, and Ig found herself smiling back.

'The reusability factor for trained bees is almost zero,' Mercutio continued to himself. 'And who has the time to raise an entire new hive of minions every time you need them?! But I've come too far to give up the idea now.'

'In the last five minutes?' Ig asked.

'Of course.' Mercutio looked at her as if she'd asked the stupidest question of all time. 'Every moment of genius has value, Heretical.'

'Merc,' Pietro groaned, 'We really don't have time for this…'

'Why don't you make the worker bees out of robots, too?' Ig asked. 'Use normal bees as, like, a template.'

Mercutio nodded absently, still not looking up. 'Like inspiration.'

'Guys,' Pietro groaned, 'we need to go if we want to get back. I don't want to go back to solitary confinement just because you two were…'

'Yeah!' Ig said, bending down to look at the bees with Mercutio. 'So they still follow their queen, but if you use metal, they can be, I don't know, recharged?'

'Because it's Minion Husbandry,' Mercutio said, 'not Cybernetics. I'd have to… to…' He turned and looked at Ig. His mouth opened, and then closed again. 'Cyborg bees,' he muttered. 'Pietro! Desk manoeuvres.' Pietro sighed, but obediently turned around, and Mercutio produced a notepad and pen from his lab coat pocket and began frantically scribbling on his back. 'Part robot, part insect. Coat the stingers in titanium so they don't break off and kill the… that's it!' He strode away from them towards the village, not looking back to check they were following. 'Come! We must visit the hardware store in Rossborough.'

'The hardware store in Rossborough?!' Pietro chirped sarcastically. 'But Mercutio, when will we find the time?!'

'I'll need to ask Uncle Rayner to ship us the titanium of course,' Mercutio continued, 'but I need electrical wire, pliers, a beekeeping hat… what're those called, again? Pietro, I need to find out what a beekeeping hat is called when we return.'

'Yes, boss,' Pietro said, saluting at his brother's back.

'Why do you do that?' Ig asked, as the three of them marched towards the village.

'What?'

'Let him order you about.'

Pietro shrugged, his eyes still fixed on his brother. 'He's the genius. I pass water bottles and carry the bags. That's what I was made to do. Now come on, before we lose him again.'

Chapter Seventeen

Rossborough was a pretty little village, if a little twee for Ig's tastes; with brightly coloured bunting strung from lamppost to lamppost, people in Barbour jackets and immaculate wellies walking their Springer Spaniels and their Labradors, and a single, long street filled with tiny, boxy shops. Ig saw a butcher, a florist, the bakery Pietro had mentioned, all lined up on the same street facing a pub with a hand-painted sign and promises of Karaoke every Friday night written in chalk pen on the window.

'Can't wait to go there,' Pietro said dryly, nudging Ig, 'as soon as I'm allowed to drink.'

'I'm not a singer,' she admitted.

'Neither am I.' Pietro winked at her. 'We'll duet. Give the old farts something to talk about.'

'Can we focus?' Mercutio grumbled. 'Heretical needs to atone for her sins—'

'Don't put it like that, please.'

'—and then I need to go to the hardware store. It's important.' Mercutio looked over at his brother. 'Fox?'

'Fox,' Pietro agreed. Ig wondered if she'd suddenly lost the ability to understand English, so she also said "fox" and hoped it was right. Mercutio rolled his eyes at her, and she felt herself blushing.

'Foxed Page,' Pietro said. 'The bookshop. It's the only place you're going to find anything halfway interesting around here, unless you think you can earn Vivi's forgiveness with a rack of lamb.'

'Probably not.'

'That settles it!' Pietro pointed down the street, towards a shopfront with an elegantly painted fox adorning the window. 'Onward!'

As they walked, Ig noticed a ripple of nervousness following them down the street; people ducking into shops and crossing the road to avoid them, a rush of furious, gossipy whispers at their backs. It was only then Ig remembered what she was wearing was quite literally the uniform of Villains. One woman tutted as they walked past – only to turn and tut even louder when neither of the twins reacted.

'Are you allowed in the village unsupervised?' she sniped. Mercutio opened his mouth to retort, but Pietro neatly spun on his heel and stepped in front of his brother before he could.

'Only first years need a chaperone, *Margaret!*' he smiled. 'I know it's been a few millennia since you were sixteen, but we're practically grownups, now.'

'Oh, aye.' The woman took a step towards them. 'You're that motherless freak, aren't you? Soon enough you'll be out of that school and the Heroes will make short work of you–'

'Careful,' snarled Mercutio, leaning around his brother and getting right in the woman's face, 'we know where you live, remember? Once we're out, you'll make excellent target practice for my shrink ray, Margaret.' Merc mimed dropping something on the floor and grinding it into paste with his shoe. The woman started and stumbled backwards, darting into the florists with a whimper. Pietro turned to his brother.

'A shrink ray? Bit cliche, don't you think?'

Mercutio shrugged. 'First thing that came to mind.'

Ig moved to apologise to the civilian; to comfort her, to reassure her that no harm would come her way, at least not today. But the boys had walked off without her, and she needed to find a gift for Vivi. So she ran to catch up with them instead.

Foxed Page was the bookshop of Ig's childhood dreams; windows full of brightly coloured picture books, jigsaw puzzles and ridiculously soft looking cuddly toys. The tables were stocked high with perfect pyramids of paperbacks, and as Ig wandered dazedly into the shop itself, the smell of paper and ink filled her nose like perfume. There was a bookshop in Newcastle – a huge, dramatic looking building in the centre of town, with a whole floor for kids' books and another for a café that sold cakes with cute, book-related puns for names. Ig used to go there all the time. But then her dad had done a signing there for some biography that had been written about him, and the staff had followed Ig and her mam around like a bad smell. Even after her dad and his publicist explained who they were, the manager glowered every time her mam so much as picked up a book to look at the cover. Ig, being the hot-headed nine-year-old she was at the time, swore she'd never go back; though a pang of jealousy slithered up her spine every time Pisces used to talk wistfully about wandering the aisles for hours, sitting in their window seats and sipping on lattes from dark green earthenware mugs.

'Right!' said Pietro, rubbing his hands together. 'Whatcha wanna steal?'

'Steal?!' Ig squeaked, darting back out of the shop – where Mercutio was waiting, examining his cyborg bee notes. 'I can't steal something!'

'And why's that, Ig?' Pietro said smugly, gaze darting to his brother and back. 'Tell us, in detail.' Ig said nothing. 'You live with us,' Pietro continued, kicking her shoe gently, 'you have to be like us. Besides, Fox doesn't suffer from it. They get a bursary from the school to cover anything that gets nicked – it's usually the younger kids, but in the name of repairing a friendship I can be persuaded to regress.' His smile suddenly turned a little more feral, and Ig saw more resemblance between the two von Ryans than she ever had before. 'And oh – look who's working, Merc…'

'Who?' Mercutio stuck his head into the doorway, then rapidly retreated. His face was pale, and Ig swore she could see a bead of sweat forming on his brow. 'Oh, sweet Mary Shelley,' he cursed. 'Her, of all people…'

Ig looked back into the shop. At the desk, flicking through a romance novel that Ig knew was *very* spicy in a heterosexual sort of way (and thus had been handed around the girls' dorms like contraband goods), was a petite girl, a little older than they were, with curly blonde hair and dimples. 'The cute girl?' she asked.

Pietro looked at her blankly. 'Do you have a type, or is it just anything with X chromosomes? Anyway. That,' he whispered, turning Mercutio back to face the door, 'is Clara. And Clara *liiiiiikes* Mercutio…'

'Shut. Up. Pietro.'

'She thinks he's dangerous,' Pietro said, his voice trembling with laughter. 'It's amazing.'

Well, that was correct. Mercutio von Ryan *was* dangerous. But, apparently, a boy who threatened to squish pensioners under his boot was perfect romance material. Weird.

'Oh, look – look!' Pietro said, pointing. 'Over in the Sci-Fi section.'

Underneath a row of weighty fantasy books with elaborate covers was a shelf of, well, stuff. Notebooks with sigils on them, board games and prints and…

'Mugs,' Ig breathed. One in particular stood out to her; shiny and black, with a glow-in-the-dark design of a long-necked creature on it. Underneath the cute monster, the text '*I Believe In You!*' was written in cutesy script. 'That's Nessie, right? It's sort of like a Mothman.'

'Well,' Mercutio replied, 'the Loch Ness Monster is from Scotland, and is theorised to be a stranded plesiosaur, while the Mothman is a cryptid from Point Pleasant in West Virginia–*aaaagh!*'

Pietro had snuck up behind his brother and shoved him into the shop. Mercutio stumbled towards the desk, colliding with it and causing poor Clara to squeak and turn puce at the sight of him. Ig clapped a hand over her mouth to stop the shriek of laughter that was racing up her throat, and gave Pietro a scandalised look. 'That,' she said in a high-pitched whisper, 'was *mean!*'

'We needed bait,' he said with a shrug. 'Come on, while she's distracted.' Pietro and Ig bolted for the nearest bit of cover – an A-frame full of huge artbooks on different places to take your campervan – and rounded the back of it to get to the Sci-Fi section, which was tucked away, unloved, in a corner.

'You sure this is okay?' Ig hissed, as Pietro fussed with the shelf, looking for a Nessie mug that still had its original box.

'Hm? Oh, yeah, yeah,' he said, flapping an arm in her direction. 'The bursary, it's all good. Come on, help me look.'

Ig bent down to look, only to be distracted by a tinkle of very flirtatious laughter from the desk. She stuck her head around the A-frame in time to see Clara practically climb on the desk while she talked to Mercutio – twirling a lock of soft-looking golden hair and saying something about locking innocent girls in dungeons and 'having them at your mercy' – while Mercutio himself turned a sickly shade of green and looked like he'd rather be anywhere else on the planet.

'What's so wrong with that?' Ig said wistfully, pulling her backpack off her shoulder. 'I'd kill to be flirted with in a bookshop.'

'Well,' Pietro said, giving up on finding a box and examining a notebook for a very famous fantasy series Ig's mam had been obsessed with a few years ago, 'depends if you've been in love with your best friend since you were learning your times tables. Merc's a one-woman guy – even if that woman has absolutely no idea how he feels about her.'

'Oh.' Ig looked back. Clara was laughing hysterically at something Mercutio had said – something that probably wasn't funny to begin with. 'I know what that's like.'

'Oh?' Pietro asked. 'Someone back at the old place?

Ig looked back down at the floor and sighed. It wasn't exactly like there were girls flirting with her back home – but even if there were, it probably wouldn't have mattered. She only had eyes for Pisces. It might only ever be Pisces. 'You care a lot about romance,' Ig said, 'for someone who apparently doesn't want it.'

Pietro laughed distractedly, picking up a beautiful brown hardback embossed with a golden stag. 'It's just funny though, isn't it? People acting like they're protagonists in books. All these big, dumb feelings, people swooning and cooing over each other. It's just so much fun to mess with them; especially if they want to act all stupid about it. Like, look at Clara.' He blew a dismissive raspberry. 'Acting like being attracted to Merc is so intense and all-consuming or whatever – it's silly, isn't it? As if people really feel like that in real life.'

Ig peeked through the slats of the A-frame. Clara was biting her lip, looking at a horrified Merc like she wanted to devour him – or she wanted *him* to devour *her*. 'I don't think that's pretend, Pietro.'

Pietro joined her at the slat. 'Really?' he said, genuinely surprised. 'Oh. Ohhh. Interesting. You learn something every day. So you and your girl at the old place?' He flapped his hand towards Clara. 'Like that?'

Ig blushed 'Not the same. But similar.'

'Ohhhh. Weird.'

As another customer entered the shop – forcing Clara begrudgingly to have to do her job for a spell – Mercutio seized his opportunity and bolted around the A-frame, rejoined the group and slammed his hands onto Pietro's shoulders.

'We have to go. Now.'

'What happened?' Pietro asked, slipping the hardback into his satchel with a confidence that Ig found unworldly.

'Clara invited me to…ugh, *karaoke*,' Mercutio winced. 'At the *pub*. And I was so appalled that I couldn't formulate an answer, and she appears to have taken it as an affirmative. So now we have to leave.'

Pietro looked over at Ig with a cocked eyebrow. 'Now or never, Villain.'

Ig looked down at the mug, then at her open bag. Was she really going to do this? Did her friendship with Vivi matter to her this much? This was wrong, this was illegal, this was against everything she'd–

She could hear Clara's footsteps as she rounded the A-frame. Ig pushed the boxless mug into her backpack, feeling the weight of it fall gently between a notebook and the lining of the pocket.

'Merc? Merc, are you going to give me your number so we can… what're you doing over here?'

Ig leapt to her feet, smiling so broadly her cheeks hurt. 'Nothing! Nothing. We're just going. Merc will text you. Or call the shop, if he doesn't have your… to organise the karaoke date, you know.'

Clara looked from him, to Ig, then down at her bag. Ig followed her gaze and saw a very definite, mug-shaped outline at the bottom of her backpack. A block of icy fear formed in Ig's chest.

'I think,' Clara said slowly, 'I need to do a bag check before you go…'

'Run!' yelled Pietro, and the three scrambled around the back of the A-frame and bolted for the door. The boys made it; leaping out into the street. Ig, however, was not so lucky. Clara grabbed her by the straps of her satchel and pulled, twisting Ig around to face her painfully. 'I don't even know who you are!' she cried.

Ig looked her in the eyes, noticed how pretty this girl looked when she was flustered, then yanked the bag out of Clara's hands so hard that Ig lost her footing and stumbled backwards into Pietro's arms.

'Nicely done!' he said, setting her on her feet and giving her a shove. 'Now move.' The three of them bolted up the high street of Rossborough; the shops and the people whizzing past in a blur of burning lungs and almost-catastrophically tripping feet. Mercutio began to slow as they passed a shop with a spanner painted onto a dark blue sign, but Pietro grabbed him by the collar and pulled him along like a particularly ill-mannered chihuahua.

'Not now, Merc.'

'But my pliers!'

'Should've thought about that before being a little hussy in Fox, shouldn't you? Hey Ig,' Pietro called, 'you know how I said there's a bursary?'

'Yep?'

Pietro grinned, barely out of breath. 'I lied. You just did a theft.'

Ig punched him hard in the ribs and kept running.

Chapter Eighteen

Walking back up a hill to school after running for their lives was not fun. 'Hang on,' Ig said, leaning against a fencepost about halfway up, 'I need another breather.'

'Ugh, really?' Mercutio groaned. 'I thought your previous establishment would have prepared you for physical effort.'

Oh great. Why not shout it from the rooftops? 'Well, I wasn't very good at it, Merc,' Ig sniped, taking off her trainers and rubbing the bottom of her foot. 'That's why I'm here.'

Mercutio stood over her disdainfully. 'I'm sorry,' he said, twirling his wrist in the air, 'what was that you called me? I think you were missing a few syllables. Merc… utio…'

'I'm sorry, Mercutio von Smartarse!'

'Oooh, cutting.'

'You know,' Pietro said, light and breezy as he flopped down beside Ig in the grass, 'if I literally didn't know better, I'd think you two bickered like that because you liked each other.'

Twin expressions of horror snapped to face him.

'Oh my god!'

'That's disgusting, Pietro!'

'Alright, alright, I'm very sorry,' Pietro laughed. 'Forget I said anything.' He dug around in his satchel and pulled out a book – the brown-and-gold hardback from Fox – and began to read. Ig pulled her shoes back on and looked in her own satchel at the mug, nestled near the bottom. She'd stolen something. She'd actually broken the law. But it was for a good cause. Right? She wanted to make Vivi happy again. She wanted them to be friends. And right then, she didn't particularly care that she was a Hero and Vivi Section was a Villain. She wasn't sure if that was selfless, or the most selfish thing in the world. All Ig knew was that she was very used to people suddenly deciding that she was bad – but usually she couldn't quite quantify why. She had done too well in a test, or not well enough. Her tone had been up at the end of a sentence when it should have gone down. She'd been so distant she was called 'cold' or so familiar she was called 'needy'. All nebulous, mysterious things. This time, she knew what she'd done was wrong. And that meant she could fix it. Hopefully.

'Come on,' she said, attempting to rise, 'let's get–'

'You know,' Mercutio said – straining as if the words were painful to say – 'I do like your idea. About the bees. It might be…it might be something to work on.'

Ig looked at him, stunned. 'Well, thank you,' she said haltingly. 'That's good of you to say.'

'The tricky part will be doing it humanely,' Mercutio said, deep in thought. 'We don't know a lot about the pain receptors of insects.'

'Why do you care about that?' Ig asked. Mercutio shot her a sharp look.

'Because it's an *animal*,' he said, slowly and clearly, as if Ig were stupid. 'It's a simple little creature that doesn't deserve to be hurt for no good reason. Animals don't deserve to be *punished*.' His voice became raw, a little scratchy, and his eyes filled with an indignation Ig didn't expect from cool-as-a-cucumber von Ryan. 'It's not like it's a *person*, Heretical.'

Ig blinked. Pietro looked up, making sure their conversation wasn't getting so heated that he needed to intervene. After a second or two, Mercutio sighed. 'Forget I said anything,' he said, walking a step or two away to lean against a tree. Pietro shook his head with a sigh and fell back in the grass, never losing his place in the book.

She felt like Mercutio had, without warning, opened up the top of his head and showed her the folds of his brain. From the second she'd met him, she'd pegged him as a megalomaniac, out for scientific glory at any cost. And that might still be true. But it fascinated her to learn, however suddenly, that there was something else going on with this strange boy who seemed to have collided with her life. Something a little more fragile.

After a moment or two of silence – except for the sounds of birdsong above her head – Mercutio coughed.

'I'll need a smoker,' he said. 'Use it like a general anaesthetic, so the bees don't feel the augmentation.'

Was he trying to keep the conversation going?

'Maybe we'll start a small fire somewhere,' Ig offered. Mercutio laughed at that – he laughed!

'Collect the smoke in jars and…' he mimed unscrewing a top and popping invisible bees inside. 'It could work.'

Yeah, Ig thought, as the three of them restarted their walk back up to school, *I suppose it could*.

'Now, with the titanium stingers – a screwtop formation over the abdomen, or simply use very tiny bolts?'

Back at Shackleton that evening, after classes were finished for the day, Ig and the von Ryans stood outside the dorm Ig shared with Vivi. Inside, she could hear thrashing guitars and a woman singing at the top of her lungs, pleading for someone to call her name and save her from the dark. 'Ouch,' Pietro winced. 'We've gone from Dad Rock to Sad Rock. This fight was serious.'

Ig winced.

Pietro knocked and opened the door with a creak. 'Viv? We've got something for you.'

Vivi was lying on her bunk bed; head hanging upside down, hair falling down like weeping willow fronds into space. She glanced at her guests, and Ig noticed with a pang that her eyes were red-rimmed and puffy. 'Hi, guys.'

'Um, Vivi,' Ig said, sitting on her bed and blowing strands of Vivi's hair out of her eyes, 'I wanted to say I'm sorry. For, um, breaking your mug. And saying the things I did. I have, um, my own things I'm going through. But that's not your fault. I shouldn't have snapped. So I bought you–'

Mercutio cleared his throat pointedly in the doorway.

'…I *got* you,' Ig corrected herself, 'a little something.' She held out her bag, arms straight and rigid. Vivi sat up and climbed down her bunk bed's ladders.

'What is it?' she asked, inspecting Ig's backpack like it might explode at any minute. 'What did you… oh! Oh, Ig – it's so cute!' She produced the mug with a flourish and a grin. 'It's Nessie! Look, guys, it's Nessie.'

'I can see,' Pietro said, nodding indulgently. Standing next to him, Mercutio was gazing at Vivi like he was prepared to burn the whole world down for her.

"*I Believe In You,*" Vivi read, a wide, wobbly grin spreading over her lips. 'Oh, Ig! This means so much, thank you! Apart from Mothman, Nessie is my favourite cryptid! How did you know?' She flung her arms around Ig's shoulders, and Ig found herself reaching up and hugging her back. Just a little. God bless Vivi's ever-fluctuating emotions.

Later, after the boys had left, Ig and Vivi were sitting on the floor while Vivi painted Ig's nails venomous green. 'Thank you for my mug,' Vivi said, blowing on Ig's toes to make the polish dry a little faster. 'It means a lot, after–'

'Oh, no, really,' Ig said, accidentally talking over her. 'It's nothing, after what happened. Let's just–'

'Ig, will you let me talk, please?'

Ig shut up. Vivi sighed, screwing the top back on the nail polish and reaching up to put it back on the desk – along with the others that had been discarded once they were deemed as being 'not Ig's shade.'

'I know to you,' she said, 'being 'nice' doesn't seem like a very Villainous thing to do. But I've always been, I don't know, drawn to the weird little spiky things in the world. Like this Sea Holly.' She affectionately prodded the stem of the blueish, thorny plant she was growing by her desk. 'Or like Pietro and

Merc. They're the things the world hates the most. The things it can't make pretty or nice. And I like to, you know, nurture them. Make them strong, so we can fight back together. And yeah, when you got here, I wanted to show you that Shackleton is just a school, like yours. But now...' she looked up at Ig. 'I think you're more of a weird, spiky thing than you'd like to admit. Now,' she said, clapping her hands so loudly it made Ig jump, 'we've done your nails. What about some eyeliner?'

'Oh no; it's okay, Vivi,' Ig protested, scooching back away from the gigantic bag of makeup Vivi hauled down from her desk, 'I've never worn eyeliner before.'

'Really?! Well, allow me to be your education. Let's see; I think you'd suit wings. Yes, black wings sharp enough to kill a man...'

'What?!'

'Don't worry; when you get back to your Hero school, you can do them in gold or whatever.'

'Get away from me!'

'Let me make you beautiful, Ignatia!'

As the two girls wrestled and scrapped on the floor – and, later, as Ig sat nicely and let Vivi paint markings on her face – she rolled that phrase around in her head.

A weird, spiky thing. People had always thought that about her, it was nothing new. Only this was the first time someone had ever said it to Ig as a compliment.

Chapter Nineteen

As the weeks passed, Ig realised that the von Ryan twins (were they technically twins? They had the same genetic material, after all) had ingratiated themselves into her everyday life as much as Vivi had. It wasn't until they were actively talking to her every day that she realised how many classes they shared; as well as Monologue, there was Poisonology, and Minion Husbandry, and–

'Villain History,' Mr. Paraxis said, underlining the word on the blackboard, 'is a rich tapestry, class. Dating back as far as the scheming alchemists and black mages of old, right up until – well, present day. And, one day, you will be a part of that tapestry, too. Now, are we ready to learn? Ahem. You're meant to say "*yes, Mr. Paraxis*".'

A vague, non-committal mutter from the class. For someone with such an imposing name, Mr. Paraxis looked and acted like he should be someone's dad. Not Ig's dad, though. Luca Peterson was more male model than model trains.

Ig scribbled the date in her notebook, a flutter of interest flickering in her stomach. She hadn't counted on finding Villain History so interesting. But the more Mr. Paraxis talked about interpreting myths and legends as the first battles between good and evil – 'King Arthur may well have been one of the first Heroes!' – the more she found herself sitting up in her seat. Whatever. A rest from observing every little thing was good for the mind, she supposed.

Something hit the back of her head. Ig turned to see Pietro grinning at her, a handful of tiny, screwed-up pieces of paper in his palm. 'So boring!' he mouthed. Ig rolled her eyes and returned to her notes.

'Now,' Mr. Paraxis was saying, 'I want you to spend the next ten minutes writing down what you hope to accomplish when it's finally your time to pick up that needle and thread,' – he was really running with this metaphor – 'and exactly why you want to impact the world for the worse. And after that, we'll be talking about a very influential Northern Villain who studied right here at Shackleton. Ten minutes; starting now.'

Oh. Hm. Ig looked around the classroom at everyone else scribbling frantically in their notebooks – Vivi, sitting next to her, seemed to be drawing tiny stick figures running away from a giant potted plant that was somehow breathing fire. She had a yellow flower in her hair, today, as well as the red spider-lily; her Gelsemium plant had just bloomed, and Vivi had acted like she'd given birth to it herself.

Ig chewed her pencil for a while, then doodled a frowny face in the corner of the page. Then, she gave it mean looking eyebrows, hoping it would inspire her. It didn't. It occurred to her, as she added swirls and lightning bolts around the frowny face, that she'd never been asked at Lunalist what she wanted to achieve after her Power Revelation Ceremony. Apart from 'do good in the world' and 'appear in promotional material and ad campaigns after doing said good', Ig really had no idea how she'd fill her time. Maybe that was why her dad visited Planet Mocha so many times in a week.

A pair of fuzzy, white paws thumped onto on the edge of her desk.

'Miss Hewetical,' Pietro said in a baby voice, jiggling an unimpressed Onslaught up and down, 'dis is sooo borwing!'

'Pietro–'

'Can we go eat cawwots and tewwowise some villagers instead?'

'Pietro, go away.'

'I'm vewwy scawy. I can dwaw blood if I bites you.' Pietro popped his head up, resting his chin on the desk. 'Do you think if she bit someone, she could turn them into a zombie too?' His face lit up. 'Would they be a rabbit zombie?!'

'No,' Mercutio said from the back of the room, without looking up from the schematics for a hive that he'd been pouring over all week. 'And bring my minion back, please. She's not a toy.'

'Haven't you got work to do?' Vivi asked, finishing the detail on a stick figure who was being eaten alive by her monster plant. Pietro scoffed, rolling his eyes. 'I finished in one sentence. 'Help Mercutio von Ryan dominate the world with his loyal army of undead creatures.' He shrugged. 'That's all I need.'

'Pietro?' Mr. Paraxis called from his desk. 'Back to your seat, please. Quietly. You don't want another stint in solitary confinement, do you?'

'Anything but that, Sir.'

'Well, then. Seat. Please.'

'Just because your marks get lumped in with your genius brother's,' Vivi whispered, 'doesn't mean you don't get to try.'

'Fine, fine, I'm going.' Pietro hoisted Onslaught on his shoulder like a baby. 'Come along, Onslaught. I know when we're not wanted.'

'He gets graded along with Mercutio?' Ig asked, as Pietro made his way back to his seat, nudging a furiously blushing Mercutio and hissing. 'Hear that? She called you a genius,' as he sat down.

Vivi nodded. 'Because he technically didn't enrol here,' she whispered. 'He's legally classed as an extension of Merc.'

'Oh.' Suddenly, a lot about Pietro's attitude to studying made sense.

'Alright, class; pens down, please,' Mr. Paraxis said. 'Now, today's subject influenced much of Northern Villain culture in what came to be a relatively short amount of time. We're going to spend today talking about The Witch Queen, also known as–'

What?!

Somehow, Ig was now on the floor, under her desk. 'Miss Heretical?' her teacher asked. 'Are you alright? I know it's embarrassing but–'

'Yep,' Ig squeaked. 'I'll get up now.' But it was no use. Ig was paralysed. Even though she knew that she was being ridiculous, hiding at the mere mention of her mother, her body had just… reacted. A pencil clattered to the floor, and Vivi slid out of her seat, muttering something about being clumsy. 'Sorry, Sir, Sorry! Hey,' she whispered, slotting her hand into Ig's and squeezing, 'now we're both on the floor, let's just listen from here. It's like a podcast in a sensory deprivation tank!'

Ig smiled and squeezed Vivi back.

'So The Witch Queen graduated in 1999 – yes, so very long ago, class. She then took a year off to consult dark and forbidden texts in a family-owned cottage in the Cheviots…'

Ig had been to the cottage a few times when she was little, before her grandad died. He'd make the shadows in the wall dance like puppets to make her laugh.

'…consulting with useful demons, making connections in the dark and eldritch underworld. Remember; networking is very important. Then, in a standard move for a young Villain, she robbed a bank.'

A rumble of interested chatter rippled around the room. Ig found herself sitting up a little straighter, her head brushing the top of the desk. She didn't know this story. Mr. Paraxis crossed over to his desk, where an ancient tape recorder was sitting. 'Now, I have a clip here from an interview the Witch Queen gave to the BBC in 2009, talking about her debut. Ah. Now. How do I make this play the clip–'

Suddenly, a voice filled the room. A low, musical, young voice. Ig's heart lurched painfully.

'–thing about robbing a bank,' the Witch Queen was saying, 'is that it's very customisable. It's a nice, effective way to show off what you can do, how formidable you are, without getting muddied up with the 'statement' of your first crime. Sometimes you can spend so long trying to get your crimes on theme, you miss your big moment to shine. And everyone needs money, don't they?' Around the classroom, students laughed. 'After that, I worked my way up to acts of shock and awe. Once you have your theme, and the public have something of an idea who you are, you can really go wild. I turned the City Hall into my throne room for a week; passed swift and bloodthirsty judgment upon those who wronged me. That was fun. I amassed a devoted following – I still keep in touch with a few of them – and then when I was in my thirties, I met my... um, my husband. Well, I'd known him for a long time. But that was when we started, er, seeing each other romantically.'

Gross, Ig shuddered.

'I retired from Villainy, and I had my family. Which was very important to me; I was a career girl, but I always knew I wanted to have children and settle down. But if that isn't in your fate, that's fine too. We need all types to make the world a darker place, don't we?'

Ig blinked, and was shocked to feel a tear tumble down her cheek. She missed her mam so, so much, and she hadn't even realised.

'Right!' Mr. Paraxis was saying, somewhere above her head. 'Very interesting, very interesting indeed. Now; I want those plans for your own evil legacy left on your desks, please – yes, Pietro, even yours. See you next week!'

Ig climbed out from under the desk, her backside aching from sitting on the cold floor. 'Is that conducive to better study, Heretical?' Mercutio asked sarcastically, as the boys joined them at the front of the classroom. 'I may have to try it.'

'Ignore him,' Pietro said, bumping Ig with his elbow. 'You okay?'

'Yeah,' Ig replied, hoping the others couldn't see the tears in her eyes. 'I'm fine. I just–'

'Wasn't that your mother?' Falcon Reeve asked, making a beeline for Ig as soon as they were dismissed. Ig's stomach swooped into her shoes. 'You've never mentioned it before. If my mum was as dangerous as that, I'd be yelling about it from the rooftops. Plus, with that voice?' Falcon lolled his head back and made a very unpleasant noise in his throat. 'She could make me her minion any time–'

'Oh, Falcon,' chirped Vivi, appearing from nowhere with a pretty, floral box in her hand. 'I made you something.'

Falcon's eyes narrowed. 'You made me something?'

'Yep!' Vivi beamed, all sunshine and kittens. 'A little something to say sorry for making you puke in the fountain.' Inside the box were four cupcakes; their chocolate icing perfectly swirled, with a delicate edible pansy perched on top of each one. They looked perfect. Too perfect.

'My mami's special recipe!' Vivi trilled. 'Try one! They're super good.'

She blinked up at him with innocent, sparkling eyes. Falcon snorted through his nose.

'I don't trust you.'

'Aw, why?'

'Because you made me throw up in the–! Never mind. You,' Falcon said, snapping his fingers at one of his cronies – a girl with sandy blonde hair and glasses. 'Amelia. Eat one of these cupcakes.'

The girl blanched. 'But Falcon…'

'Now.'

Falcon's Power took hold of the girl, and she walked stiffly over to Vivi, who picked up a cupcake and handed it to her. Without saying thank you, Amelia stuffed it robotically into her mouth.

'Ugh,' said Pietro with a wince, as he shouldered his and Mercutio's bags. 'Chewing noises. Gross.'

Amelia blinked. She shook her head. Her eyes cleared, and she smiled at Falcon. 'They're really good!' she exclaimed. 'Really, really good. Vivi, can I have another one for my free period–'

'Back off,' Falcon said haughtily, 'the rest are for me.' He picked up a cupcake and delicately put it into his mouth. 'I appreciate – oh, these are so good – I appreciate the gesture, Vivi. You're right; toilet humour is beneath you. Wow,' he said with a happy swallow, 'they really are–'

His face fell. His stomach gurgled – so loudly students in the hallway giggled as they passed.

'Are you okay, Falcon?' Vivi asked, her voice trembling with concern – or was it laughter?

'Oh. Oh, no. Excuse me,' Falcon said through gritted teeth, sweat standing at his temples. 'I need the bathroom. Um, right now.'

With that, Falcon dashed from the room, knocking over several of his cronies as he went. Ig could hear him yelling at people to move out of his way even as he vanished down the hallway. Vivi smirked, tossing her hair over one shoulder.

'Mwahaha, Rule number one,' she purred, a wicked smile blooming across her face. 'Always include a control cupcake. Gives the victim a false sense of security. Merc taught me that one.'

At her side, Mercutio was reaching critical levels of flustered-ness. Frankly, he looked as if he were about to dissolve. 'Glad to, um…' he swallowed hard. 'Glad to be of service.'

'You really are evil,' Ig grinned at Vivi.

'Top marks, here I come. Falcon, sweetie,' she sang as she skipped out the room, 'maybe another cupcake would soothe your stomach…'

Chapter Twenty

'Falcon Reeve's been looking for you again,' Pietro said, through a mouthful of overnight oats. Vivi groaned, fluttering a hand in her friend's direction. Behind them, the fountain splashed their bags and the backs of their coats, the fangs of the dragon sparkling with water.

'Don't talk with your mouth full, you goblin. It's too early to see the inside of your mouth.'

Pietro swallowed theatrically and repeated his statement. 'Think he wants to challenge you again,' he added. 'I know he's been swotting up in Mind & Manipulation, trying to get stronger for your next Villain War. Miss Hypnatyse can't get rid of him.'

Vivi groaned, aggressively scraping the bottom of her bowl. 'Why? It's only been a week since I made his limbs lock up with the Gelsemium pollen.'

Apparently, Vivi and Falcon's little spats were an ongoing trend. Last week he'd tried to get Vivi to clean the blackboard with her tongue, and as a result they'd had to roll him to his next lesson on a trolley. It was amazing. Ig had been very glad she'd managed to mend the rift between her and Vivi; especially since she slept near the pretty, five-petaled flower that had caused all the damage.

'It's been week and a half, actually,' said Mercutio, barely looking up from his notebook. Ig usually prided herself on being able to read upside down, but his spidery scrawl was beyond even her. She leaned over to get a better look – she could maybe make out the word 'hive' – but Mercutio yanked his notebook back, out of her reach. 'He brings it up. Frequently. It's aggravating. Please stop trying to spy on me, Heretical. It doesn't suit you.'

Pietro and Vivi shot Ig a look; one that she steadfastly ignored. She had an idea why Mercutio was so 'aggravated' by Falcon's attention towards Viv. But she kept her mouth shut. The von Ryan boy might be horrendous to be around, but outing him to his crush was a low Ig wasn't prepared to stoop to; Lily Volt and her cronies throwing her feelings for Pisces back in her face at Lunalist was still too raw a memory.

The four of them had decided to sit outside for breakfast that morning; Vivi had spotted Ig squirrelling away cereal bars and pots of oats from the school shop/dungeon, and had introduced her to a round, cosy, firelit room with a bar full of sugary cereals, fruit, yoghurts and pastries that appeared every morning between six and nine and somehow never seemed to be so full you couldn't get a seat. As Ig was stuffing her fourth pastry into her mouth, she realised she never wanted to see another granola bar as long as she lived. Over time, the von Ryans had come to join them most mornings in their designated little corner; bickering and swapping treats and homework tips until the next bell rang. It was A Thing now, Ig suspected. But today was a fairly pleasant day, and the world was still green and sweet-smelling, so they decided to have a morning picnic. Until classes started (at nine-thirty. Nine-thirty! Decadence, nothing less than sinful), students were given a fairly free rein. It still unsettled Ig, ever so slightly; used as she was to rocketing out of bed, already late before she'd even begun her day. The first time she'd set her alarm for her usual time, Vivi had thrown a pillow at her and threatened to poison her breakfast.

'Well,' Vivi said, standing up and stuffing the last of her blueberry and white chocolate muffin into her mouth, 'Falcon will have to wait. We've got education-mandated fighting to do, first.'

'Unless you crash from all that sugar,' Ig said with a playful roll of her eyes.

'Oh, yeah; because a pain au raisin is so much better.'

'It's got fruit in it!'

'And, like, a ton of sugar.'

'But the fruit! Hang on; what did you say about fighting?'

'Oh, yeah,' Pietro drawled sarcastically. 'Combat Class day. My favourite.'

'Combat Class?' Ig said, mentally raking through her timetable for a class she'd apparently managed to miss. 'I can't remember seeing that on my–'

'It's a once-a-month, year-wide brawl,' Pietro said. 'A chance to see how everyone's progressing – and get a feel of any new Powers in the year group. And until someone opened their big mouth–' he glared at Vivi, who shrugged innocently, 'I got to sit on my butt and watch from the sidelines. But now, thanks to Little Miss 'Power Lenders work on Pietro, Mr. Glasse', I have to participate.'

Vivi leaned in to Ig and stage-whispered in her ear; 'Mr. Glasse thought Pietro wasn't going to ever get a Power, because he's a clone.'

'Because his particular set of genes,' Mercutio added; having moved on from his notes to finishing off his bowl of plain Greek yoghurt, still not looking up, 'have already had their Power activated. Scoff. As if Pietro and I are the same person. We're identical, not psychically linked. Read a book, Glasse.'

'Did you just say 'scoff' out loud?'

Mercutio regarded Ig coolly. 'Yes.'

'I had it so easy!' Pietro lamented. 'Overlooked, under-appreciated, yes. But at least I got to read. Now I have to sweat like the rest of you.'

'Are we going or not?' Vivi said, kicking her friend gently in the ribs. 'I've been ready for thirty seconds.'

'Why so eager, Miss Section?' teased Pietro. 'I thought you got over that little crush you had on Mr. Glasse months ago…'

'Shut up, Pietro,' said Merc and Vivi in unison.

Ig followed the others up a gently curving flight of stairs, past a gargoyle she swore she'd never seen before, and down a completely different flight of stairs. Vivi swung open a set of large double doors to reveal a gigantic, bare room beyond it. The floors were made of dark, varnished – and, in some places, cracked – wood, while long, rectangular windows near the ceiling let in the only light. Milling around in the middle of the room were a few faces Ig recognised; Falcon Reeve and his cronies, a girl who sat behind Ig and Vivi in Torture Management, who turned away from her friends to give Ig a wave so enthusiastic and friendly Ig simply looked away and pretended she hadn't seen. Ig's stomach swooped in a funny, giddy sort of way as she realised one of the girls in that group was Katalina; the gorgeous, leggy girl from Ms. Schwab's class who crawled all over a chair and gave Ig serious palpitations.

'Hey, Kat,' said Pietro with a wave, 'Team No Power for life, right?'

'I hope not, Pietro,' replied Katalina, flicking her long, impossibly straight hair out of her eyes as her gaze settled on Ig. 'Oh – you're the new girl from Monologue, aren't you? Ignatia?'

'Haaa,' Ig replied.

Katalina laughed. Was she wearing makeup? To a class that sounded like it was going to be very, um, physical? Ig decided then and there not to ever think about this girl sitting at her desk, slowly applying lipstick at eight in the morning while Ig herself was still all sleep-fuzzy and half-dreaming. Nope, she'd never, ever think about that, especially not when she was trying to get to sleep and her imagination was more than willing to run wild with the concept. It would not end well.

'You don't have a Power either, right?' Katalina asked. 'You'll have to protect me from having to pair up with this idiot. Promise?'

'Heee,' Ig continued, marvelling at her own eloquence. She'd better start praying she never came across this girl in the field, or she'd be a goner. Katalina turned back to her friends, and Ig leaned against the nearest surface – which turned out to be Vivi. 'Be honest,' she said. 'Did I just make an idiot of myself?'

'Oh, Ig.' Vivi's warm, gentle hand clasped her by the shoulder.

'Of course you did.'

'Ignatia Heretical,' Pietro said, leaning into the conversation and framing an imaginary poster with his hands. 'Never met a girl she couldn't humiliate herself in front of.'

'Pietro, don't embarrass her.'

'What? You're fifteen, Ig. You're allowed to be embarrassing. If you're afraid of being embarrassing now, you might as well skip your teens and be, I dunno, thirty or something, where the embarrassing is built in.'

'Glad to know your opinions on thirty-somethings, Pietro.' A man had entered the classroom; he was tall, but wire-thin, with pale skin and a neat, immaculate goatee. Tucked behind his ear was an unlit cigarette. Ig realised she'd been expecting Mr. Glasse to look something like Coach Cloudspear – that is, an adult version of the boys at Lunalist, all muscles and blond hair and self-importance.

'Oh, Sir,' said Pietro, clearly warming to the topic. 'Are you over thirty? I wouldn't have put you at a day over twenty-nine.'

'One more word,' said the teacher, walking past the students with his hands in his pockets, 'and I'll have to partner with you myself, to keep an eye on you.'

'And distract the rest of the class with how awesome I am?' Pietro called back. To Ig's horror, he shot finger guns in the direction of their teacher, who simply rolled his eyes and kept moving.

'You should have been here last month,' Vivi whispered in Ig's ear, 'when we were out in the gardens for Combat Class. Pietro got in trouble for sneaking off.'

'Hey, wait a second. I did not 'get in trouble',' Pietro scoffed, flicking air quotes in Vivi's direction. 'Mr. Glasse strongly advised that I pay attention to the class, and predicted that my free time privileges would be forfeit if I did not acquiesce to his teaching methods.'

Vivi shot him a withering look. 'Pietro. That's getting in trouble.'

'Sounds fake.' Pietro swooshed his hair out of his face. 'I never get in trouble.'

'Class,' Mr. Glasse called from the front, 'I personally don't mind if we talk all lesson. But I did plan on giving some of you invisibility powers for the session today, if you want to actually concentrate.'

Immediately every single non-Powered student in the room turned to face Ig's group, glared and told them, in no uncertain terms, to shut up. Pietro huffed, crossing his arms and turning away with a roll of his eyes. 'I was just stating a fact.'

'Okay,' Mr. Glasse said, holding up a wooden box about the length of Ig's arm, 'line up one at a time – one at a time, class! – and receive your discs for your Lenders, if you need one. The sooner we get this part done, the sooner we can have some fun, alright?'

Ig managed to hold out her hand, take her Lender disc and say 'thank you, sir' without doing something awkward and spontaneously combusting on the spot. She smiled at the familiar feeling of the tiny magnet on the bottom clicking into place in her band and then, after that, there was that lovely feeling of a Power taking hold of your body; a delicious electric tingle up and down your arm, making the hairs on the back of your neck stand up and filling you with the feeling of being invincible.

Vivi and Pietro were snickering to each other; while Mercutio stubbornly pretended not to notice. 'What?' Ig whispered, and Vivi began to sputter.

'You know how each Power Lender is registered to a single student?' she said. Ig nodded.

'Well,' Pietro said, smoothing his hand over his face to try and keep his grin at bay, 'when we first started at Shackleton, a certain someone had delusions of grandeur…'

'Surely,' Mercutio growled, 'you are not telling this story again.'

In unison, Vivi and Pietro mimed slapping five Power Lender bracelets on each arm. 'At long last!' Pietro scream-whispered, contorting his face into a manic grin, 'I, Mercutio von Ryan, have been granted the power I so greatly deserve!'

'Now, tremble before your new overlord – with the power of five Villains in the body of a single boy!' Vivi stretched out her arms. 'I am the Master of all I–'

'Beep doop beep doop bwaaaaah,' sang Pietro sadly, pretending to power down and flopping limply from the waist. 'Unregistered use of Power Lenders. Shutting down.' Ig turned to Mercutio, incredulous.

'You tried to steal Power Lenders? Why did you think that would work?'

'It was worth a try,' he grumbled.

'Did you get in trouble?' Ig asked. Mercutio turned to her and grinned a sharp, wolfish grin.

'I got extra marks added to my assignments for the rest of the term, Heretical. Initiative goes a long way at Shackleton.'

'Okay!' Mr. Glasse yelled, clearly already frustrated with all the chatter, 'pair up! Let's push ourselves with a new opponent today, shall we? Someone from outside your little friend group.'

'Kaaaat,' Pietro cried, running off to join the gorgeous girl from before. 'Be my friend!'

'Pietro, no!'

'Pleeeeease?'

Mercutio had already stalked off to assess his options. Ig knew he was smart, but what could he do in a Combat Class? Hope his opponent died of a heart attack and bring them back as an undead slave?

'Okay,' Vivi said, taking Ig's hands in hers. 'You and me, let's go.'

'But the teacher said not to–'

'But we're not friends, are we?' Vivi winked. 'We're arch-nemeses in the making.'

Ig paused; then laughed, squeezing Vivi's hands. 'Okay.' At least it meant she wouldn't have to make a fool of herself in front of someone new.

'Line up,' called Mr. Glasse. 'Facing your partner, please.'

The class did as they were told; Mercutio on Ig's left, Vivi in front of her, Pietro and Katalina off to the right somewhere. 'Now, we're going to do this in short bursts. Turn invisible now, Power Lender people, and when I blow my first whistle, you will begin attacking your opponent. I hope none of these pairs both have Power Lenders, or you won't be able to see each other and this fight will be very boring indeed. One my second whistle, you stop. That doesn't mean 'let me get in one more hit, Mr. Glasse.' It means stop. It's a safety thing, I don't want to get fired.'

'This is going to be easy,' Vivi said with a sunny grin.

'How?' Ig asked. 'You haven't even got any plants on you.'

With all the flourish of a circus performer, Vivi produced a single flower from her blazer pocket. 'Aha!' she said, brandishing it in the air. 'Look upon the instrument of your doom, Heretical – and despair!'

Off to the side, Ig watched Mr. Glasse pinch the bridge of his nose and sigh to himself. 'I'll definitely need a tab break after this.'

Chapter Twenty-One

Becoming invisible didn't feel any different from being visible. All of Ig's limbs held the same amount of weight, her footsteps still sounded on the wooden floor. But looking down at herself, she looked… sketchy. Like she hadn't been coloured in, yet. To everyone else, she would be hard to spot; especially when there were at least twelve other basically-unseeable students running around in the same place. Still, Ig knew from a handful of invisibility classes back at Lunalist (before she got left behind after one lesson and the tutors decided that Ig simply didn't make herself noticeable enough to be invisible) that there were lots of ways she could give herself away, if she wasn't careful. Like–

'Got you!'

Vivi's face lit up with manic glee and, to Ig's surprise, she didn't go immediately for a plant-based attack. No; instead, she leapt forward and tackled Ig to the ground. Ig bit back a yelp as her tail bone connected hard with the floor.

'Sloppy, Miss Section,' called Mr. Glasse from across the room. 'Good on you for finding her, but I can tell you haven't been working on your form.'

'But Sir,' Vivi whined, as Ig wriggled like a hooked fish beneath her, 'I got her! I won!'

She was distracted just long enough for Ig to lick her finger and stick it in Vivi's ear. 'Oh my god!' Vivi yelled in outrage, as Ig thrashed herself loose and took off across the Combat class floor, 'that was disgusting, Ig! What is it with you and slobber?!'

'…and now she got away,' Mr. Glasse drawled. 'Keep trying.'

Ig stuck to the perimeter of the classroom, feeling safe against the wall. Around her, everything was carnage. There were students flying high above her, invisible opponents caught in their grip; students who were blasting each other with bolts of dark-coloured light from across the room; Katalina and Pietro, who were basically wrestling on the floor – though Kat seemed to have a distinct advantage as she bent Pietro's fingers backwards, grinning all the while. God, she had perfect teeth. Ig knew she and Pisces would get along swimmingly – and send her into heart failure simply from being in the same room together. Over in the corner, one student stood, open mouthed, as a stream of spiders spilled from their lips; running in a rippling line to where their opponent, now merely a writhing mass of bugs, lay curled in the foetal position on the floor. Next to them squatted Mercutio, furiously taking notes as their own partner huffed impatiently, complaining that 'you're not even playing right, von Ryan!'

It was a free for all. It was madness. There was no way Vivi could find her again in this. All she had to do was wait it out and–

'Hey,' someone whispered in her ear, 'did you know that when you're thinking, you talk to yourself?'

Ig turned – facing straight into a cloud of orange-yellow dust. Immediately her eyes started to stream, and her nose filled up with snot so fast she couldn't catch her breath. Everything was blurry, and her head was suddenly full of cotton wool; her thoughts were thick and fuzzy. She turned, sneezing hard into her sleeve, as Vivi pushed her to the floor and pounced on top of her so Ig's face was pinned against the floor. Vivi pulled Ig's arms behind her back so hard that her shoulders popped. 'Oilseed,' she said, pulling on Ig as the pair grappled on the floor. 'It gives some people hayfever. Well, I mean – mine gives everyone hayfever, I suppose.'

Ig's eyes widened with the pain – surely Vivi wasn't going to actually pull her arms out their sockets? – and then widened even further as an idea popped into her head fully formed.

'That's clever,' she wheezed, as Vivi's knee pushed into her ribs. 'Are you growing that in our dorm?'

'Oh, no – I didn't know if you got hayfever for real life or not. There's a farmer just outside Rossborough, he has these huge fields filled with it. I like to go there when I need a break from the school, you know? So I snuck out a few nights ago and pilfered a few–'

Ig had had follow-up questions to keep Vivi talking, but apparently she hadn't needed them. But, as she suspected, Vivi's grip on her arms loosened when she was distracted.

When Ig was small, her mam had taken her to Edinburgh Zoo. She always remembered the sunbears – these huge, black creatures with long tongues and sloping shoulders. All the other little kids had been scared. But not Ig. She'd listened, fascinated, as the zookeeper told her that sunbears could turn in their own skin; so if a tiger had them by the neck, they could twist around and defend themselves. That was the creature that Ignatia Heretical channelled as she slipped her arms out of her blazer's sleeves, twisted, and sneezed right in Vivi Section's face. The other girl screamed – the angriest Ig had ever heard her – and rocketed backwards as Ig made her escape. 'You are foul!' Vivi cried. 'Absolutely foul, Ig! I am going to put chili powder in your bedsheets, you see if I won't – Mr. Glasse! Ig isn't playing fair!'

'Oh?' their teacher shrugged, looking around him. 'Am I at Lunalist? Did I get incredibly lost and end up in Newcastle?'

'Sir…'

'Because I thought this was a school for Villains. I must be confused…'

'Sir!'

Safely on the other side of the room, Ig took in a big breath – her nose now clear – and assessed the situation. Vivi's flower was too effective for her to get close to her opponent again; she needed a new approach. The perimeter wasn't safe anymore, so she ducked and weaved her way through the crowds, getting knocked and tripped as she went. Vivi was easy to escape when she wasn't using her Power. She needed to get rid of…

Mr. Glasse had his back turned to her, trying and failing to get Mercutio to participate in the class. His hands were on his hips, pulling up his black polo neck just enough that Ig could see what was sticking out of his back pockets. A keyring. A shiny, green, folded piece of paper with 'tobacco' printed on the side. And a lighter. Quieter than she'd ever done anything in her life, Ig crept across the room, held her breath, and gently, slowly – but not too slowly! – eased the lighter out of Mr. Glasse's pocket. She crept around to the side of the teacher, only exhaling once she was far enough away to know she hadn't been spotted. Then, she took off her Power Lender.

Disabling your Power Lender always felt like waking up from a particularly nice dream; the disappointing 'oh, right' of going back to normal, to being exactly who you really were. But this time, Ig barely noticed. She was too busy scanning the room for Vivi.

She was over on the other side of the room, temporarily distracted by Katalina sitting on Pietro's back. Then, her head snapped up, and Ig felt herself smile. Her face set in a determined grimace, Vivi crossed the Combat class room until Ig was within striking distance. Ig, for her part, didn't move – which would have surely set off alarm bells in Vivi's head if she weren't still so outraged about the sneezing.

Vivi raised her right hand, which held the oilseed flower, and her brows knitted together in concentration. A stream of orange dust headed directly for Ig; who raised her own hand, and flicked the lighter open. The cloud of pollen caught alight as easily as paper, bursting into a ball of flame that seemed to suck all the air out of the room with a thunderous "vwoom". In less than a second, it was gone; nothing more than grey smoke drifting up towards the high windows of the classroom. Every single student fell silent; Ig could feel twenty-something pairs of eyes, all staring her way, burning into her skin. Pietro, across the room, was outright gawking. Bravado fading fast, she let the lighter clatter to the floor and stared, wide eyed, at the rest of her class.

'I...'

The rest of her words were swallowed up in wild, rapturous applause. Vivi was leaping into the air, arms flapping happily at her sides. 'Wooo!' she hollered, her hands curling into devil horns as the burnt ends of the oilseed flower fluttered from her fingers. 'That was amazing! Aaaamaaaziiing!'

Ig's stomach turned cold as she realised how red her dorm-mate's face was from the heat. She really hadn't thought this through; if she killed Vivi, she'd have to take care of all her stupid plants. She looked away shyly – and caught Katalina staring at her. The two girls made eye contact for a moment before the shrill sound of a whistle being blown brought her back to reality. 'Very good, Miss – Heretical, was it?' Mr. Glasse said, walking over to her side. 'Not the most conventional use of invisibility, but I liked it.'

'I know it wasn't right,' Ig started to babble, blood rushing to her cheeks, 'but it just came to me, and before I thought about it anymore I was...um, sorry for taking your lighter, Sir.'

Mr. Glasse paused, blinked, and then shrugged at her. 'Myeh,' he said, twisting his face. 'I shouldn't have brought it in here if I didn't want it to be used. Fair play, Miss Heretical.' Mr. Glasse held out his hand. 'But seriously, I do need it back, right now. If I needed a smoke break before you nearly set Miss Section on fire, I certainly do now.'

'Brava!' Pietro cried, walking backwards out of the classroom as they left at the end of the day – aching and slightly hysterical with exhaustion after another three rounds of Combat Class, in which everyone had been trying to outdo Ig's performance, to no avail. 'Encore, Villainous Heretical! Encore! Oh, here Merc; your towel. You must be sweaty after all that hard work.'

He fished a washcloth from his brother's bag and chucked it at Mercutio's face.

'Oh, stop it,' Ig blushed, thwacking him gently in the ribs as

Mercutio squawked indignantly. 'It wasn't anything.'

'Wasn't anything?' Vivi interjected. 'That was so clever, Ig; I would have never thought you'd use such underhanded tricks. I must be rubbing off on you.' Ig laughed awkwardly as Vivi slung an arm over her shoulder, squeezing her tight. The pride she felt at having outsmarted her was still flickering in Ig's chest like a flame. It was unusual. Dizzying. She could get used to the feeling.

'Pssh; thanks a lot, von Ryan,' snarked a student as they pushed past the twins; he had fangs jutting out over his bottom lip, and a layer of brown fuzz covering his face and arms. Ig recognised him as Mercutio's partner from Combat Class; the one who sat on the side while Mercutio scribbled in his notepad. 'Did you get all the research you needed, watching those spiders in the first round?'

'Some,' Mercutio said with a slow shrug of the right shoulder, slinging his washcloth back at Pietro. 'Enough to use in my Minion Husbandry project. So it was useful, at the least.'

The boy tutted under his breath, hackles rising. '"Your project". Right. Well, I didn't get to do anything that lesson. I thought you were meant to be smart.'

'I am smart. Pietro, what are my estimated grades?'

'A, A*, A*, A, a D in Villain Accounting but you told me never to bring that up…'

'Alright, Pietro, that's enough.'

The fanged boy looked Mercutio up and down; disappointment and disgust curdling across his face. 'And you're so modest with it. Ugh. Remind me never to partner with you again, von Ryan.'

'Alright,' Mercutio said, clearly bored with the conversation, 'I will.'

'What? Hey, no,' sputtered the boy, as Pietro snorted with laughter into his sleeve. 'That was meant to – you're meant to be – oh, forget it. Idiot.' He stalked off, joining his own group of friends, who were sniggering under their breath at him. Mercutio coolly watched him go, then turned to Pietro.

'What did I do wrong this time?'

'Briar wanted you to help him get a better grade by kicking your butt in Combat Class. Because you're the Great and Powerful Mercutio von Ryan, it would look good if he beat you.'

'And I didn't participate correctly for that to happen?'

'No.'

'And why is Briar's grade my problem?'

'Because you were his partner, Merc.'

'Ah. I see.' Mercutio didn't sound sad, or even worried about how this Briar guy might feel about him in the future. He was collecting information; nothing more. Ig wondered what it was like, to live like that. Free of the consequences of other people's feelings. It felt as far-off as not having to breathe, or eat.

'Anyway. You!' Pietro said, giving Vivi a hug so tight she was almost picked up bodily from the floor. 'The Little Poison Master.'

Vivi failed to meet his gaze. 'Psh. I need to work on my form.'

'Yeah,' Pietro scoffed, 'that's so important when you can bend plants to your will, right?' Vivi brightened slightly and Pietro continued, buoyed by her reaction. 'Come on, Viv; no-one's gonna be able to get near you in the real world. Just make your lair in, I dunno, Alnwick Poison Garden or something, and you'll be untouchable.'

'You think I could take over Alnwick Poison Garden?' Vivi said – eyes shining as if Pietro had suggested she take over the Pentagon. 'Oh I love the Poison Garden – I'd make a little nest in their belladonna patch and sleep there if I could. You really think I could do it one day?'

Pietro rolled his eyes at her affectionately. 'Course you could. She's not just a pretty face; eh, Merc?'

'Well, I wouldn't say that,' Mercutio interjected, sweeping his dark curls from his face in a way that was both flirtatious and blatantly over-rehearsed.

All three of them stared at him. 'What did you say?' Vivi asked, her voice leaping up an octave incredulously.

'Oh, come on, Merc,' Pietro muttered, hiding his face in his palms. 'I try, I really do...'

Mercutio paled. 'I... oh. You said 'not just a...' I thought you said... so that didn't... um, I have to go give the bees a bath. Or something. Goodbye.' He turned on his heel and walked back into the Combat Class, letting the doors swing shut behind him. Pietro watched him go in awe.

'I set him up so well for success,' he whispered. 'And he calls her ugly and walks into a room with only one exit. That boy amazes me every day. So! Plans for tonight, ladies?' He threw his arms around Vivi and pulled her in close. 'I've got some contraband in my room I'm willing to share; and by that I mean a pint of cookie dough ice cream I'm stashing in Merc's cryo-freezer without his permission. Any takers?'

'Cryogenically frozen ice cream does sound delightful,' Ig deadpanned, digging her planner out from its place in her satchel, 'but I think I have...homework.'

In the neat, square box labelled with today's date – along with 'picnic breakfast with P, M & V' – were two words, printed neatly and ringed with red pen.

Oh, Ig thought. *Right.*

'Call Dad.'

Chapter Twenty-Two

She'd forgotten. How had she forgotten?

Well, Ig thought, *it probably had something to do with the fact you've been gallivanting around a Villain School with Villain students doing Villain things... villainously.* She'd been having far, far too much fun, and had nearly missed her chance to talk to her dad – the only parent she had for the rest of this term, since her mam was forbidden to know where she was – to go eat ice cream with Pietro and Vivi. She was such a bad daughter, and an even worse Hero. Back at Lunalist, Pisces called her parents every Sunday, regular as clockwork. Ig could picture it perfectly; Pisces brushing out her long, red hair while her parents gushed down the phone at her about how proud they were, calling her darling and sweetheart and blowing kisses. It was like something out of a film, which made it feel all the realer. It made Ig look at her mam and dad – with their fierce, loving disapproval and cheerful obliviousness respectively – like they were actors refusing to stick to the script and just work with her, here.

When Ig and Pisces adopted their kids one day – two girls, Rose and Wren Rising – she would ask Pisces' parents for whatever parenting book they'd used. It obviously worked.

Ig made her excuses – plucking a piece of homework from the ether and pretending she'd forgotten all about it – and left Pietro and Vivi to go enjoy their sugar binge in peace. Then, she headed towards the grounds, then up the stairs to her rooftop. The sun was beginning to set, painting the dramatic Northumbrian landscape in orange and pink. Ig got comfortable, heaved out a sigh, and pressed Call on her communication device.

'Hey, honey!'

'Hi, Dad.'

Her dad was sitting in the garden; in the background, Ig could see the bushes filled with bird feeders, trees filled with nesting boxes, and the creeping ivy running up the side of the semi-detached house in Gosforth where Ig grew up. 'Mam's been on another bird feeding spree?' she asked.

'Ugh, you have no idea. She says when she spoils the crows, the blue tits and the sparrows feel "left out." Her dad raised his fingers in sarcastic air quotes, and Ig allowed herself a little smile. 'I think she just wants more familiars, personally.'

'How is she?'

'Oh, you know.' Ig's dad leaned back on the bench he'd installed in the back garden last summer. 'Coping. Sulking. She misses you.'

'Hm.' Ig wasn't sure what to say, so she opted to say nothing much and let her dad fill in the gaps. Which he did, expertly; chattering about some Hero training facility for adults he'd been invited to open down in London. 'You know, the New Dawn? You might've seen 'em in the news. Good crew, honey, nice people. They just took on someone a lil' older than you as an apprentice; Seer, or Sire, or...'

'Spire?'

'Yeah! Yeah; Spire. Sweet kid; real nice manners. Cute, too...'

'Dad–'

'Whaaat? I can't keep my eye out for a someone for my best girl to settle down with?'

Spire – Margot Margaleves – was two years older than Ig, and had never noticed she'd existed. But ever since she'd come out to her parents last Christmas, her dad had been obsessed with matchmaking Ig with every girl he met. She would never forget when she went with him to one of those awful, loud HeroCons, and every girl under eighteen in the signing queue was introduced to 'my daughter Ignatia – gonna be famous, one day! Chip off the ol' block. Say; you girls doing anything after the con? Ig here has a backstage pass to The Green Room, can getcha in to meet all your favourite Heroes…'

Ig didn't go to cons after that.

'So,' her dad asked, 'how's the you-know-what going?'

Ig nodded, then waggled her head from side to side in a non-committal way. 'Good. I think. Okay. I've got some leads. I think. I've been making some recordings, writing down notes.'

Liar.

'I knew you would crush this, honey!' Her dad beamed at her as if she'd told him she'd taken down the entire school single-handedly. 'This whole thing's gonna be a piece of cake for you, just wait an' see. You got smarts, kid.'

Um, Ig thought back to her meeting with The General. The way she'd looked at her. And she thought about all the classes she'd taken where she'd stumbled into success; all the laughing and joking and chatting with Pietro, Vivi, and Mercutio – about the fact this was the first time she'd used her communication device in a week; since she'd become so distracted by these dazzling, strange, inexplicable people – Vivi and Pietro and even Mercutio – who seemed intent on being in her orbit. At first, she'd wondered if it was a distraction tactic; to knock her off course, to give her more useless information. But the more she was around them, the more she realised that everything they said to her was strangely unguarded. Pietro and Vivi hadn't told her the story of Mercutio ineffectually stealing Power Lenders so that she'd waste The General's time with it. They'd told her about it because it was a funny story.

Was there a chance that there really wasn't anything to find out, here?

No. No, that couldn't be right. She wouldn't be here, if that were the case. She just had to keep looking. She just had to remember to look.

'Dad,' she said, faltering even as she began, 'if the mission, um, fails – if I can't find anything out that The General wants to know–'

'That's not gonna happen, honey.'

'But–'

'Don't worry about that, Ig.' Her dad looked earnestly down the lens. 'You're my daughter, and I know I didn't raise a quitter.'

'Um. Okay, Dad.' Ig wondered what her dad would think if he knew that his 'not a quitter' daughter had used those smarts he was so proud of to almost commit arson today. Mr. Glasse had kept shooting her amused, impressed little looks throughout the rest of Combat Class, and they'd made her feel a strange mix of proud, uncomfortable and – most worryingly – eager to outdo herself next time. What next time? What was there to outdo? Would she actually turn one of her classmates into a pile of ashes?

Well. Maybe Mercutio. Focus, Heretical!

'When you come home,' her dad was saying, 'we'll throw a big party, okay? We'll invite your Auntie Memoria and your little friend from school – Pisces, right? And we'll celebrate your victory over those Shackleton losers in style. A'right?'

Ig suddenly felt very, very tired – and annoyed. Why wasn't he listening to her? It wasn't that she wanted him to doubt her, that would be insane. But she wanted him to be ready to pick up the pieces if she failed. Because, sitting on this rooftop – with no information to send back home that wasn't 'I almost blew up my dorm-mate today' and a secret, guilty thought that she could be eating ice cream right now if only she didn't love her dad so bloody much – that was looking like a strong possibility. 'Okay, Dad. I'm going to go, now. Before I'm missed.'

'Hm? Oh, okay, honey. It's been nice to chat to you – I thought you'd forgotten about your old man!'

'I could never forget about you. Love you.'

'Love you too, kiddo. Go knock 'em dead!'

The screen went blank. Ig sat on the rooftop for a long while after that, her frustration simmering in her stomach as she picked idly at the skin on her knuckles. Then, she headed along to the von Ryan's dorm. There was still half a pint of Marshmallow Fluff 'n' Stuff waiting for her when she got there.

Chapter Twenty-Three

'Miss! Mercutio isn't working on his costume!'

Miss Hypnatyse sighed and put down her book. 'Mr von Ryan,' she said, 'what are you making back there?'

Mercutio, tucked away in the corner of the Intermediate Costume & Mask Design, looked up from the tiny, silver dome in his hand; one of twenty that were stacked on his desk next to a pile of needle-like stingers waiting for their turn with the soldering iron. 'Would you believe me,' he said dryly, 'if I said that it's a button?'

'No,' said Miss Hypnatyse, 'but since I'm just your substitute teacher, I can't really bring myself to care. Carry on; Mr. Decrept can mark you down when he's back next week.'

The rumble of discontent soon died down, though a few students muttered something about unfairness for the rest of the class. Merc shot Ig a conspiratorial look; which was enough of a distraction for her to drive the safety pin in her hand straight into the fleshy part of her palm. She managed not to cry out; it wasn't the first time she'd injured herself in C&MD. Why was she in Intermediate? She'd never used a needle and thread before coming here.

Come to think of it; why was Vivi here? She was sitting at Ig's side, as usual, carefully using a hot glue gun to stick pressed flowers from their dorm onto a piece of sheer green gauze. It was amazing. *If she ever wore that outside*, Ig thought, *Mercutio would have a stroke.* She rested her chin on her fist and watched her for a second; Vivi never worried about being seen as lacking; she just did her thing, and you could go along for the ride or get left behind. And, as these months wore on, Ig was realising how little she wanted to be left behind.

It really was going to be awful when they had to fight each other as adults.

Ig had never been told much about nemeses at Lunalist; only that anyone from Shackleton was bad and evil and had to be stopped at any cost. Here, the students seemed to have so much more, well, agency. They talked about their nemeses as easily as some students back home talked about their first brand deal. They had classes on how to make the best impression on the debut as a Villain. Even things like this – working with needles and pins and glue and, making their costumes into arts and crafts projects – was something she'd never done at the Academy. Lunalist Heroes all wore white and gold.

It always seemed like Heroes were reacting to problems. Villains, from what Ig had seen, placed much more value in striking first, in causing havoc and doing it in style. No wonder The General was so paranoid about them.

Wait. Did I just call The General 'paranoid?!'

'Right, class,' Miss Hypnatyse said, clapping her hands together. 'The bell's about to ring, so – do not get up, the bell is still a signal for me, not you. You can start packing your work away – slowly! Mr. von Ryan, Pietro, I will see you for Mind & Manipulation next lesson, the rest of you…well, I hope you learned something. Stitching. Weaving. Or something.'

'What do I have to do to be called 'Mr. von Ryan?' Pietro asked, as he packed away Mercutio's 'buttons.'

'Not be legally classified as my property,' Mercutio answered smoothly. Pietro blinked at him incredulously. 'What?'

'You're a dick sometimes, Merc.'

'What? What did I do?'

'Alright,' Vivi said decisively, breaking up the incoming spat between the boys by shoving her sheer flower garden into its pigeonhole and stretching her arms above her head, 'I don't know about you, but I need some fresh air.'

'I know just where to go,' Ig said.

Soon enough, the four of them lay flat in the sweet, long grass of the fields that curved down towards the village, the sheep keeping a healthy distance as they snacked on ill-gotten blackberries and kept half an eye out for any angry farmers who might spot them trespassing. Ever since her Shoplifting Adventure, Ig had been dying to come back here to untangle her nerves a little. 'So,' she asked, popping a blackberry into her mouth, 'Why are you guys doing this?'

Pietro pretended to think about her question. 'Mostly because there's only so many times you can sit on that fountain before the stones embed themselves in your–'

'No,' Ig laughed. 'I mean, this. Villainy stuff. Why did you want to come here?'

Vivi rolled over, grass seeds in her hair. 'Why do you ask?' she said carefully. Ig looked at her blankly; then, her eyes widened as she realised how it sounded. She hadn't even meant it like… like that. She just wondered. All three of them were so smart, in their own ways. Smart, and capable, and determined and…and fun. The world was their oyster, no matter what they chose to do. She'd been genuinely curious why they'd chosen to burn it down.

'I'll go first.' Mercutio sat bolt upright, like a corpse rising from the grave. 'I want to continue the legacy of my uncle, Rayner von Ryan, and wreak havoc and calamity down upon the Heroes that brought about his downfall.' Something steely and gleeful glinted in his eyes. 'First, it was undead rabbits. Then, it was the bees. Then the wolves, and the bears, and the honey badgers. Mwahaha.'

'Did you actually say 'mwahaha' out loud, dude?'

'Yes, Pietro. I did.'

'Well,' Pietro said, kicking his brother lazily in the shins, 'I suppose I'm stuck with you. Can't wait to be cleaning up zombie animal poops for all eternity.'

'You don't have to be. You could just go home.'

'What, and stay in that huge castle forever, bumbling about with Uncle Rayner? No thanks.'

'You live in a castle?!' Ig squeaked.

Pietro rolled his eyes, as if her question were tremendously boring. 'Yes. With gargoyles and dripping walls and chains and everything. Uncle Rayner's a traditionalist. He's cool, but he's 'adult cool', you know? Only in small doses.' Pietro turned towards the girls. 'What about you, Viv?'

Vivi heaved out a sigh, plucking up a daisy from under her head. 'Do you know how much damage we've done to this planet?' she said sadly, twirling the flower between forefinger and thumb. 'How many beautiful species of plants, trees, you name it have been left for dead – because we want a new motorway or a block of flats? How the soil itself is dying?' She placed the daisy on her chest and lay back, crossing her arms like she was dead in her coffin. 'If I controlled everything, none of that would matter anymore. We'd live in a British rainforest – all lush and green and bountiful, and if anyone tried to destroy it…' Vivi shrugged, as easily as breathing. 'I'd destroy them first.'

Ig thought about home – about Gosforth and its well-kept, orderly gardens and ornamental bushes – and about Newcastle's city centre, with its grey brick buildings, chewing-gum spattered pavements and fading shopfronts. She conceded that it would probably be better with a few more trees.

'And you, Heretical?' Mercutio asked. 'What do you want to do?' Ig looked up, surprised. *Mercutio von Ryan, actually acknowledging me as a person? Stop the presses.*

'Well,' she said slowly – choosing her words carefully, 'I… I want to make my parents proud of me. They, um, they worked really hard to get me where I wanted to go – to study? And the teachers. They, um, expect a lot of me. Because my – my mam. She's the Witch Queen, isn't she? So I, um, I don't want to let them down.'

'Well, that's not what I asked,' Mercutio huffed, flopping

back down into the grass.

'Wasn't it?' Ig asked.

'No. Oh, Vivi – don't move, don't move don't move.'

Vivi stiffened. Something small, round and dark was wriggling about in her hair. 'What is it? Oh nooo, I can hear its wings buzzing. Is it going in my ear?!'

'It's not going in your ear.' Mercutio crawled to her side and brushed a finger gently against her temple, and Ig could have sworn she saw Vivi's eyes widen. 'Come on,' he crooned softly. 'Come here please, I'm not going to hurt you… oh, look! It's one of mine.' Crawling across the back of his hand was a bee. A round, fuzzy bumblebee, with two balls of pollen on its back legs and a shining, silver behind, tipped with a needle-like stinger. 'Let me see…' Mercutio squinted at the insect, who was waving her front legs in the air in an attempt to look big and scary. Ig, Pietro, and Vivi crowded round for a better look. 'This is version two-point-four-point-five. I made an upgrade in the middle of the upgrade. Version one had retractable stingers, but I was finding the accommodation cumbersome and uncomfortable for the specimens. So hers is rigid, but easier to wear and more effective in battle. Also – and this is a good opportunity to test her reactivity in the field…' Mercutio fished a pair of cheap, in-ear headphones from his pocket, put them in his ears and tapped a button on the cord. The bee stiffened, took off, flew in a perfect circle overhead, did a loop-the-loop, then landed on Vivi's wrist. 'Tah-da!' Mercutio cried, grinning. 'Seamless switching from a natural state to a von-Ryan-controlled one, and back again.'

Ig applauded, and Pietro gave his brother a clap on the back. 'Very cute,' he said with a proud smile.

'She's not cute,' Mercutio said haughtily. 'She's a very advanced attack drone. Pardon the pun.'

'Why did you make her land on me?' Vivi asked, watching the bee crawling up and down the inside of her arm.

'I didn't. She wasn't under my control when she landed.' Mercutio looked over at Vivi, and his grin softened. 'She just likes you.'

Vivi blinked, staring up at Mercutio. After a long, long moment between them, where the air seemed to glitter, Mercutio coughed and looked away. 'You do wear a lot of floral perfumes, after all. Now, if you want to see what she can really do…'

He pressed the button on the headphones again, and the bee took off, flew in a straight line, and stung Pietro in the crook of his neck. 'Ow!' Pietro yelped, rocketing backwards as the bee took flight again, turned, and charged him again. 'Merc! Isn't that gonna – ow! Don't do it again, you dick!'

'It won't kill her,' Merc said smoothly, 'if that was what you're asking, because her stinger is reinforced with titanium. She can sting you as much as she likes.' By this point, Pietro was running off down the hill, startling the sheep as the tiny insect gave chase with murder on her mind. Mercutio scrambled to his feet with a dark chuckle, running after his brother while pressing the button manically, making the bee fly ever faster. Ig watched them go; turning to lie on her stomach and resting her cheek in her hand. 'For two boys who are so smart,' she said to Vivi, 'they're both very, very stupid.'

'You're right,' Vivi said, threading the daisy into the growing fringe of Ig's scruffy black hair, 'but come on; admit it. You never had this much fun at Lunalist, did you?'

Chapter Twenty-Four

Ig's tongue poked out from between her teeth as she concentrated on a particularly thorny piece of homework. 'Vivi,' she asked, 'how did Entangla use thorns to her advantage in her most famous battle with Lyrebird in 1987?'

The sigh from the bed above hers could have powered a turbine. '"Entangla used thorns to her advantage in her most famous battle with Lyrebird in 1987 by creating a collar of thorns that stopped Lyrebird from using her disabling song, thus neutralising her." Why?'

'No reason. Why did that sound like you were reading?'

A hand flopped over the side of the bed; holding an essay entitled 'Environmental Warfare; What We Can Learn From The Entangla/Lyrebird Battle of 1987,' complete with diagrams and 'A*; great work as usual!' written in the corner. 'No reason.'

'Alright, alright,' Ig huffed. 'No need to be sarky because you're in the top set.' Poisonology was one of Ig's least favourite classes; she'd discovered in these past two months that she definitely did not have a green thumb like Vivi. Everyone else in the class had a side project of some sort, growing on a wooden shelf at the back of the classroom. Rows upon rows of lush purple flowers, lethal looking cacti or endlessly twisting vines – and one bare plant pot with 'Ignatia Heretical' written on the side. It was the only class where Ig just hadn't been able to improve. Vivi swore that this sort of thing couldn't be taught; Ig refused to believe that. Everything could be learned, if you gave it the right amount of time. Even being friends with a…

Even being good roommates with a Villain.

'What are you doing for your free period?' Vivi asked. 'I wondered if you wanted to go into town with me. We could get an ice cream, go into Fox and have a look around?' She swung her legs over the side of the bed, and Ig reached up and poked her foot. Vivi pulled them back with a squeak.

'I can't,' Ig said. 'I have something to do.'

'Something exciting?'

'Um.' Ig's gaze wandered to her communication device, charging merrily in the corner of the room. 'No. Not really.'

The last time she'd spoken to The General, she'd spiralled. She didn't want that to happen again. Ig had been trying to prepare herself all week; taking so many deep, cleansing breaths, she made herself feel lightheaded, trying to do affirmations in the mornings – apart from the mornings where she woke up late and had to rush getting ready for breakfast. Or when she had homework to do before school started. Or when Pietro snuck into their room and gave her a fright by sitting at the end of her bed, watching her sleep. There was something wrong with that boy.

Vivi was down on the floor, now; misting her Widowswort plant, which had grown to about twice the size it was when Ig arrived. 'Is this Hero stuff?'

She asked it so nonchalantly, but Ig knew her well enough by now to detect the strain in her voice. Ig zipped up her backpack and went and sat beside the huge clay pot that housed the Widowswort. 'I don't have anything to tell them.'

'Good,' Vivi sniped, but her heart wasn't in it, Ig could tell.

'I've sort of realised,' Ig continued, running her finger over the smooth grooves in the pot's surface, 'I'm going to go back a failure. But that it's, um, it's not like I didn't try. And that's good. I think.'

'Did you never think to lie?' Vivi asked.

'No. Why would I do that? If I gave them fake information, they'd find me out the second they got here.' Ig pulled her knees into her chest and wrapped her arms around them. 'Then

I really would be a disappointment to everyone.' She picked at the skin of her knuckle. 'Hey, Vivi?'

'Hm?'

'If I go back a failure, that means you're going to have a really crap nemesis.'

There was a long beat of silence. Then, Vivi began to giggle, which turned into a laugh, which turned into her sliding to the floor, clutching her lungs and trying to catch her breath. Ig laughed along awkwardly, not entirely sure what was so funny. Vivi wiped her eyes on her sleeve, leaving behind a streak of eyeliner on her blazer. 'I'm fine with that,' she said at last. 'And you're not crap, Ig. Not by a long shot. Now go, before I drop that thing in the shower accidentally on purpose.'

Ig walked to her rooftop, feeling like her legs were made of lead. A few months ago, an audience with The General would be the most amazing thing to ever happen to her; now, she would rather be trying to coax life into a blatantly dead plant. This time, when she connected with the surly hacker on the other end of the line, she was expected.

'The General has been eager for an update from you,' Dana said, in a tone that made Ig cringe. 'She wondered if you'd been compromised.'

Ig swallowed her irritation and nodded. 'It won't happen again.'

'Let me connect you through.'

The screen went blank for a second, then The General's severe, expectant face filled the screen. 'Miss Heretical.'

'Hello, General.'

'You have a new update on the Shackleton situation.' A statement, not a question. Ig opened her mouth, then closed it again.

'Miss Heretical?'

'General,' Ig said, the words tripping over themselves as they fell from her mouth, 'I really don't think anything's going on, here. I mean, things are going on – but it's all, like, studying and learning and stuff.'

The General nodded, her eyes flinty. 'Studying and learning and stuff.'

Ig knew she was wading into dangerous waters, but she couldn't stop herself. She needed to tell The General what she'd found out. Which was nothing. 'There are so many students here who will be dangerous when they leave – but that's not our responsibility, is it? Once they graduate, the Villains aren't actually the Academy's problem anymore, are they?'

The General nodded. 'So,' she said, shuffling a pile of paper distractedly, 'the opposition have managed to conceal their plans from you for half a term.'

'I – no!'

'Are you sure you haven't been compromised, Miss Heretical?'

Ig's mind leapt to Vivi, back in that first week; how she and Pietro had worked everything out before they even met her. A rush of protectiveness pulsed through her body as she shook her head so violently, she heard something crack. 'No, General, not at all – I'm sure, I promise.'

The General shuffled her papers together, then looked directly into the camera, hands folded neatly under her chin. 'Miss Heretical,' she said, her voice deadly calm, 'the people at that school hate us. They hate what we stand for. They hate our discipline, our hard work and camaraderie, the order we strive to achieve every single day. Not just within the Academy, but out there in the real world. They are chaotic, envious and cruel, and they will stop at nothing to wipe us off the map. Something is happening within those walls. And you are not coming home until you find out what that is.'

Ig sat back, stunned. 'Y-yes, General,' she said, out of habit more than anything.

'On another note,' The General said, 'how are you finding your studies?'

'…what?'

The General quirked an eyebrow at her; which, months ago,

before Ig had encountered a teacher who literally had no face and was very eager to teach her about thumbscrews, would have terrified her. 'I said,' she repeated, 'how are you finding your studies?'

'Um. Alright.'

'Please don't let them overwhelm you, Miss Heretical. Those teachers have years of experience in the field; they can smell weakness like a shark scents blood in the water.'

Apart from Mr. Glasse, Ig thought to herself. The amount of cigarettes he smokes probably means he can't smell a thing anymore.

'Soldier on, Miss Heretical. The Academy is counting on you. Do not waver.'

The only thing Ig felt like 'wavering' on were her dead seeds in Poisonology. Why had The General decided she was struggling with her cover – and with her studies? 'Um. Alright.'

The General shot her one last long, hard look. 'You seem unwell. Distracted.'

'Oh – um, do I?' Ig asked, buying herself some time to think. 'Well, my dorm-mate grows plants. And I have hayfever, so I'm not sleeping well. Sorry, General.'

'Hm. I expect more information next time we speak, Miss Heretical.'

Ig nodded, eager to get off the call. 'Goodbye, General.'

The screen went blank. Ig sighed, hugging her backpack close to her chest. She felt knocked off-kilter, but she wasn't falling down that black pit of self-hate she knew was buried deep inside of her. Not like last time. That was something. She rested her head on the top of her satchel for a moment, letting herself breathe. Thoughts swirled around inside her head and, after a long while, she realised no-one had ever come up onto the roof and bothered her in all the time she'd been at Shackleton. As well as that, she'd never come across it when she hadn't meant to; like the time Vivi and Pietro were distracting her with a sing-off in the hallway and Ig had accidentally walked into the school bathrooms instead of Villain Accounting. Maybe her rooftop was a part of the school that wasn't totally under The Nyx's control.

That would probably have been a useful thing to tell The General. If she'd actually wanted to tell The General anything about this place.

Chapter Twenty-Five

'Merc?' Pietro called, tapping on the door of their shared dorm room and creaking it open, 'are you decent? It's time to go to… the…'

Mercutio whirled around guiltily. In his arms sat Onslaught, happily chewing on a blade of hay. Behind them was a cannon. This was the reason he'd missed breakfast, Ig supposed. It had become a little ritual; the four of them would meet in the Shackleton entrance for about eight before making their way to the breakfast room. Ig liked it more than she let on; she'd found it much easier to be motivated to actually get up and dressed in time to eat before lessons if she knew other people were expecting her there. But today, one of their weird little party had been missing.

'Merc,' Pietro said slowly, 'we talked about this. No projectiles in the—'

Mercutio shoved Onslaught into the mouth of the cannon without so much as blinking.

'Merc, no!' Vivi cried; but Ig noticed she was covering her mouth, smothering a scandalised giggle. Onslaught's fluffy butt stuck out the mouth of the cannon, along with a pair of white, fuzzy back feet.

'You know how The Nyx feels about experiments in the dorms,' Pietro cried, raking his hand over his face. 'We're lucky they haven't found out about the cryo-freezer yet.' One long arm shot out to point in the girls' direction.' Viv's the only one who gets a free pass, because her stupid plants double as "aesthetically pleasing ornaments".'

'Hey!' Vivi squeaked, stamping her foot. 'They're not stupid!'

Ig laid a comforting hand on her friend's shoulder. 'Of course they aren't. They're, um, lovely. Apart from the Widowswort. And the Gelsemium. And the Venus Flytrap.'

Vivi wrinkled her nose in a huff. 'Audrey has been in that dorm longer than you. She can't be replaced, but you can.'

'Very scary. What would you do without your nemesis, though?'

'I'll get another,' Vivi scowled playfully. 'I'm not too attached to this one, yet.'

All this talk of nemeses somewhere off in the distant future didn't seem to worry Ig so much anymore. It felt more like a private joke between her and Vivi than a serious promise. Ig planned to keep it that way for as long as she could. She'd had a nightmare, a few weeks back, about an adult Vivi Section – who was twenty foot tall, for some reason – sending a cloud of poisonous spores along the River Tyne, straight towards the Academy, and she'd decided then and there that she much preferred having Vivi as a cheerleader and a source of sleepytime tea than as an enemy. For now. The more of that stuff they shared, the more tragic their eventual feud would be, she supposed.

Pietro was now actively stopping Mercutio from lighting a match. 'They're gonna – stop it, Merc, you're not funny – they're gonna kick us out if they find out you smuggled a cannon into our bedroom!'

'No they're not, dear brother,' Mercutio said calmly, shrugging his brother off his back. 'Because the experiment isn't in here.'

'Wh–'

Mercutio pointed out the open dorm room window. 'It's down there.'

Ig and Vivi scrambled to the window. It was fairly easy; unlike them, the von Ryans kept their room fairly neat. Even Mercutio's cryo-freezer was neatly hidden under his bed, covered with a blanket to avoid detection.

Outside on the lawn, past the gravel drive, was a gigantic net. 'You are joking,' Ig said.

'Ooh!' Vivi squeaked. 'I think I saw this at a circus once!'

'Will she survive that drop?' Pietro asked. 'She is just a bunny, after all.'

'Correction,' Mercutio sniped, holding up a finger, 'she is an undead bunny. Much less delicate than her more vibrant counterparts.' Behind him, Onslaught's tail twitched happily.

'Where did you get the net?' Ig asked.

'The shop dungeon,' Mercutio replied with a shrug. 'Haven't you been yet? They stock all kinds of equipment for homework; pens, new notebooks, nets, knife-sharpening kits…'

'Oh. I just buy snacks from there.'

'You really should use it more. They have so many interesting things.'

'Merc,' Pietro interrupted testily, leaning on his brother's shoulder and looking out the window. 'It's not that I'm not here for shooting things with a cannon. Believe me, I am. But the main thing I'm missing right now,' he twirled his wrist in the direction of Onslaught, who was still stuck in the cannon, 'is the why of the thing.'

Mercutio shrugged. 'Projectile minions.'

Pietro blinked; once, then again, a little harder. 'Of course,' he said, when his brother offered no further explanation. 'How silly of me to not see it to begin with.'

'Now, Pietro; I'm going to need you to–'

'Go down there and catch Onslaught if your aim is off? On it, boss.' Off Pietro stomped; muttering to himself as he went. 'Blow your bloody rabbit up,' he said, slamming the door behind him and making Ig jump. 'See if I care.' About five minutes later, a tiny, Pietro-shaped blob marched over to the net and, never breaking his gaze away from the window, held up his arms in sarcastic readiness. Mercutio grinned, and shoved his goggles down into place.

'Ready, Onslaught?'

The rabbit thumped in agreement against the walls of the cannon. Mercutio patted her affectionately on the bum, then lunged across the room to snatch up the box of matches. 'Now these,' he said to Ig, waggling the box under her nose. 'These I had to smuggle in. Poison and projectiles? All good, no problems here. But one student gets caught smoking, and it's suddenly 'oh no, Mercutio; you can't have matches in your dorm rooms anymore.' He blew a derisive raspberry. 'Luckily, my uncle hid these beauties away in our last care package. You might have heard of him; Rayner von Ryan?'

'We've talked about him before, Mercutio,' said Ig. 'Do you not even remember what you've said to–'

'He's the genius,' Mercutio continued, oblivious, 'who led an entire army of super-soldier clones into battle against six – six! – of the most powerful Heroes ever to amass at the tender age of eighteen. Or at least he was.' Mercutio's face darkened. 'Before Memoria got to him.'

Auntie Memoria? She was Ig's godmother; a curvaceous, smiling woman, her natural hair always in space buns even in her forties, who always told her the best bedtime stories when she came to babysit. She could remember so much about when she and Ig's dad were at school together – down to the tiny stitches in her uniform that came undone with each fight. Ig loved her.

'Merc,' Vivi said gently, 'you don't have to put yourself through all that again. Let's just do the experiment and go downstairs, right?'

'What did she do?' Ig croaked, her throat suddenly feeling dry and painful. Vivi shot Ig a warning glare, which she tried her best to ignore.

'Memoria,' Mercutio continued, hands clenched in agitation, 'took that all away from him. One of the greatest Villainous minds of the decade! And she was just some... teenager. But she wiped away his memory like that!' He swept an arm in a short, cutting motion.

Ig's breath skittered in her throat. Auntie Memoria wouldn't do that! Would she?

Vivi came up behind Mercutio and laid a hand on his shoulder. 'Merc's uncle,' she said, 'totally forgot how to use his cloning machines, after he was beaten by Memoria. And a ton of other stuff, too.'

'He didn't even remember who my grandfather was,' Mercutio interrupted, hands beginning to shake in frustration. 'didn't remember who I–!' He shook his head violently, curls flying. 'And his machines. All forgotten. For months. I was only four. When you're that young, and your caretaker – the only adult you've been able to rely on – suddenly can't remember how to make themselves happy anymore, and you can't do anything to help them and you're so confused, you...' The sentence choked off in Merc's throat. 'He never made any more clones, the machinery never worked for him again. Apart from once.' Mercutio leaned on the windowsill and looked down onto the lawn, where Pietro was still standing, arms outstretched. 'He always says that when I was five, I got a twin brother.'

It was the most she'd heard Mercutio speak. Ig was stunned; still thinking about her beloved Auntie Memoria taking away someone's entire identity. Their purpose. The woman who tucked her into bed at night had messed with a man's mind until he didn't recognise his own father. All while wearing a Lunalist uniform. Her hands crept over one another, picking at the skin of her knuckles until they turned red, then bruised.

'I remember coming over to play one day,' Vivi was saying, trying to lighten the mood that Ig had created, 'and being so confused that there were two of you! Uncle Rayner said Pietro was going to make sure nothing bad ever happened to Merc. Even back then,' she laughed fondly, laying a hand on Mercutio's arm and steadfastly ignoring the shiver it clearly sent across his skin, 'he was always bringing you whatever you wanted, running around after you and stuff. Remember?'

'He's my assistant, isn't he? That's what he's for. Anyway!' said Mercutio briskly, drumming his hands on the top of the cannon, the storm clouds passing over his face like they'd never even been there to begin with, 'back to the explosion. Apologies for the wait, Onslaught.' The rabbit wiggled in response. 'Three, two, one... for science!'

The explosion sent Ig and Vivi reeling, as the room filled up with thick, grey smoke. Coughing and spluttering, Ig made her way to the window again, leaning out to gulp at the fresh air. 'You couldn't have given us a bit more warning?' she coughed.

Mercutio shrugged. 'I said "three, two, one".'

Ig glowered at him, and wafted away a new plume of smoke. Out on the lawn, Pietro was sitting on his butt in the grass, dazed but alive. In his arms sat Onslaught, who was pressing her nose into the crook of his arm, unbothered. Pietro looked up at the trio crowded at Mercutio's dorm window, and gave them a wobbly thumbs up.

'Hm. Not nearly enough impact damage,' Mercutio tutted, grasping for a pen and scribbling something in his notebook. 'Projectile was too fluffy? Too round?' He turned and looked at Ig. 'What do you think, Heretical? Is it worth continuing with the experiment with a fiercer cannonball, or should I pack it up completely and focus my time elsewhere?'

'Um,' Ig replied. Mercutio was asking her for advice? What was the correct answer here? Was this a trap? It was probably a trap. 'I think… you should… redirect your focus.'

Mercutio waggled his head from side to side, the midday sun glinting on his goggles. 'Hmmmm, I suppose you may be right; I mean, I'd have to go for something small but venomous to get the job done and not add more expense on a bigger cannon. And where am I going to find a rattlesnake at this time of the year, hm?'

Ig nodded, hoping she'd said the right thing. 'Yeah, I know. It's not the… not the right season.'

'Or country,' Vivi offered. Mercutio pushed his goggles off his face with a grin, mania gleaming in his dark brown eyes.

'Splendid! Then it's settled. Save the cannons for when I can get my hands on, say, a timber wolf. Or a small bear.' He clapped Ig on the shoulder so hard her legs buckled. 'I'm glad we had this chat, Heretical. So! We were going somewhere?'

Chapter Twenty-Six

The Nyx had sent around letters last night – letters! – to each of the older students, informing them that their morning lessons had been cancelled in favour of a 'special talk.'

'I hope it's not that birds and the bees thing again,' Pietro said, as the four of them walked down a corridor together. 'Coz I'm like, "didn't need it the first time, Nyx, thanks".'

Mercutio was wandering beside his brother; fussing with a tiny, purple harness that Vivi had picked up at the pet shop in Rossborough and strapped to Onslaught. She didn't feel safe letting the rabbit wander free, she said, and Mercutio had insisted his minion needed to exercise. Which didn't make much sense, since Onslaught was cradled in his arms like a baby right now. He was staring down at her, fiddling with a clasp, twisting and untwisting the strap in an effort to make her more comfortable. Ig couldn't believe how his life – his uncle's life, his granda's life, even Pietro's life before he was even created, had been affected by the actions of someone she knew so well. Someone she never thought could act so cruelly. She had to talk to him about it. She had to find out more. 'Merc,' she said, jogging a few paces to keep up with the von Ryans, 'I was wondering, could we talk about–'

'Nope,' Vivi muttered, shouldering herself in between Ig and Mercutio. 'Not happening.'

'But,' Ig said, caught off guard by the intervention, 'I just wanted to apologise for bringing up–'

'I said no, Ig.' Vivi looked into Ig's face, deadly serious. 'We're not talking about that anymore.'

Ig backed off; but the thought still worried in her head, now tinged with a nasty, poisonous strain of guilt. She thought she'd been doing so well, talking to people. But if being sociable was a class, she'd be bumped back down to Basic by the end of the day. Behind Vivi, Mercutio looked down at Ig's dorm-mate like she'd hung the moon for him. A soft, tender smile tugged at the corner of his mouth – a smile that vanished as Vivi whirled on him.

'Instead, we're gonna talk about you missing meals. Again.'

'Now, Vivi–'

'Don't 'Now, Vivi' me, Mister!' Vivi prodded Merc in the chest, and he reacted as if she'd stabbed him. 'I thought we were over this. I worked too hard last term to break that stupid habit…'

'Nothing I do is stupid, Vivi.'

Vivi glowered. 'You. Need. To. Eat. Put some fuel in that body!' It suddenly occurred to Ig that perhaps the early morning breakfast appointments weren't just for her benefit.

'I don't need sustenance to survive,' Mercutio sniffed. 'Only knowledge.'

The rest of the walk to the assembly hall – another place Ig had never been to, until now – was a loud, chaotic, four-way argument; with Ig inexplicably taking Merc's side that eating was a very easily forgettable task, while Pietro and Vivi demanded and bribed and cajoled; all to no avail, until Vivi produced an apple from her blazer pocket and shoved it into Merc's mouth mid-monologue. Pietro laughed so hard he nearly slipped down the staircase. Merc shot Ig a despairing look as he crunched his way through the apple's skin and Ig, wanting to earn back some Sociable Points, patted him on the back in commiseration. He flinched, but allowed it.

The assembly hall, as it turned out, was a huge, dark room, lit by the same ornate sconces that lined the dorm hallways. At the front, a proscenium arch rose up towards the ceiling, purple velvet curtains hanging at each side. The students were ushered in by teachers – Ig spied Ms. Schwab, fussily shushing the front row, while Mr. Throttler glowered a distracted, chattering group of lingerers into submission. Row upon row of high-backed, dining-room-style chairs spread out in front of her – Vivi pulled her to the right, making sure they could all sit together at the back. Ig settled herself, hands knotted in her lap. 'Does anyone know what this is about?' she asked. Worry skittered up her spine; what if this was how she was outed as a Lunalist spy? What if The Nyx was gathering all the oldest students together – as well as the scariest teachers and Ms. Schwab – to run her out the building? She didn't even have her communication device with her. How would she call for help? What if The Nyx used their Power to trap her in here forever, to endlessly run down corridors while the faculty and her classmates chased her down like a fox in a hunt?

'Breathe,' Vivi said, prying Ig's fingers away; apparently she'd been picking at her knuckles again, 'it's probably some sort of talk. The Nyx likes to get Villains in to tell us about getting started, how to organise your first crime, all that stuff.'

'But what if it is about…you know,' Ig asked, 'about me?' Vivi grinned, her teeth sharp and white.

'Then I'll give you a headstart.'

'Hahaha… haaaaaa. Funny.'

'Alright, Shackleton; settle down, please.' The Nyx was striding out onto stage, clapping their hands to get the attention of the chatterers. 'I know you've been knocked off schedule today, but I know that my most mature students can sit quietly and listen…' A murmur of scoffing and laughter rippled around the room. The Nyx rolled their eyes fondly and called for quiet again. 'Students. Please. Now, we've arranged for a very special guest to join us today to talk to you about joining an evil society once you leave Shackleton.' Every student around Ig started to talk excitedly, all at once – some louder than others – making her ears ring. Suddenly, with the embarrassment of pushing Merc too far and the fear of being found out, Ig was feeling a little overexposed. Everything was starting to hurt.

'Students!' The Nyx called, holding up their hand. 'Don't make me punish the whole year, please.' It was no use; the hubbub and raised voices continued, until Ig couldn't make out any words anymore. The Nyx sighed. 'Alright, then. You can't behave, so instead of listening to Mr. Mendez, we're going to have the sexual health talk. Again.'

There was a collective cry of horror.

'Okay. You asked for it. You're all at a very delicate biological stage, students. You're probably experiencing a lot of changes, such as hair growth, bodily odour and… shall I go on?'

The entire hall fell silent. Every single back was ramrod straight, every set of eyes trained on the floor. The Nyx smirked. 'That's what I thought. Let's try again. As one of the founding members of The Midnight Movement – hush! – Maximillian Mendez revolutionised how Villains were seen in the public eye. Along with Villains such as Infusion, The Dark Horse, and, for a brief spell,' they pretended to blush, causing the other teachers to laugh, 'a certain young upstart who decided they were better suited to teaching, The Midnight Movement were one of the first Villain societies in the UK, with the first use of that name being on BBC News in 1992. Mr. Mendez is here to talk to you all about how to apply to a society, the perks, and even how to set up your own. Mr. Mendez?'

A man with a grey, well-trimmed beard stepped out from behind the curtains to a robust round of applause. 'Thank you, thank you,' he said in a low, sonorous voice. 'Oh, you're far too kind. And don't let your headteacher fool you,' he said, waggling his finger at The Nyx, 'they were great. Just great. You're all very, very lucky to have them. So! A little about me.'

As he talked, Ig wondered idly if this information would be useful to The General. Surely knowing that Shackleton were actively recruiting students to work together to gain an advantage would be good to know? She wasn't sure anymore.

And besides; she could barely concentrate; there were too many people sitting so close to her, the odd whisper or giggle wrenching her attention away from what Maximillian Mendez was actually saying. Glancing down the line, she saw that Vivi, Pietro and Mercutio were hanging on his every word. Someone, somewhere, was popping chewing gum. It sounded gross. Mr. Mendez talked about the advantages super geniuses like him had when forming a society of their own; how being a planner with no real Powers besides his mind could be dangerous without some muscle to back it up. Ig wished she'd thought to bring her communication device. If apps could gather dust, the dictaphone function would be coated in it by now. Where had she put it? She hadn't seen it in a while; since she'd called The General. That was ages ago, now. Had she lost it? She couldn't have lost it, she needed it, what was the point in finding all this stupid stuff out if it wouldn't help her to–

'Okay; why don't we open it up to the floor?' Maximillian Mendez was saying. 'Anyone got any questions for an old man like me?'

Mercutio's hand shot up. Ig didn't hear what he asked. Mr. Mendez laughed and answered in a way that Ig assumed made sense, then moved on to someone in the front row. Pietro whispered something to his brother, and the pair laughed under their breath together. It felt like someone ran a knife over Ig's skin.

'Anyone else? Anyone... hang on.' Maximillian Mendez squinted into the crowd, then actually sat down on the edge of the stage. To Ig's horror, he made eye contact with her. 'Is that little Ignatia Heretical?'

Every student in the assembly room whipped around to stare at her.

'It is, isn't it? Viola's girl?'

Ig's ribs felt like they were in a vice.

'Oh, you probably don't remember me. Your mother and I are friends from years ago, before she met your...'

'Stop talking!' Ig wanted to scream. She could feel people whispering about her. She could feel the words 'Witch Queen,' 'of course she is' and 'looks just like her' slithering across her bare arms, over her shoulders. Vivi tried to take her hand, and she flinched. It was suddenly very hard to breathe.

'How is your mother?' Mendez continued, clearly unable to see – or unbothered by – her expression of absolute terror. Ig supposed bearing down on someone frozen in fear was par for the course for someone like him. You probably barely even noticed it, anymore. 'You know kids; I campaigned to get Viola Heretical to join The Midnight Movement, back in the day. But she said no – because you were on the way, Ignatia.'

Oh God.

'I know your father was adamant you were going to that Hero school in Newcastle–'

Oh God, oh God, oh God. A rumble of gossipy conversation flowed through the room. She was going to get caught. Ig could already see The Nyx looking her way; their brow furrowed.

'But I'm happy to see you followed the path of darkness after all.' Mendez smirked, all smug charisma, and a few of the girls and a handful of boys began to giggle. 'You look too much like your mother to go straight.'

She had to leave. She had to get out of there, right now. Ig pushed her chair backwards with an awful screech, stared for one awful, paralysing second at The Nyx, and bolted from the room. She could hear Vivi yelling her name as she shoved open the assembly room doors, her footsteps muffled on the carpet as she dashed up the main staircase. She had no idea where she was going – only that she wanted to get somewhere safe, somewhere where the teachers couldn't find her and drag her back into that awful room to listen to some stranger tell her how much like her mother she was. Because she wasn't anything like her. She was good. She was good! She was…

She wasn't good. She was a frightened little girl in disguise, blundering through life hurting people's feelings and lying and stealing and hoping against hope she could grow up to be just like her Daddy. Nothing like Viola Heretical, the wonder and the terror of the North. She could never be like her, never. She wouldn't let herself be like her.

Suddenly, Ig couldn't catch her breath. She stumbled into a hallway corner, sinking to the floor. Ig took in big, whooping gulps of air, shoulders tight and tense around her ears. Her vision was blurred with frustrated, angry tears. She wanted to be a force for good in the world, someone brave and quick and happy and confident, who made friends easily and never let idiots like Maximilian Mendez or Lily Volt get her down. Ig punched her legs, the dull ache spreading out over her thighs. Stupid. She was so stupid.

The panic was finally starting to subside, leaving only exhaustion and shame in its wake. She really hoped no-one was looking for her. Maybe, if she made it back to the dorm before assembly was over, she could have a shower and a glass of water before Vivi figured out where she was. It wouldn't make it all better, but she could be slightly more normal before she had to explain herself. Ig stood up, shook herself out, and walked back the way she came.

Weird. She could have sworn she ran straight along this corridor, collapsing right at the very end. But now, Ig realised there was a right-angle turn up ahead. She took it; only to find herself at the beginning of the block of classrooms where Mercutio and Pietro usually hung out during free periods; conducting their experiments and bickering with each other. She definitely hadn't come this way, so she turned back. And bumped right into a set of double doors. Ig reared back with a gasp, then shoved them open with a frustrated little growl. She found herself back in a hallway, lined with dorm rooms… on the ground floor. Ig spun, heart beginning to pound. She spotted the main entrance and dashed for it like she was being chased, hanging onto the banister as she ran up the staircase like it would stop her from falling to her death.

I knew I didn't belong here. The words came from inside her brain, yet Ig jumped as if they'd been hissed in her ear. Then, she kept running.

She reached the top, took the left that she knew – she knew, as well as she knew her own name – took her to the room she shared with Vivi…and opened the doors onto the Combat Class room. Ig stamped her feet and roared; her voice cracking and splintering as she screamed, kicking the huge double doors over and over until her legs hurt. Then, she sunk to the floor and sobbed; thick, wet, humiliating tears streaming down her face.

She was lost.

Chapter Twenty-Seven

Her hands ached. Ig looked down through the sludge of tears to see her hands were bruised up to the wrist. Numb to her own emotions, she turned them this way and that, looking at the mottled, blackish-purple stains with a detached, idle stare. She flexed her fingers, and she felt her pulse jumping in the veins along her arm. It was so strange. Mam said it was bad circulation, but it only ever happened when she was upset – or, at least, that was when she noticed it…

'This seat taken?'

A tall, gangly figure was towering over her. Ig couldn't remember how long she'd been here; only that she'd stopped crying a while back.

'What do you want?'

'Rude. I thought you'd get yourself lost,' Pietro said, sitting down on the floor beside Ig, 'so I came to find you. At least no-one else is around; always helpful when you need a good cry.'

'I'm not crying,' Ig began, before pausing to blow her nose loudly and snottily on her tie, which she'd wrenched from around her neck ages ago.

Pietro wrinkled his nose. 'It's a bold choice for customisation, Heretical, but at least you'll stand out.'

'Shut up, Pietro.'

'You sound like Merc. Next, you'll be raiding hives for bee larvae and strapping re-purposed thimbles to their arses.' Pietro looked for a laugh from Ig, but didn't get one. 'So,' he drawled, 'wanna talk about it?'

'No.'

'Okay.' Pietro shuffled next to her until their shoulders bumped. 'Then we'll sit here in silence 'til you feel better.' Which they did. For ages. Ig had never known Pietro to keep his mouth shut for so long. He took a pen from his pocket and began to twirl it around his fingers. When he got bored of that, he started to rapidly click the top up and down, making a satisfying taktaktaktak noise. Ig looked up, and Pietro glanced at her out the corner of his eye. 'Want to try?' He said, holding the pen out to her. 'Sometimes it helps if you've got something to do with your hands while you talk.'

Ig took the pen. It was the type they sold by the till in Fox; a cheap, plastic ballpoint. She still didn't want to talk. She'd been so scared that her cover was about to be blown – that The Nyx might start to think a little harder about exactly why a 'former' Hero would suddenly be transferred to Shackleton. But even worse than that would be if Maximilian Mendez had outed her just to compare her to her mam.

Too useless to be a Hero. Too cowardly to be a Villain. Ig was nowhere. Nothing. No-one.

'You know,' Pietro says, 'I know what it's like to feel overshadowed by someone.'

'I don't feel overshadowed by my mam,' Ig snapped. Pietro blew a dismissive raspberry at her.

'I know that, Heretical; we're talking about my problems right now, don't be so egocentric.' Ig sulked and went back to her pen. 'I think,' Pietro continued, 'that sometimes people think that because I came from Merc, that I must be just like him. Then, when they find out I'm not, they gloss over me. They all focus on the Great and Powerful Mercutio von Ryan, and they don't see me in the wings, holding the bags.' Pietro blew a stray lock of hair out of his eyes. 'And, I mean; maybe they're right to. I don't even know if I'm going to get a Power.'

'But Mercutio said–'

'Merc says a lot of things. I'm an anomaly. Uncle Rayner

never made a Villain clone before me, so we don't know.'

'But if you think Mercutio is holding you back,' Ig asked, looking up, 'why do you stay? Didn't he say you could go home and live with your uncle anytime you wanted?'

Pietro groaned. 'Because I love my brother. Because I want to be with him. No-one seems to get that! I'm never, ever as happy as I am when I can watch him Mercutio all over the place, being the smartest idiot in the room and making things interesting.' Pietro sighed. 'He's like a shooting star, and I'm, like, a moon or something, you know? I don't want to be away from the light someone like Merc gives off. But I want to… be able to bask in it with him sometimes. And I don't know if I can.'

Ig said nothing; she was too busy thinking. She had a shooting star in her life, too – maybe more than one, if she was honest. She didn't know if she wanted to talk about that yet, though. So instead, she said; 'at least you're not totally in love with your best friend.'

'Careful,' Pietro said – though Ig could hear a laugh hidden somewhere in his voice, 'I'm allowed to take the piss out of Merc. You're not.'

'I'm not taking the piss!'

'It really sounds like you're taking the piss…'

'No I'm not! I'm sympathising! It's awful, I should know!'

The words were past her lips before Ig had realised she'd spoken. She clapped her hand to her mouth with a wince. Pisces' face flashed before her eyes; all soft red hair, big eyes and clear skin. Oh, she hadn't thought about Pisces in a while. It hurt; like when you forget you sprained your ankle and put all your weight on it suddenly.

Pietro tipped his head towards her. 'The person from the old place?' he said, voice suddenly soft and serious. Ig nodded. All the aching, longing feelings she had for Pisces came flooding back in one awful, painful wave.

'She's going to be amazing,' she said, the sound muffled by

her hand. 'She's already amazing. When we leave school, she'll be famous. And I'm just funny little Iggie, tagging along and… and holding the bags.' She swallowed hard. 'I don't even think she's asked how I am since I left.'

Pietro heaved out a sigh. 'That sounds shit, Ig. I know I can't help much with the serious feelings parts of romantic stuff – you sure I can't interest you in a scheme instead? Some there's-only-one-bed shenanigans?' Ig laughed despite herself. 'But still. That sounds really… shit.'

'I miss her so much.'

'I know.'

'Any more weirdly appropriate stories to make me feel better in your repertoire?'

'Only if you want to hear about the time Onslaught bit me because I brushed her for half a second too long,' Pietro laughed. 'I felt so rejected. She's all sweetness and light with Merc and you guys. I still have the scars.'

'We don't smell like a weird version of her master.'

'Look who's talking about weird. But yeah; I don't do proper romance advice, you know that. Though I did hear on the grapevine that Katalina Kanaan is nursing a bit of a crush…'

'On who?' Ig asked, in total sincerity. Pietro blinked at her, and Ig blinked back. Faces were hard to read. She felt like she was missing something.

'No-one,' Pietro said, after a long moment. 'Come on; Vivi'll be having palpitations if she can't find you.'

Chapter Twenty-Eight

As they walked back towards the dorms, Ig inspected her hands. The purpleish-black mottling was fading; only really surrounding the raised skin of her knuckles now. She remembered how the pain had run along under her skin like a heartbeat – it might have been the tears blurring her vision, but she was almost certain she'd seen her veins visibly begin to pulse…

'Um, hey,' Pietro said softly. 'I might be overstepping here, but Merc'll forgive you. For the Uncle Rayner stuff.'

'Really?' Ig cringed. 'How can you be so sure?'

Pietro laughed, rolling his shoulders back. 'Because if anyone knows what it's like to accidentally hurt someone's feelings, it's Merc von Ryan. Just don't bring it up again, even to apologise – he'll think you want to rake it all up again, cause drama for no reason. And don't bring it up around Viv, or she'll–' he mimed slitting his throat with an ugly, retching noise in the back of his throat. 'Rayner's practically her uncle, too. Her mums have this forge thing not too far from our castle – her mami makes the coolest weapons – and we all grew up in this weird little evil neighbourhood   situation. Uncle Rayner made us call them Auntie Cath and Auntie Isa, and I swear I thought Vivi was my actual cousin for the first six weeks after I was… after I was born.'

He trailed off.

The hallway was quiet; most of the students were still in their first class of the day, while the older students were apparently still listening to the presentation in the assembly room. The hallways had their own particular scent; like just-blown-out candles. The breakfast rooms smelled like pancakes and orange juice. The classrooms often stank like smoke or chemicals, and of course the dorm room was full of the scent of flowers and fresh dirt. Ig had been here so long, she'd forgotten to notice. It all seemed to absorb itself into the background of her daily life; like the chatter of students and the pounding of feet on carpet and the voices of the teachers–

'Miss Heretical?'

'Oh gawd,' Pietro drawled. 'We've been caught.'

'There you are,' said The Nyx, practically jogging down the hallway in their expensive shoes. 'I thought you'd keep running until you hit the village. Thank you for finding her, Pietro; you can head back to the assembly, now.'

'But Professor Nyx–' Pietro protested.

'You,' The Nyx said, their voice taking on a steely tone, 'can go back to assembly, now. Thank you.'

'Can I also go back to assembly?' Ig asked, watching Pietro skulk away; probably to veer off as soon as their headteacher wasn't looking and find somewhere quiet to read his book. As awful as Maximilian Mendez was, it was better than whatever was about to come with The Nyx. And at least her friends would be there.

'No,' The Nyx said, a hint of laughter in their voice.

'Oh. Okay.'

The Nyx led Ig along the hallway until a set of double doors opened up onto the main entrance. From there, she was ushered into The Nyx's office and told, in a tone that brokered no argument, to take a seat. The Nyx sat across from her at their ornate wooden desk, steepled their fingers together, and looked hard at Ig.

'Do you want to tell me what that was about?' they said gently, smoothing down the blazer of their suit.

Ig looked at the floor, embarrassed. 'Does it matter?' she heard herself say. Insubordination, she thought. You would have never talked to a teacher like that at the Academy.

But then again, a teacher at the Academy wouldn't ask what

was wrong in the first place.

Ig forced herself to look up at The Nyx, who cocked an eyebrow at her. 'It matters,' they said, 'because you are my student, and you've clearly been crying. You might be a Villain now, Miss Heretical, but you're still fifteen. I'm allowed to worry.'

'I'm okay,' said Ig, as easily as breathing. 'It's fine.'

'No, it's not.' The Nyx sighed. 'I apologise if Mr. Mendez's visit… caught you off guard. For all the choices you and your mother have made, I still should have accounted for your father being a Hero. It must have been awkward, hearing someone badmouth your parent like that.'

'It's not—' Ig began, before The Nyx held up their hand for silence.

'Miss Heretical. I wanted to tell you that I've been chatting with your tutors, and everyone seems to agree you're fitting in really nicely here.' The eyebrow quirked again. 'Mr. Throttler and Mr. Glasse in particular were singing your praises. 'Ruthless,' was the word they both used.'

'Oh,' Ig said quietly.

The Nyx's expression grew soft. 'Your mother was ruthless, too,' they said. 'She always was, even when we were in school. She was so beautiful, so popular – but she couldn't stand bullies, even when they picked on a scrawny young child with a bad haircut who floated somewhere between being a boy and a girl.' They winked, conspiratorially. 'Ask her about the time she set up a booby trap to catch Peregrine Reeve sometime. It's a great story. Even Villains have a moral code, Miss Heretical. It's not a traditional one, but it is there.'

Ig felt herself wilt.

'I sense,' said The Nyx wryly, 'that wasn't as much of a comfort as I imagined it'd be.'

'I'm just tired, Professor Nyx.' It was only half a lie. 'I'll go get some sleep in my free period and be fine for my next lesson.'

'If you're sure.' The Nyx stood to let them out, the door creaking as they opened it. 'Oh; one more thing before you go.'

Ig looked up into their face. The Nyx sighed, running their hand over the rasp of their stubble in contemplation. 'I should be better at this by now,' they muttered to themselves. 'I might not know your father, Miss Heretical, but I've seen footage of him thwarting some of my old schoolmates; including your mother, back in the day. He's flashy. He plays to the crowd. Always smiling and waving. He's a showman; that's probably why he connected so well with your mother. As ruthless as she was, she loves to put on a show, doesn't she?'

They had that right. A hundred different images of Viola Heretical flickered in front of her mind's eye; telling tales for her remaining devotees over a glass of wine, practicing her cackle in the mirror, and even bringing down feathered damnation on someone for parking in front of their house – that one happened often. Ig laughed, rolling her eyes fondly.

'You have a little of that in you, I think,' said The Nyx, tilting their head to the side to appraise Ig properly. 'Mr. Glasse was telling me about the pollen incident in Combat Class. But both your mother and your father rush into battles with all guns blazing, metaphorically speaking. They use their Powers first and assess the situation later. But you?' The Nyx waggled a long, manicured finger in Ig's direction. 'I think you're smarter than both of them put together, I really do. You have the flash, certainly – you couldn't keep the company you do and not pick up a few things. But it comes from a place of planning and strategy.'

'It does?' Ig asked. It was so strange to hear someone talking about her like this. Like she was more than an obstacle to be overcome, or a mistake to be corrected.

'I think so,' said The Nyx. 'Perhaps stop trying to be like them, and start thinking about the kind of Villain you are.' A warm, glowing feeling spread through Ig's chest. 'Thank you,' she managed to choke out.

'Any time, Miss Heretical.' The Nyx ushered Ig out of the room – into the hallway that her dorm was on, still quiet and peaceful and smelling of smoke. 'But please, do me a favour? Don't tell your mother I said she wasn't smart.' They winced. 'I'm under no illusions. That woman could hunt me down and have her birds peck out my liver at any point.'

'I promise,' Ig said with a grin.

'Good lass. Pietro,' The Nyx called, 'you can put your book down and collect your friend now.'

'Aw, what?!' came a shout from behind a gigantic earthenware pot of sea holly. 'How did you know I was here?'

'I know everything. And you've got solitary confinement for your next free period because you disobeyed me.'

'What?! That's absolute bull–'

'Want to spend your whole weekend there, Pietro?'

'…no.'

'Then see Miss Heretical to her room and get to your next class. Mr. von Ryan will be wondering where you are.'

As they walked the hallway together – Pietro grumbling as he headed off to solitary about how you shouldn't get in trouble for reading. It was basically homework you chose to do – Ig kept that warm feeling as close to her heart as she could.

She could be like both of her parents, and still be like neither of them.

There were teachers here who talked about her when she wasn't around – who remembered her name not because of who her parents were, but for what she'd done in their classrooms. They boasted about her.

The Nyx thought she was smart.

She – Ignatia Heretical – had convinced someone she was smart.

Chapter Twenty-Nine

'Explain to me again,' Viola Heretical said, through gritted teeth and the living room door, 'why I can't talk to my daughter?'

'Mam,' Ig said, raising her voice as much as she dared (she'd somehow managed to evade attention while sitting on her rooftop, and she wanted to keep it that way) 'you know why.'

'Yeah, baby,' her dad said, leaning back in his chair, 'it's all School Business. We're not talking about anything interesting, promise.'

'If it's not interesting, let me in.'

'Mam…'

'Fine. Fine. You're coming home for the holidays, though? We can talk freely then, can't we? Or does The General have something to say about that, too?

Ig hadn't given a lot of thought to the end of term break. When she first arrived here, she was so sure that she'd be returning home victorious; The General smiling over her, Pisces leaning on her arm, the entire Hero community singing her praises for helping to stop whatever infiltration those awful Shackleton students were planning. But she'd discovered nothing more than what she'd told The General during that first ill-fated, rushed call home. That being;

1. The students were weird,

2. The school was weird, and

3. No one had mentioned the slightest hint of a whisper of an idea about invading Lunalist. Not even gossip in the hallways between classes. And Ig had been listening – in between laughing with Vivi about how ridiculous Falcon Reeve was

being this week, or chatting with Pietro about whatever was on his mind that day, or listening to Mercutio monologue about how translating his bees' communicative dancing to indicate the direction of nearby flowers was key to getting them to listen to his commands through mimicking their footsteps with radio wave signalling… or something. But nothing had come up. And, if she was being honest about it, she was starting to think that it never would. And so – instead of calling The General and making a fool of herself – she decided that, this time, she'd call her father first.

'Oof. Your mother, Ig.' Luca Peterson stretched, and Ig heard the pop in his shoulder through the screen. 'She is not happy about all this. Last time you called? I was in the doghouse for, like, a week.'

'Is she that mad at me?' Ig winced.

'What? Oh, honey, no,' her dad soothed. 'She's mad at the school, not you. She doesn't get it. At her school, they let their students run wild; calling home whenever they want. When I was your age – maybe a year younger? – I went on this long hike up into Kielder Forest. No cellphones back then, didn't talk to my parents at all – they didn't even know where I was! And I turned out fine. Your mom'll calm down when you're home and she sees you're in one piece.'

Ig nodded, unsure. Her dad had said 'her school' as if he'd forgotten she was, technically, a Shackleton student now. 'Um, speaking of your school days, Dad…'

She watched as he leaned forward in his seat, eager to talk about The Good Old Days.

'Did you ever meet, um, Rayner von Ryan?'

Her dads's face twisted in confusion and distaste. 'Rayner von Ryan? Why'd you wanna know about him?'

'Oh, nothing,' Ig said quickly. 'It's just, um, that I met his nephews, and–'

'Nephews? Hey – now hey, they're not being funny with you,

are they?'

'Funny?'

'Honey, you know that if anyone tries to do anything with your body that you don't want them to do, you can say no, okay?'

'Oh my god, Dad!' Ig cried, horrified. The thought of either Mercutio or Pietro trying to seduce her made her want to gargle bleach. 'That's disgusting!'

'What?' Her dad looked blank for a second, then clapped his hands over his face. 'No! Oh God, no, I didn't mean like that – but if they are, you need to talk to someone about it–'

'DAD!'

'Okay, okay! What I meant was – okay. Rayner von Ryan… he did some weird stuff back in the day. Like, cloning stuff.' Ig sighed impatiently. Obviously. She knew that. 'He had this whole army at one point – and they said he took random samples from tons of people to do it. Non-Powered people. He wanted to see if he could turn them into, I dunno, super soldiers or something, through whatever goop he made them in, but it didn't work. They were still super powerful, though. A mix of so many people, blended into one and then cloned five hundred times. You couldn't defeat them easy, 'coz he'd bred all their imperfections out. Beat us once, then it took a helluva lot more of us to finally take him down for good.'

'Including Auntie Memoria?' Ig asked. 'Someone brought her name up, and I didn't know about that fight.'

She hadn't been able to get it out of her head since. She didn't know what Mercutio and Pietro's uncle looked like; so in her dreams, her lovely, kind, funny family friend – the one with all the good stories and the loudest laugh – had wiped away the mind of a boy that looked just like the ones she ate breakfast with every morning. Same curly dark hair, same bright eyes, same manic intelligence and wit and bravado. All gone. Vanished, in one wave of Memoria's hand. She needed her dad to tell her it was hard on Auntie Memoria; that she never quite got over taking away someone's entire mind, that she knew it needed to be done, but she wished there had been another way. She needed regret.

Her dad's mouth quirked up at the side. 'One of her best moments. We all knew that kid was going places, after that.'

The horror that washed over Ig felt like a bucket of cold water had been dropped over her shoulders. 'Did she…' Ig swallowed and tried again. 'Someone – the teacher – said Rayner forgot about his nephew – his dad–'

'Your Auntie was a special case,' her dad beamed; eyes misty as he recalled his youth. 'Top of her class – never missed a day, friends with everyone. Captain of the debate team, and the Chess Club, and… oh gosh, a million other things. Of course she got a mind controlling Power, being so smart an' all. But when she got it so early – fifteen I think? – and then got such a high-profile mission right out of the gate?! I was so jealous of her, you have no idea. But we knew that von Ryan was only gonna go down if we could disable his army. And I always remember; The General – well, she wasn't The General then, she was another student, but she had potential, y'know? – she said that to take out a hive, you gotta go after the king.'

'Bees don't have kings,' Ig said softly. Her right hand found the loose, dry skin of her left knuckle and began to tug and twist. 'Wait; did you say Auntie Mem got her Power revealed early?'

Her dad laughed fondly. 'If anyone was gonna, it would be her. They knew she had potential, kid! It isn't like that with everyone.'

'That must be really hard on the people who know when they're younger,' said the spectre of Vivi Section that lived inside Ig's head. 'Like me.'

'Tell you what; when you get home, we'll have Auntie Mem over for dinner, and she can tell you all about it. How's that sound?'

'Great, Dad.' Ig suddenly felt very, very tired. 'I have a class soon, so I'm going to go. I need to get ready.'

'Pffft,' her dad scoffed, 'what're they teaching you today?

Kicking Puppies 101?'

'It's Torture Management, actually,' Ig said sharply, before realising that didn't sound much better. Her dad flinched, and Ig instantly felt guilty. It was so easy to hurt his feelings. Luca Peterson was a little like Pisces – everywhere he went, he assumed that everyone was absolutely delighted to see him, and wanted nothing more than to make him happy. Because, usually, it was true. He was a Hero; he'd done amazing things, saved so many people's lives. When she was small, Ig was so used to people coming up to shake her dad by the hand. She thought it was just how people walked through the world. Until she grew up and realised no-one ever reached for her mother's hand.

Her dad was a great man. He, Ig realised in that moment, was also oblivious, thoughtless, and careless. Rayner von Ryan was, from everything she'd heard, an awful person. But Pietro and Mercutio deserved to grow up with an uncle who could remember their names. Ig apologised, and made a joke so she could hang up, knowing that her dad was smiling, all the way back in Gosforth. Then, she tucked the communication device into her bag, and climbed back down the stairs. She walked with her head down, backpack hugged tightly against her chest, following the paths that her feet knew would lead her to Torture Management. Everything her dad had said to her was swilling and turning over in her head – though something was nagging at her. Something about what he'd said wasn't quite right; at least, not right with the way Ig knew things worked now. She just needed to work through her frustration with her dad, her second-hand guilt about Memoria and Rayner, the pain in her hand from where she'd been pulling at her skin – it looked like she was going to bruise…

'Oh, Ig – Ig, hi!' Ig's head snapped up. Standing in front of her was Katalina Kanaan; the tall, gorgeous girl from her Monologue class. Her bag was propped up against the dragon fountain, and a sketchpad was lying on the lip. 'Hi!' Katalina said again, pulling her shiny black hair over her shoulder. 'You nearly walked into me, there.'

'Did I?' Ig asked. 'I wasn't paying attention, sorry.'

'No, it's okay.' Katalina laughed awkwardly. 'I wasn't concentrating, either.'

'You weren't?'

'No.'

Ig felt like this conversation wasn't going anywhere. Which was a shame, because Katalina was usually so smart. And kind. And talented. And she had the cutest nose; a little squashed, like a pug's.

'I'm sort of glad I saw you, actually.' Katalina looked away shyly. 'Do you want to see something cool?'

'Um.' Ig shouldered her backpack. 'I have to get to Torture Management.'

'It'll only take a second. Mia and Veronica are in their classes right now – they're the girls I usually… anyway. Look at what I can do!' Katalina did a high-kick, her foot reaching almost over her head – which would have impressed Ig in itself, but as her foot struck the floor again, a shower of orange flames shot from her heel, flickering and spitting against the stone of the fountain.

'Oh my god!' Ig cried. 'You got your Power?'

'I did!' Katalina squealed, jumping in a circle. As she did, tiny, candle-like flames danced around her. Ig watched them sputter and fade away on the bare concrete of the courtyard. Then Katalina caught herself and laughed, embarrassed. Ig had to admit; the silly, excitable girl in front of her was very different from the purring, skulking Villain-to-be she'd seen for the first time in Monologue Class. Both were nice. Really nice. But still. Different.

'It's silly to be so excited, I know. But I never thought I'd get fire Powers.'

'No,' Ig said, her eyes on the flames, 'neither did… neither did I.'

'I'll have to go tell The Nyx,' Katalina said, bouncing one foot up and down to make flames spurt out from under the sole of her foot.

'So they can get your Ceremony ready?'

'Ceremony?' Katalina tilted her head to the side, nose crinkling in confusion. It was very cute. 'What Ceremony? I mean, my mum and dad might take me for a fancy meal or something when I get home. Is that what you meant?'

Why was she so calm about getting her Power? Obviously Vivi was because it was so long ago – but back home, students usually didn't reveal their Powers until their Revelation Ceremony – in front of the whole school, all the parents, the press…

'I just meant The Nyx needs to disable my Power Lender; it won't work now, they can get it ready for someone new next year. I know the flames are little,' Katalina was saying, 'but I'll get better at it. I'm actually glad they're small right now – I don't want to set fire to my room or anything! You'd have to come rescue me or something, haha.'

Ig wasn't listening. She was staring into space, watching an ember licking at the shoelace of Katalina's boot.

Katalina didn't know what Power she would get.

But her dad said they all knew Auntie Memoria would get a mind control Power. How could they know that before she got it?

Plus, Ig knew that Shackleton students got their Powers at random times; not just at sixteen. Why was a Hero getting their Power early such a big deal, then?

'Do you, er, want to sit down?' Katalina asked, hiding behind her curtain of hair. 'It'd be nice to have someone to talk to, so I don't keep fussing with my Power.'

'I can't,' Ig said. 'I have Torture Management.' What she really needed was to be somewhere where she could concentrate, and write down her thoughts in peace. And sitting on the edge of a fountain with Katalina Kanaan wasn't her first choice. She always felt strangely nervous when she was with her.

'Oh. Okay.' Katalina seemed disappointed.

'I hope your friends are free soon?' Ig offered, already moving to leave.

'Yeah, but–'

'Okay, I'll see you in Monologue on Monday, bye!'

The thoughts in Ig's head were swirling even harder; a mess of colours and thoughts and voices, all vying for her attention. She jogged through the hallways – always focusing on where she needed to go, trying hard not to let her thoughts wander – got to her classroom early, much to Mr. Throttler's surprise, threw open her notebook and snatched up a pen. Something about how Lunalist and Shackleton dealt with Powers was very, very different from each other. And she needed to work it out, before her brain exploded.

Chapter Thirty

'You're stalling.'

'What do you want?' Ig whispered; looking up from the worksheet she'd been staring at blankly for ten minutes and starting as she found herself nose to nose with Mercutio von Ryan. What was it with these brothers and personal space?! 'I'm trying to work, Mercutio.'

'Ah yes; incredibly hard, it seems. Industriousness, thy name is Heretical.'

Ig huffed. He was right. She was supposed to be working on a filtration system for the sharks in her hypothetical lair; one that wouldn't get all clogged up with bits of Hero. But her brain wouldn't make it happen. The only thing she'd written so far was the word 'the.'

Mercutio tapped her worksheet. 'You can't use Great Whites. They die in captivity. No-one knows why.'

'Yes, I can.' Ig snatched her paper from under Mercutio's hand. 'Villains use them all the time.'

'A common misconception.' Mercutio held up one finger, looking smug. Ig hated when Mercutio looked smug. 'They use tiger sharks. Or crocodiles, but that has a whole other set of problems. Heat lamps, basking areas, combating calcium deficiency…'

'Eyes on your own work, Mr. von Ryan,' drawled their teacher, a young man with a snake tattoo winding around one arm. Mercutio turned back to his own paper… for about two minutes.

'So what were you doing,' he asked, as Ig winced with irritation, 'if you weren't stalling?'

'I was thinking.'

'About?'

'About if Pietro would miss you if I fed you to a Great White Shark.'

'He would. Pietro loves me.'

'Leave me alone,' Ig hissed.

'Work hard, Miss Heretical,' their teacher said, patting her on the shoulder as he passed, 'and you'll figure it out. I know you can make really innovative enclosures; I still brag about your sun bear cave/jungle lair project in the staff room, it was inspired.'

'Thank you, sir,' Ig said, blinking up at him with more emotion than she expected. 'That... means a lot.'

'Nyeh nyeh nyeh. Nyeh nyeh nyeh nyeh,' Mercutio grumbled, finally turning back to his own paper in a huff. Everyone knew animals were his thing. Ig was too distracted to pay him much mind, though. Ever since her last conversation with The General, she had been spinning her wheels; her brain picking and poring over the way her dad had talked about her Auntie Memoria being 'a special case' and 'having potential', and that being the reason she had her Power revealed to her early. But Vivi had been a whole year younger, and apparently it wasn't a big deal. Katalina was excited to get her Power, but was surprised that Ig expected her to have a big ceremony and a fuss made of her for it.

I wanted to make a fuss of her. Wait, what? Concentrate, Ig.

Maybe Heroes needed that order and structure for their Power to manifest? Or maybe Heroes and Villains were genetically different? That one didn't make the most sense; Ig couldn't be the only child of a Hero and a Villain ever, even if she was the only one to have switched sides...

Ig froze; her pen poised above her page, right beside that lonely 'the.' Her insides turned to ice.

She'd switched sides. Well, obviously she had; the paperwork had been filed months ago. What she meant was, internally, she'd switched sides.

She didn't think of herself as a Lunalist student anymore.

In Ig's mind, her school was Shackleton School for Villains. It felt like looking over the edge into a deep, dark ravine; like being stripped of all her armour, all her masks and disguises and being seen for the very first time. It almost hurt. But it was so, so much better than anything that had happened at Lunalist.

I don't want to go back. The thought was so clear; like someone had whispered it right into her ear. But Ig knew that it was how she felt, deep down in her heart. She didn't want to go back to Lunalist. She didn't want to report back to The General about her schoolmates, about her teachers – about her friends. She wanted to keep getting good grades on her Torture Management assignments, and get better at Minion Husbandry (maybe even finish this stupid worksheet), and ask Pietro for help on her homework and go into the village with Vivi again and maybe, maybe get Mercutio to laugh at one of her jokes and… and she wanted to graduate with them.

It wasn't a happy thought. It felt like giving in. She's failed her mission. More than that; she'd failed at being a Hero. Did staying here make her a Villain? The thought felt like licking a battery; painful in a strange, poisonous way. Maybe she could be an assistant, like Pietro. Yeah! She could look after Vivi's plants. That would be fine. Wouldn't it?

It wasn't like she was ever going to get a Power, anyway.

Suddenly, the bell rang. Ig leapt out of her skin, shoving all her papers and pens into her satchel in one swift movement. She needed air.

'You fancy a walk down into town, Ig?' Vivi asked, as Ig swung her satchel onto her shoulder and made for the door. 'I've got a craving for that cheesy bread, and the new guy at the bakery has the smallest attention span ever. I bet I can snatch one right off the cooling rack–'

'No no, I'm fine,' Ig said distractedly. Vivi narrowed her eyes.

'You sure?'

'Yep!' Ig forced so much breezy positivity into her voice it cracked. 'Have fun without me.'

'If you're sure…' Vivi made to turn away, and Ig pulled her back, and idea sparking in her head.

'Oh, but…if you're going to Fox, would you pick me up a book on…' she floundered for the right word. 'On… flower… stuff?'

If Vivi's eyes narrowed anymore, they'd be shut. "Flower stuff?".

'Yeah! Like, um, you know.' Ig rolled her hands over one another, searching for the point. 'How to grow things. Look after plants, stop them dying. Composting. I thought it might be, you know, useful.'

Ten years from now, when I'm living in the bio-dome that was once the North East, misting your Widowswort and wishing my dad would call me sometime, it might be useful to know about fertiliser, I guess.

'Why do you want to know that?' Vivi asked. 'If you want something grown, you can just ask me. And it's not like it's your best subject, right?'

Ig cringed. 'Um. Yes. I suppose you're right.'

'You,' Vivi sighed wryly, 'are very strange, Ignatia Heretical.' She tapped Ig on the nose. 'Boop. See you later.'

'I… yeah. I know. Bye.' Deflated, Ig watched Vivi go; grabbing the boys as she left, laughing and joking as they all vanished into the throng of students in the hallway. Something cracked open inside Ig, and a lonely, defeated feeling flowed out.

What if she doesn't want me? she thought. I'm supposed to be her nemesis. But I can't even do that. What if she'd rather have an enemy than a hanger-on?

The voice in her head took on a nasty, gleeful tone.

Pisces didn't want a hanger-on, did she? She abandoned you as soon as you were out of her sight. Who's to say Vivi isn't exactly the same? After all – you made a pretty terrible Hero. Why would you make a good assistant? You're the same person you've always been. You surround yourself with amazing people – your parents, Pisces, Vivi, Mercutio – and then get upset when they all run rings around you. You can't even keep a plant alive, and Vivi's making up brand new species in her spare time.

Ig pushed her way through a sea of people, walking the path to her dorm as if in a daze. One stupid Minion Husbandry lesson where she wasn't totally concentrating on a task, and everything had changed. She wasn't going back to Lunalist – and not only that, she felt relieved about it – and the only other option open to her was already cut off at the knees because of, well, her whole situation.

She unlocked the dorm room door and flopped into her bed like a tonne weight. How was she going to tell her dad she wasn't going back? That would open up a whole can of worms at home. He was going to be so…confused. And to top it all off, she didn't even have a plan for what she would do instead. The best she had was trailing around after someone far more accomplished than she was. Again. Inevitably, that was what she always seemed to end up doing.

Ig's gaze drifted to the blue, thorny plant, sitting in its earthenware pot by the open door to the bathroom. Weird, spiky thing. Then, her eyelids were suddenly heavy, and Ig was falling into a deep, sad, dreamless sleep.

Chapter Thirty-One

'Ig… Ig…'

Ig flung one arm over her eyes, turning away from the voice that hovered over her head. Stupid dreams. She needed to get a good night's sleep, and she couldn't do that with the sound of boys chattering on in her head.

Hang on. Boys? That wasn't like her.

'Ignaaaaatia…waake uuup…'

Ig opened her eyes slowly; inches away from her, his nose practically touching hers, was Pietro von Ryan. Ig yelped; hitting her head on the headboard of her bed. 'Ow.' Ig glanced at Vivi's clock. Half past midnight. She rubbed the emerging bump on her temple, glowering at Pietro who sat at the bottom of her bed, head tilted, watching her like a cat. 'Whatcha dreaming about?' he asked, all sweetness and light.

'I was having a nightmare about calling Mr. Throttler 'Dad' in front of the whole school,' Ig growled, pulling the bedsheets up around her chest. 'Which was preferable to what's actually happening, I think.'

'Oh, who hasn't called that old sweetheart 'Dad' before? He gets a little teary when you do, actually – the old softie.' Pietro beamed, picking Finnie out of Ig's bed and giving him a squeeze. 'But we haven't got time to analyse that particular psychosocial nugget right now. We're having a raid.'

'A raid?' A chill ran through Ig's blood. Was this it? Her first Villainous act? She'd only decided she wanted to stay a few hours ago – she noticed it was dark outside now – and she hadn't prepared. What if this had been the plan all along? Entice her with friendship, and then as soon as she was fully converted, Vivi and Pietro and Mercutio showed their true colours and attacked the Academy? What would she say to The General? To Pisces? 'What do you mean?' she asked.

'Well,' Pietro said, pouting as Ig snatched her cuddly toy shark back, 'What I technically mean is Viv and Merc decided to have a raid, and they wanted me to wake you up so you could be involved. Shackleton traditions and all that. But I assume what you mean is; 'what is a raid'?'

Ig nodded.

'So; Uncle Rayner found a secret passageway into the shop dungeon back in the old days. It's, like, full of spiders, but no-one else seems to know it's there.'

Ig thought about her rooftop; how many tiny nooks and crannies were there at Shackleton that were out of The Nyx's control?

'The plan is,' Pietro continued, 'we all trot down to the dungeons, take anything we can carry, bring it all back to the dorms and eat so much sugar we crash in our first lesson tomorrow. It's practically a family tradition.'

Ig felt a weight lift from her chest; at least it wasn't something too bombastic. But then again, it was a social event. 'I think,' she said, kicking the gangly intruder off the bed, 'I'll pass on this one, Pietro.' At least if she got a full nights' sleep, she could listen to all of Vivi's stories in the morning without dropping off.

Pietro's face crumpled. 'Aw, no – come on Ig, it'll be fun.'

'It's okay,' Ig said, her chest already filling up with fluttery, spiky nerves. 'I don't want to spoil the fun.' In truth, she was feeling tired and overly sensitive and wasn't entirely convinced that she was wanted. She never had been before, after all. 'Really,' she said, hugging Finnie to her chest, 'it's okay.'

Pietro pouted. Ig stood her ground. 'Fine,' Pietro sighed, holding up his hands. 'But I want you to know we noticed how down you were today. Well, me and Vivi noticed. No deeper meaning, no ulterior motive, just being nice.'

'You're Villains.' Ig aimed a gentle kick at Pietro's hip. 'You're not nice. Now get out of my room.'

'Fine, fine, I'm going. But it's on your head, Heretical.' Pietro wagged a finger at her reproachfully before closing the door behind him. Ig sighed, falling back on her bed and staring up at the wooden slats above her head. What was she doing here? It was bad enough she had basically failed at her mission – she'd fobbed off The General, of all people – she'd done it for… what? A group of Villains. A group of bloodthirsty, backstabbing, vicious and malicious Villains, who would turn on her in the space of a breath and… and… and who probably didn't really like her, anyway. Who would like someone as middle-of-the-road as her? Ig couldn't get Heroes – the best examples of humanity in the whole world – to like her, so what chance did she have with this lot?

Something tapped at her window. Ig ignored it, curling tighter around herself and squeezing her eyes shut. She needed to sleep. She was asleep. She was calm and relaxed and deeply, deeply asleep–

The tapping got louder. Ig tore back her blanket and lunged towards the window, ready to shoo away whatever bat or bird or monster was trying to force its way in. 'Go away–!'

Vivi was leaning on the pane of glass. 'Hello!'

'What are you doing?' Ig hissed, as Vivi opened the window and clambered into the room. 'I thought you were having a raid, or something.'

'We are!' Vivi said, pulling her satchel – which looked as if the straps were about to burst – off her shoulder. 'You didn't come to the raid, so we're bringing the raid to you.'

'How did you even get up here?' Ig looked out the window to see a long, wooden ladder leaning against the side of the building. Clambering up it – one grinning and waving, the other clinging to the ladder and scowling – were Pietro and

Mercutio. 'Ah. Okay.'

'We stole a ladder!'

'Yes, Vivi. I can see that.'

'Why,' grumbled Mercutio, as he slid into the room, kicked the ladder away from the window and watched it fall soundlessly onto the grassy lawn, 'did we have to use a ladder for our entrance? It's merely another traceable element for the staff to use against us if we were discovered. Plus,' he shuddered, looking down at the ground below us, 'I can't exactly say I'm a fan of the, ahem, lack of contact with terra firma.'

'Because,' Pietro sighed, pushing four glass bottles into Ig's hands, 'it's not exactly a raid if we knock politely on the front door, is it?'

'C'mon, Merc!' Vivi chirped, leaning way too far into Mercutio's personal space. 'You have to live a little.' Her voice dropped to a breathy rasp, and Ig knew in that moment that Mercutio von Ryan was definitely not an emotionless robot. Because if he was, he would have blown a gasket. 'Do something… dangerous.'

'I - I,' Mercutio began, before clearing his throat and blushing furiously. 'Um, that is to say, er… ah, cake!' He thrust a glass tupperware box in Ig's direction. 'Cake,' he reiterated. 'For you. We brought it. Here. Eat it.'

'Ah, Mercutio,' Pietro sighed, sitting on Ig's bed and digging around in his own satchel, 'if only I had your way with words. I'd be unstoppable.'

'Cake?' Ig asked, opening the glass lid of the tupperware. Inside was a slice of chocolate cake, the whirls of icing on top slightly squashed from the lid of the box. 'Why did you–'

'We couldn't have you missing out on the raid,' Vivi said. 'So we went to the kitchen, grabbed a ton of stuff and put it in our bags, and brought it up here to you!' She produced an inexplicably-uncrushed bag of sweet chilli crisps from her bag and brandished them in Ig's direction. 'And you don't even have to share! Just… don't go back to bed yet, okay?'

From across the room, Pietro raised an eyebrow in Ig's direction. 'Thanks, Vivi,' Ig said, reaching out and crushing Vivi close in a one-armed hug as she tried to swallow her embarrassment – and, secretly, her delight. A warm, happy feeling began to flutter in her stomach, and Ig decided in that moment she'd see what happened if she let it bloom.

The four sat on the dorm room floor together; Vivi and Pietro producing all manner of treats from their bags like marauding pirates showing off their haul; chocolate bars and bags of crisps and muffins and, in Pietro's case, a tin of caramel sauce. 'Pietro!' Vivi crowed, as he shoved a heaping, drippy spoonful into his mouth, 'that's disgusting!'

Pietro paid her no mind; simply humming contentedly and hugging his stomach. 'It makes my tummy happy,' he said, eyes closed in bliss as he rocked from side to side.

'At least spread it on something.'

'Shan't. It dilutes the flavour.'

'Ig, tell him!'

'Actually,' Ig said, scooting across the circle, 'pass me that spoon, I want to give it a try.'

'Eww, you're not even getting a new spoon?!' Vivi screwed up her eyes, face contorted in a mask of disgust. 'That's so gross, I can't even stand it.'

'I'm going to wipe it, Vivi: I'm not an animal.'

'An indirect kiss,' Pietro snarked, cleaning the spoon on a napkin and handing it to Ig. She leaned in as if to kiss him on the lips, and he waggled his tongue at her – almost close enough to lick her nose – and made a 'blahlablahla' sort of noise. 'That's what kissing looks like, right?' he asked no-one in particular.

'I can't look anymore,' Vivi whimpered, covering her eyes with her hands. 'You two are too much for me.'

'Making the Villains wince; I knew you had it in you, Heretical,'

Mercutio said dryly, snapping off a square of chocolate and offering it to Vivi; taking one of her hands on his own and peeling it away gently to place it in her palm. 'Here. To distract you.'

Vivi looked down at the chocolate, then back up at Mercutio, and Ig could have sworn she saw something flicker in her eyes. 'Thanks, Merc,' she said, taking the square and placing it between her lips.

Ig smiled and licked the caramel from the spoon and – oh my god. It was the best thing she'd ever tasted. Obviously, she'd had caramel before, but this stuff was dark and rich, not pasty and plain like the millionaire's shortbreads Dad brought home from Planet Mocha. And with the added decadence of eating it straight from the tin? On another level.

'Okay, okay,' Pietro said, trying to snatch back the tin while Ig spooned caramel into her mouth. 'I said you could try it, not eat the whole – hey! Ig! Not fair!'

'Vivi,' Ig said, getting up and running to hide behind her dorm-mate; which was tricky, seeing as Vivi was half Ig's size. 'Hide me. He's out to get me, Vivi!' She squatted down until her vision was taken up with a mass of green hair, trying not to wobble as she laughed.

'Don't drag me into this!' Vivi joked, wrestling the tin from Ig and handing it back to Pietro. 'Just because you're my friend doesn't mean you can use me as cover.' A warm rush of emotion, sweet and thick as the caramel still staining her teeth, washed over Ig. Vivi was her friend. They were all her friends. Somehow, through blind luck, she'd managed to find people who actually wanted to be around her. The warm feeling spread into her head, where it made her a little dizzy. It felt like a sugar rush; this heady feeling of really, truly being accepted. They'd done all this tonight for her – because they'd noticed she was sad. They'd noticed her! Nothing Lunalist could ever have given her topped that moment; sitting on the floor in her bedroom, listening to Vivi and Pietro argue while Mercutio ate chocolate and watched with a cool sort of amusement.

It didn't matter if she was a Villain or an assistant, or even if she dropped out entirely and went to work in a shop or an office somewhere and became painfully normal in the process. She'd still have these three evil, chaotic idiots. She was sure of that, now.

'Hey,' Ig said, catching everyone's attention. 'I'm starting to think we haven't finished our raid for tonight, guys. I mean, I was barely involved.' She smiled. 'Let's go eat under the stars.'

Vivi's mouth dropped open into a small 'o' of excitement; Pietro was already on his feet and shoving his shoes back on. Even Mercutio looked intrigued – one eyebrow raised as he regarded her across the room. 'You have a way to get on the roof?' he said.

'Oh yes,' Ig said. 'I found it when, um…' When she'd been reporting back to The General. But that was in the past. All of it was behind her now. 'Come on; let's go.'

Chapter Thirty-Two

'So,' Pietro said, slinging an arm around Ig's shoulders as they fell behind Vivi and Mercutio, 'How do we get up there, Schemer?'

'Schemer?' Ig said, narrowing her eyes.

'Yeah,' Pietro said with an easy shrug. 'You're the schemer of the group. The cool, calculating one who always has a plan.'

'I don't know if I've ever been cool, Pietro.'

'Viv's the emotional support with a nasty side,' Pietro continued, pointing to Vivi's back as she walked ahead of them, chatting with Merc as they moved through the school gardens, 'and Merc's the megalo-manic wild card.'

'And what are you?' Ig asked. Pietro struck a pose; hands framing his face.

'I'm the face man. The good-looking one who gets us out of all our scrapes and entanglements.'

'Oh, are you?' Ig laughed, digging her elbow into Pietro's ribs. 'You've decided, then.'

'Better than being a lab assistant forever.'

'So very humble of you.'

'Hey; you should know by now that being humble gets you nowhere in our school.'

Ig felt a rush of happiness pulse through her veins and, for once, she didn't swallow it down. 'Our school.' It felt nice.

'Shouldn't we have some muscle somewhere in the mix, too?' she asked. 'Someone who can smack their way through a problem?' She thought of Katalina, with the sparks dancing around her heels. In a year or so, that could be a very useful inferno.

Pietro shrugged. 'Myeh. We're scary enough without it.'

They passed through the paved courtyard; Vivi crinkling her nose at the lack of vegetation. 'Look,' she said, flicking an annoyed hand in the direction of the fountain, 'they've drained the water now. Is a little bit of algae so bad that we can't even have a nice water feature?' She was right. Usually, the dragon spat water from his huge, toothy maw; today it was dry as a bone. 'What am I even going to do with algae? Give you a dose of B-12?'

'Hm,' Merc said with a smirk, counting off on his fingers. 'Side effects of eating too much Spirulina, as told to me by Vivian Section; headaches, muscle pain, trouble sleeping, back sweats…'

'Merc!' Vivi squeaked in outrage. 'You're not meant to remember the things I tell you.'

'I remember everything you tell me.'

There was a pause. Vivi stared at Mercutio, who seemed on the cusp of saying something more… before they both pretended to be very invested in looking at anything else but each other. 'How is it,' Pietro asked the stars above, muttering under his breath, 'that I don't even want to stick my tongue down someone's throat and my flirt game is so much better than his? Honestly Ig; I should give classes.' They made their way to the hidden door in the wall, and Ig grinned at the smattering of applause she earned as she pushed it open to reveal the dark, winding staircase beyond. She had to admit, she was glad to be finally sharing this part of her Shackleton journey with the others. Now everything was out in the open, and she could move on. Maybe, when they got up there, she'd tell them about her decision to not go back to Lunalist. They were halfway up the stairs when Vivi tensed, turning around to stare back out the doorway. 'What..?' she muttered to herself.

'What is it?' Pietro asked.

'I thought I heard something,' Vivi said. 'I'm going to go see what it was.'

'Do you want me to come with you?' Merc asked.

'No, it's okay. Go look at the stars; I'll be five minutes.'

And she was gone; disappearing back out into the night. Ig and the boys pressed on; heading up onto the shingled roof where Ig had had so many conversations and thought so many secret thoughts. She found she was really looking forward to sitting up there with the boys, telling jokes and sharing sweets, and maybe even persuading Merc to take the plunge with Vivi. It would be nice.

She lasted two minutes before she was running back down the stairs. 'Vivi?'

The grounds were oddly quiet; as if the entire school was holding its breath. Ig could hear her footsteps. 'Vivi?'

No answer. Ig strained her ears; just out of sight, around the other side of the dragon fountain, she could hear a hissed, furious conversation – and then a whimper of pain. Wishing she had brought something to protect herself – even a loose slate from the rooftop to chuck at whoever was lurking in the dark – Ig picked her way over the courtyard. She could pick out two figures, pressed up against the lip of the dragon fountain. One was Vivi – struggling in the other person's grip, her hair turned sickly green by the moonlight. Ig didn't recognise the student at first – they had their back to her, and Ig assumed it was one of Falcon Reeve's little cronies, out for their own personal Villain War. But then, the girl – a blonde girl in a white-and-gold top – spoke. 'Look, just tell me how to get in, 'kay? And I'll let you go.'

Ig would recognise her voice anywhere. It had haunted her for years at Lunalist.

Lily Volt's hand was gripping Vivi's jaw painfully. On the paved courtyard, with no plants within reach, she was powerless. Vivi thrashed against Lily's grasp, but to no avail. 'Ugh,' Lily scoffed. 'You Villains are all so annoying. Bored now.' To Ig's horror, Lily's hands began to spark; tiny yellow lightning bolts danced over her fingers. She had her Power. She had her Power! They weren't even meant to have their Revelation Ceremony until next year, oh my god she was going to hurt Vivi–

'Leave her alone, Lily.'

The words were out of Ig's mouth before she could stop them. Lily's head snapped up as she turned slowly to face her. The sparks dancing over the fingers that gripped Vivi's face faded and died.

'Are. You. Serious?' Lily gasped, before shrieking with laughter. 'You're actually still running around out here? Not, like, trapped in a basement somewhere? Oh my god. Oh my god that is actually too funny.' She shoved Vivi backwards and she tumbled back into the dried-out fountain. 'What are you doing here?' Ig asked. Lily shrugged, eyes wide, and Ig felt anger and embarrassment spark up inside her. How was it, after all these months, Lily Volt could make her feel so stupid?

'Just doing a little reconnaissance mission,' she said. 'Since you were so bad at it.'

Reconnaissance mission? But The General told her that no-one could get into Shackleton. That had been the whole point…

Vivi was sitting up, now; wiping gunk from the bottom of the fountain away from her face. 'Ig, who is this?'

'Aw, Iggie,' Lily simpered. 'You didn't tell people about me? But I thought we were friends.'

Ig was too stunned to speak; backing as far away from Lily Volt and her insufferable smirk as if she could. 'The General,' she said, before swallowing hard. 'The General told you what I told her. About the school – about The Nyx and–'

'About the spell that teacher put on this place?' Lily scoffed, her eyes raking over Ig's face. 'Dude. We've known about that trick for ages.'

What?

'Did she tell you that – hold on,' Lily giggled. 'Did The General tell you we didn't know about the school being in a liminal space?'

'Liminal… what?'

'You don't know anything, do you?' Lily Volt folded her arms and shifted her weight onto one hip, looking Ig up and down like she was a particularly disgusting insect. 'That's probably why all the intel you sent back was useless.'

'But…you got past the hedges!' Ig protested, her voice cracking. 'Even the flyers couldn't get in, so how–'

'Even the flyers couldn't get in,' Lily parroted, twisting her face into a mocking snarl. 'There's a hole in the hedge that isn't being guarded by all that weird magic stuff. Talia found it on her last mission. Duh. You really are the dumbest person ever, aren't you?'

'Don't,' Vivi hissed, 'talk to her like that.'

Lily scoffed and flicked her hand in Vivi's direction. Sparks crackled along her wrist like a bracelet, zipping along her fingers and leaping out into the air – before wrapping around Vivi's arms, pinning them to her side with crackling electricity. Vivi gasped and crumpled to the floor of the fountain.

'Vivi!' Ig cried, running to her friend's side. The same crackling whips shot out again, snagging on Ig's feet and sending her crashing down to the floor. Pain – like pins and needles crossed with a paralysing numbness – swept up and down her legs like a rash, making them useless. Ig glared as Lily towered over her, sparks flying and spitting over her arm. 'Look, Iggie; we got moved up a grade,' Lily crowed, admiring her new Power. 'The General actually saw potential in us – unlike some people – so we got shown our Powers early. Aren't you happy for us?'

Despite everything that had happened, Ig still felt a wave of jealousy rush through her. Lily Volt had potential? What had she even done to show it, apart from put on a stupid accent, flirt with the teachers and throw spiteful jabs at Ig?

For someone being groomed to be the next great Hero, Ig thought, as she swung her electrified foot out and knocked Lily Volt's legs out from under her, *you really are the worst*. She prepared herself for the inevitable crunch as Lily fell backwards. But it never happened. Lily's fall was cushioned by a wave of water that rushed around the corner, propped her up and pushed her gently back onto her feet.

'Ugh,' Lily said, piling her glossy blonde locks up onto the top of her head, 'I told you not to get my hair wet! I just got it done.'

'Did they hurt you?' asked a voice, so achingly familiar that the breath stuttered and stopped in Ig's throat.

It's not her, she thought. It can't be.

'No,' Lily said, scrubbing water from her clothes with the flat of her palm. 'They're incapacitated. Did you find a way in yet?'

Ig was going to be sick. She was sure of it.

'Not yet. If you've got hostages, maybe they'd be useful for finding out where she is?'

Lily leaned down and grinned at Ig. 'Probably,' she said, flicking water into her face.

'Oh, good,' said Pisces, as she rounded the corner of the hedge, looking as beautiful and far away as she had the last time Ig saw her. 'The sooner we can get inside, the better.'

Chapter Thirty-Three

The world went quiet. Not in a beautiful, everything-else-fell-away kind of way. More like someone had punched Ig in the side of the head. She watched, as if from under water, as Pisces and Lily talked and planned how to get into Shackleton. It felt so wrong that they were here. Even though her legs were still numb, Ig dragged them a little closer to her chest, stifling a whimper.

Pisces laid a hand on Lily's arm, tenderly inspecting her for injuries, and she noticed there was something snaking over her arms; thin plastic tubes, winding up to a long container strapped over her shoulders. It sloshed as she moved, and Ig realised it was filled with water. Pisces had been given her Power early, too. Water manipulation. Of course. Her parents would be so proud.

'—not the teachers,' Pisces was saying, a thousand miles away. 'The dorms. After we see what we can find, we get them to chase us through the classrooms before we escape; in the chaos, they might destroy their own experiments. Then we can set their work back a little, as a bonus.'

That was their plan? Lead the students directly to their projects – as well as each classroom's Power Lenders? If Ig had been able to, she would have scoffed. A foot – clad in an expensive, name-brand trainer – came down to rest on her shoulder. 'You won't say anything about it, will you?' Lily simpered. Ig scowled back up at her; watching as, at Lily's side, Pisces' expression changed.

'Iggie?' she asked, before rushing to kneel down beside her. 'Iggie, oh my god, what are you doing?'

She hadn't even realised who Lily had captured. This night was going spectacularly. Ig raised her head, confused. 'You...

you know what I'm doing here.' *What I was doing here.* 'The mission…The General…'

For a moment – a stupid, hopeful moment – Ig thought Pisces was going to ask if she was okay. Then, her perfect brow creased in confusion. 'I thought you would have given up ages ago,' she said in a whisper.

'Given up?' Ig asked. 'What–'

'Lily, get off her. She's not going to do anything, get off her.' Pisces grabbed her arm and helped Ig to her feet. Ig stumbled, and once upon a time she would have used it as an excuse to lean against Pisces' side. But now, she just wanted to stand up on her own.

'I thought you would have given up by now,' Pisces said again, softly.

'You said that,' Ig replied stiffly, pulling her arm back.

'Well,' Lily said, shooting a nonchalant spark in Vivi's direction to keep her back, 'I guess we were both wrong, Pisces. You thought she'd be long gone, and I thought she'd be falling at your feet and begging you to take her home. You know; sweep her up in those strong arms of yours.' She wrapped her arm around Pisces' waist for a brief second, pulling her close and leaning into her personal space – and in one moment of magnetic, lingering eye contact, Ig knew that Lily and Pisces had kissed. At least once.

But what was even more interesting – *don't you dare cry, Ignatia Heretical, don't you dare let them see you cry, keep focusing on what's around you* – was that the sparks circling Lily's wrist faded as she smiled into Pisces' face. *She needs to concentrate on her Power to make it work. Use that.*

Now that Lily was distracted, Vivi could drag herself to her feet and stagger to Ig's side. 'Okay, you've had your fun trying to get in,' she said. 'You can't. You've tried before. Just leave, alright? Before I–'

'Hang on. Pisces,' Ig said, pins and needles raking up and down her arms as she rubbed them. 'What do you mean, you thought I'd have given up ages ago? Given up on what?'

No-one was making any sense. Nothing at all made sense!

Pisces tilted her head to one side, red hair tumbling over her shoulder. 'Iggie…' she stated.

'Don't call me that!' Ig snapped. 'I hate when you call me that.' As the words left her mouth, she was shocked to discover that it was the truth. 'Just answer me.'

Pisces' eyes widened. 'Iggie, don't shout at me.' Ig bristled.

'Well then, don't baby me for once in your–'

'I thought you would have dropped out, alright?' Pisces snapped, frustration sharpening her words. The bottom fell out of Ig's stomach. 'You could barely handle things at Lunalist,' Pisces continued, throwing up her hands in frustration, 'how could you handle things here?'

'I've been fine, Pisces–'

'The General thought you might be dead, or a slave, or being used for parts by one of the monsters that lives here, but I told her you probably ran away–'

'Wait. The General knows you're here?!'

For the first time in ages, Ig felt like she was on an uneven footing. She felt like she was supposed to know things she could never have found out, assumed things she could have never guessed – all while being called stupid to her face. She hated it just as much as she used to. But now it made her angry.

'Duh,' Lily scoffed. 'She sent us, Iggie.' Sparks flew between Lily's fingers once more as she advanced on Ig and Vivi. 'She wants, you know, actual info? She did think she could get something useful out of you being here – before you got turned into a human slug or something gross like that – but you just told them a whole ton about stuff they already knew. Oh my god, you are, like, such a total embarrassment to the–'

'Lily, stop talking like that!' Ig screamed, fists balled tight at her side. 'You sound like a crap film from the Nineties, no-one talks like that!'

Lily, Pisces, and Vivi all stared at her, eyes wide with disbelief. Ig could feel her chest rising and falling like she'd run a marathon, frustration and confusion simmering in her stomach. Then, into the silence, Vivi did the worst thing she could have possibly done.

She laughed. A long, ugly snort, hand clapped over her mouth. And Lily Volt snapped. She closed the space between her and Vivi, her beautiful face contorted with fury, and slapped her hard with the flat of an electrified palm. Vivi was knocked backwards with a cry, curling around herself as she hit the lip of the fountain hard, sparks still spitting over her cheek.

'Who do you think you are, you little–'

Ig launched herself at Lily with a snarl, grabbing a fistful of her silky blonde hair. The two fell to the ground, a ball of fists and nails and years of resentment. Ig's head hit the ground and she saw stars, tasted the bright copper of blood in her mouth as she bit down on her tongue. In the same moment, Lily bent Ig's hand backwards so hard that the bones in her fingers popped. Ig turned and sank her teeth into Lily's wrist – the taste of shea butter body wash mixing with the blood in her mouth – when another blast of freezing water hit her in the face. Lily wrenched her arm out of Ig's mouth, crying out in pain as her teeth left long, ugly scrapes along her skin. 'This,' Lily hissed, inspecting the damage as Pisces helped her to her feet, 'is why The General wanted to get you out the way. You're an animal. Someone like you could never be like us.'

'I don't want to be like you,' Ig said. 'Not now. You were always a bully, Lily. Now, you're just a bully with Powers.'

'Ig!' Pisces said with a gasp, hand flying to her mouth – as if her beloved but untrainable pet had done something mildly naughty. 'You can't say that. Lily isn't a bully. We both wanted to help you! Don't you want that?'

And that, right there, was the point where Ig's sanity broke a little. It had been a long time coming, after all – since apparently she lived in a different world to everyone else around her. Everyone at Lunalist, anyway.

'Help? You want to help?!'

Ig began to laugh – more of a cackle, really. Her hair was a tangled snarl of knots, brushing the nape of her neck. Blood dripped from her mouth and her eyebrow where she'd hit the ground, but she didn't care. She looked around her – at her friend paralysed on the floor, at the girl she would have died for and the person who made her life miserable for years in all sorts of tiny, vicious ways – and she laughed and laughed until she felt a little sick. She probably looked like she'd lost her mind. Good, she thought. Good.

Her hands hurt. They almost burned.

'You're acting crazy,' Pisces said under her breath. She sounded in awe, like Ig was some sort of natural disaster. 'Maybe these Villains have corrupted you, after all.'

'Maybe they have,' Ig said, catching her breath.

'I thought I could be a good influence on you, Iggie,' Pisces continued, her tone full of wonder and a dawning understanding. 'The General gave up on you, but I really thought I could help.'

Her expression turned harsh and blank; like a steel shutter slamming closed. 'No wonder she wanted you out of Lunalist, if this is what you're really like. I knew you were a bit slow to catch up at school, but not this. Not this.'

Ig's laughter stopped in her throat, threatening to choke her. 'The General wanted me out of the school?'

She knew she'd been a disappointment – not living up to her dad's standards, looking so much like her mam – but The General had actively wanted her gone? Ig's heart stuttered in her chest as she thought back over every encounter she'd had with The General. They flickered in front of her vision like a film on fast-forward; all the looks, all the long, disapproving silences. How embarrassing Ig must have been to her. She'd thought she was getting a girl version of The Streak, and instead she had an awkward, flailing student with no direction, who was hard to like and even harder to assign a role to.

A foot caught her in the stomach. 'Of course she did,' Lily hissed. Ig tried to rear up, to fight back, but Pisces pushed her back down. 'You don't listen, do you? She was always talking about you pestering her with updates – when really, she wanted you to lay down in a corner and rot somewhere. Like you were ever gonna survive all these psychos.'

Ig squeezed her eyes shut tightly. She wasn't going to let them see her cry. She wasn't.

'That's why I was so surprised to see you,' Pisces said. 'I thought the Villains would have used you up by now.'

'You really think that little of me?' Ig hissed.

'Come on, Iggie,' her old friend said, in the sweetest, most innocent tone Ig had ever heard. 'Be reasonable. The General wouldn't waste her time sending you on a real mission, would she?'

The tears were boiling up inside of her, now; anger and shame and humiliation raging inside of Ig like a storm.

'You can't expect Lunalist to put all that hard work into a weak link, can you?'

Ig's eyes snapped open like Pisces had slapped her. They'd been expecting her to fail. Ig had been crashing and burning at Lunalist for a long, long time, and it had just become too embarrassing, too pitiful for the teachers to watch. So they'd chosen to send her somewhere else, get other people to finish her off for them. Her fingers found the dry, loose skin on her knuckle, and pulled; the pain distracting her for a second from the blood trickling into her eye.

Silence. Then, a low, buzzing noise caught her attention. Seconds later, Lily and Pisces heard it too; looking up in time to see a droning, black-and-silver cloud descend upon the garden. There were so many of them, they blocked out the moon, plunging the fountain into darkness. The last thing Ig heard Pisces say – before the screaming started – was a strangled 'what is that?!'

Chapter Thirty-Four

'Oh my god!' Lily cried, hitting the ground with a thud as she tried to evade the swarm. 'No, no, get away, get away – Pisces, my face! Pisces, stop them!' Pisces wasn't listening, though; she had her own battles to fight. Every time she sprayed the drones with water, they managed to evade it, moving like a tiny murmuration of starlings that swirled and curved around Pisces' attacks, coming back all the stronger. Vivi blearily sat up, hand over her cheek, wincing in pain from Lily's electrified slap. It looked like she was in a bubble; the black cloud of insects left a good few inches between their stingers and her skin. The same was true for Ig; she reached out her hand and still couldn't touch one of the drones.

In a blur, Pietro was dashing across the courtyard and vaulting into the fountain, inspecting Vivi's cheek as the swarm opened up a corridor for him. 'Are you okay?' he asked her. 'We couldn't get down off the roof quick enough. We could see what was… what did they do to your–'

'What is the matter with you?!' screeched Lily, as Pisces aimed a frustrated blast of water at the sky. 'They're just bees!'

'Wrong!'

Ig looked up. Standing atop the fountain, lab coat billowing behind him in the night wind, goggles over his eyes and a headset pinning down his hair, was Mercutio. He'd snatched up a random broom from somewhere in the garden and swung it through the air like a sword.

'Whoo!' hollered Pietro, as the swarm tornadoed around the trespassing Heroes; 'that's my brother! Mess 'em up, Merc!'

'These,' said Mercutio, voice strained with manic glee as the swarm loomed behind him, 'are cyborg bees!' With a wild cackle, he pointed the broom at Lily Volt, and the swarm of bees rushed at her like a black wave, making her almost invisible. Her screams, however, were enough to make Ig's ears bleed.

'I'm allergic, you freak!' she shrieked. She wasn't. At least, Ig was pretty sure she wasn't. 'You know what'll happen if you kill a Hero?!'

'Oh,' Mercutio said nonchalantly, stepping down off the fountain with all the grace of a performer on a stage, 'these particular bees aren't venomous.' He tapped the side of his headset and smirked wolfishly. 'Not until I tell them to be. The stingers are, however, coated in weapons-grade titanium. So they'll hurt. A lot.' He cast a quick look in the girls' direction. 'Everyone alive?'

Ig nodded. Vivi, leaning on Pietro, was gawking. Literally open-mouthed and flushed. Finally, Ig thought to herself, feeling the hysterical urge to laugh bubbling up again. Mercutio winked – he winked! – and turned his concentration back to his swarm.

Like Lily, Pisces was also screaming. But hers were shrieks of fury. She was firing blasts of water in random directions; her own flawless skin already marred by a few nasty red welts, her hair clinging wet to her forehead. She tripped over her own feet at one point, weighed down by her heavy tank of water, and fired off a string of very unbecoming swears. Ig had never seen her like this; so easily upset, so out of control. Then again, she'd never seen Pisces not get her way, either. Usually, the world seemed to bend to Pisces Rising's will, almost before she asked it to. She probably thought she'd come here – with her new Power and her new girlfriend – terrify a few Villains and go home feeling good about herself. Instead, she was trying to fight bugs and losing. Ig wondered what she had ever seen in her.

No. That wasn't true. Something in her would always yearn for Pisces Rising. The difference was that she knew how pathetic that part of her really was, now.

With one last bellow of rage, Pisces aimed her blasts in Mercutio's direction and drenched him, knocking him backwards and causing him to land painfully on the broom handle. His headset began to spark and smoke, and Mercutio just managed to scramble to his feet and wrench it from his head before it electrocuted him. In dismay, the Villains watched as the swarm of cyborg bees dissolved; the insects flying up and out of sight, heading back to the safety of their hive.

'You,' Pisces growled, advancing on Mercutio and aiming another blast at his head. 'You...you monster.' Her tone was filled with loathing and outrage. 'I'm going to drown you right here and save the world some trouble.' She raised her hand one more time and aimed it squarely at Mercutio's head.

'Merc!'

Pietro dashed forward, took up the abandoned broom and swung it with all his might – catching Pisces in the stomach and knocking her against the fountain. The container of water across her shoulders broke, and water cascaded down her back. Pisces got to her feet with a groan, pressing her hands against her soaked Lunalist uniform to wring a few more blasts out of them; now more like projectiles than a constant stream. One caught Pietro in the leg, and Lily lunged forward to grab him, trying to use Pisces' water as a conduit. Sparks flew over her palms again, but in one fluid movement, Pietro flipped the broom handle in one hand, spinning around just in time to block her attack. He brought up his leg and kicked Lily away before dropping to the ground and using the broom to knock Pisces' feet from under her. Pisces scrabbled for purchase on the slick concrete; until Pietro knocked her down again – harder, her lip bursting as she hit the side of the fountain – and pointed the jagged, broken end of his improvised weapon in her face.

'Stay away from my brother.'

Pisces scrambled to her feet, shot one panicked look at Lily, then at the remains of her shattered water container. She weighed up her options, smearing her hand across her bleeding lip. And then she ran.

Ig's mouth flapped open and closed like a fish. 'That…that…'

'That,' said a voice behind them, 'was incredible.'

Ig and Pietro turned to see Mercutio standing, slack-jawed, behind them; pointing an accusatory finger at his brother. 'Have you been able to do that the entire time?!'

Pietro looked down at the broken and battered broom handle as if he was seeing it for the first time. 'I don't…know?'

In the next instant, Mercutio had Pietro by the lapels. 'You're going to let me make some modifications to your weapon, yes?'

'Merc… it's a piece of wood. I don't want it anymore.'

'Oh, pish posh,' Mercutio scoffed with a grin, hands flapping in the air as if to wave his brother's objections away. 'I've had this idea for a Power Lender modification; giving abilities to inanimate objects; spontaneous combustion, ice powers, all that. Not my usual milieu, but give me two weeks and a contraband six-pack of energy drinks and I'll have it ready for use—'

'Merc. We're still in a fight.'

'Oh. Right.'

Lily was staggering to her feet; wincing as her hand went to her stomach where Pietro had kicked her. 'You,' she hissed, 'are going to pay for that.'

'Lily,' Ig began…before closing her mouth, tongue dry against her teeth. What was she even going to say? Something cool like 'go after your little girlfriend, it's over'? That wasn't Ig's style. Grill Lily for information? No. There was only one question Ig needed an answer to. 'Why do you hate me so much? What have I ever done to you?' Tears stung in her eyes; hot and full of anger. Everything hurt. Her skin felt like it was on fire.

A nasty, feral glitter shone in Lily's eyes as she stumbled forward. Pietro and Mercutio took a step towards each other; blocking her from reaching Ig. 'I don't hate you,' Lily snarled. 'I never even think of you. You're nothing, Iggie. You're nothing but a desperate, friendless freak, with a has-been dad and a witch mother. We all felt so sorry for Pisces, having to put up with you all that time. But it got her some Brownie points with The General, so she stuck it out.' She reached up and pushed a lock of dank, blonde hair out of her eyes. 'Know what?' she laughed hoarsely. 'I'm glad she sent you here. Because all these other psychos,' she gestured to Pietro and Merc, 'will find out how useless you really are soon enough.' Her voice began to crack. 'They'll see how pathetic you are, and they'll chew you up and spit you out, just like you deserve. Like we all wanted to back home but we're just. Too. Nice!' She spat on the floor, and smiled with bloody, bared teeth.

Ig sank to the floor; every inch of her raw and screaming. She looked down at her hands, as if in a dream, and saw that they were entirely black, up to her wrists. And they hurt. They ached and burned and hurt so much, it was like her skin had been flayed off. 'Okay,' Pietro said, low and dangerous in his throat. 'That's enough. You're outnumbered. Go join your friend licking her wounds in the village before we get the teachers to really mess you up.'

'Falling back on the grown-ups to fight your battles?' Lily sneered. When the boys remained stony-faced and unmoving, she relented. 'Fine. I'm going, I'm going–'

But in her hands, bright yellow sparks were spitting between her pretty, manicured nails.

'Nope,' muttered Vivi. clutching the side of her face. 'Not today.' She scraped her hand along the inside of the fountain, gathering up dried, half-dead algae under her own nails. She winced with concentration, twisted her hand and a wave of green dust burst forth from her palm, sent with a breath into Lily Volt's face. The Hero lunged forward, right through the cloud; and then paused, twitched, stiffened and, finally, crumpled to the ground with a groan. She didn't get up again.

'She killed her,' Pietro breathed. 'Awesome.'

'It's a paralysing spore,' Vivi said, wincing as she stood up. 'It's like cramps, but everywhere. It'll keep her down until you can get her out of here. Boys?'

'On it.' Pietro hauled the girl to her feet, then slung her over his shoulder like a sack of potatoes.

'And we're not taking her to The Nyx,' Mercutio asked with knotted eyebrows, 'because..?'

'Because then Lunalist will come looking for her,' Pietro replied. 'And it won't be two mean girls with new Powers that they send. We'll be right back.' And he was gone, disappearing through a gap in the hedges to deposit Lily somewhere far enough away to be safe. Mercutio trailed behind him, still insisting they talk about weapon modification.

Ig barely noticed. Everything that had just happened – everything she'd learned – washed over her like a black, icy tide.

The General had been trying to get rid of her. She hadn't wanted any of the information Ig had found for her – any of the information that Ig had agonised over, wondering if it was worth ruining her new friendships. She already knew all of it. What she'd wanted was to get Ig out from under her feet. And everyone at Lunalist had known about it.

Pisces had known about it. Pisces had known, the entire time, that she was going to be sent away. That she was, in the eyes of the Academy, beyond redemption. But she'd kept her mouth shut, acted like nothing was wrong because, what? It made her look good? Dealing in charity before she'd even graduated? And then the second Ig was out of her lovely red hair she'd gone running to Lily Volt, of all people.

And the others had seen. Vivi, Pietro, Mercutio…they'd all seen how little she mattered to anyone who had known her for more than a few weeks. And they would know that Pisces was right. She really was a weak link. It didn't matter what she did, what she said, they would know her real value, now. And they'd turn on her. Why would they do anything else? It was all she deserved, after all.

There was something tight and thrumming in Ig's chest. Her heart was pounding – or was it her temples? Her skin – her hands – felt on fire, and her entire brain was filled with Lily's awful, sneering voice, repeating itself over and over again until the words nearly lost their meaning, became a crazed, nonsensical babble.

Freak

Friendless freak

Chew you up and spit you out

Felt sorry for you, you freak

Freak

Freak

Freak

Freak –

Something huge and powerful and dark exploded from both her palms.

Chapter Thirty-Five

'Ig? Ig, what's going…'

'Heretical… hear us?'

Then, nothing. Nothing but a whirling, scorching blast of emotion and sensation that engulfed every inch of Ig's skin. Something was reaching up, lashing against the cold evening air, but she couldn't work out which part of her body that was. She couldn't think; couldn't see, couldn't process anything that was happening around her apart from feeling so, so stupid. Stupid and naïve, and useless and unlovable and weird. She'd always been so weird and there was nothing – nothing! – she could do about it, it was just how she was, no amount of trying and trying and trying was ever going to fix that…

They'd lied to her! They'd told her, all this time, that all she needed to do was apply herself more; try that tiny bit harder, keep striving to be normal, to be a real, worthy Hero and everything would fall into place and she'd earn their love, earn their friendship, be forgiven for the sin of being who she was. But that was never going to happen, was it?

That distant, cold part of her body writhed again; a distant shudder of pain. Ig cracked one eye open; distantly curious about how she could reach up so high into the air while sitting on the ground – and a sick, horror-filled feeling speared her through the heart. Above her shoulders, thrashing wildly and grabbing at nothing, were two gigantic tendrils. Around them swirled a thick, black smoke; coming off the tendrils themselves in viscous gobs, floating in space and drifting up towards the full moon. Ig closed her eyes again, willing them away with a sob.

This couldn't be happening.

She could still feel them, though; whipping through the air, terrible and huge, threatening to rip her apart. What was happening to her?! And why did it feel good? The pull of her emotions felt like how she imagined a riptide would feel; strong and powerful and intoxicating, pulling her down and stopping any attempt Ig had left in her to fight it. Maybe this was what was meant to be. Maybe she was always meant to be like this.

She wanted to break something. She wanted to rip and tear; to smash something brittle and sharp into a thousand tiny pieces, over and over and over again. Distantly, she felt a wrenching, tugging sensation – and then a scream, and the shattering of stone, the impact reverberating up the tendrils and into her shoulder. It felt satisfying; in an awful, destructive way. Ig did it again. And again. And again, until the tendrils couldn't find anything more to break. One tendril dug into the ground – she could feel it raking through the earth, pulling up mud and grass and brambles and slamming them into the ground, throwing them with wet splats against the building behind her.

'Everyone okay?' she heard someone ask. 'Ig, Ig try and breathe – it just happened, guys, I wasn't even looking, and she started screaming… Pietro, don't touch her!'

Somehow, about a foot away from her, Ig faintly registered coming into contact with something solid; shoving it back and away from her hard. She didn't want anyone near her. Her brain couldn't take it.

'Okay,' that distant voice was saying, 'can anyone see a mint plant or something? I need to…'

Was that Vivi? Oh, she didn't want Vivi seeing her like this. She'd know that everything that Lily and Pisces had said about her was true. She was a freak, after all. Ig couldn't take it if Vivi left. Or the boys. If they left her, she'd destroy everything she could see. Everything she could touch.

Then, a blast of something cold and almost spicy – like toothpaste, times a thousand – hit her straight in the face. Ig gasped; the smell went up her nose and into her lungs, scalding and freezing her all at once. She reeled, eyes snapping open as the grass then the trees then the night sky whirled past as she fell over onto her back.

'Ig!'

Ig's vision was suddenly filled with three worried faces. Mercutio's brow was furrowed, Pietro was nursing a black eye – how'd he get that? – and Vivi had been crying. In her hand, she was clutching a fistful of mint leaves so tightly, her knuckles were turning white. Across her cheek, Ig could see the angry red marks from Lily's electrified slap. Behind them lay the shattered remains of the fountain, the dragon now reduced to rubble and fractured pieces of stone. A few of the brambles and hedges had been uprooted and shredded, and the stone of the school behind her was smeared with thick clods of dirt. And the tendrils were gone.

Ig closed her eyes again, slower this time. She suddenly felt very, very tired. She turned onto her side and curled up in the foetal position, knees touching her chin.

'Was that…' Pietro said, trailing off into an uncomfortable silence for a moment or two, before trying again. 'Ig, was that your–'

'Don't,' Ig managed, the words feeling heavy in her mouth. She knew already. She knew what it was. It hadn't felt anything like using a Power Lender – easy and fluid and wonderful. Her Power – her Power – was all pain and strangeness. Fitting, really.

'What,' said a voice from behind them, 'is going on?'

Ig looked up. Standing by the courtyard, clad in a robe and a pair of pinstriped silk pyjama bottoms, was The Nyx. They looked horrified. 'You…' they took in the sight of the ruined dragon statue and swallowed hard. 'Explain. Now.'

'My Power,' Ig managed to whisper. She was the only one who could tell the whole story, and right now she just didn't have the strength. So, she went with the least complicated answer. 'I got my Power, Professor Nyx.'

The Nyx drew their robe tighter around themselves, and something haunted flickered across their face. 'Oh, Ignatia,' they said – almost to themselves – before clearing their throat. 'You need to get her back to the dorms. We can talk about this once she's rested. Mr. von Ryan, can you help her up?'

'Yes, Professor Nyx.' Mercutio stooped down to Ig's level. 'I'm going to put my arms under your armpits, to keep you upright. Alright?' Ig nodded, and Mercutio hoisted her to her feet. 'One foot in front of the other,' he said, and Ig leaned back against his chest – affection and shame flickering somewhere underneath the thick, dead tiredness aching through her body. This was supposed to be a fun night with her friends. And they'd ended up fighting for her, instead. They didn't even get to sit under the stars.

'I'm not carrying you, Heretical,' Mercutio snapped. The fact that he sounded more irritated now than when she was destroying everything around her made Ig laugh. Not a long, loud laugh, or the half-mad cackle from before. More of a huff of breath carried by a smile.

'…meant to be a hug, Merc.'

Mercutio sniffed. 'Well, I don't do those. So walk.'

All four of them filed past The Nyx in silence, and made their way back inside. As they walked up the stairs, they glanced out a window overlooking the gardens; assessing the damage that their fight had left behind. The pools of water from Pisces' tank, the sad, broken fountain and the long, ugly tears in the grass. The Nyx was still out there, staring at the wreckage. Ig turned her head away with a wince. 'How's your face?' she managed to ask Vivi, in a voice that felt like a dead weight.

Vivi smiled; wincing a little at the effort. 'It's a burn. I have some fast-acting aloe vera plants growing in the dorm, they'll fix it up fine. I made them when Merc burned off his first and only attempt at a beard with a Bunsen burner; remember that, guys?'

Behind her, the boys laughed; softly, half-heartedly, humouring Vivi more than anything. Back at the dorm, Ig sunk into her mattress, folding her knees up close to her chest again. It would have felt good to be home, if she could feel anything at all. Mercutio hung back in the doorway, eyes fixed on her. There was a tiny crease of concern lining his forehead. Ig wanted to tease him; tell him that's how you get wrinkles, but she couldn't summon the strength. Vivi had vanished into her plants, looking for something. Pietro started methodically piling things at her feet; a bottle of water, Finnie, a clean t-shirt and, when he ran out of ideas, her toothbrush. 'We need calming music. Viv,' he said, voice thin with tension as he rifled through Vivi's record collection, 'why is everything you own so bloody angry?! Don't you have some, I don't know, whale noises or classical music or…'

'Pietro,' Vivi interrupted, glancing at Ig – who was sitting on her bed, blanket draped over her head, staring blankly down at her hands. They were pale again. Like nothing had even happened. 'Let Ig have some quiet. Please.'

'Okay.' Pietro sat at Ig's feet, watching her carefully. Waiting for something terrible to happen so he could step in and fix it. She felt like one of Mercutio's bees. 'Ig,' he whispered, after a grand total of thirty seconds of silence, 'can I get you anything?'

'Pietro,' warned Vivi. 'Stop.'

'Tea? What about some tea?' He squinted her, trying to smile through the pain of the bruise puffing up around his eye. 'Chamomile with honey, to calm your nerves. That's what Uncle Rayner used to make us when we were kids, it always worked. I'll go make you some.'

'Pietro, I'm on it. Leave her alone.'

'Anything at all, Ig, you let me know and it's yours, okay? I'm gonna stay right here by your side until you need me to–'

'Okay,' Mercutio said, finally losing patience and hauling his brother up by the collar, 'that's enough. She needs sleep. We'll assess the situation in the morning, Pietro.'

'Merc—!'

'You've forced me to take on the role of the emotionally intelligent twin, and it unsettles me. You know where we are if you need us, Vivi.' Mercutio paused in the doorway and shot Ig a look she was too drained to interpret right now. Then, he closed the door.

The General thought you might be dead, or a slave, or being used for parts by one of the monsters that lives here, but I told her you probably ran away.

If she still wanted to stay here, did that make Ig a monster, too?

The only noise in the quiet that followed was the tinkle of a spoon against china, over somewhere behind the plants that filled up their dorm. 'A Vivi Section special,' her friend said, emerging with a steaming mug – the Nessie one – cupped in both hands. 'This always helps me when I'm overwhelmed.'

'Overwhelmed' seemed like such a small word for how Ig felt. She was hollowed out. She felt like all her nerves had been flooded with sensation, and now they were dead. Ig realised she had never really made the choice to leave the Academy behind. It had been made for her, by people who had written her off months ago – and she hadn't even noticed. She really was stupid.

The tears came, then; loud and painful, like coughing. 'Oh, Ig,' Vivi said softly, setting down the mug and sitting next to her on the bed. 'I'm here, just let it all out.'

Ig fell against Vivi and cried until her throat screamed.

Chapter Thirty-Six

Ig and Vivi stayed up late into the night. They didn't say much of anything to each other; sitting with the endless mugs of tea, staring into the wafting steam and holding each other's hands. Even after Vivi was curled up on her bed like a cat, snoring softly, Ig stayed awake; staring down at her hands. She had a Power. After all this time. And it was dark, and scary and violent, and unlike anything she could have ever imagined. Unlike anything Lunalist could have imagined for her.

Slowly, she slipped off the bed. Vivi snuffled in her sleep, but didn't stir; not even when the dorm door opened, then clicked shut. Ig loved her friends dearly, but there was only one person she wanted to talk to tonight. Before she called home, Ig sat on the roof for a while and looked up into the stars. Like they had a million times before, her thoughts drifted to Pisces. Nice, sweet, kind Pisces, who did the right thing by pretending to be Ig's friend. Being spurned by the girl she had feelings for wasn't what made Ig lose control, back at the gardens. She'd had a thousand hopeless crushes in her time, and she'd have a thousand more. No; what Ig was really angry about – the thing she was really mourning – was the loss of a friendship that had never really existed. Her only solace in that school had been a girl who was gritting her teeth the entire time, comforting herself with thoughts of how sympathetic she was being to a loser like Ignatia Heretical. It hurt far more than anything Lily Volt had ever said to her.

Ig pressed the Call button on her tablet. 'Ig?' her dad asked, blearily looking into the camera as he rubbed his eyes. 'It's the middle of the night, honey. Is everything okay?'

He was in the living room; he must have grabbed the tablet and dashed downstairs in case her mam heard what they were talking about. Ig's chest tightened painfully. 'Dad…' Her voice pitched up into a sob, but she swallowed it thickly.

'Okay; Hero protocol.' Her dad actually looked serious for once. 'Are you hurt?'

'No, not really…'

'Is someone else hurt?'

'No.'

'Do I need to come up there and kick someone's butt?'

It was meant to make her laugh, but the thought of The Streak storming Shackleton Academy – and immediately being overwhelmed by teachers and students alike – made Ig feel a little queasy. 'No.'

'Okay, hon.' Ig watched as her dad settled himself into his favourite armchair. 'I'm here. What–'

'Luca Peterson. Let. Me. In.'

Ig's dad's face dropped as the big living room light began to flicker off and on. 'Oh, boy.'

'You will not keep me from my daughter, Luca.' The door to the living room began to rattle in place. Beyond that, in the hallway, Ig could hear the flapping of wings. 'That wretched school will not deny me for a second longer. Open the door, Luca.'

'Viola, please–'

'Open the door,' said the voice, reverberating and distorting like the sound of ice breaking, 'or I will break it down.'

'Okay, okay!' Ig's dad cried, lunging back over the armchair and wrenching the door open. 'It's open, alright? It's open.' Ig's mam was standing in the doorway. Or, rather, she was floating. Her toes just brushed the ground, and her hair was standing up on end as if she'd been electrocuted. Her eyes were black, and her face was beautiful and furious and terrible, and Ig hadn't wanted to run into her arms this much since she was small.

'I hear your pain, daughter,' she said, drifting into the room. 'I will not rest until I have cleansed the earth of those who wronged… you.' Looking at the screen, Viola blinked hard. Her eyes cleared, becoming their usual jade green colour, as her hair tumbled around her shoulders again. 'Are you on a roof?' she asked in her normal Geordie twang.

'Hi, Mam.'

'I knew something was going on. Tell me all about it – wait.' Ig's mother squinted, taking in the scene around Ig. 'I know that roof. You're at…'

The life seemed to drain out of her. Her skin was usually pale, but suddenly it seemed paper-white. Tears sprung into her eyes as she whispered, 'Blessed Hecate. You're at Shackleton. They've sent you to Shackleton.'

'Baby, we can explain,' Ig's dad began, but Ig cut him off.

'They told me it was a reconnaissance mission,' she said, swallowing hard, so she didn't start crying again, 'but it was a lie, Mam – to get me out of the way. They didn't want me there, they didn't think I was good enough, so they…'

'Oh, poppet.' Ig's mam's gaze refocused; she'd clearly pulled up another tab on the screen. 'Hold on. I'm going to book us both the first train in the morning to Rossborough and we'll sort this out. Stay where you are – well, not where you are, you're on a roof. But stay somewhere safe, and we'll come help you. That school won't know what's hit it once we–'

'Mam, stop. Can we, um, talk?' Ig looked apologetically at her dad. 'On our own?'

Her parents shared a look; a kind of silent argument Ig had seen many times when she was growing up. Then, with a final 'love you, kid,' her dad left the room and shut the door behind him. It was the first time Ig had been alone with her mother in months.

I needed you, Ig thought. And they kept me from you. The grief and the love and the fury roiling in her stomach was almost too much to bear. 'What is it?' Ig's mother asked. 'Um. I don't,'

Ig began, before taking a deep breath and continuing. 'I don't want to leave Shackleton. I've made friends here, and my grades are actually really good–' Ig's mam grinned, then covered it up with a cough, 'and… and no-one bullies me, here. I mean, Falcon Reeve is awful, but he's awful to everyone. And after I found out about the Academy, I might have, um…' Ig picked at her knuckles nervously. 'My Power came out for the first time.'

Ig watched her mother take a deep, stabilising breath. 'Alright. Can I ask what it is?'

'It's like, um,' Ig spread her palms out and made a 'woosh' noise, rolling her eyes back into her head. Her mam leaned closer to the screen.

'And how was it?' Awful. Terrible. Scary. Brilliant. 'Intense,' Ig said finally. 'And dark.'

Viola Heretical smiled. It wasn't brilliant and beaming, like her dad's. It was small, and secretive. A smile that said, 'I know exactly what you mean.'

'I'm sure it's beautiful, my love. I'm sure you understand now how lovely darkness can be.'

'Ha. You could say that.'

'I want to see you use it. Soon.'

'You will.' There was a long moment of quiet between them. Then, her mother spoke, her eyes wet with unshed tears.

'Ignatia. I'm not going to pretend I was ever happy about you going to that school. But having to stand by and watch as Lunalist ground you down – those teachers, and those awful girls, and the constant back-and-forth between classes – I've never felt pain like it. Including when your dad pushed me off the Angel of the North during our first battle.' Ig snorted, wiping away her tears with the back of her arm. 'So when I say I am happy for you, I mean it. I'm not smug, I won't be crowing to your father. But I am so, so angry, my darling.' Viola Heretical steepled her fingers, staring right down the lens of the camera. 'Are you angry too?' she asked, her voice growing low and soft. 'You can tell me.'

Ig nodded. She was angry. Even as Ig had felt all that sadness – all that pain at being pushed away, embarrassed and abandoned – she'd felt a bolt of brilliant, dark, dangerous fury. The fury that had made her want to destroy everything around her. And the part she hadn't admitted to anyone – not to Vivi, not even to herself – was that she'd enjoyed it. It felt good to be angry. She deserved to feel angry. And she didn't need to admit that to her mother. Because she already knew. That was what she had needed, tonight. She loved her father deeply. But she was a Villain's daughter, too. It was time she embraced that.

'Am I right in thinking,' Ig's mother said, her voice low and musical, 'that there's something else?'

'I was hoping,' Ig said slowly, 'that you and Dad wouldn't let on that you know about what Lunalist did. For a while.'

Ig's mother's lips curved into a smile. 'My girl has a plan.'

Ig grinned back at her. 'Of course I do. I'm the schemer.' Half an hour later – after her mother had finally said goodbye and Ig was left alone, in the dark and the quiet – she opened her right palm up to the night sky, and concentrated. She still felt deadened, but somewhere deep down inside her, that storm of emotions still raged. Ig closed her eyes, and let it flow up into her hand. Slowly – deadly slow – a black tendril unfurled, like one of Vivi's flowers. It was smaller than the last time, but it still towered over Ig's head. It wafted gently in the gentle Northern wind, the not-quite-smoke coming off it in lazy globs. Ig reached out a finger on her left hand and touched the black core of the tendril. She could feel it, in an abstract sort of way; like when you can sense someone is standing behind you, even if they aren't touching you. Slowly, she ran her finger up and down the tentacle, from the delicate, curled tip to the base of her palm. Wonder, gentle and fragile, bloomed in her chest. There, with the Northumberland sky behind her, Ignatia Heretical felt complete for the first time in her life – and a plot of vengeance began to form in her mind. It was slow, at first; no more than a flicker of a breath of a thought. But slowly, it began to take shape. Ig rolled it around in her mind for a while, letting it jump from idea to idea; quietly, taking all the time it needed. She had time, now. She had a cover story – if she could be sure of anything, it was that Pisces and Lily went back to Lunalist with stories of how she was the same hopeless, helpless girl she'd always been. And she had friends. Real, true friends, who had seen her at her literal worst and had simply offered her a cup of tea.

Together, she and her friends could do anything. Anything at all.

Chapter Thirty-Seven

After about half an hour, Ig began to shiver. It was the middle of the night in Northumberland, after all. She scooted back across the rooftop, but her tendril kept snagging on the shingles. Hm. Last time, Vivi knocking Ig out of her trance had been enough to make her Power go away. Ig placed her hand level with her nose and concentrated, watching through slitted eyes as the tendril slowly inched back into her hand. It felt ticklish; like slurping up a strand of spaghetti. But the spaghetti was huge, and also part of your skin. Once it had completely vanished, Ig made her way to the trap door and down to the staircase.

Her entire body was aching, and her mind was sore and empty. Ig kept trying to think, but it was like persuading a car to start without any petrol in the tank; thoughts just shuddered and sputtered and died. She needed rest. And a good breakfast in the morning. And then she could really start to plan– 'I thought I told you to rest.' Ig froze in her tracks. Sitting amongst the destroyed fountain was The Nyx; knees tucked up under their sharp chin, mud on their expensive pyjamas. Ig had purposely, stupidly made an effort not to look at the at the broken remains of the dragon fountain as she'd made her way to her secret door. She felt like she'd hurt an old friend. Only this time, a stolen mug wouldn't fix things.

'I couldn't sleep,' Ig said, opting for a half-truth. 'So I waited until Vivi was asleep and I snuck back out.'

'You aren't worried about losing control again? Destroying something else without your friends here to protect you?'

Ig thought for a second. 'It's better than shredding all of

Vivi's plants. She's a lot scarier than my Power, sometimes.' The Nyx laughed softly. Sadly. 'That's true.' They rested their chin on their knees again. 'Miss Heretical, you are a lot of things. Mindlessly destructive is not one of them. So you'll have to forgive me if I don't entirely believe that you and your friends were out here, having a perfectly lovely night, and you suddenly lost control over nothing at all.'

Ig stayed silent. The Nyx kicked a stone loose, and watched it tumble away into a trench her tendril had carved in the earth. 'I had this fountain commissioned, you know. The year I became head teacher. Some of the other teachers – I won't name names – didn't like it. They said it was tacky, that it didn't fit with the rest of the gardens. They said the dragon was "a bit much, even for a Villain school". But I knew there would be students who loved it. So, I gritted my teeth, picked my battles, sweet-talked when I needed to.' They let out another sad laugh. 'Shouted when I needed to, as well. And, in the end, I got my way. The fountain was installed. And the right students fell in love with it.' They looked up at a window, high in the school building. 'My room is just up there, and it did my heart so much good to see you and your friends sitting here. But,' The Nyx sighed, 'after all this time, it seems that there are still those who think they can simply change what they think is unsuitable. And if they can't, they'll destroy it.' They turned away from Ig slightly, resting their chin in their hands. Somewhere, off in the dark, a vixen screamed. 'It's nights like this that my hope wavers, Ignatia Heretical.'

Ig stood off to the side awkwardly, hands knotting together at her stomach. She'd had no idea how important this fountain was to The Nyx when she destroyed it. She hated the awful, sickly guilt that swirled in her stomach, knowing that something that had meant so much to someone had been ruined because of her.

No. Not because of her. Because of Lily and Pisces, and what they'd pushed her to. Ig had no idea how her Power would have manifested itself if she hadn't been out here tonight – maybe once she was high off all that caramel she'd been eating, they'd pop out in her sleep and try to strangle Mercutio or something. But Ig knew that without Pisces and Lily's interference – their decision to come to her school and act as if they were entitled to their deference, to her fear – nothing would have been destroyed. It was their fault. Slowly, Ig picked her way over the shattered remains of the dragon and sat down near her teacher. The Nyx barely stirred.

'I wish I could make this better,' Ig said. 'I'm not very good at comforting people. Or making people feel comfortable, actually.' She looked down at her feet, and saw, trapped under The Nyx's boot, a bloodied scrap of gold and white fabric. 'But I can promise you something.'

'Can you, now?'

Ig nodded.

'And what is that?' Ig raised her hands; turning them this way and that, admiring them. 'The people who did this? Who decided that something that doesn't fit must be useless and needs to be destroyed? I'm going to make them pay. Somehow.'

Finally, The Nyx smiled. 'What did I tell you when you first arrived here, Miss Heretical? About bullies?'

Ig turned to her head teacher and grinned 'Make sure you hit them twice as fast and three times as hard. Semper Scelestus,'

It was the first time those words had left Ig's lips. The Nyx looked at her for the first time, reaching out to ruffle Ig's hair. 'You look like your mother, you know.'

'Thank you,' Ig said. 'I know.'

The Nyx's smile faded away. 'But since you seem to know a lot about what happened and you're clearly not telling the whole truth, some penance will be needed, you know.'

'What?!'

'Get some sleep,' The Nyx said, stretching out their long limbs, 'but I want this mess gone before your first class. Please.' A few hours later – which felt like seconds, by the time she had got herself off to bed and finally drifted off – Ig was staring down the mass of rubble and clods of earth while holding the brush end of the broom that Pietro had used to beat up her former classmates with his hitherto-unseen ninja skills. She was having a very weird twelve hours. The Nyx's deal had been to keep what happened to the fountain a secret – 'I'm assuming there's a reason you don't want to tell me what you know, so I'm being a good headteacher and trusting my student' – if the problem was at least tidied away before the student body were up and about. Ig, tired as she was, decided to use the time, and the peace and quiet, to think. If there was one thing she'd learned about herself while she was at Shackleton, it was that she was very good at thinking–

'Morning, Ig!'

Katalina Kanaan rounded the corner, and every thought Ig had ever had flew right out her head. Katalina was already washed and ready for school – Ig was starting to think she slept in that perfect makeup of hers – and her long hair was tied back in a loose plait. 'H-hey!' she squeaked. 'How's the…how's the fire going?' Katalina tilted her head at her. 'What're you doing?'

'Nothing!' Ig attempted to hide the rock she was hauling behind her back.

'What happened to the fountain?'

'Nothing!'

Katalina laughed softly. 'Ig, come on. You can tell me, you know. I won't bite.'

For some reason, that last sentence made everything infinitely worse and better at the same time. Ig chucked the rock over onto the pile with a groan. 'Something got in and the fountain was attacked last night,' she said, choosing her words carefully so she wasn't actually lying to Katalina. 'The Nyx was super upset, so I said I'd clear it up for them.'

After they told me I had to.

Katalina smiled warmly. 'Well, aren't you cute? Though I don't know where I'm going to draw now.' She held up her sketchpad.

'You could keep me company?' Ig asked, feeling bold. Katalina shrugged, and sat on the grass. Quietly thrilled, Ig went back to piling up rocks. Apparently Mr. Glasse had heard about them, and dropped some serious hints that morning that the debris could be used for a decent outdoor terrain for Combat Classes – one that was off-school that he could charge Shackleton for using each month – and was now arguing very publicly with Mr. Throttler, who wanted them for his rose garden back at home. Either way, they needed to be in one place for pickup.

'They'll be really sad, you know,' Katalina said, watching as Ig worked with her sketchpad in her lap. 'The Nyx loved that fountain. And after everything that's happened with them, it's such a shame that it got wrecked.' Ig paused in her work. 'What do you mean, everything that's happened?'

Katalina paled. 'Oh. I forgot you didn't grow up around a lot of Villains.' She threaded her plait through her hands nervously. 'So when The Nyx was little – like, really little, first year little – Lunalist contacted the school wanting to arrange a transfer.'

'What?' Ig cried, nearly dropping a particularly sizable stone on her foot.

'Obviously, the school said no,' Katalina continued. 'And their parents, too. But then one night, they just… vanished. From their bedroom. No-one knew where they went. They were gone for days.'

'Oh my god,' Ig said. 'That's awful! What happened?'

Katalina looked at Ig quizzically. 'Your mam, she… Ig, has your mam really never talked to you about all this?'

'No?' Ig took a step towards the other girl. 'Kat, what happened with my mam?'

'Ig! Ig, come quick!'

Ig's attention snapped behind Katalina's shoulder. Pietro was running towards them; still in his pyjamas, hair ruffled. His cheekbone was mottled with yellow and purple bruising, but at least it looked like he could see properly this morning. 'Ig! Come quick! Something's… oh wow, out of breath… something's happening! Hi,

Kat. Nice of you to keep Ig company. But come quick!'

'What's happened?' Ig asked. Her stomach lurched painfully. Had Lily and Pisces returned? Did they have reinforcements? Was someone in danger? Did they have Vivi? She was meant to be joining Ig so she could persuade the brambles to grow over the hole that Pisces and Lily had used to get in – what if they'd come back through and caught her?

'Mr. Glasse and Mr. Throttler,' Pietro said breathlessly, 'are fighting!'

Ig blinked. 'What?'

'They're fighting. Proper fighting! Something about a rose garden, and always being selfish, and…oh, come on,' Pietro huffed, throwing up his hands, 'am I the only one whose always wanted to watch a Teacher Fight? You're all so boring.' He turned on his heel and flounced off. 'Wanted to place bets and everything,' he mumbled grumpily.

Ig turned back to Katalina shyly. 'I think I should go.' Even if she was safe, she should probably find Vivi, anyway.

'Oh, alright.' Katalina got to her feet. 'Well,' she said, her gaze on the grass, 'it was nice talking to you, Ig. It's always nice to talk to you.'

'You too.' Something fizzy and exciting passed between the girls. Ig found herself wanting to linger in it. 'Well. Bye.'

'Bye.' Katalina's eyes dropped from Ig's eyes to her lips and back again.

Something hot and sharp flared in Ig's stomach. 'Bye.'

'Ig, I want you to know–'

'OH MY GOD, MR. THROTTLER PUT MR. GLASSE IN A HEADLOCK!' Katalina winced.

'You know what?' she laughed. 'Just go. It's okay. The moment's gone.'

'What moment?'

'Ig! You are being a very bad friend, right now!'

'Coming, coming…'

Chapter Thirty-Eight

'Did you hear about what happened to the fountain?'

'Yeah – I heard it was some student going nuts.'

'Do you think it was the Hero school?'

'Nah – The Nyx would have told us.'

Ig's teeth sunk into the wood of her pencil, leaving the latest in a ring of bite marks that had almost reduced it to splinters.

'My cousin in the top year said it was a big cat – you hear about all these panthers and things running about on the moors, Rossborough has to have one, right?'

'I heard it was aliens! You know; on, like, a fact-finding mission. Scoping us out – seeing if we're ready to join their interplanetary regime.'

'Aliens? Come on, Aiden; be realistic.'

Apparently, none of the students knew about what had happened two days ago in the middle of the night, out in the maze. And right now – with her Power still wildly out of control – Ig was more than happy to keep it that way. So she nodded absently when her classmates asked for her opinion on what happened, and kept her eyes on the short, white-haired man writing complicated percentages on the ancient blackboard at the front of the room. Villain Accounting had never seemed so interesting. 'We have a very big exam next week, students,' Mr. Tyrante said, underlining a particularly thorny equation on the board for emphasis. 'So if you don't have a firm grasp on this type of tax fraud, now is the time to…' Muffled guitars and thumping drums resonated through the wall, making the eraser tumble from its holder onto the floor. Mr. Tyrante pinched the bridge of his nose, hard. 'I'm assuming Mr. von Ryan has commandeered the classroom next door for his free period?'

Ig smiled, despite herself. Mr. Tyrante was the only teacher she'd come across in her time at Shackleton who wasn't utterly charmed by Mercutio and his antics. 'If I let you miss out on this last question,' Mr. Tyrante sighed, 'will someone please go and tell him to turn his music down?'

Ig's hand was in the air before he'd finished speaking. She knew what Merc was working on and wanted a sneak peek.

The music was very definitely ancient; 80s at least, but not the kind of thrumming, yowling, thrashing stuff that Vivi liked. This was bouncier, livelier. Not exactly what she'd expected the sarcastic, intense Mercutio von Ryan to be listening to in his downtime.

As she opened the door, the sound smacked her in the face, hard as a slap. 'Merc?' Ig called, hands coming to her ears. 'Mr. Tyrante says you have to turn… it… down.'

The classroom was in chaos. Leaves of loose paper were strewn on every surface, along with pens and screwed up chocolate bar wrappers and textbooks open to random pages. In one corner, forgotten, was a whiteboard with the words 'HERETICAL HANDS – RESEARCH – IMPORTANT!!!' scrawled across it. On the table was Mercutio's headset that he used to control his swarm – in pieces – along with a tiny, slumbering cyborg bee, taped to a piece of card standing in for an operating table. And, whirling like a dervish with his back to her, was Mercutio. Dancing to novelty vintage pop rock.

His white lab coat billowing out around him. Merc spun in circles, shoulders moving to the beat, feet tapping, hips shimmying. Over in her cage, Onslaught watched the madness with the calm, bored stare of a pet who has seen every inch of her owner's insanity. Behind her, Ig sensed someone standing just at her shoulder.

'Ig! Ig, it's a free period next. Do you want to grab… a… oh.' Ig turned to see Vivi standing at her shoulder, staring into the room. A bright pink blush was spotting along the apples of her cheeks, and Ig swore she hadn't blinked for at least ten seconds. People who were attracted to boys were weird. Mercutio hopped in weird little jumps along the length of his desk, looking happier and, at the same time, more deranged than Ig had ever seen him. It was, frankly, terrifying.

'Oooh-oooh-oooh, Weird Scienc–AAGH!' Mercutio yelped; finally opening his eyes and spotted Ig leaning against the doorframe, lips pressed tightly together. His arms shot up into the air reflexively, sending the marker pen he'd been using as a microphone flying across the room.

'Are you,' Ig said, closing the door behind her – Vivi managing to squeeze herself inside just in time, 'always doing, like, the strangest things when no-one's looking?'

'Hmph. Of course I am,' Mercutio huffed, straightening out his lab coat and rearranging his features into something resembling his usual haughtiness as he turned his music down. 'That's the best time to do it.'

'Mr. Tyrante says turn the music down. But,' Ig said, walking over to Onslaught's cage and waggling her fingers through the bars, 'I wondered if maybe we could talk about your theories about…what happened the other night.' Something painful twinged in her chest, so she unlocked the cage, picked up Onslaught and buried her face in the rabbit's soft, fluffy fur. 'Yes I diiiid, yes I did, Onslaught, hiiii poppet…' Onslaught snuffled happily against her ear, and Ig's chest relaxed. Maybe Mercutio could engineer another Onslaught, just for her.

After seeing what Ig could do, Mercutio had – of course – taken it upon himself to research what had happened with… whatever it was. That dark, powerful force that had erupted from her hands. But, judging by the music and the disassembled headset, that had fallen by the wayside. Still, he was Ig's only hope. Who else was she going to tell? The teachers? 'Hey, Mr. Throttler; so the school got invaded by my former classmates – I was actually a Hero spying on you all, but I got over that whole thing – but don't worry, we fought them off, honest. Hey, could you have a look at these gigantic tentacles growing out of my hands?'

Ugh. No. She'd take her chances with Merc.

'Capital idea, Heretical,' Merc agreed. 'Let me see to this little fellow. Two minutes, and I'm all yours – your humble servant, I swear; your wish is my command.'

Vivi made a weird little peep noise in the back of her throat.

Merc bent over his tiny, sleeping charge again, looking from it to a pile of shiny, silver thimbles with needles attached to their bases. 'Hm,' he muttered. 'I suppose pairing you to the new and improved headset system will have to wait. Rushing the process will only yield unsuitable results.' He gently removed the tape that stuck the bee to the cardboard, and placed a glass jar over it before scooping Onslaught out of Ig's hands and putting her back into her cage.

'Nooo,' Ig whined. 'Give me back my baby.'

'Shan't.' Mercutio said. 'Onslaught; you are a distraction. Watch over the specimen. Alert me when she awakes and I'll send her back to the hive.' Onslaught wiggled her nose in affirmation, and Mercutio spun to face the girls, sitting on the floor in one fluid motion and beckoning them to join him.

'So,' Ig began, 'I was wondering if you'd made any progress with–'

'Physiologically? No. I can't find any records of anyone – Villain or Hero – whose Power manifested as a weird, half-solid tentacle-smoke… thing.' Mercutio waved his hand dismissively in the air; then snapped his fingers and waggled a pointer finger in Ig's direction. 'However! However, I have been poring over the events of that night, and I have a hypothesis.'

Ig scooted closer, eager to hear more.

'The evidence seems to suggest,' Mercutio continued, 'that your Power was triggered by something in the courtyard that night. Now, it wasn't your friend being in peril – from what I saw, you were willing to rip that girl's hair out with your bare hands to save our dear Vivi, no additional appendages required.' Ig blushed and reached out to give Vivi an awkward squeeze. 'And it wasn't to save the school or anything that noble. Which leaves what that girl was saying to you – and how it made you feel.' Mercutio held up a hand and counted off on his fingers, 'Inadequacy, insecurity, anger, betrayal, shock – could all be factors.'

Ig felt uncomfortably perceived – and by Mercutio von Ryan, of all people. She didn't like it.

'So, where does that leave us?' Vivi asked.

'If I have your permission, I'd like to conduct a few small tests?' Mercutio asked Ig. She nodded. Part of her was nervous – whatever it was, that Power had been so much bigger than she'd anticipated. Nothing at all like using a Power Lender. More potent, and so difficult to control. But another part of her – a small, vicious, curious part of her – would walk over hot coals if Mercutio von Ryan thought it would give that Power to her again. 'Alright, here we go.'

'Right now?!' Ig squeaked.

'No time like the present. Palms up, please.' Ig did as she was told. Mercutio cleared his throat and, with great effort, looked Ig right in the eyes. 'Ignatia Heretical… I hate the way you do your hair.'

Ig started. To the side, she heard Vivi sputter into her hand. 'What?!'

'I hate your hair,' Mercutio reiterated. 'It does nothing to flatter your face, which is far too round for a shoulder-length bob. You should grow it. The fact you haven't altered your uniform yet is not the mysterious, unknowable statement you think it is, you just look boring. The book you lent to Pietro? I read the first few chapters; the writing style is severely lacking – I've read Hero/ Villain enemies-to-lovers fan fiction with better characterisation, and it made me think less of your reading comprehension skills. The way you waggle your hand so a teacher will see that you know the answer in class and call on you is the most annoyingly desperate thing I've ever… excuse me, you're meant to be trying to harness your powers. Not blushing.'

It was true. Ig had gone bright red – she could feel it creeping up towards her ears – sitting bolt upright with her fists clenched. This was Mercutio's big plan? To insult her? She didn't even know she waggled her hand at teachers! 'I'll keep going,' Mercutio said, clearly annoyed Ig wasn't destroying the classroom after thirty seconds of nitpicking.

'Merc–' Vivi warned.

'You babytalk to Onslaught too much. She is a fully matured, adult rabbit, and should not be patronised in this way by–'

'Merc,' Vivi said, sharper than Ig had ever heard her speak, 'I think you're being a bit of a dick, right now. It's not actually helpful.'

'It's the scientific method!' Mercutio protested.

'Scientifically dickish, you mean.'

'Language!'

'Don't you 'language' me, I'm four months older than you…'

While they bickered, Ig sat quietly between them, rolling around what Mercutio had said inside her mind. Inadequacy. Anger. Shock. Betrayal.

Because all these other psychos will find out how useless you really are soon enough. They'll see how pathetic you are, and they'll chew you up and spit you out, just like you deserve... For once, Ig didn't shy away from the feelings that Lily's words sparked in her. Didn't panic, didn't try to think of a new way to be useful or worthy of existing. She sat there and felt it. They'd lied to her. They'd pushed her away, brushed her aside. They'd sent her here – to a place that they knew was dangerous! – and hoped that she'd become someone else's problem. And you know what? Ig had thrived here! She really had. She was doing well in her classes, she'd made friends, she'd even decided something about her future – before Lily Volt and… and Pisces… had spoiled it all.

Pisces. Pisces had felt sorry for her. All this time. She'd never felt anything for Ig, apart from pity. Something flexed in Ig's chest. Pisces had looked at her the other night – after everything Ig had been through, all the ways she'd endured and grown and changed – and felt sorry for her. Her! The girl who'd walked into the lion's den when those cowards had had to creep in under the cover of darkness. The girl who was making her way despite everyone thinking she couldn't. After years of those people at Lunalist thinking she was worth nothing. Had they been too blind to see her potential, or were they too cruel and proud to admit that they were wrong about her?

She was going to do this. She was going to unleash her Power on her terms – not just when Pisces Rising hurt her. She was going to train. She would make her tendrils do as she commanded. And once she could, everyone in the North East would see what happened when you underestimated Ignatia Heretical. Realising she actually liked herself wasn't a moment of peace for Ignatia Heretical. In that moment, when she saw herself for who she really was, all she could feel was rage. She opened her palms again; keeping her eyes closed, so she felt her Power rather than seeing it. She noticed so many more tiny sensations this time around; the feeling of every tendon in her hands flexing as one, a new muscle reaching and writhing out of her palm, the strange scent of smoke filling her nostrils, the blood burning in her veins. This felt so much more real than the last time, and far less terrifying. Her right tendril caught something up, wrapping around it and lifting it high into the air – she should really open her eyes and see what she had picked up, but Ig didn't want to, she wanted to stay in this moment of indignant anger until it swallowed her, until it swallowed everything– 'YES!' The dream broken, Ig opened her eyes. Suspended ten feet in the air, her tendril wrapped tightly around his middle, was Mercutio. Grinning.

'You did it!' he cried, feet kicking happily against the back of her tendril. Ig noticed dimly that she could feel it – but only just, like an insect was walking over her skin. 'I knew you could do it, Heretical! You're a phenomenon! A force of nature!' In his excitement, Mercutio inhaled a lungful of smoke. 'Ack – oh, oh god, it tastes like burned garlic, oh that's so – blahahaurrgh…'

As he hacked and coughed and laughed, Ig looked over at Vivi. Her eyes were shining, her fingers pressed against her lips. 'You did it,' she echoed. 'I'm so proud of you, Ig.'

Chapter Thirty-Nine

The first task was to work out how to put Mercutio down. Then, he and Vivi scribbled frantic notes as they asked Ig to perform various tasks with her Power; huge swipes that took out entire tables, then opening a window without smashing the glass, working up slowly to something delicate like picking up the glass to let Mercutio's bee escape and fly home, back to wherever he'd stashed the hive. That was tricky, and involved a lot of concentration. Her emotions were still present – she still needed them to summon the tendrils – but they were simmering at the back of her brain, while she focused on what she wanted to do. Sheer force was something Ig wasn't lacking when it came to her Power; but she'd need delicacy and control, if she wanted to be anything more than muscle on a brighter mind's team. And Ignatia Heretical was no-one's sidekick. She wouldn't be reduced to a convenient tool, or a useful but unloved pet. Not anymore.

Once the bee was freed, Ig watched her zoom out the window into the Northumberland air. She wondered at the trust that Mercutio had in her, to not destroy one of his projects like that. *This was the same boy who hadn't given me permission to use his first name when we met.*

'Well, this has been truly enlightening, Heretical,' Mercutio was saying, gathering up papers and beekeeping equipment. 'But I'll have to collect my things, now. Miss Hypnatyse needs this room at three.'

'Oh,' Vivi said. 'So you're… you're not free now? I thought we could, um, go for a walk. Or something.'

Merc blinked at her. 'No. This was my free period for the day.' He waved an arm around them. '"Hence Heretical Studies".'

'"Heretical Studies" – that's so funny!' Vivi hooted, laughing so loudly she made Onslaught start in her cage. Mercutio jumped too – clearly unaware of anything he'd said that was funny. 'Like she's a – like she's a lab rat or something! Hahaha. Ha.'

'Vivi,' Ig said from the floor, 'it isn't even our free period. We have Torture Management.'

'Oh, do we?'

'Yes. We need to go now.'

'Oh. Okay. I need to go now,' Vivi repeated to Mercutio, heading towards the door. 'I have to, um, get to Torture Management.'

'I gathered.' Merc held the papers close to his chest, looking after her as she bumped awkwardly into the closed classroom door and turned to apologise to it. 'Well, um… it was nice to have you here, Vivi. While we worked. Even if you accused me of being a–'

'A dick?' Vivi said with a giggle, looking Mercutio up and down. 'Well. You can be. But I wouldn't change you. At all.'

'…oh. Alright.' Mercutio flushed red, eyes turning glassy. 'That's… that's good to know.'

Both of them blinked at each other for a second, then Vivi fumbled her way to the doorknob and was gone in a flash. *She didn't even wait for me*, Ig thought. But actual flirting had taken place! Worth it. Ig made a mental note to congratulate Vivi when they were back at the dorms.

'Heretical?' Mercutio said, still staring at the door.

'Von Ryan?'

'Is Vivi… ah. Is she seeing anyone right now? Or does she have plans to… see… someone… soon?'

Ig laughed – which she realised was a horrible error when Mercutio's face fell and, for one awful second, he didn't look like the cocky, aloof-and-yet-somehow-annoyingly-hyperactive scientist she'd come to know. Mercutio, for once in his life, looked like a sixteen-year-old boy. 'It's Falcon Reeve, isn't it?' he muttered, shoulders slumping in defeat. 'His little scheme with those, quote-unquote, 'Villain Wars?' I knew it, Pietro said I was wrong, but I knew it.' In three strides, he crossed the room to Onslaught's cage, opened it, picked up the rabbit and smushed his face into the soft fluff of her belly. Onslaught, for her part, looked serene about the whole thing. This was not her first time being a von Ryan comfort item, it would seem. Ig took in the scene for a second, then hopped up onto a table with a sigh.

'Merc. Vivi isn't seeing someone. And she definitely doesn't like Falcon Reeve.'

Mercutio let out a long, muffled groan.

'I mean it! I think she likes guys who are a little more, um…' Crazed? Arrogant? Unhinged? '…creative.'

Mercutio blew a raspberry – either in derision or because Onslaught's fur went up his nose. 'Don't be ridiculous, Heretical. Who wouldn't be infatuated with Reeve? He's cool. He's handsome and unflappable and always says the right things.' His shoulders slumped. 'And he's not so very…much.'

Ig tipped her head to the side. 'She watched him puke in a fountain, Merc.'

'And I bet he did it with style.' Mercutio sadly slipped Onslaught back into her cage. 'Anyway. Doesn't matter. Onwards and upwards, all that.'

'Merc.'

'I don't need pity, Heretical. You of all people, must know how that can sting.'

'I wasn't going to say that.' It didn't feel right to out Vivi's feelings – especially now, when she was just getting to grips with them. 'I wanted to say thank you.'

'Hm? Oh, no problem,' Mercutio said, distractedly, fussing the latch on Onslaught's cage.

'No,' Ig said, laying a hand on Mercutio's shoulder so he'd actually look at her. 'I mean it. Thank you. I don't… I don't think like you do, Merc. I know that, if this had been up to me, I never would have made the connection with Lily and what she said. I would be too scared to.' Mercutio looked from her hand to her face and back again, teeth working at his bottom lip self-consciously. 'So, anyway. I hope you know…I'm happy to know someone whose brain works like yours does. I don't think you're 'much.' I think you're brilliant.'

After a long moment, a small smile crept across Mercutio's face. 'Likewise, Heretical.' He looked her up and down, a thoughtful expression crossing his face as he tapped his chin with a forefinger. 'You know,' he said, 'I've been wondering about your particular brand of brilliant. Your brain is definitely a unique one…'

'Oh, cheers Merc,' Ig scoffed.

'Coupled with your developmentally lacking social skills,' Mercutio continued, 'the emotional regulation issues, your love of soft and fuzzy things like our dear Onslaught…' Mercutio nodded as if he'd solved a particularly thorny problem. 'You may be autistic, you know.'

Despite herself, years of lectures on Lunalist's zero-tolerance bullying policy drifted to the front of Ig's mind. 'I hope you're not still trying to insult me, Merc.' A defensive, exposed feeling slithered across her skin; quickly followed by something different; more eager, questioning. She hoped Mercutio would say more, and she hoped he never brought it up again.

'Why would I be doing that?' Mercutio raked his hand through his curls. 'I'm autistic. And I'm the most amazing person you know.'

The sun drifted through the huge windows of the classroom, warming Ig's face. Something about that word – 'autistic' – felt right, somehow. Fitting. A little raw, like a fresh bruise, but it was a satisfying kind of soreness. Like the first time Pietro had called her 'Villain.' It turned out Ignatia Heretical had a lot to learn about herself – more than anyone at Lunalist had ever realised.

'Just something to think about.' Mercutio flicked one hand sarcastically in her direction, and Ig saw a little mischief dancing in his eyes. 'Besides; I don't need to be ableist when my next tactic for addressing your insecurities was to bring up your abysmal track record with women–'

A tendril shot out of Ig's right hand, wrapped around Mercutio's arm, and tossed him across the room.

'Oh my god!' Ig cried, running over to where her friend lay sprawled across the floor. 'Oh, Merc – I'm so, so sorry, I can't completely control it yet, but I'll get better, I'm so sorry!' Mercutio blinked up at her slowly. Like a lizard. Then, his shoulders began to shake. Ig pressed her lips tightly together to stop the laugher sputtering out, which just made everything funnier. Ten minutes later, Miss Hypnatyse and her Mind & Manipulation class walked into a classroom in disarray, two manically giggling students, and a very world-weary undead rabbit.

Chapter Forty

Ig lay on her bed, watching as one tendril undulated slowly in patterns in the air. When she was little, she'd had trouble talking, so her mam had worked on the vowels with her every morning after breakfast for months – slowly mouthing 'a, e, i, o, u' and getting Ig to copy her. She'd decided to do something similar with her new Power over the last week and a half; spelling out words, drawing crude zig-zags and spirals, getting better control so she didn't accidentally slam it against the base of Vivi's bed. Again. The tendrils didn't hurt, exactly, when she hit them off things; it was like the memory of hurting, a distant, throbbing, nagging ache. Still, it didn't feel nice. So, Ig trained – night after night, until she had just the amount of control that she wanted. It was about an hour before lights-out, and the sweet, earthy smell of the room and the gentle sound of the misters watering her plants was making Ig feel drowsy in a lazy, comfortable sort of way. It was the first peace she'd felt in days. The weekend had been spent mostly in Mercutio and Pietro's dorm, practicing extending and withdrawing her tendrils until it became second nature – with begrudging breaks to head down to the snack dungeon for supplies – so it was nice to finally be back in her own space.

'Have you thought about what you're going to tell everyone?' Vivi asked from her bunk.

'What about?'

'In Combat Class tomorrow,' Vivi replied. 'Your Power Lender won't work, remember? Because of the…' a hand reached over the side of her bunk and wiggled. Ig chewed on her lip, deep in thought. She'd forgotten about that; her tendrils taking up

267

the space in her brain that was usually free for a Power Lender to take advantage of. She'd hoped to be able to keep her Power a secret – for a little while, at least. Partially out of fear that somehow the news would make its way back to Lunalist. Something was forming in the back of her mind; a vicious little idea that nipped and gnawed at her whenever she was idle – and sometimes when she was meant to be studying. Old habits died hard, and Ig always found it easier to concentrate on the thing she wanted to think about. But as well as all that, she felt like she was still getting to know her Power. It was this new, secret, strange part of her – she didn't know if she wanted to share, yet. She ended up dreading it all weekend; barely listening to Merc pontificating about his theories about her Power, missing her cue to laugh when Pietro told a joke. And on Sunday night, she couldn't sleep for thinking about how other people would react. I mean, it wasn't like she was the weirdest girl at the school or anything – that student with the spiders in their mouth was far, far weirder – but that old, familiar fear of being misunderstood came creeping back in, making her heart skitter in her chest. In the end, she slipped silently from bed early the next morning, put on her uniform, and left the dorm before Vivi was awake.

The school seemed to lead her to the breakfast room; Ig barely had to concentrate, now. She liked it when the school was quiet like this; listening to the muffled pad of her feet on the carpet, the distant caw of birds outside. It was a good time to think. Ig grabbed herself a pain au raisin (Vivi thought they were gross, Ig liked the soft, custardy pastry inside the flaky shell) and settled herself in a chair – directly opposite Mr. Throttler, who looked up sharply as she sat.

'Oh,' Ig said. 'Sorry, Sir. I'll move.'

Mr. Throttler waved his arm, a soft mumble reverberating inside his hood. Ig sat back down, and the pair ate in relatively comfortable silence. Mr. Throttler, for his part, kept his eyes – or what Ig assumed were his eyes – on his magazine; 'Maiming

& Mutilating Monthly', the title said. 'The Iron Maiden; worth the hype? Plus, we test the blood-cleaning hack EVERYONE'S been talking about.' After a while, he looked up again, to see Ig toying with her coffee cup, deep in thought. He tilted his head at her curiously, and Ig sighed, throwing herself back in a chair.

'Do I have to tell you, Sir?' she asked. Mr. Throttler weighed up the question, then shrugged. 'Fine,' Ig said. 'I'll tell you. But please – don't tell anyone else. Let's call it, um, student-teacher confidentiality or something. Please?'

Mr. Throttler mimed zipping his lips shut. As Ig spoke, she watched him carefully, considering her story, nodding encouragingly as she talked; eventually fishing a pen from somewhere in his cowl and making notes on the edge of his magazine. Maybe it was because he couldn't talk, Ig thought, but Mr. Throttler was probably the best teacher she'd ever had. At least she felt like he actually listened to her when she spoke. '…but I suppose that all sounds silly, doesn't it?' she said, after about five minutes of non-stop monologuing at this poor adult, who only wanted to read in peace before she showed up. 'I should be proud of my Power right away, shouldn't I? Ready to, I don't know, take on the world before I've even begun. Isn't that what happens? You get your Power, and you race out to find the nearest Hero to beat up?' Mr. Throttler cocked his head at her, then gestured around them like she was a fool. 'Right,' Ig said, drawing her knees up to her chest. 'That's what a school's for. I forgot that getting a Power wasn't the end of my story, like it is at… like it is at other places.'

Mr. Throttler glanced over Ig's head, then motioned for someone to join them. Ig looked over the back of her chair to see Mr. Glasse – looking immaculate and awake in a black polo neck, even at this ridiculous hour – holding a cup of steaming black coffee. 'Throttler,' he said, nodding in greeting. 'Oh, and Miss Heretical; how nice to see you.'

Mr. Throttler was writing something on his magazine again;

he tore the page out and handed it to Mr. Glasse, who studied it intently. 'Private Combat classes?' he asked, shooting a look at his colleague. Mr. Throttler nodded. Mr. Glasse darted a look at Ig, and then shrugged. 'Yeah, okay.' Ig started, confused, and Mr. Glasse rolled his eyes at her. 'What, you think you're the only student who's a little shy about their Power?'

'How did you–'

'Actually, it sort of works out. I've got a student doing one-on-ones that you can work with – as long as you respect each other's privacy.' Mr. Glass drained his coffee in one swallow and put the cup down on Mr. Throttler's magazine. 'See you at nine-thirty.'

The rest of the class were told to meet in the school grounds, while Ig was shown into the same classroom where The Infamous Lighter Incident had gone down. Ig wondered who this other student could be. Someone with a Power they didn't want to let the rest of the school know about. It could be someone really powerful, she thought – someone she had seen in classes all term, who suddenly took on this new, strange identity.

Maybe it's Katalina, she thought, surprised by the sudden thrill of shyness that ran through her.

'Well, well,' Pietro von Ryan cried, idly twirling a baseball bat one-handed, 'They really do let any old Villains in here, eh?'

Ah. No such luck.

Ig had to admit, her friend looked well. Very well, in fact. A little sheen of sweat suited him, and he was carrying himself with a lighter, bouncier step than usual. Maybe it was because he wasn't weighed down with two backpacks' worth of school materials.

'What're you doing here?' Ig asked. 'Is everything okay with Merc?'

'Why wouldn't it be?' Pietro said sunnily. 'You know those sick moves I pulled off in the garden?'

'When you beat up two Heroes with a broomstick? I recall.'

'Well, that was my Power!' Pietro twirled his bat with a flourish. 'I asked Mr. Glasse if I could work on it before I, you know, try anything fancy in Combat Class. It's all still so new, you know?' His smile faded. 'Why do you think Merc would be here? I don't need him to hold my hand, you know.'

'I don't know.' Ig picked up a bat herself and failed miserably when she tried to copy Pietro's twirls. 'I just thought, if you were here – practicing in private – maybe he asked you to get better before you…'

'Oh, no no no. It was my idea.' Pietro flopped onto the floor and began stretching out his calves. 'Merc's crazy about the whole situation. He's still positive he's going to make me a glowing bō staff, or something. But, you know, I don't want to show him up.' Pietro grew shy all of a sudden. 'I knew how to be Pietro, Mercutio's assistant. I don't know how to be one part of The Von Ryan Twins, With Their Crazy Powers. So I'm gonna train up, all on my lonesome, until we can burst out into the world together.' He lifted his head and gave Ig a strange look. 'You still don't entirely get him, do you?'

'No. But I like him a lot more now.'

'Okay, people,' Mr. Glasse said, closing the doors to the Combat Classroom, 'are you warmed up? Or were you too busy chatting?'

'Too busy chatting, sir,' Pietro grinned.

'Good to know.' When Ig turned to look at her teacher, he was gone. 'Sir?' she said, turning in a circle. 'What're you–' Something thwacked Ig on the back of the head. 'Ow!' Mr. Glasse reappeared at her side – only for a second. As soon as Ig tried to lash out at him – a tendril growing at rapid pace from her hand, clumsily slashing at the air – he had vanished again. An unseen pair of arms grabbed her from behind, spinning her around and throwing her to the ground. Reflexively, Ig held out her hands to break her fall – and instead found herself propped up on two sturdy tentacles, all her weight bearing down on them. Interesting. She did an awkward sort of push-up to right herself, and turned to Pietro, who simply shrugged.

'He goes invisible,' he said.

'I established that, Pietro.'

'Thought you might need some context clues – hang on.' Pietro whirled, striking with his bat as he dropped low to the ground. To the side of him, something fell heavily to the ground. 'Ha! Very good, Mr. von Ryan,' came Mr. Glasse's voice. 'I thought I would catch you off guard with that one.'

'It'll take more than that, Sir.' Pietro slung his bat over one shoulder, and Ig couldn't help the pride that filled her up at the sight of him basking in praise like that. But, at the same time, something pinged in her head. A hypothesis she'd have to test. Mr. Glasse turned visible again, slightly out of breath.

'Right, you two; consider that your warm-up. I'm off to see to your classmates. When I come back, I want to see two warriors in front of me, got it?'

'Yes, Sir.'

Mr. Glasse pointed a casual finger-gun at Ig. 'Nice defensive measures, Heretical.' Ig did double finger-guns back at him and instantly regretted it. 'Can you do a handstand?'

'Not since I was six.'

'Well, next time you find yourself in the position you were just in, try moving into a handstand from there. See if you can right yourself.'

Ig nodded. As Mr. Glasse left, she turned to see Pietro standing behind her, grinning like a cat. 'Ready?' he asked. Then, he struck.

The last time Ig was in Combat Class, fighting with Vivi, it had felt like a test. When she was fighting Lily Volt – scrapping on the ground, blood running into her eyes – it was desperate, raw and messy. Fighting with Pietro felt like play. His style was light and quick, full of spins and ducks and dodges, blocking her attempts to kick or punch him in the face. He forced Ig backwards so fast and with such force, she barely had time to catch her breath. 'Come on,' he said, pushing his hair out of his eyes with the back of one hand, 'use your Power. I know you can control it.'

'Maybe. A little,' Ig said, out of breath. 'Enough, I think.'

Pietro cocked his head and widened his eyes at her.

'Come on, then. I even give you permission to give me another black eye.'

Ig grinned, holding up her palm and shivering as a tendril lashed out like a whip, whipping Pietro's legs out from under him. He sprung back up and aimed the bat into her shoulder, hoping to knock her back – a move that Ig blocked, raising up her arm and keeping him safely out of striking range. Before Pietro could rush back into her space, Ig pushed her arm out straight and sent a tendril, straight and vicious as a dagger, towards his chest. For a second, Pietro's playfulness and bravado vanished, and he genuinely looked shocked as he dived out of the way. Ig was pleased at that… until Pietro grinned, slamming his bat into the floor at such an angle that it bounced up into the air, shattering a light fixture above Ig's head. She dodged the falling shards of glass with a growl, and came after Pietro with murder in her eyes – or, at the very least, very painful bruising.

They continued like that for a while – slashing and whirling, jumping and rolling and laughing at each other – until Pietro finally knocked Ig off balance, his bat coming within inches of her nose. She pitched backwards, arms windmilling behind her – and the tendrils caught her like they had before, leaving her in a weird, crablike position. 'Don't move, don't move don't move!' Pietro shouted. 'Try and get out of it without retracting the tentacles.'

'I'm stuck!' Ig yelled.

'You're not. Just like Mr. Glasse said; do a handstand. The momentum will flip you over.'

'A backwards handstand?!'

'Try it, you big baby!'

Ig closed her eyes, kicked her legs up into the air…and ended up doing a weird scissor-kick. She tried again, nearly kicking Pietro in the face. In the end, he grabbed her ankles and pushed her up and over; Ig screaming the whole time. It occurred to her, as her knees flew past her head, that it wasn't handstands she used to do when she was six. They were forward rolls, which were totally different.

This was it. She was going to break her neck, before she'd even had a chance to really live–

And then, just like that, her feet were on the ground. She was right-side up, hands – and tendrils – sticking up in the air. And Pietro was grinning in her face. 'You did a flip!' he yelled. 'See, Heretical? You have to believe in yourself–'

He was off guard; now or never. As Pietro reached for her, Ig lowered her arm to her side and directed her tendril at a sharp right angle, aiming it squarely at a very sensitive area of Pietro's anatomy – faster and fiercer than she'd ever used her Power before. Pietro knocked her aside, almost without thinking. 'Hey! That was sneaky!' he laughed, outraged. 'What'd I done to deserve that?'

Ig shrugged. 'I had a thought,' she said.

'Oof, dangerous.'

'Shut up. Do you remember when we were in the gardens, and Lily was…' Ig shoved the memory of her bully smiling into Pisces' adoring face aside. 'When she was distracted. She lost her grip on her Powers. But when Mr. Glasse caught you off guard…'

'I could still fight,' Pietro finished for her. 'Hm. What do you think that means?'

'I'm not sure yet.' Ig smiled her very best Villain smile; the one she'd been practicing in the mirror before bed. 'But it's interesting, isn't it?'

Her friend's grin was insidious – just like her own. 'Very interesting.'

Chapter Forty-One

'No, I'm telling you,' Pietro was saying, as he and Ig cooled off after their fight, 'miso caramel – it's going to be the next big thing.'

'Pietro, that sounds disgusting.'

'And I bet you felt the same about salted caramel, once upon a time. And now look.' Pietro gestured, raking his hand through his curls as he did. 'Everywhere.' He offered her some of his bottled water. 'You need to hydrate.' Ig wrinkled her nose. 'I'll get a drink back at the dorm. I don't want your slobbers, thanks.'

'What, you mean you don't want to drink the spit of a sweaty teenage boy? Fair enough, we are pretty disgusting. So,' Pietro said, untying and retying his shoe, 'we're going to make those shiny-haired brats from Lunalist pay, right?' Ig leaned back, feeling a not-unpleasant stretch in her back. 'I'm thinking about it.' She hadn't wanted to bring it up first; scared that, after everything she'd put them through, her friends might not want to fight her battles for her. But since the discovery of her Power, she'd been practicing with Mercutio every time their free periods lined up – sometimes with Vivi cheering her on from the sidelines, sometimes alone. And speaking of Vivi, her dorm-mate had been constantly telling Ig about this 'cool new grounding exercise' she'd just happened to come across in a mindfulness book she just happened to be reading, making sure to slather her with compliments and motivational quotes like Pietro slathered a spoon with – ugh – miso caramel. At first, Ig had been distrustful of the whole situation – still suspicious of kindness, after all this time – until Vivi had literally sat her down and explained she was trying to keep her at an emotional baseline, so she could learn better when she was training.

Everyone she cared about at this school had involved themselves, without her even asking them to. So, Ig supposed, it was only fair to let them in on what she was planning. 'I'll tell you next weekend,' she said. Pietro flopped backwards with a groan.

'Next weekend? Ig whyyy?'

'Because!'

'I wanna know noooowwww…'

'I need the proper setting!'

'Noooooo…'

'Hey!' Ig crawled to her friend's side and booped him on the nose. 'You were the one who wanted me to be evil. I need the right place to reveal my dastardly plan.'

Pietro grinned up at her. 'But it's gonna hurt them, right?' Ig smiled. When she thought about what she was planning, she felt a very unique, gleeful kind of nastiness. She often thought back to when she'd yelled at Vivi, all those months ago; how it had felt so perversely good to be awful to her. What she felt now, in those moments when her plan unfurled in her mind's eye, was a little like that. But with Pisces and Lily, Ig was done caring how uncomfortable she made them. In fact, she was beyond that; she wanted them to fear her.

Pietro sat up, an eager glint in his eye. 'So,' he asked, 'can I at least know what's happening next weekend that's so special?'

'I'm taking you all shopping.'

'What?'

'I have to go.'

'No, wait, Ig! Gah, I hate cryptic clues.'

'Pietro, listen to me.' Ig placed her hands on her friend's shoulders. 'I need to tell you something.'

'Is it about–'

'It's not about the plan!' Ig shook Pietro back and forth with irritation. 'If you'd shut up for a second, I wanted to tell you I'm proud of you!'

She was. She hadn't missed Mr. Glasse calling Pietro 'Mr. von Ryan' and giving him praise for his own work, not his brother's. The two bag-carriers had made something of themselves. And it would be very, very useful to have someone with Pietro's skills around. Someone who could smack their way out of a problem.

Pietro looked at her, eyes suddenly shimmering. A trembling, wavering, thrilled expression crossed his face for a second, before he coughed it away. 'Thanks, Heretical. Now please, go have some water, before you shrivel up and die.'

The rest of the day passed with ease; a few classes, lunch with Vivi out by the sad, grey little stump that remained of their fountain, followed by a free period of lashing her tendrils at a bullseye Merc had drawn on a blackboard while he and Vivi pretended with all their might that they weren't flirting with each other.

As they went to leave, Vivi reached up and hugged Mercutio tightly – pressing a quick kiss to the corner of his mouth. She'd been aiming for his cheek – Ig knew this because she'd somehow been roped into letting Vivi 'practice goodbye hugs' on her for most of their lunch break. The problem was Ig was a lot shorter than Merc and so, upon realising she'd missed her target, Vivi bravely and maturely ran away from the situation, leaving a thunderstruck Mercutio and a despairing Ig in her wake.

'I have no idea,' Ig bemoaned later that evening, as Vivi threw herself on her bed and went over the not-quite-a-kiss for the thirteenth time, 'how I'm the less disastrous one when it comes to relationships. Did you make me up that vial of stuff, by the way? I was going to use it tonight.'

'What did you say to him?' Vivi wailed; mascara smudging under her eyes in wet smears. 'After I left? Does he think I'm an idiot? He does, doesn't he; he thinks I'm a total idiot who goes about kissing her friends for the fun of it. Oh, and it's in my blazer pocket.' She flapped her hand at where she'd slung her uniform once they got home. 'The little yellow bottle? Inside pocket. Yeah, that one.'

'Thanks.' Ig found the vial and shook it gently. Back at the classroom, once Vivi had made her escape, Ig had given Mercutio a meaningful glare and said 'she doesn't do that to Falcon Reeve' before walking away, leaving him to his thoughts – of which she assumed there were many. But Vivi didn't need to know that Ignatia 'fell in love with her bully's girlfriend' Heretical was interfering in her dating life.

'That's going to hurt, you know,' Vivi said, wiping off the last of her makeup on her pillowcase and shooting the yellow vial a sideways glance as Ig slotted it into her own pocket..

'I know.' Ig changed the subject as quickly as she could. 'And with Merc…well, you sort of are a total idiot who kisses her friends for fun. Use your cleanser, you goblin, or you'll get spots.'

'Ig!'

'Until he knows you want to be his girlfriend and make weird plant-bunny hybrids together, it does look like you randomly decided to kiss him.'

Later, as the sun set across Shackleton and Vivi curled up on her bed to read some ridiculous horror novel (something about vampires and New Orleans), Ig walked out of their dorm room and down the main flight of stairs and out into the gardens. The world around her was quiet, the only sound coming from the blackbirds singing in the hedges. Ig silently walked around the fountain and, after checking no-one was around to see her, turned her palms towards the floor. Two strong, beautifully dark tendrils coiled out of her hands and pressed into the earth, supporting her until she felt brave enough to allow them to lift her from the floor. Ig rose into the air; wobbling slightly as she realised quite how high she was but regaining her balance easily. She stepped out onto her rooftop and left out a long, happy exhale – she knew that would work. She fished her communication device and the yellow vial Vivi gave her out of her backpack and pressed Call. Then, as the Lunalist logo flashed onto the screen, she tipped her head back and emptied the bottle of pollen directly onto her face.

'War Room – oh my god!' cried the hacker girl on the other end of the call. 'What the hell happened to you?' Ig looked into the lens – or, at least, she thought she did. Her eyes were streaming so badly, everything was a wet, tearful blur. Vivi's oilseed was even more powerful than it had been during Combat Class. Ugh, she'd need an hour-long shower after this. She hoped Vivi hadn't used all the hot water. 'I need–' Ig said through her tears, making sure that her sniffles sounded particularly snotty, 'I need to talk to The General. Now.'

The General's face filled the screen. 'Miss Heretical,' she said, so calmly Ig felt a chill run down her spine, 'what is the meaning of this?'

'General,' Ig sobbed, 'I want to come home. I want to come home right now, please don't make me stay here – call Pisces, tell her to come get me, she'll come get me, I know she will…'

'Calm down,' The General said, 'take a deep breath, compose yourself – that's it – and tell me what's happened. I can't help until I know.'

'General,' Ig said, smearing her sleeve across her eyes, 'You were right about them. You were right about everything. They're insane here; you don't know all the things they've said to me, what they've done…' She took in a big, shuddering breath. 'General, I'm so scared, all the time. My dorm-mate is the worst of them all – she drugs me so I can't sleep, and when I do, I have these nightmares, these awful nightmares. Then in the lessons – they're so scary, General, and they talk about things I don't understand – when I fall asleep at my desk, the teachers say they're going to punish me.'

'How are they going to punish you?'

'I don't know…make me one of their experiments, maybe? I don't know, I can't follow along with anything they're saying. I'm so confused…'

Ig had been rehearsing this call for nearly a week now. The

words tripped off her tongue, the helpless crack in her voice coming naturally. Miss Schwab's lessons had paid off. If this all wasn't so stupid, it would be funny.

'I knew those lessons would be too much for you,' The General said, almost to herself. But she didn't look sad about it, or worried. She looked relieved. Ig swallowed the lump in her throat and continued.

'What're they going to do to me, General?' She forced a tremor into her voice, hoping she sounded as scared and as upset and pathetic as she looked.

'I don't know, Miss Heretical. But I know one thing to be true. You have to keep going with your mission.'

All Ig's breath left her lungs in a rush. Now she knew for certain that Pisces had been right. No amount of terror or crying or awful stories would force The General to bring her back to Lunalist. Because as long as she was here, she wasn't their problem. She pulled a shuddering sob from somewhere deep inside her chest, hands flying to her mouth. 'Wh-what?'

The General raised an eyebrow. 'I thought you wanted to help us, Miss Heretical.'

'I do,' Ig lied.

'Then prove that you can hold firm. Use this vicious turn to your advantage, and report back with your findings.'

Stay where you are, get bullied and brutalised and experimented on... it'll be good intel for us. Ig felt her anger rising in her chest, and shoved it down as hard as she could. She needed to be pathetic and scared right now, not bubbling with rage. She had to hold her nerve.

'I've been telling everyone how promising your findings are,' The General said gently, tilting her head to the side like a bird spotting prey. 'The tutors, Miss Rising, your father. If you buckle now, you'll be making me out to be a fool to believe in you. You don't want that, do you?'

What Ig wanted was to smash the tablet into a million tiny

pieces with one of her tendrils – to throw it as far as she could into the Rossborough wilds. But instead, she balled her hands into fists just out of the camera's sight and shook her head, snivelling. Her knuckles began to turn black.

'Alright,' The General said. 'No more crying, Miss Heretical. Go and show them that a Lunalist student cannot be broken.'

But you don't think of me as a Lunalist student, Ig thought. You think of me as a problem.

'Goodbye, Miss Heretical. I'll be in touch.' The screen went blank. As soon as she wasn't being watched, Ig's face smoothed over into careful, thoughtful blankness, tears still drying on her cheeks. She hadn't expected it to be that easy to plant thoughts of her mental collapse into The General's head. But, she pondered to herself, as she made her way back to her dorm, that's what happens when a person shoves you into a tiny box of their choosing, labelling you 'weak' or 'useless' or 'not worth the effort.' It makes them stubborn, and it makes them stupid. And stubborn, stupid people are perfect victims for a Villain.

Chapter Forty-Two

'Ugh, finally,' Pietro complained, as the four of them staggered off the bus together, 'we've been on that bus for days.'

The bus shuddered and hissed to a halt just steps away from Grey's Monument; down a tiny, claustrophobic street lined with bus stops and cantankerous commuters. Beside them was a huge, glass shopping centre, opposite was the bookshop and a patch of grass littered with kids in band t-shirts and pigeons, and behind them, there it was; Grey's Monument. The centre of all Ig's plans.

'One hour, fifteen minutes,' growled Mercutio through gritted teeth, shooting a venomous look back at the bus driver. 'Would have been faster without your nine-minute so-called 'tab break', Dave. Don't you know who you're ferrying around in your shoddy little vehicle that stinks of–'

The driver closed the bus doors on Mercutio's immaculate white lab coat with a petty grin. Mercutio bit back a curse as he yanked on the tails of his coat, examining the dirty streaks the door had left behind. 'Are we positive that there isn't a better way to get to the city centre from Rossborough?'

'Positive,' Ig said, her attention already coaxed away from her friends and their complaints.

It felt so strange to be back here in Newcastle. It was so… busy, and so loud. She missed Rossborough already; but this little trip was important. She had things to plan, and she could only plan them if she came back here. Lily and Pisces were more than happy to trample all over her new home; why shouldn't she return the favour? She walked away from the bus stop, across the pavement and up onto the steps that led to

Monument itself; craning her neck to look up at the top of the huge, stone spire that acted as Newcastle's infamous landmark, meeting place and, most Saturdays, protest venue. She turned slowly in place so she could take everything in, form a mental map of the area to take back to her dorm. The entrance to the shopping centre, with its neon lights and gaudy advertisements; the street with all the buses and taxis and delivery bikes. The bookshop – with its windows filled with a new kids' book penned by one of dad's old co-workers, the title painted on the window in bright yellows and greens. There was the fancy clothes shop, then the road again, sloping away towards the Laing Art Gallery then out towards the motorway…and the bank, steps away and just off to her right, with its wide glass windows and black-and-red branding. And next to it, an alleyway that Ig knew led to nothing but the Tyneside Cinema, where the General had saved those old women all those years ago. All very important. 'Right,' Vivi chirped, trying to keep the boys chipper. 'What first? Sushi? Shopping? Oh, there's a Planet Mocha down that street,' – she pointed down a street jutting off of Monument that was full of fashionable coffee shops, expensive clothes outlets and, weirdly, vape shops – 'I haven't had a Venti Cinnamon Latte in ages…'

Ig turned, the spell of her plans broken. There, only a few buildings away down a street she hadn't planned on using (one that led to Lunalist – no good for an escape route) was a sleek, green-and-white coffee shop. Outside, people sipped on their iced coffees and tapped frantically at their keyboards and phone screens, all looking terribly busy and important. A huge sign in the window, complete with a caped, cartoon silhouette, said 'Discount for Our Local Heroes! Students of Lunalist Academy are eligible with receipt of latest school report.' That was new. Planet Mocha had long been a favourite of Heroes – her dad was practically keeping the one in Gosforth in business – but since Ig had been gone, they must have decided to make it an official collaboration, rather than an unwritten rule that Heroes get free stuff whenever they want it.

The door clanged open, and a couple emerged; two girls, one blonde, one redheaded, arm in arm. The redhead was laughing at something the blonde had said and for a moment, Ig felt sick. Then, the redhead turned, hair shining in the sun, and Ig released a breath that she hadn't realised she was holding. Not her. Not them. She was fine. Everything was–

'Ig?'

Ig shook herself out of her thoughts. Vivi was holding her shoulder, while the boys lingered awkwardly behind her. 'You okay?'

'Go on,' she said, rolling her eyes in a self-deprecating way, 'I don't want a coffee, but you three go have one and I'll catch up, okay?' It'd be a good chance for her to scope out the site of her plan without drawing attention.

Vivi looked down the street at the coffee shop – at the sign – and then back to her friend. 'Nah,' she said, jutting her chin out contrarily, 'it's alright. Something tells me we wouldn't be welcome.'

'We're not in uniform, though. We could be, well, normal.'

It was true. Vivi was wearing a faded old band t-shirt and jeans, while Pietro had opted for an open checked shirt and scuffed, white trainers, while Mercutio…well, Mercutio was still wearing his lab jacket. 'There's nothing wrong with my dress sense,' he'd said haughtily, back at Shackleton. 'Though I will sacrifice the goggles if I must.' Ig had agreed that he must. Ig, for her part, had chucked on an old, black t-shirt dress she'd found in the bottom of her luggage when she unpacked back at the start of term. It felt like they were in disguise.

'No, but they can tell.' Vivi said, teeth pressing down hard on her bottom lip. 'They can always tell, you know.'

'Something in the, you know,' Pietro waved his arm vaguely in the direction of his face. 'This whole situation.'

'Really?' Ig asked. That was interesting.

'They've done studies,' Mercutio said, sitting down on the

Monument steps to scrub the dirt out his lab coat. 'Putting non-Villains in Shackleton uniforms, Villains in civilian clothing. It's unquantifiable, but there nonetheless. 'Innate sinisterness,' I think is the quote. I'll link you the study back home. It's interesting. Sad. Weird. But interesting.'

Ig looked around and realised that, even though Monument was crowded, no-one was sitting near them, People skirted around them like water near oil; shooting them nervous, uncomfortable looks. Looks that Ig had known her whole life. These people weren't seeing Vivi, the ray of perpetual sunshine; or Pietro, the funniest, most caring boy she'd ever met; or even Mercutio with his boundless faith in his friends, hard to earn but all the worthier for it. Just like they'd never seen anything in her beyond this strange, unsettling quality she had. One that she couldn't change, no matter how hard she had tried in the past. One glance, and they'd made their mind up about her. About them.

Innate sinisterness. Well, if that was all they wanted to see – why not give it to them?

'Get up,' she said. 'I changed my mind. I'd love a coffee.'

They walked around Grey's monument in a slow circle, while Ig made the final adjustments to her plans, nodding and humming to herself. Yes; this would do nicely. Then, they all walked down the street into Planet Mocha, letting the door swing shut behind them. Seconds later, passers-by on the street heard a boy scream; 'oh my god; is that a rat in the blueberry muffins?!' and the entire shop exploded with people. They dashed out onto the street, screaming and retching and recording on their phones, talking in outraged tones about how they all knew Planet Mocha had been going downhill for years – which was more than enough pandemonium for four teenagers to bolt from the coffee shop; stolen goods in hand. Ig had clambered over the counter and swiped the last raspberry and white chocolate cookie; Vivi was stuffing chocolate-covered coffee beans into her mouth. Mercutio had been sharp enough to snatch a brand-new takeout drink right out of a barista's hand, and Pietro had, inexplicably, grabbed two huge bottles of hazelnut syrup. They ran down the street that Ig knew led to the Quayside; their legs windmilling underneath them as the slope become steeper than they'd accounted for, laughing and screaming for each other to hurry up or get left behind – which, of course, was a total lie. Restaurants and taxi hubs flashed by in a blur, people tutting and cars blaring their horns in their wake.

They didn't arrive at the River Tyne so much as crash into it; leaning against the railings and laughing, breathless and sore. The Quayside was far less chaotic than the city centre; with its sleek, minimalist law firm offices, all eager to make a connection with Lunalist. One Ig's right was the Tyne Bridge – old and grand and covered with kittiwake nests – and to the left was the sleek, shining Millennium Bridge – the one that led to the very school that, up until a few short months ago, Ig had called home. It curled up into the air, thin and silver as a crescent moon.

'You know we'll have to walk back up that hill, right?' Pietro asked. Looking behind them, the street seemed almost vertical.

Ig shrugged. 'It was the quickest escape route. Besides, you've been getting fit at your sessions with Mr. Glasse, haven't you?'

'Yeah, I know,' Pietro scoffed, nudging his brother in the ribs. 'I was thinking of Merc. Egghead here doesn't do cardio.'

'Pietro, I will put Onslaught droppings in your overnight oats, I swear on my Keith Henry Stockman Campbell autograph.'

'Oh, what? Overreaction of the century!'

'It is not–'

Vivi leaned on her shoulder; breath smelling warmly of chocolate and coffee. On the other side of the river, Lunalist glittered in the sunshine like a memory from a dream. 'Does it feel weird,' Vivi asked Ig, 'to be back here?'

Ig looked out over the river. In her mind, she could plot the route from the entrance to her dorm, and from her dorm to each of her classrooms. The quickest way to each – Lunalist was a lot more open-plan than Shackleton. No winding hallways or tiny, cosy nooks to eat breakfast in here. She could see the tutors patrolling the halls in their downtime, the students hanging about in little cliques, sniping and gossiping. The General in her War Room. Pisces, meditating every morning with her Green Goddess smoothie and her bright, beautiful future spreading out before her like a sunrise. Ig reached down deep inside herself, searching for a scrap of homesickness, an iota of regret that things had worked out the way they had. She found nothing at all. Just anger, and a deep, fierce love for the Villains beside her. She shook her head, and Vivi let it go.

'So,' Mercutio asked, sipping at his drink, 'are we permitted to learn of the plan, yet? Oh; it's a caramel latte. Excellent.'

'It's still percolating,' Ig said.

'No, it's pretty well-brewed.'

'My idea, Merc; not the coffee.'

'Oh, come on,' Pietro argued, flicking the lid of his syrup bottle into the river and taking a big, disgusting swig, 'what's going on in that beautiful brain of yours, Ig?'

'We won't judge,' Vivi added, slotting her hand into Ig's. 'You know that.'

Ig did. So she looked out at the place she used to call home, and smiled at it. 'What did my mam say?' she asked. 'About how the best Villains make their debut. What's the best way to show off what you're capable of – and get the attention of every Hero in the city while they do it?'

'Just tell us, Heretical,' Mercutio asked dryly, humouring her. Knowing she'd been planning exactly how her big reveal would go. Ig smiled – small and mean.

'They rob a bank.'

Chapter Forty-Three

Ig was ready. Her plan had begun falling into place that week, she had her friends by her side, and she was about to take sweet, bombastic, chaotic revenge on the people that had wronged her. So naturally, the night before it all went down, she couldn't sleep. Her mind was whirring at a million miles an hour, images and sounds and snatches of speech flickering through her head like a projection. In the end, she threw back her bedsheets with a quiet groan and sat up. If she wasn't going to get to sleep, she might as well get up and train a little more. There was usually a teacher patrolling the dorms at night; but it was more for appearances than anything else. Weirdly, the only time she'd seen someone get into real trouble was when a first year was caught smoking out their bedroom window and had to 'volunteer' for Mr. Throttler's waterboarding demonstrations for the rest of the week.

As Ig stood up, one of Vivi's abandoned pins came into contact with the soft flesh on the arch of her foot. Ig yelped, swearing under her breath as she stumbled to her desk seat. 'Oh my god, these stupid things…oh, crap. Vivi? Did that wake you up?' Silence. Ig extracted the pin from her foot and craned her neck to look into the top bunk. 'Vivi?' Empty. Vivi must have had the same idea about getting up. Not surprising, really; she'd done nothing but moon about for weeks, now – ever since Mercutio had rescued them from Lily and Pisces' attack. Oh well. It was better than her mumbling Merc's name in her sleep, like she did last night. That was disturbing.

Ig pulled on some clothes and slipped out her dorm-room window, padding through the grounds as quietly as she could.

Her nerves were still nipping at her mind, though, and after a while she felt a bit like a hamster on a wheel, going around and around the gardens. She needed space.

Ig found herself walking along the quiet road that led to the sheep fields near Shackleton; head full of plans and memories, going over each tiny step of her debut. She could have wandered anywhere in Rossborough, but deep down, she was hungry for the smell of clean grass and the gentle snoring of sheep. She and the others hadn't been to their field in a while, and she missed it.

Ig went to hop over the long, irrigated ditch that surrounded their field, using one tendril to support herself…when a hand wrapped around her ankle and pulled her down. Ig tried to scream, but a hand was clapped over her mouth.

'Shhh!' said the voice. 'You'll spoil it.'

Ig found herself looking into the big, brown eyes of Pietro von Ryan. 'Piehro? Whu'reyouhdooin'–'

'I'm going to let go,' Pietro hissed, 'but you have to stay quiet. Okay?'

'Muh–'

'Quiet.'

Ig rolled her eyes, but nodded. Pietro carefully took his hand away, as if he were expecting her to bite him. 'You're lucky I didn't strangle you,' Ig whispered, pulling her tendril back into her palm. 'What's going on? What are you doing here?'

Pietro looked shifty. 'Nothing.'

'Pietro–'

'Vivi and Merc definitely aren't on a date in the field.'

'What?!' Ig went to stand, trying to get a better look, but Pietro pulled her back down.

'I said they weren't on a date!'

'And I think you're lying!' Why was this so exciting? It wasn't even her relationship. But the idea of all the mooning and sighing and pining finally coming to an end made Ig feel like she was sneaking a peek at her Christmas presents after her parents thought she was sleeping. 'I want to look.'

'Well, you can't. It's disrespectful and a violation of privacy and I almost got caught twice already.' Pietro made himself comfortable in the grass. 'You'll just have to listen.'

'Fine.' Ig made herself comfortable and strained her ears.

'…about this weekend?' Vivi was asking. Ig realised they were talking about the plan. Their debut.

'I haven't thought about it much,' Mercutio drawled, cool and unaffected.

'That is a filthy lie, Mercutio von Ryan…'

Mercutio laughed – not his usual manic cackle, or even a dark chuckle. This was warm and light. 'Alright, fine. You're correct. I've been fine-tuning the hive's reaction times all week, trying to make sure they are perfect. What about you?'

'Not really too worried, I suppose. I know Ig's got it all covered.' There was a soft noise; someone shifting in the grass. 'But it's still my debut, you know? You only get one. I'm nervous.'

'Understandable. But you needn't be worried. You're going to make a formidable Villain, Vivi. I mean, who wouldn't be impressed by you?'

'Really?'

'I would know. I've been, um, impressed by you my whole life.' Mercutio sighed, sounding almost defeated. 'Totally, utterly, stupidly impressed. Sometimes I thought I'd die from being so impressed.'

'Pietro,' Ig hissed. 'I meant to ask you. Have you been practicing with the new bat this week? It's heavier than your old one.'

'Ignatia,' Pietro hissed back, his entire body tense and his gaze fixed on the invisible couple, 'I love you. But shut up.'

Ig shut up. There was a lull in conversation; the only sounds to be heard being the bleating of drowsy sheep and the wind in the grass.

'I did make you something, though,' Mercutio said, all in a rush, 'not that I think you need a modification! But I thought it would help. Ever since Heretical's Heroes ambushed us, I was thinking about your Power being hindered by a lack of vegetation, so I… I was thinking of ways that I could… here.'

The faint clink of metal. 'It's a safety pin,' Vivi said slowly. 'A little bottle on a safety pin.'

'Okay, so; let me explain.'

'Here we go,' Pietro mouthed, rolling his eyes. 'This is where he blows it.'

'The bottle is glass, topped with a beeswax seal,' Mercutio babbled. 'My idea was that it could either be used as a mini terrarium, for long-haul expeditions when you won't have access to your plants, or it could be used like a keepsake vial for specific cuttings when you know what you'll need. For example, when we're in the middle of Newcastle with nothing but badly-watered grass to hand?'

'Oh. Oh, Merc.' Ig could hear the warmth in her friend's voice. 'That's actually really sweet.'

'What do you mean, 'actually?' Did you think it wouldn't be sweet? Am I not sweet? I can be sweet…can't I?'

'No! No, I – oh, god..'

Ig groaned softly into her hands. Out of the pair of them, she hadn't expected Vivi to be the one to ruin the moment.

'What I meant,' Vivi tried again, 'is thank you. I love it. Is it from Fox?'

'Well, the safety pin is from the dungeon's First Aid Kit. But the bottle is from Fox, yes. It used to contain a scroll with some saccharine literary quotation on it – I still have it if you want it, I think it's from Alice in Wonderland…'

'No, it's okay. I like it as it is. Why'd you use beeswax for the stopper?' There was a pause. 'So you'd remember that I gave you it.'

Another pause; longer, heavier, more meaningful. 'I couldn't forget that. I'm impressed by you too, Merc.'

'Oh. Oh, right.'

'Yeah.'

'He's done it,' Pietro whispered; peeking over the top of the hedge, eyes gleaming with delight in the darkness. 'He actually managed to make this crap romantic. Go on, brother, seal the deal…here we go…yes! We have contact!'

Ig sat up straighter. 'A kiss?' *If Mercutio ever hurts her*, she thought, *I won't need my tendrils to get revenge. I'll rip him apart with my bare hands.*

If Pietro noticed her sudden murderous intentions, he didn't seem to care much. 'A kiss, baby!' he beamed, still peering over the hedge. 'They finally…oh. Oh, okay, now this is weird. Oh, gross, I forgot how disgusting kissing is.' Pietro sat back down in the dirt. 'So! Let's chat while they…do that. How're you feeling about seeing your girlfriend on Saturday?'

'She's not my girlfriend.' Pietro cocked an eyebrow at her, and Ig sighed. 'Nervous,' she admitted. 'There are a lot of 'what ifs', and when I think I've planned for all of them, I think of something else.'

'You know it's going to go exactly as you think it will, right?' Pietro leaned back, wincing as he put his hand in a puddle of mud. 'They aren't that smart. Plus, they won't be able to resist the optics of the whole thing. Justice for one of their own, the awful Villains brought down by the devoted protector of poor, sad Iggie Heretical. Yeah?'

That was right. At least, Ig thought so. But Ig had never been one of their own. And if she had been poor and sad once, she wasn't anymore. So instead of replying, she leaned against Pietro's side and looked up into the stars. She'd done everything she could do; planned until her brain spun in her skull. She just had to hope she had more value as a plot point for Lunalist than she ever had as a person.

After a while, the quiet in the field beyond them was unsettling, rather than sweet. Vivi and Merc were talking in low, soft voices, and Ig felt like it was something she wasn't really supposed to hear. So she led Pietro back towards the school. He seemed to be growing bored, anyway; now that he'd achieved his goal of getting his brother a girlfriend, the actually romantic part seemed inconsequential.

'Hey,' Pietro said, as they walked up the main staircase, 'if we're both flying solo tonight, want to come over to my dorm for snacks? We could paint each other's nails, gossip, play the world's most boring game of Spin The Bottle…'

'Where we give each other firm but friendly handshakes instead of kissing?'

'She's done this before. Oh, but,' Pietro said with a smirk, pulling up short as he spotted Katalina Kanaan lingering awkwardly outside Ig's door, 'maybe you have more exciting plans…'

'What do you mean?' Ig asked. But Pietro had already spun on his heel and was walking away; hands clasped behind his back, whistling innocently.

'Pietro? Pietro! Pi–'

'Ig?' Katalina asked. 'I was wondering if we could, um, talk?'

'Well, you are outside my room. So… I suppose so.' Katalina usually wore such dramatic makeup to school. Sharp eyeliner, red lips. Ig didn't know how she had the time, or the patience, to do all those intricate, pretty things to her skin. But tonight, her face was bare – scrubbed clean and fresh-looking. Ig wanted to press a finger into the apple of her cheek, and see if it was as soft as it looked.

Wait. What?! You are such a creep, Heretical.

'I've been thinking a lot about you,' Katalina was saying. 'Since I got my Power. You were so kind to me, so supportive and excited and… it was so sweet.' She took a step forward. 'You're so sweet.'

Something twinged in Ig's stomach. She'd never been called sweet before.

'And I've realised some things and…and I know you've got your debut tomorrow, and I wanted to wish you good luck.' Was she blushing? Oh god, she was blushing. Why was blushing suddenly so terrifying?! 'That's… really nice of you,' Ig faltered.

When Katalina didn't say anything more, she fumbled in her jacket pocket for her dorm room key. The conversation was clearly over, and she didn't want to keep Katalina from her twenty-seven step skincare routine, or whatever she did to make her face look like that. 'Well, I… um, I appreciate your support.'

Talk like a normal person for once in your life! her brain screamed at her.

'I'll come and find you when we get back, and let you know how it–'As she unlocked the door, Katalina reached over her shoulder and pushed it open with a soft creak. Ig, still not entirely sure what was happening, stepped backwards so the other girl could come in; her back bumping off the doorway as she did. Katalina pulled Ig to her, closed the door behind them and, in the quiet and the dark, pressed her lips against Ig's.

It wasn't fireworks and applause from an adoring crowd, like it had been in all Ig's fantasies about Pisces. It was gentle, and quiet and lingering. There may have been some very embarrassing sighing and leaning involved, especially when Katalina cupped Ig's jaw with her hand to tip her head back a little. When she finally opened her eyes a blissful eternity later, Ig realised the room was lit with a warm, orange light.

'Sorry,' Katalina laughed, pulling her hands away and wringing them over each other, their glow sending shadows over the walls, 'it happens when I'm happy. Is that weird?'

It wasn't weird. It was beautiful. But words were suddenly very difficult. Before she could stop herself, Ig brought Katalina's palm up to her lips and kissed it. 'How did you know it's my debut tomorrow?' she whispered. 'We didn't tell anyone.'

'Pietro told me.' Katalina's fingers brushed Ig's cheek, leaving streaks of warmth across her skin. 'For someone who hates kissing, he was very excited when I told him I liked you.'

Why wouldn't he be happy? Mercutio and Vivi were practically together, and Pietro had been given a new set of dolls to bump against each other until they kissed. Instead of being a lethal weapon, Pietro should have got manipulation Powers. 'Of course he – wait a second,' Ig said, snapping out of her first-ever-kiss delirium with a shake of the head. 'Did you just say you like me? Like, like-like me?' Katalina laughed softly, and kissed Ig again – lightly, sweetly, barely even a peck. 'I'll see you when you get back,' she said. Then, the door was opening, and she was gone. Ig slid down the wall, hair fanning out behind her on the wall. Giddy with excitement, she squealed into her hands, drumming her feet against the floor. She'd just had her first kiss. Her first kiss! And Katalina liked her. Liked-liked her! She'd never felt like this before; like her insides were made of bubbles and her head was full of candyfloss and her lips still tasted like... 'I take it that went well?' said a muffled voice on the other side of the door. Ig felt her cheeks growing hot as she thumped the door with the heel of her hand.

'Go away, Pietro!'

'My second matchmaking triumph of the night. I really am a genius, after all...'

'Go away, Pietro!'

She swore she could hear him laughing all the way back to his dorm.

Chapter Forty-Four

'I still don't see why I can't wear my lab coat.'

'Because then we won't match, Merc.' Ig gestured down at herself; clad in a plain black t-shirt and black jeans. 'We can't afford fancy matching uniforms–'

'Yet!' Vivi piped up.

'…yet. So we have to look like we're acting as a unit. If you wear a white lab coat, you'll look like a separate thing.'

'Scoff,' Mercutio huffed, adjusting his new and improved headset. 'I don't see why that's a bad thing.'

'Because,' Pietro sniped, punching his brother in the shoulder, 'for once, this isn't The Mercutio von Ryan Show. This is Ig's thing.'

'It's my debut too!'

'You've got your bees on standby, right? And you got to bring the rabbit, so stop whinging.'

'Whinging?' Mercutio's voice screeched up an octave as he clutched Onslaught to his chest, one hand pinning her ears to her head so she couldn't hear the insults being thrown her way. '"Whinging?!" That lab coat has been around longer than you have, Pietro…'

'Merc, babe?' Vivi purred, leaning in to Mercutio and placing a hand on his chest, 'drop it. Okay?'

Her nose brushed against his, and a hundred emotions flashed across Mercutio's face; surprise, longing, giddy and ridiculous adoration… then, with a cough, he composed himself with a nod. Ever since he and Vivi became an official item, Ig had seen a plethora of new emotions from her favourite mad scientist.

'Fine. For you.' The four turned and walked away from the bus stop, into narrow alleyway by the bank at Grey's Monument. '"Babe?"' Ig whispered. 'Really?'

Vivi laughed, blushing prettily. 'I knew it would stop him in his tracks.'

'Pfft. I thought I was meant to be the schemer here.'

The vibe on the journey to Newcastle that Saturday morning had been light-hearted and playful – hyperactive, to be honest. Excitement fizzed and buzzed between the four of them; Pietro jumping on Mercutio and messing up his hair, Vivi blasting her music from an ancient CD player and Ig singing along to the snatches of lyrics she knew, earning them glares and tuts from the adults stuck on the bus with them from Rossborough that were staunchly ignored. This was the last time any of them could move through the world as merely annoying teenagers; after today, they'd be Villains. All of them.

Ig swallowed; rolling her shoulders to feel the shift of pressure in her back. After today, Lunalist would see her as she really was. She just hoped she'd predicted their next move correctly. She flexed her palms, and tiny, comforting coils curled around her thumbs. They reached the end of the alley – a tiny cinema to their right, a wall plastered with posters for upcoming artsy films opposite, the bank tucked out of sight on their immediate left – and Ig paused. 'Are you ready?' she asked her friends. They turned back to look at her; all wide smiles and barely contained energy.

'Of course we are,' Mercutio said.

'You remember the plan?'

Pietro drew a shiny new baseball bat from his backpack, letting the now-empty bag drop to the floor. He kicked it behind a wheelie bin. 'I go in first and get their attention.'

Vivi ran her fingers over the pin placed over her heart – the glass pendant filled to the brim with cuttings from her Red Spider Lily plant. 'I'm on crowd control.' She giggled. 'Or lack thereof.'

'And I,' Mercutio finished, 'am camped out across the street, doing nothing useful–'

'Merc.'

'I mean, ready to give the signal when our friends arrive. We have it all under control, Heretical; we did go through the plan several times last night.'

Ig couldn't resist. 'When you and Vivi weren't off smooching, you mean,' she teased.

'Smooching?!'

'Okay, okay,' Vivi said, spinning Mercutio around and shoving him towards the entrance to the alley. 'Time to go. We can argue about this later.' She was right. Once the city had been thrown into chaos and two of Lunalist's brightest were utterly humiliated; then, and only then, could Ig tease her friends about how adorable they were together. The von Ryans vanished around the corner without a second glance. Only Vivi – ridiculous, earnest, protective Vivi Section, who gave her a chance when everyone else had written her off – lingered for a second. The two girls looked at each other. Then, Ig ran into her arms. 'Love you,' Ig said, squeezing Vivi tightly.

'Love you too,' Vivi said back, before taking a step backwards. 'You ready to make some chaos, Ignatia Heretical?'

'It's been a long time coming.'

Vivi smiled, and disappeared. Ig exhaled, leaning against the cold brickwork of the alley. She tapped the back pocket of her jeans, feeling the round, smooth weight that sat there. Her Plan B – the one the others didn't know about. One way or another, this was going to be her day.

Beyond her hiding spot was Grey's Monument itself; a sprawling, bustling hive of activity, especially on a sunny Saturday like this one; people lounging around the monument itself, waiting for friends, kissing hello and goodbye, drinking their coffees or eating their lunch while indignant protesters yelled through awful, tinny megaphones and shoppers bustled to and fro in front of them, all grim-faced and regretting their life choices. Beyond them lay the study in opposites that was Newcastle; the shining glass shopping centre across the road from the bookshop, hyperactive teenagers mixing with dead-eyed retail workers, raggedy-looking pigeons perching on corporate-funded sun loungers. Ig couldn't think of a better spot for her debut. She pressed herself against the alley, readying herself. She'd know when the robbery had started when–

The pretty sound of shattering glass filled the air. 'Alright, people,' Pietro yelled – his voice sounding rougher and more aggressive than she'd ever imagined from her witty, affable friend – 'if you hadn't guessed already, this is a robbery. Unless your ISA is worth your life, get down on the floor. I said–!' The sound of more glass breaking and people beginning to scream drowned out the rest of his speech. Ig smothered a grin with her hand, watching heads snap up over at Monument. Who knew Pietro had been paying so much attention in Ms. Schwab's classes? His projection was perfect.

Across the street, people began to take out their phones; some to call the police, who'd dispatch the Heroes…but most were filming whatever chaos Pietro was causing. Good. From the way the glass shattered and the lights suddenly cut out, he'd probably used that trick of bouncing the bat off the floor to cause as much chaos as he could. She liked that she knew him so well, these days.

It wasn't long before a cloud of reddish spores poured out of the now-obliterated windows of the bank. Seconds later, a chorus of retching drifted by on the wind – the wind that, mercifully, didn't stink of vomit, even as some of the victims stumbled out onto the pavement with sick coating the bottoms of their shoes. Ig felt a twinge of sympathy for her friends, trapped in a bank slick with other people's puke. It wouldn't be for much longer, though. Not if Ig was right about what was coming next. She heard the echoes of a scuffle, a few cries of pain and anger as someone in the bank evidently tried to stand up to Pietro and his bat. Across the street, leaning against the cafe that looked out onto Monument itself with Onslaught tucked under his arm, Mercutio was staring intently at the bank; leg bouncing up and down, rabbit-fast and agitated. He wanted to get in on the fight; protect his girlfriend and his brother and flex his own muscles a little. Ig had intentionally held him back for the second phase of the plan – once Vivi had potentially exhausted her supplies and Pietro's menace had lost some of its novelty with the terrified crowd – but that didn't mean he had to like it, did it? Suddenly, his gaze snapped up to the skies. He squinted, and Ig's stomach dropped. Before Mercutio even gave the signal – a single hand, extended above his head like he was shading his eyes – she knew what was coming. Two huge shadows passed over the street, and the crowd – now pressed against the elevated sides of Monument itself, scared out of their minds but not so much that they'd dare miss a spectacle – gasped, and then cheered. Ig recognised one of the flyers passing overhead as Talia – the flyer from her first meeting with The General. The other flyer she didn't recognise…but she knew exactly who they were carrying, even before they rolled out of their convoys' arms and plummeted to the earth to a roar of applause from the crowd, landing in perfect formation in their gleaming, brand-new uniforms. Neither Pisces Rising nor Lily Volt could fly. But that wasn't going to stop the darlings of Lunalist from having a perfect Hero landing on their first ever mission. Ig smiled, wire-thin and sharp. She knew it. She knew they'd come running.

'Well,' Pietro snarked, walking into Ig's line of sight as he idly twirled his bat with one hand, 'this is a nice surprise, isn't it Vivi?'

'It is, von Ryan,' Vivi replied – oof, Mercutio wouldn't like his brother hogging the first use of the family name like that. 'Two green little Heroes, sent out on their first mission alone. What, are we not worth bringing out the big guns?'

'We'll have to change that, Viv.'

'You have to stop this,' Lily said, her voice as clear as a bell and as rehearsed as a West End show. 'Come quietly, and let these people go in peace.'

'Peace?' laughed Vivi. 'Did you say peace? Why would I be interested in that?' She took a step or two forward, and Ig knew Pisces well enough to catch the twist of distaste in her upper lip. 'Hmm; that's a nice new setup you've got there,' Vivi said, stepping forward and jutting her chin out at Pisces' water tanks. They were sleeker than last time; two long tubes snaking over her shoulders and down her back. 'They'll make nice watering cans for my new garden.' She tilted her head, regarding Pisces with a manic smile. 'I think I'll put it right where your precious school is now.'

'Your corruption won't touch Lunalist,' Pisces said – and Ig's treacherous heart lurched towards the sound. 'We won't let you. We won't let you hurt our fellow students like you did with Iggie.'

'Iggie?' Vivi shrieked with manic, piercing laughter – hand curled theatrically in front of her mouth, eyes sparkling with gleeful contempt. It wasn't subtle; Ig assumed that was why she wasn't in the Advanced classes for Monologue. All the same, Ig watched Mercutio melt a little across the street and willed him to focus. 'Who's that?'

'She was my friend!' Pisces cried; turning slightly so the crowd could see the tears shining in her eyes. 'She was sweet and kind and innocent, and you hurt her. And now,' she said darkly, pointing her hands towards Vivi and Pietro in readiness, 'you'll pay for it.'

Ig took that as her cue. She turned her palms to the concrete and pressed her tendrils into the ground. And, with a cackle that shook the foundations of Grey's Monument itself – a cackle could change the course of fate, that would make a father weep and a mother scream with pride – Ignatia Heretical ascended.

Chapter Forty-Five

For the rest of her life – no matter what happened next – Ig would remember the look on Pisces Rising's face as she rose from the alleyway behind the bank at Grey's Monument. That look of absolute, world-shaking shock; the tiny step backwards, the slack jaw, her lips forming Ig's name, the sounds lost on the wind rushing through Ig's hair and the screams from the crowd below. She looked like she was staring at a monster. It was glorious.

Ig raised herself a little higher – higher than she'd ever gone before – and laughed in absolute delight. "Innocent?" she cried. "Sweet and kind?" She leaned her weight to the left, bringing up her right hand and striking the ground with her tendril. Pisces leapt backwards with a cry as the pavement under her feet cracked. 'How naïve can you possibly be?'

Ig pulled her hand back, bringing her tendril towards her and readying for another strike. 'I'm the Witch Queen's daughter. And you thought you could treat me like your little pet.' She cracked her tendril in the air like a whip, smiling as the crowd collectively leapt out of their skin at the sound. She advanced, using her tendrils like terrible stilts, as the crowed backed away and Pietro and Vivi flanked her on either side.

'I'm no-one's pet, Pisces.' Pisces hadn't recovered from her shock enough to use her Power; she was still staring up at Ig as if she was stuck in some awful dream. Vivi and Pietro seized their opportunity to distract her, which seemed to take the form of Vivi tackling her with all the ferocity of a rugby player while Pietro yelled support. Lily Volt, on the other hand, had had enough. She brought her hands together with a clap, electricity fizzing over her fingers. She muttered something under her breath – something insufferable, Ig assumed – and prepared to attack. Her blue eyes glinted with malice as she stared Ig down… but before she could take aim, a droning cloud of bees encircled her. Ig heard the indignant shriek from inside the buzzing ball of insects as Mercutio placed Onslaught on the ground and sauntered into position; taking his time, of course. This part, at least, was still The Mercutio von Ryan Show. He tapped his headset and the bees parted, revealing an enraged Lily Volt.

'Remember me?' he said, leaning down to lock eyes with the Hero. Even from up high, Ig could see the fury in Lily's face, contorting her pretty features into a snarl. For the first time, Ig noticed a spray of red marks dusted over Lily's cheeks and across the bridge of her nose.

'You,' she hissed. Mercutio's smirk grew sharp as a knife, eyes dark and mocking. 'Me.'

Vivi – who was now climbing on Pisces' back in an attempt to unplug her water tanks – turned her head to gaze at her boyfriend. 'Oh my god, he's so hot,' she whispered to herself dreamily, before being smacked backwards with a burst of water from Pisces' palm aimed directly into her face. Meanwhile, Lily Volt was being cooked alive by bees. The swarm flew around her in a tight ball, and the waves of warmth from the bee's furry bodies and their frantically buzzing wings were taking their toll. When the swarm parted for a moment – so Mercutio could appear behind Lily and yank on her perfect blonde ponytail – she was already covered in a sheen of sweat. When Ig had left Lunalist, Lily had been obsessed with the 'clean girl' trend; showing off how naturally dewy and plump her skin was. Now, she had foundation and blush streaking down her face, mascara bleeding across her cheeks – further revealing a smattering of red marks across the bridge of her nose, with more running down her jaw like a rash.

'You ruined my face!' Lily shrieked. Which was a lie; Lily looked fine. Normal-person pretty, rather than social-media-superstar pretty. But, like every other mean girl at The Academy, she was nothing without perfection. 'Do you know how much concealer I need to use now, to cover up all those – get away from me, you stupid… stupid bee losers!' She fired off another bolt with a scream; one that Mercutio easily evaded.

'Are you talking about those scars peppering your cheeks?' he deadpanned. 'The ones from the first time you encountered my swarm? Good to know titanium stingers leave lasting damage.'

'I lost my brand deals, you telekinetic freak! I was going to have my own line of skincare! I was going–' Lily raged, blue and yellow sparks snaking up her arms, dancing off her fingertips, 'to be the top selling brand–' she fired wildly into the swarm, sweat dripping from the tip of her nose, 'in the twelve-to-sixteen age bracket!'

Conducted by the moisture on her skin, Lily's lightning zipped back up her arms and over her shoulders, making her yelp in pain. She tried again, harder – and electrocuted herself again, harder. Shaking with rage, she stamped her feet and roared. 'Oh my god I hate this!'

'Well, that's not accurate,' Mercutio said smugly, stepping away from the hole in his swarm that he'd created to watch Lily lose her mind. 'Because telekinesis would mean I'm literally moving the bees with my mind, would it not?'

Lily moved toward the sound of his voice, but the constant movement of the bees – not to mention their low, insistent droning – masked his movements. 'Stand still!'

'And I'm not doing that. That would take a lot of work, wouldn't it?' Lily spun wildly in a circle; another hole opened up in the swarm and Mercutio leaned in and shoved Lily to the ground. 'Honestly. You Heroes never think things through.' About ten bees darted forward from the safety of the swarm to sting Lily on the hands, causing her to yelp in pain. 'It's mind control. Obviously. If you're going to insult me, at least use the proper terminology.'

'That's what I – stand still, I said!'

Ig really hoped someone in the crowd was filming so she could find the footage later. She needed the sight of the two most infuriating people she knew going toe to toe burned into her brain.

The sound of a torrent of rushing water yanked her out of her amusement. Pietro had taken over distracting Pisces; aiming a blow at the tanks on her shoulders, only to be knocked back by a cricket ball-sized blast of water to the chest. Pisces assaulted him with shot after shot, pushing him backwards towards Monument itself. Pietro managed to hit a few of them away with his bat, but they were coming too fast for him. The crowd jostled nervously like antelopes on the edge of a hunt. Ig wrapped a tendril around Pisces' leg and pulled her to the ground, giving Pietro a chance to catch his breath and move to help Vivi to her feet. Ig hissed in pain, her palms burning more than ever as Pisces dangled from the end of her tendril like a doll; limp and helpless, as Ig dragged her across the pavement, lifting her up so she hung, upside-down, in front of Ig's face. The crowd gasped in horror.

'Do you like my Power, Pisces?' Ig asked. 'I suppose I have you to thank for it, really.'

'Ig–'

'I'm talking now,' Ig said, her voice low and dangerous. 'You thought I was weak. Poor, naïve little Iggie; your own personal charity case. Well, look at me now.' Pisces struggled against the tendril, so Ig shook her. 'Look! Look at me, Pisces. You can give me that, at least.' Pisces did look at her, then. Those beautiful blue eyes were full of tears – tears of fear and, Ig realised, of sorrow.

'What did they do to you?' Pisces whispered, and her lip had the audacity to tremble. 'Ig… Iggie, if you're still in there, tell us who did this.' She looked down at the fight below; Lily had broken free of the swarm and was stalking towards Mercutio with murder in her eyes, Pietro and Vivi hot on her tail. 'Was it…was it one of them? We can help you!' She struggled against the tendril; but it was weak, almost tentative. She wasn't using her Power to free herself, like Ig had assumed she would. Where was the frustration, the indignance, the anger that Ig had expected?

'Tell us what they did and we can cure you, it's not too late, we can go back to how things were—'

She kicked feebly at the tendril holding her other foot and, with a jolt, Ig realised that Pisces was trying not to hurt her.

'How things were?' she asked softly, her face contorting with rage. 'You think I want to go back to how things were?'

'Ig, please…'

Even now – in the middle of her debut, having orchestrated a bank robbery just to get her into the right place at the right time, surrounded by all this terror and chaos – Pisces still thought Ig was being manipulated. Still thought she was a weak link. Anger, hot and smoking, rushed through Ig's bloodstream. Her Power raced up her arms, turning the veins in her arms black right up to her elbows.

'I would rather turn this city to ashes,' Ig whispered, watching Pisces' face curdle from sympathy to horror, 'than go back to being pitied by you.'

In one fluid movement, Ignatia Heretical reared her tendril back over her head, aimed, and flung Pisces Rising with all of her strength. Her limp body – with her lovely red hair flowing behind her – flew past Grey's Monument and over the busy road, hitting the window of the bookshop with a crash that was heard across the city.

Chapter Forty-Six

Grey's Monument was usually such a noisy place. It was the centre of the city, after all; always full of chatter and shouting and music playing from terrible speakers and the sound of buses roaring past. But in the moments after Ig threw Pisces, the only sound that could be heard was the tinkle of freshly shattered glass. The window, which seconds ago had been bright and cheerful, looked like an open wound; blank and gaping, torn pages fluttering in the breeze. The crowd, still clustered around the Monument, were frozen in place. Even Lily stopped fighting; staring up at Ig along with Vivi, Pietro and Mercutio.

Ig's throat was sore; like she'd been screaming. Maybe she had been screaming. She lowered herself to the ground. She could sense her friends on either side of her as she walked towards the road that separated her and the bookshop, but she didn't turn to look at them. Even in her shock, that dark, nasty part of Ig was howling in triumph. All this time she'd been playing along with her friends; making out that this was all a game, a glorified prank. Pretending that she would be happy with embarrassing Lily and Pisces, showing them up in their first ever Heroes mission. Being a greasy little smear on their perfect academic record. But no. It was always going to lead to this; to destruction. The Nyx hadn't seen it in her. But she'd known it was there for a long time.

'Pisces?'

But it couldn't be this easy. Pisces wasn't going to give up without a proper fight. Was she?

'Pisces!'

Destroyed books hung limply out the remains of the window,

their spines broken and their insides gutted. Deep inside the shop, she could see a display that had caved in on itself; umbrellas and board games and expensive notebooks falling from their broken shelves where Pisces must have landed. As soon as Ig's right foot made contact with the paved tarmac of the road, a gigantic jet of water blasted through the broken window and hit her in the face. Ig fell backwards, landing hard, head snapping back and connecting with the road. Something cracked in her back pocket, and panic spiked through her veins. Colours swam in front of her eyes as she tried to right herself, the dull roar of applause ringing in her ears as Pisces climbed back through the window, stumbling slightly as her foot skidded across the back cover of what used to be a bestselling novel about people having affairs and being rich. The only mark on her was an ugly-looking cut across her forehead; a bright red bead of blood running past the corner of her eye and stopping just short of the birthmark on her cheek. She even bled prettily. Ig hated her so, so much.

Suddenly, pain snaked up her spine and gripped her like a giant fist. Ig cried out as Lily Volt's electricity shot through her, sending her collapsing to the floor again. Sodden scraps of paper pressed against her hands; now that she was soaking wet, the pain was blinding. Somewhere far away, she heard someone calling her name, and the sensation of Lily's foot on her back, grinding her down. 'You,' Lily hissed, 'don't get to win, Iggie.'

The crowed behind her cheered for their Heroes. Lily turned and waved to them, beaming.

'Keep her there, Lily.' Pisces was walking away from the bookshop towards them. Her eyes were fixed on Ig, her expression unreadable – but Ig never did have a very good grasp on what Pisces was thinking, did she? 'She did a terrible job as a spy,' she was saying, 'but at least she'll make a good hostage. People of Newcastle,' she called to the crowd, 'we're apprehending a very dangerous Villain here. Please, stay back – and keep her accomplices from helping her.'

'You heard her!' said the crowd.

'Get back!'

'Don't let them run around the back of you!'

'You mess with one Geordie, you mess with all of us!'

A human shield? Ig thought, gritting her teeth against the pain to glare up at Pisces. Classy. Very classy. 'Ig? Ig!' A shout of indignant anger – probably Vivi's – went up as the crowd moved to block her friend's path. Jeers started up from the bystanders.

'Who do you think you are, coming here?'

'Keep them back – they're just kids!'

'You get the girl, we'll handle the lads.'

'Crazy, all of them…'

'Bloody mental teenagers…'

The sound of retching and the drone of bee's wings drifted to Ig's ears as her friends fought to reach her – but then, everything became one indistinguishable mass; just noise and nonsense and shouts of pain.

It had all gone wrong so quickly. All her planning, ruined, and for what? A moment of petty satisfaction. Defeated, Ig's gaze drifted away from Pisces' face; over her shoulder…to the water tanks attached to her back. The right-hand tank, the one Pisces favoured, was almost empty. The other was about half full. Still useful to her.

Ig gritted her teeth, forced her palm to lift, and shot a tendril towards the tank on the left, straight and sharp as a knife. The crowd behind her cried out in dismay as, one more time, the city centre was filled with the sound of breaking glass.

The majority of Pisces' water soaked the back of her uniform, running down the backs of her legs to puddle on the concrete. Lily Volt jerked back in shock, her mouth a perfect 'o'. As she did, her electric grip on Ig loosened. The tendril whipped back, hitting Lily in the face and knocking her to the floor.

Pisces was frozen in place; her eyes wide as she took a shaking step backwards. Glass crunched under the heel of her expensive, brand-new white trainers. Ig watched as anger rose to the surface; turning Pisces' lovely pale skin an angry crimson, her pretty lips curling in a snarl.

'You…' Pisces whispered. 'You ruined everything.' With a feral howl, Pisces leapt at Ig; her hands curled into claws. But Ig was ready. She braced her hands against the floor and, in the space of a second, saw the moment when Pisces got sloppy. It was right there; as she pitched forward, one foot off the ground, the other pressing into the concrete with only her toes to keep her balance. The moment where Ig saw Pisces smile. It was a furious, awful grimace of a smile, but it was there. She couldn't charm Ig into submission anymore, and she was more than happy to punish her for it. And that was the moment where Ig pushed herself up and back, tendrils supporting her weight as her legs came up over her head in a backwards handstand. The momentum carried her, and her boots connected hard with Pisces' perfect, flat stomach. They both crashed back to the ground. The second water tank cracked, and Ig heard a yelp of triumph – the crowd had moved closer to get a better look at the fight, and her friends had managed to carve a way to her side. Pietro looked like he was about to explode from worry; Mercutio looked disappointed that the fight seemed to be over. And Vivi…Vivi looked like she was ready to smash another window. Ig smiled, and tasted blood on her tongue. She might have totally botched their debut with her temper; but at least they were all still standing.

Pisces scrambled to her feet; shaken, trembling with anger, looking over at Lily for backup. 'Lily,' she said, panicked. 'I need water. I need you to get me some–'

'What the hell, babe?' Lily sniped, getting to her feet and kicking a large, lethal-looking piece of glass out of the road.

Vivi wrinkled her nose. 'Ew. I'm totally not calling you babe anymore, Merc.'

Merc pulled her into a one-sided hug. 'I'm devastated. Truly.'

'Look at all this,' Lily continued, spreading her arms wide in case Pisces hadn't noticed the carnage. 'What did you think you were doing?'

Pisces' mouth dropped open. 'I… Lily? Baby, I–'

'Do you know how expensive all this kit is?' Lily folded her arms, shifting her weight onto one hip. 'Specially after you got the last model broke, too.'

Ig heard a dismissive scoff behind her. 'I think you mean 'after you broke the last model–' A ball of lightning shot over Ig's head. Mercutio barely had time to shove Vivi out of the way before it hit him in the chest and he crumpled to the ground, head bouncing off a nearby planter as he went down. 'You shut up, nerd!' Lily screamed, as Ig managed to haul herself to her feet and crawl to her friends.

Vivi unpinned the badge over her heart and brandished the pin at Lily. 'I'm gonna puncture her eyes for that,' she growled. 'Then we'll see what precious brand deals she gets.'

Lily rolled her eyes at her. 'Oh my god, it's you. Are you his little girlfriend or something? Ugh, so gross – oh my god, Pisces, get off me!'

Pisces was at her side, now; trying desperately to grab her girlfriend's hand. 'Lily – Lily, look at me. I'm sorry, it's just… you know what Ig is like. You know how she gets under my skin, I'll work on it for the next fight, I promise…'

'Get offa me, I said.' Lily wrenched her hands free, wiping them on her uniform as if Pisces was dirty. Pisces watched her, heartbroken. 'I can't believe you lost control like that, Pisces. Like, it's so unlike you. We are so not cool right now. I–'

Whatever else Lily Volt was going to say, it was strangled into a choked-off yelp as a white blur hit her in the stomach like a cannonball. Lily writhed on the floor, trying to pry the ball of white, fluffy fur and fury from her chest as Onslaught tackled her to the ground. Lily tried to get away, crawling over broken glass and cutting up the palms of her hands, but Onslaught was relentless; chasing her down and leaping onto her back, rearing back her adorable, round little head and extending a long proboscis from her mouth, complete with a row of long, shining, needle-sharp teeth. She bit down on Lily's shoulder, and Ig couldn't help but wince as Lily shrieked in pain and outrage. Pietro, for his part, burst out laughing.

'What… what?!' he cried, slapping a bleary-eyed Mercutio on the back and knocking him off balance. 'What is this madness?!'

His brother shrugged, blinking with one eye and then the other. 'I made some… ugh. My head. Some adjustments to her genetic makeup. You ever heard of tardigrades, Heretical? Tardigrades are…interesting. Ow.' Lily lashed out at Onslaught, catching her in the stomach; she hopped away and thumped her foot on the ground, angry at her meal being disturbed. There was a smear of red across her tiny, twitching nose. Vivi leapt into action, grinning wickedly and brandishing her pin. 'Hang on, Onslaught! I'll hold her arms back for you!'

Watching her go, Merc grinned soppily. 'Do you know that I love her?' he asked Ig, head lolling to the side.

'The bunny or the girl?'

'Yes.'

Pisces' gaze snapped so violently between her girlfriend struggling against a rabbit and a green-haired eco warrior on the floor, the broken glass around her feet, and Ig collapsing into the arms of two identical boys – one woozy, one utterly delighted at the spectacle before him – that Ig swore she could hear her joints cracking. She didn't look angry, anymore; just confused. Never in her wildest dreams – in all the times her future was laid out for her, perfect as her ironed and pressed uniform – would she have ever thought her first mission would go like this. For a moment, Pisces froze. Then, she bolted across the street, straight into the crowd; Ig could hear her yelling at them to move, to get out of her way, to stop touching her. She vanished after that; heading down a street that Ig knew led to the Tyne. To Lunalist.

She was running away. Because that was what bullies do when things don't go their way.

Ig shook off her friends, lifted herself up onto her tendrils, and gave chase.

Chapter Forty-Seven

Ig's tendrils windmilled wildly underneath her as she chased Pisces back towards Lunalist – down the same steep slope heading towards the River Tyne that she'd dashed down with her friends only days before. People dove out of her way, screaming with fright, swerving wildly in their cars as Ig leapt across busy roads; flipping cars onto their sides as she went, just out of spite. Ahead of her, Pisces was running at full tilt, dodging and weaving through the throng of people heading down to the Quayside to take selfies on the Millennium Bridge, with the most famous school for Heroes in the world shining in the background. At one point, she hopped neatly over the bonnet of a car that had screeched to a halt in front of her, leaving a sweaty handprint on the paint, legs flinging out gracefully in front of her. Now that she wasn't impeded by her tanks, her natural agility was on show again. In another life, she could have been a gymnast, or a dancer. But here, in this reality, she was the perfect student, the Hero, the girl Ig had loved once and, somehow, the person she could have been – if only she'd been born completely differently and had a totally different personality. That was how they got you; telling you to work a little harder, be a different person, hurt yourself a little more. Hate yourself into becoming who others wanted you to be.

They reached the Quayside itself, Pisces scaled the black railings of the fence that lined the river and leapt into the water like a mermaid, without so much as looking back. Ig paused; throat burning, arms aching. She couldn't even see a ripple where Pisces had entered the water; how was she meant to–

Pisces rose out of the river with her hands already braced, shooting balls of water in Ig's direction before diving back underwater – but her aim was off, and they splattered against the sides of the railings, showering Ig in a light, ineffectual spray. Pisces surfaced with a growl of anger, firing again. Ig rose into the air – but just as she crossed the Tyne, tendrils reaching for the far bank, something tugged her down towards the water. Ig yelped – more with surprise than shock. Whatever it was had grabbed hold of her…

'No. Don't you dare.'

Pisces was climbing her right tendril. She shimmied up it like a fireman's pole, feet scrabbling for purchase, coughing as the clouds of smoke billowing around her caught in her lungs.

'What are you doing?!' Ig cried. Pisces' grip was light; like the ghost of a fly crawling across your skin. Still, panic rose in her chest. Pisces was touching her. She didn't want Pisces anywhere near her! The tendrils grew as Ig rose herself higher into the air. 'Get off me, get off!'

'People,' Pisces said through gritted teeth, far below her, 'need to stop saying that to me today.' She dug her hands into the solid mass of the tendril, her eyes glittering with manic determination, 'I'm only…' Ig pitched to the side, putting her weight on her left tendril as she lifted the right one into the air, 'trying…' Pisces bit back a scream as Ig tried to shake her off like a dog shaking off a flea, 'to help!'

The entire Quayside had come to a standstill, watching this new Hero and Villain fighting in the middle of the river. As she pitched from side to side, Ig was painfully aware of how many cameras were probably on her right now – all the videos of her parents were dated but well-edited news clips, she was going to have shakey-cam YouTube videos. The river was far below her now; a strip of blue-grey-green paint. Ig keeled to one side as Pisces grew closer, dodging angrily squawking kittiwakes trying to fly home to roost. The sudden movement made her lose her balance, pitching wildly. The other side of the river swooped up to meet her as Pisces reached the base of Ig's tendril, and as she looked up she caught her reflection in the shining panels of the Lunalist Academy for the Gifted and Talented. Her hair was a mess, tangled and standing up in places. Her face was bruised and her eyes looked sunken and wild. She looked like a Villain.

They both hit the roof, scrabbling down the shiny surface of the Academy. Pisces had grabbed Ig's wrist in a vice-like grip, and her feet skidded over the glass with a hellish squeal. Ig's stomach lurched as the world tipped around her, becoming a swirl of blue sky and green grass and silver walls. She hit the ground with a thud – twisting at the last second so she didn't land on her back again – her teeth clacking painfully together; though, mercifully, Pisces' grip on her wrist slackened, and was gone.

'Oh my god!'

'What's happening?'

'Pisces?'

'Is that–'

'Oh my god!' With a groan, Ig realised they'd landed on the astroturf behind the school, where Ig and Pisces used to have Flyer Class. Students hung in midair, their mouths wide with shock. For a second – one wild, insane, reality-bending second – Ig wondered if the past few months had been a dream. Maybe she'd fallen out of the sky after that stupid Flyer Class, and she'd imagined everything with Shackleton. Maybe Vivi and Pietro and Merc weren't real. Maybe she was still alone. Still weak. But then Pisces dashed past her, soaking wet and bloodied, still carrying the remains of her water tanks, and she knew with a rush of relief that it wasn't true. She knew in her bones that her friends were coming for her, as surely as she knew her tendrils would support her weight. She scrambled to her feet and crashed through the Academy after Pisces. A few times, Ig shot a tendril out in front of her, trying to grab at her leg, her arm, her pretty red hair; but Pisces was too quick. A blur of memories rushed past Ig; hallways and rooms she recognised, familiar faces from her classes, teachers who screamed her name as she dashed past them. As if they were worthy of any respect now. How many of them had known about The General sending her away? How many had been relieved?

They careened up a long spiral staircase that led to the War Room – almost colliding with the staff coming down the other way, having clearly been told to evacuate. For a fleeting second, Ig made eye contact with Dana – the hacker she'd only seen through a screen for months now – and it was so surreal she found herself laughing wildly as she chased Pisces up the stairs. It was like seeing a celebrity in the flesh. *Hey, Dana – can I get your autograph?*

As they entered the now-empty War Room, Pisces slammed into one of two identical closed doors. 'General,' she cried, the doorknob slippery under her wet palms, 'General, please, are you in there? General!' She managed to wrench the door open and fall through into the darkened room. Ig glanced at the other office, where she'd signed the forms that had sent her to Shackleton; if Pisces was looking for The General, she'd chosen the wrong room. This one was dark, almost pitch-black, with strange shapes shoved into the corner. Nevertheless, Ig followed her in like a bullet from a gun, colliding with her back. The two girls fell to the floor, wrapped in Ig's tendrils; too close and too tired to even hurt each other, really. They could only struggle to keep the other down, their breath mingling as their faces pressed close together. After her swim in the Tyne, the gash across Pisces' head had stopped bleeding. But her pretty face was smeared with dirt and waterlogged makeup, and all the gunk in that river couldn't possibly be good for you. Ig hoped she had sepsis.

Pisces attempted to wriggle away, but Ig pulled her back. She grabbed Pisces' arms with her hands; enjoying the feeling of the bones in the other girl's wrists moving under her grip. She even squeezed a little harder than she needed to, just because she knew it hurt.

'You think you know so much about me,' Ig hissed. 'You think I'm so easy to figure out. But you didn't see any of this coming, did you Pisces?' Pisces set her jaw defiantly and thrashed like a fish on a hook. Ig lost her grip. 'Answer me!'

'I don't,' Pisces spat, 'need to justify anything to a Villain.'

She was so childish. 'But you were happy enough to… to…'

Ig's thumb had slid down Pisces' right wrist, hovering over the spot where her pulse was thrumming; fast and delicate, like everything else about Pisces. But there, underneath the skin, was a solid, hard ridge. Ig cocked her head, watching her thumb move back and forth over the solid mass under Pisces' skin. Suddenly, everything was clear; like the adrenaline in her system had evaporated.

It didn't feel like bone. It was too uniform, too neat, too circular to be natural. She prodded it.

'Ig what are you–'

'Shut up.' Ig took her hand off Pisces' left wrist, using both hands to pinch the circle hard.

'Ow! Stop that!' Pisces went to pull her hand back, but Ig stopped her.

'What have they done to you?' she muttered. The fight forgotten about, she traced the outline of the circle again with a finger. It was small – about the size of her thumbnail – and subtle, but now that she'd seen it, she had no idea how she hadn't noticed it earlier. 'If I didn't know any better, I'd say that was…'

Her stomach plunged into ice water.

'Pisces… is that a Power Lender disc?'

Chapter Forty-Eight

Ig crawled backwards as if she was afraid Pisces' skin would poison her, cradling her own wrist in her hand. 'Pisces, what have they done to you?'

Pisces stood up, brushing invisible dirt from her uniform – which did nothing to move the stains of dirty water, blood and sweat that were actually spattered all over her clothes. 'Look,' she said, 'if this is some sort of Villain trick–'

'Can you just answer me normally for once, please?' Ig snapped. 'Why is that thing–' she jabbed a finger in Pisces' direction, 'under your skin?!'

Pisces stared at her as if she were stupid. 'Lily told you,' she said slowly. 'We had our Power Revelation Ceremonies moved up. The General said–'

'Oh, please,' Ig said sarcastically, waving her hands about in a pantomime of enthusiasm, 'do tell me what The General said. She's such a bastion of truth and integrity.'

'Don't talk about her like that!'

'I'll talk about her however I want!' Ig stormed up to the Hero girl and prodded her in the chest. 'She kicked me out, Pisces! She didn't want me here, so she told me a pack of lies and served me up to her enemies. For all she knew, I was going to be eaten alive at Shackleton.'

'Instead, you turned your back on everything you knew for a bunch of freaks–'

'Oh my god,' Ig yelled, pulling Pisces' arm back towards her with a hastily summoned tendril. 'Tell me what this is right now or I'll wrench your arm off and find out for myself.'

Pisces looked at her, hurt filling her big blue eyes like tears. 'You never used to be like this,' she whispered.

Ig glared at her. 'What,' she snarled, 'did you ever know about me?'

Silence. Then, Pisces sighed. 'I told you. I had my Power Revelation Ceremony. You've got your Power, Ig – shouldn't you know what happens?'

'I didn't have a stupid Ceremony,' Ig said. 'Your girlfriend called me a freak, and it just happened.' She produced another tendril from her left hand and waved it about like the world's weirdest flag. 'Didn't yours just… happen?'

'No?' Pisces looked down at her arm as if she'd never seen it before. 'No, it's… at your Power Revelation Ceremony. An implanted Power Lender tames the Power in your body, sorts it from potential energy into something that's concrete.'

Ig twisted her face in disgust. 'Permanent, you mean. It's the Power they choose for you, or nothing.'

Pisces nodded, confusion still clouding her features. 'It's how it's always been done. They look over your school reports and your grades and think about what sort of Hero you should be and then they…Ig, you're telling me those Villains didn't put something in you to make you like this?'

'No!'

'So why did you decide on… that?'

'I didn't!' Ig let go of Pisces' arm. 'It just happened.' She looked up at Pisces. 'So that thing gave you your water Powers?'

Pisces nodded, and something clicked into place in Ig's brain. The way that Lily had to concentrate on her Powers, how Pisces wasn't as good at aiming her jets of water as she was at climbing or jumping…

'Why did they choose water?' she asked.

Pisces shrugged, and Ig could have sworn she saw something bitter flicker behind her eyes. 'I do Swimming Club. I'm good at it. My name's Pisces Rising, they said it was obvious. And…' she flicked her hand at her birthmark. 'It all just makes sense, doesn't it?'

'But that's cyclical thinking,' Ig said. Agitation flowed through her veins, making her pace. 'They asked you to do Swimming Club, you didn't choose to do it. So they made you go to Swimming Club because they thought water would suit you, and they thought water would suit you because you do Swimming Club…' she looked at the Hero in front of her. That dark, gleeful, angry feeling swirled inside her again. 'Pisces,' she said evenly, 'do you sometimes wish you'd got heightened agility, or something?'

Pisces flinched like Ig had hit her.

'You were always so good at that stuff. I remember how much you liked Flyer Class, because everyone saw that you were the fastest girl in our team. And you got to do all those amazing tricks, didn't you? Back before you had a Power.'

Pisces nodded, teeth pressing into her bottom lip.

'I bet you don't get to do that now.'

Pisces shook her head, eyes glassy with tears.

'My friend Pietro has something like that,' Ig continued, voice growing smooth and soft. 'Heightened abilities. But he came by it naturally. He picked up a broom handle and knocked you both around like it was nothing.'

'Stop it,' Pisces whispered.

'He's amazing. Strong and graceful and…oh, he's so cool, Pisces, you wouldn't even believe it. At the fountain, back at Shackleton; when he attacked Lily, did you look at him and think that maybe you could have–'

'Stop it!' Pisces screamed, covering her ears. 'Stop trying to get in my head, it won't work, just stop it!'

Ig huffed out a laugh. 'Worth a try.' It was the most normal conversation they'd ever had.

'Miss Heretical,' came a voice from behind her, in the doorway to the room. 'I have to admit, you surprised me.' The light turned on, filling the room with a blinding, clinical white light. Ig whirled; there in the doorway was The General – standing with her arms crossed, looking down at her and Pisces as if they'd been caught fighting in the halls. 'I pride myself on being able to read my students,' The General said, walking into the room and around Ig in a slow circle. 'Their temperaments, their goals and ambitions, their estimated targets. I was certain that Shackleton would be too much for you.'

It was like she was trying to make Ig feel guilty for surviving. 'Well,' Ig said, turning to face The General in a slow pivot, 'maybe you can't read people like me.' As her old headteacher moved around the room, Ig could see behind her a chair, not unlike the one she'd sit in when she went to the dentist – except for the fact that the dentist never had to strap Ig in with leather and buckles. A long arm extended out from it on a hinge, with an array of bright, shiny objects balanced on a tray that glinted in the sun. A glass of water. Scalpels. Needles. And a plastic sleeve filled with blank, white Power Lender discs.

The General laughed. 'Well, perhaps that's a blessing in disguise. Why did you come back here, Miss Heretical?'

Ig looked over at Pisces. There was no thought needed, no excuses or rationalisation. 'She's my nemesis,' she said simply. Pisces blinked, her face growing blank with realisation and shock. It was true. No-one would ever make either of them as angry as they made each other. No-one would ever want to stop Ig's chaos more than Pisces, and no-one would ever want to make Pisces' life more miserable than Ig. They were stuck together. Ig was glad she finally saw that.

Pisces' hand moved slowly to touch the ugly-looking cut on her forehead. It was definitely going to scar.

'Ah,' The General tutted. 'Well, Miss Rising, you really are set for life. A nemesis at the tender age of sixteen – and one with such a cult following, too.'

'A cult following?' Pisces asked. 'What do you mean?'

'Well,' The General said, her tone never wavering as she walked back towards the door, 'she has her band of reprobates

– who are currently making their way here I'd imagine, eager to show their loyalty by taking out a few Academy students. Then you have the mother's acolytes–'

'Don't bring my mam into this,' Ig said in a low, dangerous whisper.

'Your mother,' The General snapped, glaring daggers in her direction, 'brought herself into this. Were there no megalomaniacs available for her to seduce, that she had to align herself with a respected Hero like your father?'

'My dad–'

'Could have gone on to save the world. But now, he's shackled to the United Kingdom because his unwavering duty and honour has been used against him. When he told me he had a child on the way with her, I almost–'

Ig's tendril cracked like a whip through the air, aimed directly at The General's head. Her mask of nonchalance slotting neatly back into place, The General held up her hand, and a beautiful arc of water – small, but as well-crafted as an arc of ice – curved through the air and blocked Ig's attack. Ig spun; Pisces was behind her, glass of water in hand. The General sighed, bored and irritated. 'Miss Heretical,' she said, smoothing her iron-grey hair back into place, 'you really need to learn to control your temper.'

And that was when Ig saw it. The scar on The General's wrist; that only imperfection, that spiderweb of raised skin tissue. The trophy from her days as the country's youngest Hero. The scar that sat above her pulse point. Exactly where Pisces' Power Lender was.

Pisces wasn't the only Hero this had happened to. She said so herself. It happened to everyone. It had happened to The General. And then something else had happened to her, and the Power Lender under her skin had been destroyed.

The General didn't have a Power. Not anymore. She'd lost it.

Just then, the lights went out.

Chapter Forty-Nine

The room was filled with the sound of a thousand terrible, flapping wings. The lights began to flicker off and on, so rapidly that the shadows it cast seemed to move with a life of their own; shifting and flapping, turning the room into a vortex of dark feathers; echoing with the sound of clacking beaks and the glint of a hundred cruel, beady eyes. The General flinched. Pisces spun in a tight, panicked circle. But Ig stayed still, a smile spreading across her face. She knew what was coming next.

'Get away,' a voice said, hidden somewhere inside the shadows, 'from my daughter.' The room plummeted into darkness one more time. Then, at Ig's shoulder, stood The Witch Queen; beautiful and terrible in her black dress, her hair undulating around her head as she floated a foot from the ground. A rush of love coursed through Ig's veins, so hot it burned her heart.

'Give me one reason,' The Witch Queen said, her voice like the crack of an earthquake, 'why I shouldn't turn this school to rubble.' The General took a step forward. 'Viola–' The Witch Queen flicked her wrist, and the dentist's chair hurtled across the room in an angry screech of metal on tile, flinging itself between Ig and her old teacher.

'Stay back.'

The scalpels and needles slowly rose, turning like a child's mobile in the air to face The General. One drifted across the space and came to a stop mere inches from Pisces' adorable button nose. 'I've seen you too, little girl,' Ig's mother said, without turning to face the Hero standing at her back. 'Don't move.' The Witch Queen made a swooping motion with her other hand, and The General lifted into the air, hands flying to her throat. 'You turned my daughter against me,' The Witch Queen said. 'You warped her mind until her own worth was nothing but dirt under your foot. You made her keep your little secrets and your lies, and then you abandoned her.'

'Viola…' The General croaked.

'Enough. You should suffer, General. You should suffer as my daughter has suffered. Terrified and alone in the wilderness, with no one to care if you live or…'

'Ig!'

'Your cavalry has arrived, Heretical!'

The Witch Queen's brow creased; her gaze flitting to the open door. Ig's heart lurched as she craned her neck to look past The General, still floating in midair.

'Hey! You! Tell me where Ig Heretical is, or I'll launch this bat somewhere very uncomfortable indeed…'

Three sets of footsteps pounded across the War Room and there – bruised and battered but ready to fight – were her friends. Pietro's bat was dented and chipped, Vivi was covered in scratch marks and scrapes, and Mercutio had exactly none of his usual snark and composure left after running halfway across the city immediately after being electrocuted. But they were here. Ig dashed from her mother's side, pushed past the motionless General, and flung herself into their arms.

'Oh my god, is everyone okay?'

'You just ran off!'

'I'm sorry Vivi, I needed to–'

'Never do that again. Never ever ever!'

'Okay, okay…'

'I know we're Villains, Heretical, but that doesn't mean you get to leave us behind. Do you know how much venom my drones had to use up so we could make our way to the Quayside unscathed? A lot!'

'Okay, Merc,' Ig said, smearing a tear across her cheek, 'I'm sorry. I'll do better.'

'Well. Good. I'm not being emotional, stop saying that.'

Vivi, who until now had been clinging to Ig like a baby sloth, raised her head and looked into the room beyond her. 'Um… what have we walked into?'

The General managed to painfully twist her neck to glare down at the four Villains. Pisces looked like she was about to burst into tears. And The Witch Queen was looking at them quizzically, her hair falling along her back like silk as her feet touched the floor. 'Oh,' she muttered, blinking hard as her eyes returned to their usual dark brown colour, 'so you weren't alone, after all. You found your own little Villain society.'

Ig felt Vivi's hand squeeze around her own – watched as Pietro and Mercutio stood a little closer to her – and realised that she was right. The air seemed to leave her lungs in a woosh, then her whole body felt light as a balloon. She had a society. She had friends. She had a family.

The room suddenly grew bright again. 'Hello,' The Witch Queen said, holding up one hand in a wave. 'I'm Ig's mam. I've heard nothing about any of you.'

'Ooooh my god,' Vivi whispered, gripping Mercutio by the lapels. 'Merc. The Witch Queen is talking. To me. Can you believe it?' She shook her boyfriend a little, and Ig winced as Merc's head snapped violently back and forth. 'Can you believe it?!'

'Y-yes, love. I c-can. I h-have ey-yes.'

Ig's mam laughed. 'Aw, bless. It's been a while since I've had that reaction from a teenager. Aren't you just so canny, Miss, um..?'

'Vivi, Mrs. Heretical. I mean, Mrs. Witch Queen. I mean… Vivi Section. Is my name.'

'Oh! I think I know your Mami! Isabela Garcia? Or I suppose it's Isabela Section, these days…'

'Mam,' Ig groaned, rolling her eyes. 'Can you stop, please?'

'Just one second, poppet.' The Witch Queen flicked her wrist again, and The General flew across the room and crashed into the wall. 'I need to decide,' she said, advancing on The General like a wolf on the hunt, 'what I am to do with this one.' The General groaned, wincing up at Ig's mother. 'Viola.' The Witch Queen narrowed her eyes. 'Carol.'

'Carol?!' Pietro sputtered, his loud laughter making Ig wince. 'Ig, this is the person that all you Heroes are so scared of – the one who was the freakin' mastermind behind all of this – and she's called Carol?! That's the most boring old lady name ever! What, is she going to ask to see the manager if her Venti macchiato with whipped cream and a caramel drizzle isn't the right–'

The Witch Queen glared at him and for once, Pietro von Ryan shut his mouth when he was asked to.

'My husband trusted you, Carol,' Viola said, turning back to The General. 'He told me of your school days, how close you were. And I wanted to believe, for his sake and my daughter's, that your mania for control had cooled. That you had moved on from what happened that night, blossomed in your new role at the school. Now I see how foolish I was.'

'You never understood what you did to me, Viola,' The General said, attempting to stand. 'You never knew what it was like.'

'We were all Powerless once, Carol–'

'And some of us,' The General spat, 'have been Powerless for nearly twenty years!'

Something clicked into place in Ig's head. 'Mam,' she whispered, placing a hand on The Witch Queen's arm, 'did you... did you take The General's Power away?' Her mother sighed, never looking at Ig, but said nothing.

'You,' The General said, 'were always the same, Viola. Chaotic. Unhinged. Violent. Everything we stand against. You saw what made the Academy great – that made Heroes like me great – and you hated us for it.'

'That isn't true. You stormed Shackleton, Carol,' the Witch Queen said evenly. 'You stole Nyx from us. We had to get them back.'

Ig's eyes widened. The Nyx's words from the night of the Lunalist raid – the night she got her Power – sang inside her skull.

'After all this time,' The Nyx had said, 'it seems that there are still those who think they can simply change what they think is unsuitable. And if they can't, they'll destroy it.'

'Wait,' said Vivi slowly. 'Nyx? Like, Professor Nyx? Like our headteacher?'

'You kidnapped someone?' asked Pisces, still rooted to her spot behind Ig. Her voice was small, and trembling. 'Is that…is that why Shackleton invaded the school, General? When you were younger?'

'Nyx had potential,' The General said, as if that explained anything at all. 'Their Power could have changed the world – and they wanted to stay in the middle of nowhere, bothering sheep and terrorising villagers. They just needed to see things our way–'

'You kidnapped them from their bed, Carol!' The Witch Queen cried. 'A twelve-year-old child!'

'And what about me, Viola? I was fourteen–'

'We were fourteen, Carol–'

'–starting my career. I was going to be great, Viola; and then you snapped my wrist like a dry twig.' The General held up her arm in furious, steely vindication. 'They couldn't remove all the fragments of my Power Lender, Viola. It couldn't be replaced. I can never get my Power back. Never. Because of you.'

'You seem to have done well from it,' The Witch Queen said dryly, 'what with an entire Hero empire at your beck and call.'

'No thanks to you – you and your pride. Your jealousy over Nyx cost me my Power.'

The Witch Queen gritted her teeth. 'It wasn't personal, Carol. Why can't you accept that? I will not apologise for protecting one of my own.'

'Will you apologise, then,' The General said, staggering to her feet, 'for turning a Hero's daughter,' she pointed a vicious finger at Ig, 'into that?'

Silence fell over the room. A hand splayed across Ig's back, and she was shocked to find it was Mercutio's. Vivi, in contrast, moved forward, fists clenched and jaw set, but Ig pulled her back sharply. 'Hang on,' she whispered. 'Just hang on. Let them talk.'

The Witch Queen's lip curled in disgust. 'My marriage,' she said softly, dangerously, 'is not a personal slight against you, Carol.'

'It wasn't enough to make me Powerless,' The General continued, as if she hadn't spoken. 'You had to ruin Luca's chance to be a father to a child worth having?' She laughed harshly. 'Your daughter was weak, Viola. Easily persuaded with a little bit of praise. And now, she's fallen in with that crowd of degenerates, and it made her a monster. She was an insult, a mockery to everything we stand for. To me. And she still is.'

Ig felt the bile rising in her throat. With a groan of effort, The General rose to her feet, slowly and painfully. 'And now,' she hissed, 'with one snap of my fingers, I can raise the alarm and every single student who deserves to be here – who have actually accomplished something with their time here – will converge on this room and tear your band of Villain brats apart.'

Ig's mother crossed her arms with a scoff. 'Call your little army of children,' she said, and the room darkened again around her. 'Let them have a taste of fear before they graduate.'

'Um, Mrs. Witch Queen,' Pietro said, casting a look down the hallway as if scores of Heroes were already on their way, 'they have teachers here too, right? And even if it's just students, there's like…' Pietro did a quick head count. 'One, two, three, four… about a million times more of them than there are of us.'

'We're outnumbered,' Merc said simply.

The very air seemed to cool, and The General smirked.

'I can't fight,' Pisces said lamely, breaking the silence, 'unless I have water. Can I have another tank, General?'

The General's smile vanished. 'Have you earned one?' she asked.

Pisces looked at the floor. 'But I want to help,' she whispered. No-one answered her.

'Great,' snarked Pietro. 'One de-Powered Hero. That increases our odds by, oh, point-one percent.'

'We're still going to try, right?' Vivi said, moving a little closer to Ig. 'Right, Ig? We're still going to try and fight?'

Ig's mind swooped through the Academy campus; mentally taking stock of classrooms upon classrooms of students. Even the ones who didn't have Powers yet would throw themselves into a fight, if it got them some small sort of acclaim; something to put them above the rest, to make them seem the most important. Everyone who ever studied at Lunalist knew the impact of having something exceptional on your record as early as you could. What could be more important than saving a member of staff – the headteacher, no less – from a bloodthirsty Villain attack? Then, on top of that, you had a whole crowd of seasoned Hero teachers to contend with. Apart from her mam, Vivi was the most powerful among them. Pietro had had his Power for a few weeks. And speaking of her mam – would she even protect the others? Knowing The Witch Queen, she'd throw everything she had into protecting Ig… and let her friends suffer as a consequence. She was a good mam, but she was an even better Villain, after all.

They were going to lose.

'Wait,' said Ig. 'Wait a second. I want to make a deal.'

Chapter Fifty

Six pairs of eyes turned towards Ig. 'What,' said The General, 'could you possibly have to bargain with, Miss Heretical?'

'Poppet,' her mam asked, 'what are you doing?'

'We can fight!' Vivi cried, opening her glass pendant on her pin (which was surprisingly gore-free; Ig assumed she hadn't used it to blind Lily Volt) and inspecting the last few spider lily plants that were still alive. 'I promise, Ig! We can, give me a second to–'

'My deal is,' Ig said, walking forward as if no-one had spoken, 'is that you let us walk out of here, unharmed, just this once. And I don't destroy this entire school.' Behind her, Pisces laughed; hysterically, as if this were the funniest thing Ig could have said. 'No-one else wants to fight, General,' Ig continued. 'They only came here to defend me. And I know this place is the one thing that matters to you.' More to you than your own pride, she thought. More than the actual students.

'You are a strong monster, Miss Heretical,' The General said, 'but you're young, and you're green. Even with those… things I saw you using over the river, you can't hope to have any real impact on a school as well-armed as–'

'I'm not going to physically destroy it.' Ig said, speaking slowly and clearly, 'obviously.' The General raised an eyebrow. 'I'm going to destroy its reputation.'

The General blinked, face frozen in confusion. Then, she laughed. 'Miss Heretical,' she said, shooting a glare at The Witch Queen as she did, 'there are people in this room with easily sullied reputations, I'll give you that. But none of them are registered at this Academy.' She made chilling eye contact with Ig, who felt her fists clench at her side. 'How do you think invading the region's most beloved institution to attack children will look? There won't be a civilian or Hero alive that won't be out for your blood.'

Ig pretended to think. 'Hm. It would look about as good as experimenting on children and altering their bodies to fit your marketing deals, I suppose.'

It was brief. Barely more than a flicker of an eye. But Ig saw The General flinch. Ig dug her hand into the back pocket of her jeans, fishing out a small, silver disc, not unlike a compact mirror. It was damaged, now; the case had a huge, ugly crack down the centre, and somewhere along the way the 'call' button had popped out entirely. But it still worked, and the battery was at the halfway point. Impressive, since Ig had launched the dictaphone app on her communication device back on the bus from Rossborough to Newcastle. She was glad the thing had finally proven itself useful; she'd barely used it back at school.

She cycled back through her recording; right through the fight at Monument, through her chasing Pisces down to the Quayside, and through the chaos of her running through the Academy hallways. She found the point she was looking for – trying not to catch Pietro's eye as the sounds of her and Pisces scuffling filled the room. She knew how it sounded; she wasn't stupid. 'I told you,' the recording of Pisces said at last. 'I had my Power Revelation Ceremony. You've got your Power, Ig – shouldn't you know what happens?'

'I didn't have a stupid Ceremony. Your girlfriend called me a freak and it just happened.'

Ig couldn't help herself. She looked over at Pisces as Lily Volt was mentioned. She wanted to watch as the pain and the shame washed over her face. 'Isn't that the girlfriend who watched you lose your first fight and told you how embarrassing it was for her, Pisces?' Pisces looked down at the ground, pink spots forming on her wet cheeks. 'I hate you, Ig.'

'Good. At least you feel something for me now.'

'…it's where you get your Power,' the Pisces on the recording was saying. 'They reveal it to you. An implanted Power Lender tames the Power in your body, sorts it from potential energy into something that's concrete.'

'Permanent, you mean. It's the Power they choose for you, or nothing.'

'It's how it's always been done. They look over your school reports and your grades and think about what sort of Hero you should be and then they…Ig, you're telling me those Villains didn't put something in you to make you like this?'

'No!' Ig shut off the recording. 'There's more,' she said coolly, 'but I don't need to play my entire hand. Pisces gave me a lot of information.' The General's face had gone ashen.

'A lot of students here have Hero parents, don't they?' Ig said, beginning her own slow walk around the room. 'People who were also given this 'treatment' with the Power Lenders. I'm not stupid enough to think that you came up with that yourself. I know my Dad used Power Lenders when he was here, and I'm assuming if I checked his arm, I'd find a Power Lender disc. Also, none of our parents ever raised hell about you implanting microchips in us, so they must see it as normal. Not worth talking about. But,' she continued, looking pointedly at Pisces again, 'what about everyday, normal people? How will they feel when they hear about children being strapped into chairs and operated on? Do you know,' she laughed harshly, 'for all your pearl-clutching and fear-mongering, the only thing I ever saw being experimented on at Shackleton was a rabbit, or a couple of bees.'

'General,' Pisces began, her speech rapid and slurred with panic as she seized on a chance to grab hold of the narrative, 'she's talking about the horrible monsters that attacked Lily–'

'Wait a second, Pisces,' Ig said, holding up a finger for silence.

'I'm not done. Speaking of normal, everyday people… did your parents sign a permission waiver when you started here? I know mine didn't. I know they're so proud of their little girl being a Hero, but how would they feel,' Ig said, advancing on her former dorm-mate, 'if they found out their fifteen-year-old had been given life-changing surgery? You never mentioned that in your little calls home. Do you think your dad would like that? Do you think his doctor friends at the RVI would have something to say?'

Pisces glowered, but said nothing.

'Neither side knows how things are done at the other school. Not really; not like I do.' Ig laughed. 'You were so certain I was stupid that you let me find out more about the differences between Heroes and Villains than any other person on the planet.' She held up her communication device. 'Until I release this tape, that is. How will parents – or the news, for that matter, the ones that have been covering Power Revelations for years – feel when they find out Powers can come naturally for us, but they might be too big or too loud or too inconvenient for the best Hero School in the world. And what about when they find out your solution is to stick plastic and wires in our veins, General? Was Pisces close to getting a Power that didn't fit her image? Was that why you put her under the knife? What about Lily?' Outrage seeped into her voice, making it crack. 'What about me? What would you have done with me?!'

The very air seemed to thicken with tension. 'We never force Powers upon our slower students,' The General said carefully after a long, hard swallow; already preparing for the media maelstrom Ig intended to unleash. 'Miss Heretical, your constant jealousy of Miss Rising and Miss Volt has… has turned into a mania. They have always been so far above you that–'

'That you strapped them to that monstrosity early,' Ig said darkly, flinging a hand out towards the dentist's chair. 'That was their reward, General.'

Pietro was standing open-mouthed at Ig's side. 'Hang on,' he said – playing it up for the crowd, typical von Ryan behaviour. 'They put microchips in the Heroes? In the underage Heroes?' His mouth cracked into a smile. 'Oh, wait 'til I tell Uncle Rayner he isn't the worst mad scientist on the block anymore…'

The realisation of how that would sound to the world outside the room they were standing in washed over The General like a cold, black tide.

Ig looked at The General and smirked. If she were Mercutio, she'd hold for applause. If she were her dad, she'd be adamant that this was all one big misunderstanding that could be ironed out for everyone's benefit. If she were her mother, The General would be dead by now. But she wasn't any of those people. She was Ignatia Heretical.

Chapter Fifty-One

The General gritted her teeth. 'You're going to release that audio whether I let you go now or not,' she said. 'Do you honestly think I'd trust a Villain?'

'The only reason I'm not releasing it now,' Ig said coolly, 'is so my friends get to go back to Shackleton in one piece. They have homework to hand in.' She swore she heard Vivi smother a laugh. 'You have to trust that I really do value their safety over taking down the people who ruined my life. Besides,' she shrugged, 'I might need something else from you in the future. Then, I can perhaps give you the only copy as a reward, and you can have Pisces here drown it in the Tyne.'

The General stared at her for a long moment. 'What about the other students?' she asked. 'The ones that have their Ceremonies between now and… whenever you decided to blackmail us. We're not going to stop progress to accommodate you, Miss Heretical.'

'I know.' Ig lifted her shoulder in a shrug. 'And I'm not interested in saving Heroes. Lunalist students didn't care about me when I was here. Why should I care about them now I'm gone?'

Pisces had the good grace to look a little sick at that. 'You really are a Villain,' she whispered.

'Glad you've finally realised that,' Ig spat back.

The General looked like she was about to say something more. Then, her shoulders slumped. 'That's the longest I've ever heard you speak without saying "um",' she said, laughing softly to herself.

'I've learned a lot while I was away.'

The General stared at the communication device as if she wished she could explode it with her mind. She moved forward, but the von Ryan boys stepped in front of Ig protectively, and she felt her heart swoop with love for them. They were idiots, but they were her idiots. And, when they needed her to, she knew she'd do the same for them. After a long moment of staring them down, The General flicked her wrist. 'Pisces,' she said, 'escort them off the school grounds. Then come meet me in the War Room – after you've cleaned up your face.' She walked slowly to Ig's side, leaning down to stare her full in the face. 'I cannot believe,' she whispered, 'you would do this to us, Miss Heretical. I can't believe you hate us so much that you'd align yourself with them.' Her gaze flicked over Ig like she was a smear of excrement on the floor. 'You could have disappeared into anonymity if you were struggling so much here. But no. Your arrogance and your hate will now be your downfall.'

Ig steeled herself, staring blankly back into her old headteacher's eyes. 'I know,' she said. 'And I've never been happier.'

The General straightened. 'Pisces.'

'Yes, General.' Pisces walked over to the group of Villains. 'Come on,' she said, taking Ig by the arm and leading her into the corridor. 'Remember; you said you'd go quietly.' She dug her nails into the soft flesh of Ig's arm.

'Oh, absolutely not,' cried Vivi, storming towards them both, jabbing a finger into Pisces' chest. 'Listen here, Pretty Girl. I know you've never had a bad hair day in your life and it's given you a God Complex, but that doesn't mean everyone else is going to let you get away with–'

Ig pushed her friend gently backwards with the flat of her palm. 'I just negotiated our way out of here, Vivi,' she said. 'Please don't spoil it defending my honour.'

'But she…she's such a…you can't let her…' Vivi stamped her feet. 'This is so frustrating!'

'Pietro,' Ig said, looking back over her shoulder. 'you bring up the rear. Make sure no-one tries anything on the way out.'

'Got it.'

'Merc, you hold Vivi… Merc?'

Mercutio was attempting to drag the dentist's chair out the door.

'Merc!'

The scientist jumped, hands up in the air like Ig had threatened to shoot him. 'What?' he cried. 'I'm not allowed to take home a little trophy? Haven't you heard of the spoils of war? Look at this thing!' he said, giving it an affectionate kick. 'Real leather straps, a good quality light-and-mirror setup, a handy-dandy tray for all your instruments…I could really use this thing back at school.' He held up a Power Lender disc and grinned. 'Note to self; bees with Powers. Super strong bees. Tiny, fire-breathing bees. Invisible bees. Mwahaha.' Pietro punched his brother in the shoulder, snapping him out of his daydream. 'Go get your girlfriend, idiot. I'm not having that in the dorm, anyways.'

'…fine,' Mercutio grumbled. 'Don't worry, I've got her.' He wrapped his arms around Vivi's shoulders and frog-walked her out the room. 'I know, love, I know,' he murmured into her hair. 'I wish I could let you kill her. You know how much I hate being the sensible one in any social dynamic. Please stop growling. It's unsettling and deeply attractive at the same time and I'm having conflicting emotions…'

Pisces dragged Ig out into the War Room. 'Why are all these Villains so weird?' she whispered.

'You get used to them,' Ig replied. They walked towards the staircase in silence, lost in their own thoughts. Ig had often dreamed of being on Pisces' arm. It had never looked like this.

Onslaught was patrolling the corridors, keeping students in their classrooms with a snarl and a menacing thump of her back feet; baring her bloodstained proboscis at anyone who got a little too close. Mercutio snapped his fingers and she fell into line, nuzzling happily against Vivi's ankle as they walked.

Even though she'd asked Pietro to bring up the rear, Ig's mam was the last one to reach the staircase. Silently, she walked with them, head held high, until she reached her daughter's side. 'I'm going to go, poppet,' she said.

Ig felt her heart twist painfully. 'So soon?' She'd barely spent any time with her mother in months. They hadn't even really talked about what had happened at Shackleton. When she was away from the world – when she didn't have to play the part of the scheming, manipulative Villain anymore – Ig had really, really wanted a cuddle.

'I'll visit the school soon,' her mam said, gently cupping her cheek. 'I think The Nyx and I have a lot to talk about.'

So much about her headteacher made sense to Ig, now. Their protectiveness over the school, their dedication to keeping students safe when they could have been the member of a powerful Villain society. The way they'd offered sanctuary to a student fleeing the same aggressive favouritism and obsession with conformity that they'd seen in their short, friendless time at Lunalist. There was a story there, somewhere, between her mother and The Nyx. Maybe one day – when they weren't outsmarting Heroes – Ig would ask to hear it.

'And,' Ig's mam continued, 'I think I'm going to need to have a talk with your father tonight.'

Ig winced. 'Oh. Right. Dad. Will he be–'

'Devastated. Distraught. Betrayed.' A spasm of sadness flickered in Ig's throat. She swallowed it before it could turn into guilt. 'But he'll grow used to it. It takes time, but wounds like this scab over and heal into scars. I should know, after all. Love is all about healed scars.'

'Did you notice…' Ig held up her free arm questioningly, and her mother nodded.

'It was your father's choice. Nothing has ever made him as happy as being a Hero did. Who am I to spoil that for my husband? It's not like I don't have practices he objects to,' The Witch Queen said with a laugh.

Ig nodded. 'Oh,' she said, 'before you go. Um. There might be… I might have met a…' her mind flickered back to Katalina; gorgeous, sweet Katalina, kissing her in the dark. 'A girl.'

The Witch Queen raised an eyebrow. 'Hm? Well, we can talk about that part later,' her mother said. She turned to Pisces. 'I heard a lot about you from my daughter over the years, Miss

Rising. You really are as pretty as she said you were. And I want you to know that I never liked you.' Pisces' shoulders twitched like she'd been struck.

With one last meaningful look, The Witch Queen stepped back, out of Ig's reach. 'Your hair's grown out,' she said, her eyes shining as she stroked a finger down Ig's cheek. 'It suits you.' The lights flickered off and on again, and she was gone. Ig sighed, and kept walking. After a while, they passed the mural of The Streak, and Ig forced herself not to look away. Her father had made his choices, and she had made hers. That was that.

'Hey; she's really just going to let us go?' Pietro said out the corner of his mouth, as he jogged to catch up. 'Your ex, I mean.'

'I'm not her ex,' Pisces snapped. Pietro made a very rude gesture at her.

'I thought you were covering our backs,' Ig muttered. 'But yes. Right up until we cross the Lunalist threshold. Then, she'll set every Hero in this place on us; on top of, well… them.'

She jutted her chin towards a window facing the river. The other bank – the one that led back into town – was now swarming with vans, camera crews, journalists and onlookers. Ig would be surprised if any other part of Newcastle was busy at all. 'The General is probably hoping we get torn apart by the press.'

'Are we seriously not leaking the tape?'

'And give up a nice piece of blackmail material right at the beginning of our careers?' Ig winked. 'Of course not.'

'Spoken like a true Villain,' Pietro laughed, nudging her in the side.

'That's not a good thing,' said Pisces under her breath. 'Why are you all acting like it's a good thing?' She tugged Ig forward a little, so their heads were nearly touching. 'I'm not giving up on you,' she said, her voice low and angry. 'You'll pay for ruining my first mission.' Typical, selfish Pisces. 'And you'll never release that recording, as long as I'm around.'

'You could come with us,' Ig offered. 'Be a rebel for once in your life, fight back against a school that shoves kids like us into moulds that don't fit them.' She looked back at Vivi, still struggling against Mercutio's grip and shooting Pisces daggers. 'Vivi might take some time to forgive you, but…'

Something flickered across Pisces' face. It looked, to Ig, like regret. Perhaps pain, or longing. But it was smothered quickly and forever. Ig had already known the answer. But she needed to ask anyway. 'I'm here to do good,' Pisces said, straightening her back and gazing into the middle distance. 'I won't turn my back on the impact I can have on this world just because the way I got there was… difficult. I'm not a quitter, like you are. I'm a Hero. Heroes don't run from hard times.'

'Is that so?' Ig asked. 'It's not because there aren't any brand deals and press tours and laps of honour for traitors?'

Pisces said nothing. 'You were right, before,' she said. 'We are nemeses, aren't we?'

'Neither of us have to like it. But there we are. You going to chase me all the way back up to Monument?' Ig asked. Pisces sighed, like it really did hurt her to let Ig and her friends go.

'You might get away this time. But only because I need a new tank before I can take you on again.'

'I'm sure your owner will provide you with one, if you're good enough. You're not much use to her otherwise.'

Pisces made a disgusted noise in the back of her throat. 'I liked you better when you could barely talk to me.' Ig laughed bitterly. 'Of course you did. Well, those days are gone.' In her mind's eye, she looked ahead to years full of schemes and diabolical plots, endlessly quoted monologues and battles won and lost, all stretching on forever; the two of them more entwined than they'd ever been before. She realised that before anything else, Pisces Rising would always be the girl who would never love her back. There would always be a part of Ig – however small – that would always be howling in pain, asking why she wasn't enough. The last tiny part of Ig's heart broke. Then, it stitched itself back together, dark as smoke, and she was ready for her future.

Chapter Fifty-Two

The second they crossed the threshold of the school – back out into the real world, with the River Tyne shining at their side – they broke into a run. Adrenaline shot through Ig's veins, and for a brief second, she felt like nothing more than a fifteen-year-old girl, running from the consequences of her actions with her friends. She could have been anyone; taking her friend's hand, shrieking with playful terror as, across the river, a hundred different voices shouted her name.

'Ignatia!'

'There she is!'

'That's her? Really?'

'Ignatia! Hey! Hey, over here!'

'We need to know why, sweetheart – look into the camera and tell us why!'

'Why do you hate Newcastle so much?'

'Ignatia, What's your relationship with Pisces Rising and Lily Volt?'

'Hey, look over here!' Reaching the base of the Millennium Bridge, Ig watched with a grim smile as scores of Heroes, students and tutors alike poured out of the doors of the Lunalist Academy For The Gifted and Talented – some even taking flight and rising over the shining back of the school. They probably wouldn't attack them. Probably. It wouldn't do for noble, gallant Heroes to exploit a loophole in their deal and attack them just outside the limits of their bargain. Especially in front of all those cameras. No; they'd get away, this time. But once the story spread; of how this gang of thugs had humiliated two of Lunalist's brightest young stars and stormed the most important Hero landmark in the North, Ig could picture the spin Lunalist would put on their actions. They'd be the most wanted Villains around. And that was fine with Ig. It would be nice to be wanted for a change.

She wrapped a tendril around her friends and lifted them into the air with the other, propelling them forward and up into the Newcastle sky. Years later, it would be the picture that everyone associated with the rise of Ignatia Heretical, The Kraken herself. A young, dark-haired, incredible girl flying through the air – fleeing from the Academy she betrayed, landing on top of the Millennium Bridge with the rest of her band of scoundrels. It would be the beginning of the greatest Villain Society the United Kingdom ever knew. But that was years away. Right now, they were just four teenagers, bunking off from school for a day to get revenge on people who deserved it. What could be more joyful than that?

'This is…' Mercutio said, looking down at the river far below them, 'really high up.'

'I can put you down, if you want,' Ig said with a grin, as more and more Heroes gathered in the courtyard of the Academy; most bristling with fury at their beloved institution being violated by a bunch of scruffy ne'er-do-wells, while some – the younger ones, really – just gawked up at them. It was probably the first time any of them had seen a Villain before. Ig had never seen a Villain up close until she'd shared a room with one.

Across the Tyne, a loudspeaker crackled and squalled. 'Mercutio von Ryan!' shrieked a painfully shrill American accent, 'I'm gonna get you for this!' Pushing through the crowd of journalists and onlookers, Lily Volt almost launched herself over the railings on the bank of the river; someone pulled her back with a pitying wince. Lily's hair was matted and snarled, and her perfect skin was pocked with bee stings and rabbit/tardigrade bites. She looked a mess. She looked unhinged. It was amazing. 'I'm gonna follow you to the ends of the earth to stop you, you total weirdo! I'm gonna ruin you – I'll rip you apart! I'll blast your stupid eyebrows off! You'll never set foot in Newcastle again, you freak!'

'Oh no,' Mercutio drawled, 'I am terrified. Please, Lily – not my City Centre Privileges. How will I live without regularly inhaling six different types of smog?'

Far below, Lily lowered her bullhorn a fraction, confusion clouding her pretty features. 'What?!' she yelled. 'I can't hear you. Speak louder!'

'On second thought, Heretical,' Merc said, pulling Vivi close and resting his head on top of hers, 'I'm fine up here.'

'Answer me, von Ryan!'

Ig was barely listening to Lily's dramatics anymore. She was watching a figure standing at one of the huge windows to the War Room; a girl with red hair and a birthmark under her eye that Ig once thought was the most beautiful thing in the world. She was looking right at Ig. She could feel it. Then, her expression unchanging, Pisces turned and walked back into the school, disappearing from sight.

'See you soon, Pisces,' Ig whispered.

The thing Lunalist loved most, even more than helping people, was a good narrative. From the first second you were enrolled, they were working out what the best story was to tell about you. They told you who was good and who was bad, who was worthy and who wasn't, who deserved love and who didn't. And who would argue with them? They were Heroes, after all. And, Ig assumed, it must be very, very easy to cling to a narrative that tells you, right from the start, that you're special and beautiful and that the people around you are there to be used; mirrors to prop up your ego.

Pisces Rising was probably going to do a lot of good in this world. She was probably going to save a lot of people. And they'd love her for it. She was a Hero. If she left Lunalist behind, she would just be a girl. And who would want that?

Vivi laced her fingers through Ig's, squeezing her hand tightly. 'I knew it,' she said softly. 'All along. I knew you weren't like them. Even before you knew it yourself.'

Ig suddenly found her throat was clogged with unshed tears. So she squeezed Vivi back and said nothing. There was nothing that needed to be said between them, anyway.

'So,' Pietro drawled, knocking a fist against Ig's leg, 'you do realise Lunalist was right, don't you?'

'About what?' Ig asked, kicking her legs through the air. Pietro grinned.

'About Shackleton students invading the school.'

A laugh burst out of Ig's chest. 'Yeah, you're right.'

She looked out over the amassing crowds; on her left, the Heroes, out to get her. On the right, hundreds of civilians, all looking at her. Most of them were holding up their phones, ready to spread her face all over their social media accounts – to talk about how they saw it all, and give their takes on what had happened. Others were just watching – waiting to see what they did next. A single, lean figure was pushing their way through the crowd; Luca Peterson, desperately shouting her name.

'Ig! Ig, honey, let's talk about this,' he was saying, voice cracking from yelling loud enough for her to hear. 'I know you're angry or scared or whatever…'

In that moment – as all teenagers must – Ig realised that her Dad, who she loved so deeply, had never really known her at all.

'…but whatever's happened, it can still be fixed. Okay? You're not in trouble, I'm just… disappointed. I thought… I thought we were buddies. Can't we talk about this, before you do something stupid?'

I'm not in trouble, Dad? Ig thought to herself. *No, I suppose I'm not. Not yet. But I plan to be very, very soon.* She turned her head from her dad, and fixed her gaze on the River Tyne; winding backwards from the ocean at her back, up into the city and beyond. A shining trail, leading her forward with her friends. It all looked like terrible, amazing possibility.

END

Acknowledgements

Just before I started writing this book, I started to suspect that I was autistic. Well, that's not true. I'd suspected for a long, long while, and just before writing this book it got to the point where I needed to start asking some serious questions. Part of this revelation – and what led to my eventual formal diagnosis – was discovering fictional characters who were neurodivergent. Brilliant, funny, engaging characters who love sharks and robots and dancing and books and don't just fall into the stereotype of the rude, mathematics-obsessed characters (often boys) that we've seen in the past. Finding them was like feeling the sun come out.

I wanted to write a character who went through life just like I do – who thinks and feels a lot like I do - and gift her with people who will love her for her brilliant brain just the way it is. So, I want to start this page off by thanking Ignatia Heretical. Bringing you into the world probably saved my life, or at least my sanity.

Now, onto the non-fictional folk. First off, my brilliant agent Laura at The Liverpool Literary Agency, who had a potentially unmarketable manuscript dumped in her inbox one afternoon and just rolled with it. Your instant support of Heretical made everything click into place at a time when I was doubting if the words that I'd written even made sense. Thank you to everyone at Northodox for their boundless enthusiasm for my work – and especially to James for my stunning cover, which captures the chaotic vibes of this novel perfectly.

Thank you to all the staff at Kith & Kin in Whitley Bay for giving me a wonderful space to write every morning before work – the first draft of this book was powered entirely by oat milk hot chocolates!

A gigantic thank you to my Disaster Twin Melanie, who has been there since I was 'just playing about' with a new book idea and who was drawing fanart before the first draft was even finished. Thank you to Harley for endless evenings of proofreading, plothole-picking and pizza; your support means the world to me, and I'm sorry Devon Casterbury isn't in this one. Thank you to Lisette Auton for changing how I think about editing, and for just being a lovely human being in general. We need more authors like you in the world. Thank you to Martha, Adele and Tsam for helping me survive – Pisces crashing through that window is dedicated to you. Thank you to Sophie for being the Vivi to my Ig.

Thank you to my YA Book Club – you are the most brilliant, opinionated, intelligent group of readers I could ever want. I can't wait to hear your thoughts. As always, thank you to Nina Zenik for keeping me company as I write. Writing isn't a lonely business with you around.

But the biggest thank you goes to you, my readers. I've had the honour of meeting some of you, and I hope to meet many more. Always remember; the people who define you as a Villain are not the ones who matter. The ones who love you no matter what are. And they're out there. You might just have to look for them in places you wouldn't expect.

FIND US ON SOCIAL MEDIA

@northodoxpress

@northodoxpressofficial

@northodoxpress

@northodoxpress

www.northodox.co.uk

NORTHODOX PRESS

SUBMISSIONS

CONTEMPORARY
CRIME & THRILLER
FANTASY
LGBTQ+
ROMANCE
YOUNG ADULT
SCI-FI & HORROR
HISTORICAL
LITERARY

SUBMISSIONS@NORTHODOX.CO.UK

SUBMISSIONS

Northodox.co.uk

CALLING ALL NORTHERN AUTHORS!

DO YOU LIVE IN OR COME FROM NORTHERN ENGLAND?

DO YOU HAVE AN INTERESTING STORY TO TELL?

Email *submissions@northodox.co.uk*

- ☐ The first 3 chapters OR 5,000 words
- ☐ *1 page synopsis*
- ☐ *Author bio (tell us where you're based)*

* No non-fiction, poetry, or memoirs

SUBMISSIONS@NORTHODOX.CO.UK

COTTONOPOLIS

S F LAYZELL

Printed in Great Britain
by Amazon

46109324R00209